WHAT THE CAPTAIN REALLY MEANS

For Madelyn Pressey,

Ken Weber

KENNETH L. WEBER

CHICAGO SPECTRUM PRESS
LOUISVILLE, KENTUCKY 40207

CHICAGO SPECTRUM PRESS
4824 BROWNSBORO CENTER
LOUISVILLE, KENTUCKY 40207
502-899-1919

Printed in the U.S.A.

10 9 8 7 6 5 4 3 2 1

Library of Congress Control Number (LCCN): 2004108020

ISBN: 1-58374-104-6

Dustjacket photos by M.A. Chojnowski

TO MARY WEBER
My Wife and Soulmate
Who Prioritized Her Dreams and Duties

Duty then is the sublimest word in the
English language. You should do your duty in all things.
You can never do more. You should never wish to do less.

–General Robert E. Lee

ACKNOWLEDGMENTS

The library at The University of Louisville bears the name of my freshman English professor, William F. Ekstrom. A gentleman, scholar, and master teacher, Dr. Ekstrom became my role model. Ten years later, Professor John M. Muste shepherded me through Ohio State's Graduate English program, blessed my thesis, and prepared me to teach writing and literature at the Air Force Academy.

In seminars and workshops over the last two decades, accomplished writers and teachers have honed my skills and challenged me to fan the spark of an idea struck some thirty-six years ago. At Harvard, best selling author John Minahan read, copy edited, and critiqued my first efforts. His encouraging words have remained my beacon. Professor George Garrett, whose *Death of the Fox* can only be called a masterpiece, rightly told me "It will take everything you've got." On two occasions, Dr. Dennis E. Hensley, Vietnam veteran, prolific writer, and inspirational teacher, liked what he saw and recharged my batteries.

At Indiana University Southeast, Professor James H. Bowden became my friend and confidant. He read, advised, and critiqued the penultimate revision. Kiva Wyndotte considered the portrayal of female characters. Professor Diane S. Reid critiqued one of the late revisions.

Virginia S. Jones, whom I met at a writing conference at Antioch University, and whose descriptive writing talent is unsurpassed, volunteered a detailed critique of an early manuscript and has remained my "pen pal" since. To Sam Guyton, you've been there, done that, and made it out. I'd fly your wing any time, any place. My close friend since first grade, renowned commercial artist and straight arrow Eric Wehder, has always been in my corner. His son, Rick, who reads beneath the surface like a laser, gave me a critique I'd like to send to every editor in the country—or better, every book club. The comments of Margaret "Peg" MacLeish, a classmate at Louisville whose appreciation of Doctor Ekstrom matches my own, initiated my final push toward publication. Dorothy Kavka, my publisher, made my work a reality. To these people, and others along the way, I offer my deepest thanks.

The comrades with whom I associated in military service have defined for me the words "dedication"and "sacrifice." They have carried a heavy load in peacetime, cold war, and combat. Many accomplished seemingly impossible tasks. Others died trying—rest in peace, Gene Reed.

Finally I acknowledge my reader, who I ask to visualize this story through the eyes of characters struggling against daunting obstacles in a cataclysmic time when many of Faulkner's "old verities" are being tested, if not ripped apart.

Serious novelists invest unrealizable amounts of time searching for the precise incident, phrase, or metaphor to explore and analyze the human experience. They do it for their own understanding primarily, but if they are altruistic—which most are—they do it in hopes of enlightening readers who are investing their precious time to consider another's point of view. If you, the individual reader, find something of value in this work, I thank you for considering my words and wish you Godspeed.

–Ken Weber
Borden, Indiana
May, 2004

CHAPTER ONE

THE SEVENTEEN SPIRES of the Air Force Academy chapel shimmered at rigid attention above the solemn nave where Captain Thomas Sawyer, class of '62, had yesterday lain flag draped. Blinking his eyes rapidly, Frank Harbinger turned his wheezing Corvair into the dimly illuminated parking garage beneath Fairchild Hall then accelerated toward the slot reserved for the head of the department of history.

His briefcase seemed unusually heavy as he crossed to the elevator. Tomorrow, he promised himself, he'd start using the stairs again. Gaining the sixth floor, he stopped at the men's room to catch his breath, comb his hair, and give his shoes a swipe before standing his secretary's inspection. Under Rachel's eye, a frayed cuff or wisp of hair touching the top of his ears would precipitate a lecture. "Honestly, Colonel," she'd say, "don't you know you're a role model and not some scruffy old professor?"

"Good morning, Rachel," he said as he emerged from the maze of partitions screening his office.

"Major Larson dropped off the Military Symposium agenda," she said without looking up, "and your physical's set for o-eight-hundred tomorrow."

"I wasn't aware my annual was due."

"It's not."

"Then why . . . "

"Because!" exasperation propelled the word. "You haven't been yourself lately. Everyone's noticed."

Harbinger shrugged then walked the three steps to his door. Safe inside he removed his blouse, seated himself gingerly at his desk, and began to scan his proposal to establish a group of historians in Saigon to record what he called "contemporary history." As he moved to the second page, Rachel approached with his morning coffee and an envelope already slit.

"I thought you might like to see this. It's from Major Cannard."

"That's kind of you, Rachel. I've had Alex on my mind since Captain Sawyer . . . " He quickly raised the cup, took a tentative sip, then slammed it back on its saucer. "What is this mess?"

"Herbal tea. You're drinking too much caffeine."

"Damn it, Rachel, I'll decide . . . " But she was already gone.

Pushing himself away from the desk and into the light flooding through the tall windows, he began to read:

Bien Hoa Air Base, RVN
15 April 1968
Dear Colonel Harbinger,

Finally took my AC-47 to war last night. Our gunship is a vintage "Gooney Bird" loaded with illumination flares and three of the meanest machine guns you ever saw. Job's to keep the bad guys from rocketing the cities or overrunning our outposts at night. The grunts sometimes call us "Guardian Angel" instead of our "Spooky" call sign.

In theory the job's simple. Race to the scene, whip the old gal into a tight left-hand circle, toss out a flare, and blast away. In practice, it's downright intimidating to a virgin co-pilot. Last night, perched on my seat cushion and straining to see out the pilot's side window, I felt like a trained monkey. Jim Hubbard—"Mother Hubbard" to the troops—had his hands full pinpointing the target, coordinating with our cabin crew, and teaching me what I needed to know. On hot targets, we share airspace with forward air controllers, fighter-bombers, helicopter gunships, and enemy bullets.

With the Paris peace negotiations starting, I'm lucky to see combat. I feared I'd be left like Bill Faulkner to brood over missing my chance for glory. Plenty of opportunities, I'm told, to snag a Distinguished Flying Cross and a bunch of Vietnamese decorations.

Time to pack it in. Give my best to Iris, Rachel, and the gang. I'd appreciate your not mentioning any of this to Merrilane. Last week Pleiku lost an AC-47 to an enemy gunner and another to a mortar shell on landing. So I'm feeding her a sanitized story about flying routine patrols protecting Saigon from rockets. Like LBJ says, no use worrying the home folks.

  Cheers,

  Alex

Harbinger swivelled his chair allowing sunlight to fall on his face. Closing his eyes he rotated the chair again. He remembered having switched places with Lossberg in the top turret, then swinging aft to check the formation. Stair-stepped behind him plowed the other bombers of his group: high-winged B-24s, engines spinning condensation trails, slab-sided fuselages cleaving ice crystals 28,000 feet above Frankfurt, twin stabilizers betraying their identity as wallowing Liberators rather than the celebrated Flying Fortresses:

"Fighters twelve o'clock high!" someone had shouted as he settled into the co-pilot's seat. Sucking pure oxygen, he wiggles into his parachute, gropes for the lap belt, and clamps it together. High decibel jamming reverberates in his headset. He senses rather than sees the spread of shark-nosed Messerschmitts. Herrick defends from the nose—long bursts, cordite stench, continual vibration. Clattering shell cases pool beneath the thrashing upper turret. Temples throb, heartbeats synchronize with stammering guns, genitals shrivel, anus tightens.

Twenty-millimeter slugs perforate the cockpit disintegrating the windscreen into shards of jagged Plexiglas. Fred McCrimmon jerks upright—once, twice—then crumples onto the control wheel his flayed torso scarcely deflecting the autopilot. Straining propellers flail into clear air dragging the tattered wings and riddled fuselage which bucks and rolls but holds to the bomb run heading. Grey speckled fighters again sift through the formation, rolling inverted for home.

Beads of sweat, tinted by McCrimmon's spattered blood, seep around the edges of his goggles, fogging the lens, stinging his eyes. Flak pockmarks the sky—close—bursting level directly in front, now streaming past his side window like dark cumulus on an instrument approach. Shrapnel crashes against and through thin aluminum. "Bombay doors coming open." He feels the buffet, senses the drag.

More flak. Concussion assaults his ears, making the aircraft a giant bass drum jostled mercilessly by a marching drummer. Oil pressure drops on the right-hand inboard. Quick look: cowl shot away, glistening oil, pouring black smoke. Hit the red button, cut the fuel, switch off the ignition. Power up the other three, dial in rudder trim, keep her straight, hold the airspeed. "Loose Woman" overrunning close alongside, nothing amiss, four props churning, even as her left wing folds over and back just before the explosion. "Bombs away!" Twelve 500-pounders spill from their racks, arming mechanisms spinning merrily.

Having missed the direct experience, Professor Frank Harbinger muses, William Faulkner chose afterwards to live vicariously in the past, able in his innocence to romanticize it, to write novels that probed the primordial consciousness, to become an alcoholic just from thinking about man's condition. Yet even if unperceived by his own cognizance, he was nevertheless comforted by the absolute certainty that, no matter how perverted and malicious his characters, he himself had never held another soul in bondage, had—perhaps because of pure chance or divine intervention—never stripped away the life of another human being.

So Alex Cannard has seen his first combat, has been fascinated by it because he has not really seen it at all . . . has just orbited like a trained monkey watching Homo sapiens' passion for destruction. And, isolated by his innocence—his naiveté—now thinks a proof of manhood is somehow involved.

Harbinger had thought often about manhood as he read military history from the point of view of his own experience. As he delved into accounts of battles—Balaclava, Stalingrad, Dien Bien Phu—he perceived a pattern of incompetence, flawed communication, and stubborn deference to tradition such that even the lowest private soldier could foretell needless casualties and ultimate defeat. Whereas Alexander had lamented the dearth of worlds to conquer, Harbinger had wept while walking the battlefield contemplating the 60,000 first-day casualties on the Somme. Truly manhood is involved: the uncommon manhood to stand against those justifying ill-conceived action.

What was his name? The ex-bomber pilot who had proclaimed himself first citizen of the world after the Second War? Davis? Garry Davis? Poor, disturbed, naive Davis always pictured being led manacled away from some United Nations meeting or other because he demanded concrete action. Who would be the second citizen of the world?

Not Frank Harbinger. He could hear whistling death closing in behind, sitting in his blind spot, pumping explosive tracers into his chest. Too bad it had to happen now. But he had no complaint. Why Fred McCrimmon and not Frank Harbinger? Why *Loose Woman* and not the leader's *Return to Duty*? He had been spared then. For what? To pour more death from the skies? To come back to Iris, whose letters had revealed a passion surpassing his own? To raise a son who roams the corporate world never calling or writing? To guide a new generation of officers toward an understanding of past blunders and missed opportunities? To allow them to articulate fresh strategies in an age when economic inter-dependency, instant communication, and creative statesmanship might combine to end past cycles of distrust and war? Not Frank Harbinger.

And probably not his protégé who was already filling the squares in an all-consuming game of careerism. Would Alex Cannard, remote from the carnage in his circling gunship, ever come to know the realities of war without quarter? To lead a sustained raid against a significant target—boring through bursting flak, flashing fighters, and exploding bombers? To cradle the bloody head of a comrade whose body had been broken by an implacable foe? To close with the enemy, clamping fingers of vengeance upon his windpipe? Would his spirit survive seeing the waste, the capriciousness of fate, the futility of protracted war, and whatever the year of separation would bring to his wife and children? Could his faith and optimism emerge from the debris intact, or would he, like Hawthorne's Goodman Brown, spend his remaining years as a darkly meditative, distrustful, desperate man?

Is there a chance he might prevail? Might emerge as a hero for the modern world: Alexander the Good?

Harbinger studied the letter for a long time before folding it back into its envelope and marking a bold "EYES ONLY" in red felt-tip pen above the address. He placed it in his out-basket, signed the memo without reading the second page, then rose and walked to the doorway.

"Please pack my briefcase for me, Rachel. I'm going to spend today at home with Iris."

CHAPTER TWO

HEARING THE POSTMAN'S JEEP cresting the hill, Merrilane Cannard flipped her muddy trowel into the dirt, stripped off her soggy gloves, and abandoned the flat of marigolds she had intended to cluster beside the front walk. She had dressed for spring—Levi's, print blouse, sneakers—hoping her optimism would rush the season. But the morning's sunlight had surrendered its warmth to the frigid gusts that burst from the encroaching forest, chilling her arms where Alex's down vest left her unprotected. Gardening had never delighted her or provided a release of tension as it did for her neighbor, Iris Harbinger, whose very name appeared to summon balmy zephyrs and clusters of fragrant blossoms.

She trotted the short distance to the mailbox and stood, stamping her feet to restore circulation and tossing her head to clear the stray hairs that had slipped from the carelessly tied bandanna. The driver had bypassed the Harbingers but swerved across the gravel road to catch the Taylors, as if purposefully whetting her anticipation. She folded her arms across her chest and held her legs tightly together, fighting both the cold and the spasm of nervous energy rippling like static electricity.

Earlier she had done her full regimen of yoga, exercising nude on the white bedroom carpet, feeling the sun's warming glow invigorating her as she slipped effortlessly from the plough to the cobra and finally into the relaxing lotus. With the rising sun stimulating her optic nerves even through closed eyelids, she had fallen into deep meditation. Surely, somewhere in the mystical process, she must have conjured a fat letter into the carrier's bulging pouch. Enduring the last painful seconds, she surveyed the familiar landscape: the swaying pine trees, crowns like massed brushes beginning to apply a wash of thin cirrus over the sky's intense blue, the descending sweep of the

13

road shimmering in the undiluted sunlight, the dappled patches of lighter green peeking through the trees and suggesting the meadow that lay beyond.

"I've got something you're looking for," shouted Mr. Post Toasties, so christened by Alex because of his ruddy complexion and crinkled red beard. He held out a stack of throwaways, two magazines, and—balanced precariously on top—an envelope with a flag-striped border and the word "free" scrawled where the stamp should have been.

"That's it!" she squealed. But as she reached for her bounty, he withdrew the prize and leaned back inside to shut off the ignition.

"Hold on, little lady." His watery eyes squinted from beneath grey-tinged brows. "The Post Office Department can't be giving away free mail without positive identification."

"Oh, come on, Mr. Carson! You're not so hard-hearted as to keep me waiting any longer."

"Why, I reckon not." He extended the bundle, but slipped the letter off the top as she took the stack in both hands and steadied it with her chin.

"Hey, that's not fair."

"Whoever said the world's fair, little lady? If the world was fair, you'd ignore this thin excuse for a letter and ask your tired old servant in for a cup of hot coffee."

"Now what would the neighbors think if I took to entertaining virile men with my husband gone just three weeks?" She stretched her right hand to stroke Carson's whiskered cheek, then collected the surrendered letter.

"Your choice, little lady, but I think that fly-boy of yours made a big mistake leavin' a filly like you."

Winking her thanks, she turned away and retreated at a deliberate canter—small steps, legs close together, shoulders and hips swaying. Once inside the comfortably furnished greenhouse adjacent to the kitchen, she settled into a wicker chair, slit the envelope with a carefully manicured nail, removed the two folded sheets, and began to read:

Bien Hoa Air Base
15 April 1968
Dearest Merrilane,

Arrived here from Nha Trang on Good Friday and flew my first mission last night (Easter). Too pushed to write till now. Bien Hoa's huge with Long Bien army post just to the east and Saigon with its Tan Son Nhut airbase 35 miles southwest. The area's secure, and we enjoy a base exchange, club, theater, chapel, and 12,000-foot runway.

I live in the Spook House with ten other officers. Each has a cot, steel locker, and whatever he can scrounge. Plywood sheeting divides the interior into cubicles. A dilapidated air-conditioner chugs and coughs constantly. Showers and latrines are out back.

Just beyond the partition beside my bed is the obligatory lounge where our mamasans gather each morning to shine shoes and boots after doing the laundry. My mamasan's actually a pretty girlsan, Miss Long-Lo-ngoc, a Catholic whose family fled the Communist take-over in '54. I'll need to pay her four or five dollars a month.

Other monthly costs will be two dollars for Club dues and enough for food and incidentals. A T-bone at the Club goes for two dollars; the dinner special's a buck and a quarter. Lunch of sandwich, dessert, and drink is forty cents. The chow hall charges twenty-seven cents for breakfast, sixty cents for lunch, and forty-five cents for dinner. Your allowance should be about seven fifty monthly.

Our war's rather tame—even boring. Mostly we orbit Bien Hoa and Saigon nightly to discourage surprise attacks. I can't see Ho Chi Minh holding out much longer. A year of garrison duty may be my fate.

Gotta go now. I miss you so much I try to keep from thinking about you. But that's impossible. To know how I feel, read again the second letter I wrote from Nha Trang.

Tell Kim and Jeffrey Dad says "Hi" and hopes the Easter Bunny was good to them.

All My Love,
Alex

She squirmed in the chair, shifting to prop her legs on the shabby camel saddle he had wagged home from Morocco in

1959. She had hated it then; she detested it now as a symbol of their separations.

"You've got to watch the spending," he had said as they loitered behind the boarding passengers. "Combat pay'll help."

"We'll be all right," she said. "Tell me you love me."

"The car's running rough. Take it to the dealer and ask . . . "

"I can handle it. Tell me you'll come home."

"Call Dad if you get in a bind. He doesn't have much, but you know its . . . "

"Can you hold out without me?"

She roused herself, blinked the moisture from her eyes, and began to read the letter again. Her husband's words evoked no images, not even his own. No second letter had come from Nha Trang. Not even a first. Were they lost in the inscrutable vacuum that had sucked up her dreams? Then an image congealed: lean and hungry girls squatting in a circle, chattering together as they fondled her lover's boots.

Shaking off the chill that permeated the room now that clouds had swallowed the sun, she rose from her chair intending to resume her planting. They had built the house in 1965 anticipating a four-year tour, but that evening when he closed the door then leaned heavily against it, she realized the war had found them. She remembered taking his briefcase, then dropping it on the foyer tiles and locking her arms around his waist."You volunteered for Vietnam."

"Two weeks ago. Assignment came today. AC-Forty-sevens. Obsolete gunships in the South. I'd prayed for a Phantom—anything to give me some fighter time before I'm too old."

"You're already too old," she said. "Thirty-six with two children."

"Others make the transition. Chance of a lifetime. Back on active service with the Academy on my record and a combat tour in fighters. Sure-fire promotion!"

"How could you do this without consulting me?"

He stroked her back, high up near the shoulder blades. "Calm down, Sweetheart. I'm a soldier. It's not right to be among these cadets unless you've pulled your tour."

"But our home. You're abandoning us. Running out on me. Just like my father!"

"It's only a year. Iron-clad guarantee our war's over in fifty-two weeks."

"It's not iron-clad."

Looking up, she saw Iris scurrying across the lawn.

Iris swept in, coughing for breath. Her style was western outdoors: faded denim wrap-around, plaid shirt with pearl buttons and open collar, and a loosely woven, red cardigan draped across her shoulders. Her frosted hair, skillfully applied cosmetics, and dazzling smile canceled age lines and sagging eye pockets that would have intimidated less confident women.

She hugged Merrilane, drawing the younger woman full into her body, then settled into a huge red pillow lying on the floor. "I'm betting you got something from Alex."

Merrilane dropped cross-legged beside her and summarized Alex's note. "And so you see, he's into the routine, and I'm in a countdown with three hundred and forty-two days to go."

"My dear, I waited at home during two wars, and I won't let you do that to yourself. I just won't hear of it!"

"You'd think I'd be used to separations. But I never bargained for a whole year of his flying airplanes left over from World War Two. I've watched Walter Cronkite!"

"He's a soldier, my dear. And a military historian. Don't you see he had to go?"

"He didn't!" Her lower lip quivered. It's this competition thing. Ticket punching they call it. It's not as if he's contributing anything. He's already dissatisfied with the routine. Well I'm bored to distraction, and it's only been three weeks."

Iris grasped her friend's trembling hands and squeezed hard. "You might want to consider getting a job. Harvey

Tucker's planning a recreation program that'll keep the children out of mischief all summer."

Merrilane dabbed at her eyes with a napkin. "I'd thought of getting a real estate license. Something part-time. Then yesterday I heard from a divorced classmate who opened a fitness center. She's nominated for Ohio's businesswoman of the year. Makes me want to tackle something really big—-really important."

"Too much wheel spinning in real estate." Iris pulled her sweater tight around her shoulders, "You need something to keep your mind from leaping off to Vietnam every whipstitch."

"You're right, of course, but here I sit with a fifteen-year-old physical education degree and no experience in my field. I made a big mistake getting married right out of college."

"Civilian grass always looks greener to a military wife with time on her hands. I'll have to ride close herd on you."

"It's hard to explain, Iris. I want something that's all mine. A new twist that'll make people sit up and take notice. I'm tired of the same old merry-go-round of housework and dinner parties and PTA and Wives' Club charities. I'm tired of being in Alex's shadow—being Mrs. Major Cannard.

"I understand, my dear. It's just that all this 'women in the marketplace' is foreign to what I'm used to."

"You've been blessed, Iris. Frank returned from the wars, and now you're living happily ever after. What if I'm not so lucky?"

"Hold on!" Iris's eyes flashed as she rose to her knees. "Harvey's brainchild! Janice said he needed someone to head a dependent's recreation program. A person to 'take the ball and run with it'—her exact words. Interested?"

"Where's the casting couch?"

"Atta girl!" Iris reached for the telephone. "I'll get you an interview before anyone else knows the job exists. Just think! The Athletic Department with all those beautiful men!"

CHAPTER THREE

WAITING OUTSIDE RODNEY PIKE'S DOOR, Merrilane flipped the pages of a ragged copy of *Sports Illustrated*. She had expected to see the director immediately, but a half-hour had passed, and no one seemed to care. Ten minutes earlier a man had rushed from the office, no doubt crashing on a project. She had not expected a mid-level civilian to be too busy to acknowledge his visitors. *Maybe it's a good omen*, she thought. *An overworked director surely needs help.*

But Pike's appearance had increased the apprehension that caused her frequently to cross and uncross her legs. He had the slender build of a distance runner and a pinched, cheerless face to match. She had dared to fantasize about working with a father-figure, someone who would provide guidance and allow her freedom to innovate. Such men existed. Usually victims of capricious fate. Ross Kincaid, her mentor at Ohio State, had treated her as a colleague rather than an intruder. She needed no dour-faced supervisors to further complicate her life.

"Merrilane! Come in, come in." The man's greeting overpowered the typewriters' staccato and the incessantly ringing telephones. "Excuse the delay. Harvey Tucker's on my case, and Pete Abbott shot out of here apoplectic because our brochure's not out."

She rose with a puzzled look but quickly realized the giant towering in the doorway was the real Rodney Pike. He smiled then thrust his hairy arm around her shoulders enveloping her in a scent of Skin Bracer diluted by pungent male sweat. Somewhat roughly he guided her into his office slamming the door behind them.

Her eyes darted among the dozens of plaques, trophies, and framed certificates proclaiming Rod Pike had been, was, and forever would be, a Super Jock. Indeed his office seemed an extension of the locker room. In one corner three stacks of yel-lowed newspapers rose halfway to the ceiling. A chalkboard—its green surface obscured by a patina of eraser dust—contained boldly drawn diagrams from the past football season. A peeling leather couch dominated the wall next to the cluttered desk. Fortunately for her sense of propriety, he had not managed to obscure or make trivial the spectacular view of green fields already animated by players in white or blue shirts.

"Have a seat on the couch, sweetie." He pulled up a captain's chair for himself. She attempted to ease herself onto the edge of the massive seat cushion, much as she would ma-neuver into a sports car. But the cushion betrayed her—hissing and deflating itself, shifting and rolling her backwards, con-suming her like a bee sucked into a jungle plant.

She ended with knees raised high and pleated white skirt hiked well above the middle of her thighs.

Roaring with laughter, Pike slid gracefully into the chair, resting his massive hands on its arms, and drawing so close he blocked the morning sunlight. "I'm sorry," he said between chuckles. "Shouldn't do things like that. But that blessed sofa's given me a million laughs. You oughta see Harvey Tucker when he sits down. It swallows the old bastard every time. And what it does to unsuspecting women always provides a few cheap thrills."

"I wouldn't have thought the director of recreation services needed cheap thrills."

"Now don't go getting serious on me, sweetie; that sofa gives me the upper hand when I negotiate with the toy soldiers." Again he chuckled as if recalling particularly pleasing incidents.

Yet he made no offer to move her to a less compromising position. Instead he inched his own chair even closer until their knees were almost touching. Although he appeared to main-tain devastating eye contact, she felt his peripheral vision simultaneously appraising her contours.

"As an advocate, Harvey's pretty transparent," he said. "Telling me you're perfect for the job but then insisting the decision's all mine. One thing about Harvey, that good-ole-boy talk is mostly for public consumption. He let me know the wants this job done on time, on budget, and without glitches."

"I see . . . "

"We're already late. No time for nine-to-five bankers' hours or running home to feed the kiddies. Think you can handle the details, sweetie?"

"I understand the requirements, Mr. Pike. With a husband in Vietnam, I've time on my hands."

"That's good. Suppose you summarize your qualifications."

Rotating her torso obliquely, she raised her legs onto the cushion deftly tucking them under her skirt until only her white pumps were visible. "Graduated Ohio State in nineteen fifty-three with a phys-ed major. As Professor Ross Kincaid's intern, I developed modules that could be combined to form any size recreation program. You know, numbers of coaches needed, administrative overhead, compatible sports for different age groups, lists of required equipment. Sort of a quick reference planning guide."

"Interesting."

"I dug out my notes last night and believe they mesh perfectly with your project. Could save us a week of donkey work."

"Sounds good," Pike said, uncrossing his legs. He had taken his eyes off her and focused them outside, somewhere far beyond the playing fields.

No longer the object of his exercise in domination, she was free to study him. Early forties no doubt. Swirls of honey-colored hair streaked with white near the temples, fashionably long over the ears, foaming into lighter tangles where it touched his collar like surf hitting a barrier reef. Blond bushy eyebrows, thick neck, and wide shoulders carried out the lion motif. Crow's-feet radiated from his eyes, refreshingly caused no doubt by years of skiing and golfing rather than squinting into the sun, as aviators did, searching for bandits. Nose, broken sometime in the past and imperfectly healed, enhanced the macho image—like a dueling scar.

21

He obviously had purchased the blue athletic department T-shirt a size too small as it seemed molded to his chest and almost constricting at the biceps. No telltale ripples swelled at the belt line as she had noticed when her husband had reluctantly dressed on the morning of his departure. Snugly tailored white trousers and spotless bucks completed his ensemble.

"Merrilane," he roused himself, "if you'll share those notes and put in some overtime, we could send the brochure to the printer tomorrow. Monday you hit the schools in Pine and Douglas valleys, previewing our plans and estimating how many kids will enroll. By Thursday, we'll firm up the schedule of sports, team assignments, and playing fields. Friday's our clean-up day, and if it's pulled together by five, I'll treat you to the Broadmoor's finest meal."

"You move fast once you make a decision."

He laughed. "Faster than a speeding bullet."

Uncoiling from his chair he extended his hands to Merrilane, who allowed him to extricate her. He preceded her to the door, then paused with his hand on the knob. "Run home, get those notes, and hurry back pronto. I'll help with the initial planning, but then you're on your own. Tell Rita to have the employment forms on my desk before she goes to lunch."

"I don't know how to thank you, Mr. Pike."

"Cut the 'Mr. Pike' stuff; he's my Dad. Everybody calls me Rod."

"Just one request before we get started . . . Rod."

"Sure, sweetie, you name it."

"Don't call me 'sweetie'."

"You got it, honey," Pike laughed. "Only kidding . . . only kidding."

After working with Rod through the dinner hour and finally wrapping up at almost nine, Merrilane collected the children from Iris, deflected her questions by pleading fatigue, and bundled the sleepy boy and girl off to bed once she got them home. She fixed a snack—apples, raisins, Chablis—scanned the paper, then settled herself in bed and started a note:

April 29, 1968

Alex My Love,

I not only got the position I wrote you about last night, but I also put in my first overtime! Rod Pike was really happy with my ideas. I foresee loads of midnight oil initially, but that'll make time fly.

I'm basing the kids at Iris's. I'll see them every day at the program. Incidently, Frank's not feeling well. Had a complete physical, but they're still running tests. You might drop him a line. He thinks so much of you.

Excuse my begging off, but I'm exhausted, and I've an early wake-up. I'll be working all day with Rod and probably half the night too.

Scanning the letter she realized her husband had been absent from her thoughts since the interview. She hesitated for a moment, then signed the usual "All My Love," sealed the envelope, placed it on the bedside table, and snapped off the light.

She had trouble falling asleep. Like fragmented pieces of a Grecian mosaic, Rod Pike's handsomeness had imbedded itself in her mind. She recalled his superb upper-chest development, the flexed biceps straining the sleeves of his shirt, the tight span of Dacron closely tailored to emphasize trim buttocks. All the pieces exuded his pungent scent. She thrashed from side to side before finally rolling onto her back.

Ridiculous! Women my age don't fantasize about men almost a decade older. But Alex could never afford a dinner at the Broadmoor. Alex . . . . Dear Alex . . . . What are you doing tonight? But it's not night out there. So damned confusing with the time change. Ten-hour difference? When it's midnight here it's . . . oh, who cares? Why aren't you here? Then I wouldn't need to conjure up other men. Are you thinking about me . . . Rod? Are my legs running through your mind right now? Are you with someone but thinking of me? Dangerous thoughts, sweetie. Frustrated fantasy thoughts. She tossed once again then rolled to Alex's side of the bed, stretching full length on her back, gripping his pillow, trying to detect a trace of his scent.

CHAPTER FOUR

MAJOR ALEX CANNARD leaned against the rough boards of the Spook House and considered the one-page note. The sun hung just above the horizon, and residual heat from the sand-bags upon which he sat surged through his flying suit, so that he sensed he was being roasted back and front.

He looked left, down the narrow passage toward the Ranch Hands' hooch, seeing where their neglected parapet had shifted and fallen. The sun had bleached the olive colored bags to a muddy brown then progressively weakened the cloth until gaps developed and grains of sand began trickling out. No doubt a passerby had disturbed the balance, causing a corner of the construction to tumble seven or eight bags into the pathway. Men no longer stepped over the obstruction but instead walked upon it, disbursing the sand and grinding the rotted fabric into the earth.

His mind drifted back to the letter that had held so much promise. Someone had placed it beside his alarm clock, so that he had awakened to see the graceful curves of Merrilane's script inviting him again to share a private portion of her life. He had delayed opening the envelope, delighting in the anticipation, until he had showered, shaved, and put on a fresh uniform.

He had wanted—really desperately needed—a long, sen-suous letter, perhaps written by candlelight as his beloved wove her thoughts into a tapestry praising him as man, lover, and soul mate. He had wanted a letter he could put in a special place to be read whenever the black dog returned to bay in the night.

He had scrambled as copilot to Archer, the laconic second in command, who—ignoring the checklist and positioning all switches and controls himself—had acted as if he were alone in the cockpit. Stung, he became increasingly frustrated with the hodgepodge of switches, knobs, and buttons that, in theory, should have allowed him to talk simultaneously with Saigon radar, the airborne Forward Air Controller, and the American advisor crouched inside the compound they had been dispatched to protect.

"You're too late, Spooky," the Green Beret announced. "All I need's illumination for a Dust Off. Got three Whiskeys and two Kilos." He looked across the cockpit.

"Wounded and killed," Archer murmured, speaking so softly that Alex had to infer what he said. He wondered why Archer chose to punish him rather than doing something about the grossly inadequate stateside training.

After dropping flares for the evacuation helicopter and then loitering for no discernable reason, they came home just before daybreak. Archer flew effortlessly: his left hand barely touching the worn control wheel, his right sometimes caressing the elevator trim as the aircraft droned through the still air. The pilots abandoned themselves to the witching hour, the moments just before the sun peeks above the horizon when eyelids droop, bodies slouch pot-bellied, and minds wander thousands of miles away. The cabin crew dozed, their forms draped over their equipment like Legionnaires dead on desert battlements.

Lulled by the pulsing drone of the engines, Alex disengaged his mind, freeing it to drift back to Merrilane. She was nice to come home to, in reality or, as was so often the case because of his duty, in fantasy. Either way he always found her shower-sweet, ready to please. This time she reclined on their pillowed bed, a perfumed candle suffusing the air with musk, its spiral flame transformed by the room's flanking mirrors into a baroque chandelier. From time to time she cocked her head as if listening for the sound of tires crunching in the gravel driveway.

Failing to perceive his presence, she resumed preening herself, drawing up her right foot, trimming each nail, and shaping its cuticle. Moving stealthily, now playing the dark Lamont Cranston to her lovely Margo Lane, he projected himself into the room. His shadow's drifting across her body startled her;

she drew the sheet around her nakedness, but the wave of apprehension flushing her face dissolved as she stretched upward to meet his kiss.

The left engine coughed once, and the image faded only to return dimly focused as if seen through milky cataracts. She stood before him as she had the morning of his departure, tear streaks tracking her puffy cheeks, the smell of their lovemaking still upon her. His shower had steamed the bathroom mirror. He flicked the vent fan's switch, then flicked again. He reached for her. She pulled away, grasping the shower door for support. Kim called from the hallway, "Hurry, Mommy, or we'll miss Daddy's airplane." He pushed her into the shower, entering close behind, groping for one last remembrance. Frigid water forced them together, drowned her cries, pooled on the hard black tile.

The suggestion of a pitch change scrambled the images and focused Alex's mind once again on his duties, but he abandoned reading the Before Landing checklist when he realized Archer was paying no attention. "Check the tie-down straps and get the crew ready for landing," he shouted to the flight engineer who stood behind the pilots rubbing his eyes.

Archer set up a long, straight-in approach to the east gaging his descent to place the aircraft's wheels on the runway's huge white numbers. Feeling no more connection to the operation of the machine than a passenger, Alex suspended all thoughts of war and allowed his aviator's soul to respond to the beauty of the landscape that welcomed him. He could make out the countryside now: sparkling green fields, miniature vehicles scooting along the perimeter road, sentries and their dogs stopping to peer up at the black underside and camouflaged fuselage of the returning gunship.

Perfectly trimmed, impeccably aligned, the aircraft skimmed just above touchdown as the sun poked over the horizon directly off the far end of the runway, flaming the low cloud deck a shimmering golden peach, and sending a wave of brilliance racing across the awakening land and into Alex's unprotected eyes.

"You got it," Archer muttered.

He grabbed the control wheel jerking its column just enough to upset all the merging parameters. The aircraft skipped lightly and bounded back into the air. Its rising nose swung left, airspeed evaporated, and the tired old bird pranged onto the runway in a wrenching imitation of its albatross namesake.

"I've got it," Archer had announced over the crew's interphone.

Remembering the whistles and catcalls that had sifted up from the cabin, Alex tried to find the humor. But the incident was still too fresh, too ego-crushing, to allow a smile just ten hours later. His embarrassment snapped him back to the reality of Bien Hoa air base, the pile of sandbags ringing the Spook House, and the pastel blue envelope he held in his right hand.

Why be depressed by Archer's actions? He was just another personality to come to terms with. But shouldn't a man be able to count on his wife to anticipate his needs and soothe his feelings even when she's ten thousand miles away? His thoughts again drifted, going far back to early childhood when he had impatiently awaited his mother's return from the hotel's Coffee Shop. As the room's shadows grew long, he would run to the window every few minutes. Between unrewarding trips, he listened for the downstairs latch to turn. "What did you bring me, Mother!" he would cry as he flung himself into her outstretched arms to be hugged and rewarded with a scrap of Danish, a stack of menus, or a nickel from her meager tips.

Only later did he learn the extent of the Depression. He had been selfish, of course, but he was a little boy, and his mother seemed to enjoy so much just loving him.

During previous deployments Merrilane, too, had propped him up. She had made the household decisions, managed the children, and wrote light-hearted letters daily. From their college meeting in the sophomore psychology course, through a three-year courtship, a gypsy-like existence at two flight training bases, frequent separations mandated by Strategic Air Command, and finally the miracle posting to graduate school and then the Academy, she had filled all the roles.

He knew he was overreacting badly to his wife's letter, but he was restless, hot, and bone-tired. Manhandling the AC-47 night after night, sometimes for as many as three sorties in a twelve-hour period, was stressful, crushing work, and he had needed something special.

Again he read the letter. It was short, but she had been tired. He could understand that. Her job will "make time fly." He could identify with that too, as his own busy weeks had passed in a twinkling. Of course he was disturbed by the reference to Frank's health, but there was something else.

A helicopter, dashing low across the compound in the direction of Saigon, scattered his thoughts. As the sound of its slapping rotors receded in the southwest, he realized the irritant was her twice mentioning Rod Pike. The name disturbed him; something percolated through his memory cells but would not filter out.

His duties as a faculty member had allowed him little contact with the various coaches and administrators who worked for the Director of Athletics. He had flown with a few of them and had met Harvey Tucker at a party, but he could not place Rodney Pike. Yet he was positive there was something, some bit of trivia or gossip surrounding that name.

"Pike . . . Rodney Pike," he repeated to himself; but it would not lock in. The only Pike he could remember was a minor character in *The Catcher in the Rye*.

CHAPTER FIVE

ROLLING INTO A LEFT BANK and adding a touch of elevator trim to maintain 3,500 feet, Alex concentrated on the mathematics of the orbit pattern while Archer dozed in the left seat. Their association had begun when Alex, less than a week in-country and clad in jungle fatigues reeking of strong dyes and cellophane wrappings, had hitched a ride to Bien Hoa on a gunship flown by the detachment's operations officer.

Shortly after takeoff, he had gone forward to stand behind the pilots. "What's it like flaring for fighters?" he asked. "How close can you fire to the friendlies? Do the . . . do the wrong guys—our guys—ever get hit?"

The dark-jowled Archer, faded coveralls bearing gaudy stateside insignia rather than subdued combat-zone patches, glanced sideways at him as if he were a teenage Explorer Scout. Turning back to scan his instruments, he rummaged for, found, unwrapped, and folded into his mouth a stick of Juicy Fruit, then returned the pack to his left sleeve pocket.

Alex retreated aft, past the three Gatling guns poised like cannon on a frigate's deck, to stand at the open cargo door watching the jungle unscroll. Only when Archer chopped the throttles and slanted the aircraft downward did he return to the canvas slings rigged as passenger seats. After landing, he shifted sideways and peered through the clouded plexiglass of the rectangular cabin window.

A bustling airport materialized as if projected on a ten-inch television monitor. But its reception was faulty; a sepia wash obscured true colors, and heat waves distorted the image. They held on the taxiway to allow a bloated C-130 transport to hunker past, its dark green and sand-colored camouflage pattern compromised by the unmistakable outline of an inquisitive duck's head, complete with beady eye, on its vertical fin. Trailing the duck waddled three smaller C-123 transports outfitted for the aerial defoliation mission, their stubby wings wavering like the balancing poles of a team of tightrope walkers. Ragged holes decorated the left wing of the third aircraft; allowing chemicals to syphon from a ruptured spray line and vaporize on the blistering hot concrete. A dank and fetid smell suffused the cabin causing Alex's lips to burn and his nostrils to twitch.

When the procession had passed, Archer spurted across the taxiway and swept onto the main parking ramp. A line of gigantic hangars faced the tarmac which was dotted with yellow starting carts. Vietnamese A-1 fighter-bombers, wings folded as if in supplication, sat scattered like plastic models small boys had snapped together then discarded. Snuggled between the spindly control tower and the firehouse with its sagging volleyball net, an HH-43 crash rescue helicopter dozed with drooping rotors. Next to a loading dock, a serpent-shaped C-141 transport lay sunning itself while consuming stacks of rectangular aluminum boxes that winked at Alex as each disappeared.

Once Archer cut the engines, Alex deplaned, handed his B-4 bag and aviator's kit to a bronzed airman, and trudged toward a blue and white trailer whose sign depicted a Klan-like figure under the motto "We Are Proud to be a Fly-by-Night Outfit." A blast of frigid air and the sight of a cadaverous lieutenant colonel with deep-set eyes and receding hairline greeted him as he stepped inside.

"I'm Mother Hubbard." The apparition had said, "Welcome to Grimm's Fairy Tales."

.

Time seemed suspended as the ancient transport droned around its orbit. Alex tried to focus his mind on the dull glow of the flight instruments, but his thoughts again wandered. He noticed the perimeter lights of the Long Binh army base were almost the same size and shape as those marking the outline of the Air Force Academy. He examined the phenomenon his next time around, even extending the pattern eastward in order to probe for further similarities. He located the cadet area, the community center where the commissary and exchange were sited, the black hole where the football stadium would be nestled, and the cluster of lights denoting Pine Valley where he and Merrilane had lived before building in the Black Forest. Archer jostled his left shoulder.

"Get a load of this," he yelled above the droning of the engines. "Turn your selector to Liaison."

Mystified, Alex did as he was told, rotating the interphone mixer switch so that it now allowed the sounds of the high frequency radio to enter his headset.

". . .don't know what them pea-brained kids is doin' while I'm at the shop," a woman's voice screeched. "Brenda's boy-crazy. An' lazy. Plays them Beetles over an' over knowin' full well it's a shatterin' the insides of my head."

"What's that?" Alex yelled as he twisted the switch, '*All My Children*'"?

"That's the MARS Follies," Archer gleefully shouted as he reached across Alex's body to reposition the switch.

". . .day long. Music an' boys, boys an' music. Thank the good Lord for a boss like Karl. Sometimes we jist sit a talkin' after the phones quit ringin'. Such a comfort. Over."

Alex realized Archer had tapped into the network of amateur radio operators who enabled lonely GIs to patch directly into their home telephones. During previous overseas deployments, he had found it crude, impersonal, and unreliable. More like a radio than a telephone, the conversation worked only if the participants remembered to say the word "Over" when they wanted the other person to reply.

"I'm real sorry you're a havin' trouble, honey. Things ain't exactly copesetic here neither. They's good kids. Just need you to pay 'em some mind. Over."

"Pay 'em some mind!" The signal faded, but came drifting back to settle on a higher level of stridency: ". . . and Brenda sure don't want me to pay no mind when she locks herself in her bedroom with that sneaky-faced Willard Dickens and them records. Another thing . . . "

Alex flipped the switch and glared in the darkness at Archer who was chuckling with almost uncontrollable glee. "Give it to him, Sister. Make his year a nightmare while you cozy up to good ole Karl." Then Archer withdrew a black grease pencil from his sleeve pocket and prepared to write on the side of his sliding window. "What's your phone number, Cannard?"

"What's it to you?"

"I'm gonna ring up your wife and see if she's better company than you are."

Reluctantly Alex supplied the number, hoping the call would get through but recognizing the improbability. Four orbits later, as they approached the "Air Force Academy," Archer shook the control column and motioned toward Alex's mixer switch. "I've got it; come up on liaison and talk to your Mrs."

"Hello, are you on, Merrilane? Over."

"Hello, honey; is that really you? I can't believe this is happening! I haven't had any mail for three or four days! The man on the phone said you were on a combat mission. Where are you? Over."

Astounded, he could only grin at Archer who was intent on clearing the aircraft for a left turn. Despite the opportunity, he was inhibited by years of training that had taught him not to discuss inappropriate information on the easily monitored high frequencies. "We're just doing a little pattern work, and Colonel Archer arranged this call. Everything's fine with me; how are you and the children? Over."

"It's marvelous to hear your voice, sweetheart. I talked quite some time with Colonel Archer. He's a delightful man. Said you caught on quick and were a fine pilot. Over."

"That's nice, but tell me about the kids before we lose the signal. Over."

"Oh, Alex, you wouldn't believe the job! I'm putting in at least twelve hours a day at the office and brought work home this weekend. Rod's dropping by later to go over the final schedule. We brief Colonel Tucker tomorrow morning. Over."

"How are the children? Do they miss me? Over."

33

"They're both fine. I'm watching my diet and exercising every day. I let myself go after you left—gained six pounds—but with all the trim people around the department . . .Oh, listen to me ramble; tell me about yourself. Over."

"I'm having dinner with Dan Strait tomorrow. He'll give me the lowdown on your boss. He's familiar with that whole crowd. Over."

"He'll know Rod for sure. Rod knows everybody worth knowing and everything that's going on. The mayor told him there's talk of forming a permanent training ground for Olympic athletes in the Springs. It could be a natural for me. Over."

Knowing he was supposed to be protecting the air base rather than discussing the training of jocks for 1984, Alex moved to end the conversation. "That's wishful thinking, Merrilane. Strategic Air Command will tell us where we go once this tour is over." Hearing the magic word, the ground radio operator returned the transmission to Merrilane.

"Hello . . . hello Alex, I didn't get all of that, but I know you're excited for me. I don't know what I'd have done without Rod's help. He's not much older than you and me, but he has all kinds of experience and just exudes confidence. He's promised me dinner at the Broadmoor if I bring in this project. Last night we went to the Peppercorn Inn, a new place in Palmer Lake. We'd worked late . . . "

"Sorry to intrude, Lover Boy," Archer's gruff voice over-rode Merrilane's, "but we've got troops in contact near Dau Tieng. Ring off with your dolly and get Three DASC to shut down the artillery out of Xeon."

"Mateus Rose reminded me of our . . . " With no way of interrupting, Alex twisted his radio selector switch to the UHF position leaving the operator to explain why "Lover Boy" had run out on the description of her most recent dinner date.

"Pawnee Target, Pawnee Target," Alex called in his most authoritative voice, "Spooky Seven Three proceeding to troops in contact. Request you suspend any fire missions out of Xeon for next one-five minutes."

Showing more enthusiasm than Alex had yet seen, Archer shoved the levers controlling fuel mixture, propeller pitch, and throttle setting to maximum cruise, stood the ancient Goon on her left wingtip, and rolled onto an intercept heading to the target. Knowing the cabin crew was unable to monitor cockpit radio conversations, Alex rotated the mixer switch to the "interphone" position. "Crew, this is co-pilot we have . . . "

"Get off the command channel," Archer yelled as he slapped Alex's hand off the microphone switch.

Feeling hot blood flooding his face, he repositioned the selector one click, and pressed the mic switch again. "We've got troops in contact at Dau Tieng. Prepare for flare and gunnery operations."

"Call Paris Control and give 'em our flight plan change," Archer yelled against the roar of the straining engines. Then, patting the side of Alex's left leg, he added, "This may be a hot one, so watch everything I do. I'll handle my own flares until you get the hang of it; I'll also talk to the navigator and the flare-kicker on interphone. You work the Fox Mike radio with the guy on the ground. His name's Shaggy Morgan Six. 'Six' is always part of the ground commander's call sign."

Blackie Charmoli, the navigator teamed most often with Archer, had stowed his magazines and come forward from his cozy desk to stand in the aisle leaning over the pilot's shoulder. "Darker than the inside of a cow," he mumbled to no one in particular.

"Shaggy Morgan Six," Alex called. "Spooky Seven Three with forty-eight flares and eighteen thousand rounds."

"Spooky Seven Three," the voice was strong, southern. "Glad you boys could make it. We had a probe about twenty minutes ago, and they're still out there. I got a visual on your running lights."

Moving his hand up to the switches, Alex looked left for Archer's nod, then cut the exterior lights and red rotating beacon.

"Ask him to give us something . . . "

A spectacular series of mortar impacts provided the fix Archer needed. "Get clearance to fire," he shouted as he banked hard left.

"Spooky has muzzle flashes Southwest. We clear to fire?"

"Roger, Spooky. Hose 'em good."

Alex flicked up the red safety guard and toggled the master arming switch.

"All guns fast fire," Archer commanded.

A deep, bass moan erupted from the cabin. The sound continued, unearthly and unremitting, for five seconds.

"Holy Mackerel, boss!" Alex recognized the voice of Sergeant Viega. "You stirred up a hornets' nest. Tracers all over the place."

Lacking the essentials of range, bearing, number of guns firing, and whether they constituted a threat, the loadmaster's call was worthless.

"Two fifty-calibers firing on you, Spooky," Shaggy Morgan called. "One's directly south about half a klik; the other's to the east-southeast, possibly on the canal bank near an ambush patrol of mine. Do not fire east of my compound."

Continuing his bank, Archer pulled one propeller lever a quarter of an inch behind the other. Startled by the resulting cacophony, Alex reached to parallel the handles.

"Leave 'em alone," Archer rasped. "The disharmony keeps the black hats from homing on our sound."

Alex added another technique to his growing list of things not taught in training.

"Spooky, this is Six. We got a strong probe from due west. Give us a flare, and we'll wax 'em."

Archer's fingers toggled a switch on the overhead panel illuminating a green light in the cabin directly above the entrance door to the pilots' compartment. At the signal, Sergeant Viega jettisoned a three-foot-long aluminum canister containing a magnesium flare set to ignite some 1,500 feet below the aircraft and provide two-million candlepower for almost three minutes as it floated beneath its parachute.

After dropping the fourth canister, Archer transferred the job to Alex who concentrated on maneuvering the aircraft within a pear-shaped pattern which allowed his flares to drift across the compound. Later, the two pilots scrambled over each other to exchange seats, so that—for the first time in combat— Alex manned the commander's position and squinted through the primitive gunsight mounted abeam his left shoulder. At Shaggy Morgan's request, he moved the gunship's orbit and strafed the enemy's escape route.

He never learned what damage he wrought, or to whom. Much of the area was a free-fire zone, so no one really cared. Archer, however, was later credited with twenty KBA—Killed by Air—and three mortar positions destroyed. Alex flew home to Bien Hoa, this time greasing his main gear so smoothly on the numbers that not even the muted kiss of the tires disturbed the dreams of the cabin crew.

When he finally collapsed on his cot in the Spook House, he fell into a sound sleep without first conversing with his God or thinking of Merrilane.

CHAPTER SIX

THE SMELL OF GRILLING STEAKS led Alex to the patio behind the hooch where Dan Strait stood in the midst of swirling smoke. "Does Westmoreland know how terrific you look in a skirt?" Alex yelled above the throbbing beats of generic Rock and Roll.

Dan curtsied while spreading the apron to show the dancing red lobsters then dragged his friend toward three men clustered around an ice chest. "Listen up, Sports Fans. This here's Alex Cannard, the second best B-Forty-seven jockey who ever pushed a crew in Strategic Air Command."

In his pressed slacks, beige sports shirt, and glistening penny loafers, Alex felt out of place joining men wearing cut-offs, tank tops, and sneakers without socks. "Wait a minute, Danny Boy. They're already working for SAC's second best!"

Ignoring Alex's jibe, the host introduced Dick Martinez, Red Hale, and Harley Davidson. Each extended his hand on cue and mumbled some courtesy vaguely remembered. "We also invited girls, but all the mamasans have to be off base by sundown."

"So they can feed papasan before he pulls third shift with the Viet Cong," the tall redhead drawled.

"VC don't bother me no more," yelled Scooter Davidson. "Not when we got our own private Spooky." His tan masked a ruddy complexion, but slurred speech betrayed the incipient alcoholic. "Right now I wanna see every man with a beer in his hand," he shouted.

"Pity all we got to drink is horse piss," Martinez said.

Scooter dipped into the cooler, pulled out a dripping can of Black Label, punctured its top, and thrust it forward.

"Cheers," Alex said before taking a quick sip. "Say, guys, what's the story? Black Label seems to be the only game in town."

"The story," Scooter leaned into Alex's face, "is the beer baron for all Vieet-Nam, the number-one mother, the honcho, the dude in charge of making sure the tap never runs dry, he likes things simple. Just one brand, right? He keeps ordering the Black Label and juggling the books. Ordering and juggling, right? Soon he'll own the brewery. And all us sons of bitches who survive this cesspool can expect early kidney failure."

"I'll drink to kidney failure," Martinez said. "Beats being skinned alive by Charlie."

Dan's eyes flashed; Martinez looked away.

"Hear, Hear!" Red Hale raised his drink. "Why begrudge a poor ol' supply sergeant for makin' his pile? Plenty big boys skim the foam off the top."

"You got that right, pal." Martinez's unblinking eyes challenged Dan.

"Let's can the economic commentary," Strait said as he stripped off his apron. "I happen to like Black Label."

"Me too, Chief," Scooter was in Dan's face now, spraying him with tiny flecks of his favorite beverage. "It's like makin' love in a canoe." He pulled back, struggling to remember his lines. "Fuckin' near water!"

"At ease, Scooter," Dan's temper beat across his forehead, but submerged leaving only a wake of deep furrows Alex did not remember. "Steaks are done. We've got baked potatoes, green beans, and French bread from Bien Hoa's Number One Bakery and Home-built Grenade Factory."

"Call this done?" Hale groused as he shuffled around the brazier. "Looks like a water buffalo after a strafing pass."

"Man, I'll trade you," Martinez yelled. "Mine looks like a crispy critter fried in nape."

Dan raised his hands for silence and looked toward Alex. "Would you like to say grace?"

"Thank you, Dan." Alex searched for a sign he was being led down the primrose path. "But I'll defer to the host."

"Dear Lord, we stand as humble soldiers thanking You for our blessings. Sustain our comrades imprisoned in the North. Comfort our loved ones. Bless the people of this troubled land. Amen." Two thunderous blasts reverberated as Dan crossed himself quickly. "Only afterburners . . . just afterburners."

The prayer lowered a blanket of silence, a spell even Scooter was loath to break. Gradually, however, the group settled into the usual pilot talk: flight characteristics of their airplanes, tactics, and the difficulty of measuring combat effectiveness.

"You guys know the lay of the land," Alex said. "So what's the score? Are we winning?"

"Jesus, Maj," Martinez said. "You're asking for an answer Westmoreland can't give Johnson. Why is it every Fuckin' New Guy wants a score? You got a three-hundred-sixty-five-day sentence; the only score is how many days you got left on your short calendar."

"Get off the major's back," the redhead cut in. "SAC weenies got to have numbers for their management control system. Nothing exists if they don't have numbers."

"Come on, guys," Alex vainly looked for a hint of laughter. "If you Forward Air Controllers don't know what's happening, who does."

"Oh, that's easy," Martinez said. "Nobody knows what's happening, so everybody makes up their own story. But we all agree it's a fuckin' game."

"What the Captain really means," Davidson slurred, "is that it's all a fuckin' game."

Even Dan joined in the laughter as if Scooter were supplying the punch line from a joke known only to the initiates.

"That's a pretty callous way of looking at it." Alex backpedaled knowing he had raised the wrong subject. But the Black Label seemed to demand he persevere. "Surely not everyone thinks it's a game."

"Sorry to upset your illusions, Maj," Martinez continued. "But open your eyes. Aren't you supposed to be the history prof? It's the classic case of trying to kill the alligators when the idea was to drain the swamp."

"What the Captain really means," laughter broke out again as Scooter sallied forth like Quixote charging the windmills, "is that a bunch of Civil Air Patrol cadets could plan a better fuckin' strategy than we've got."

"Strategy, strategy?" Hale overturned the cooler. "Who's got the strategy?"

"Everything we do here is tactical," Martinez said. "We figure high-tech ways to zap individual trucks on the Ho Chi Minh trail. Even your precious SAC got sucked in. Can you beat it? B-Fifty-twos dumping on road junctions and tunnel complexes like blind artillery. That rumbling you hear is Billy Mitchell rolling in his grave. It's all a bunch of bullshit."

"What the Captain really means," Scooter and Hale chorused, "is it's all a bunch of bullshit!" The three officers touched their Black Labels, drained them, and threw the empties over their right shoulders.

"Okay, guys," Alex wanted to de-escalate. "Who's this know-it-all captain."

"He's the absolute final word on this fiasco," Hale said. "Buncha hot rocks up at Cam Ranh pissin' an' moanin' cause they always flew close air support an' never got fragged for MiG sweeps. Then some stud gets an idea, and they concoct this audio tape recording of a reporter interviewing a fighter pilot while a Public Information Officer listens in. The reporter's asking the jock all these silly-ass questions about the war. Powerful stuff like tactics, targets, rules of engagement, all that shit."

"An' the Captain," Martinez cut in, "a real fighter pilot— full of piss and vinegar, horny as a rhinoceros, an' truthful to a fault—he answers in direct fuckin' language. After every answer this fag PIO says 'What the Captain really means,' and then gives the official Johnson-McNamara line."

"Tell me, Captain, what's your opinion of the F-Four C Phantom?" Hale dead panned.

"It's so fuckin' maneuverable, you can fly up your own ass with it!" Martinez responded.

"What the Captain really means," Scooter spoke in a high-pitched, effeminate voice, "is he has found the F-Four C to be highly maneuverable at all altitudes, and he considers it an excellent aircraft for all missions assigned."

"After this goes on and on," Hale resumed the narrative, "the reporter finally asks what the pilot thinks of the war. Quick as a flash, the jock shoots back 'It's a fucked-up war.'"

"An' the PIO," Scooter waved a fresh Black Label, "tellin' the truth for the first time since he got in-country, he says 'What the Captain really means, is it's a fucked-up war!'"

Dan arose as the laughter subsided. "I think we've enlightened our guest enough for one night, gentlemen. For dessert, I've got what's left of my mom's applesauce cake followed by cigars and brandy."

"Dan," Alex was sitting close to his friend in the gathering darkness as the others drifted in and out of the hooch. "I'm having a hard time integrating this whole thing. We're supposed to be winning, yet all I hear is cynicism."

Dan took a long drag on his cigar; the ash glowed red. "It's hard to remain true to the profession after realizing dilettantes are calling the shots. They ignore the principles of war, and we suffer the consequences."

"Is anyone falling on his sword?"

"Of course not. Everyone understands that if he does, three others will leap to do whatever the administration wants. Tell 'em what they want to hear, don't make waves, and get your tickets punched as far from combat as possible. That's the new mode of Command. No more generals like your Macedonian namesake who always led the assault—at least not on our side."

"That's probably a blessing considering most historians now consider Alexander the Great to have been a ruthless, cold-blooded killer who slaughtered his enemies, murdered their women and children, and leveled their cities."

"Sounds like just what we need to end this mess."

"What about Westmoreland?"

"He of the starched fatigues and nineteenth-century rhetoric? Unlike his counterpart in the North, he's not really in charge of much. When Giap says 'Shit,' everybody squats from Hanoi south."

"But Westmoreland's on the cover of *Time* and *Newsweek*."

"He's just the field force commander in South Vietnam, one voice in the wilderness so to speak. What passes for strategy is made way above his pay grade. Everybody's carved out a hunk of turf. CINCPAC in Hawaii controls the navy, the Air Force manages tactical air, SAC holds the reins of the B-Fifty-twos. At present we've got Thieu shuffling Vietnamese forces. Then there's the CIA mucking around with their own private armies, and Air America shuttling hither and yon in birds with no markings.

"Yes, but Westmoreland has half a million troops . . . "

"You think he can go into Cambodia, or Laos, or North Vietnam and kick ass? Some White House egghead who's never heard a shot fired in anger is whispering in Johnson's big ears. You think William Tecumseh Sherman or George S. Patton could fight under these conditions?

"I know there're constraints, but . . . "

"In the meantime, Johnson and his cronies are running the out-country air war like he orchestrated elections in Texas."

"Is this my old pal: West Point, the Long Grey Line, all that Duty, Honor, Country business?"

"Listen my naive friend, you're talking to the original Mr. Military. Johnson says 'Jump,' and I say 'How far.' But I'm in it to win. MacArthur said it all: 'There's no substitute for victory.'"

"Maybe MacArthur was wrong. We re-established the status quo in Korea and kept China in her cage. Times change. If Sherman or Patton had ripped it on the battlefield, at least nuclear missiles wouldn't have blown up the world."

"Whose side are you on, Alex? All we did in Korea was tie up resources forever. Can't the distinguished professor of history see what's happened here? We snubbed Ho Chi Minh in 1946 when he campaigned in Paris for Vietnamese national unity. Instead we sided with France whose goal was always to regain control of her former colonies. Later we disregarded the French debacle and got ourselves bogged down. Now we can't win because we won't employ naked power the way Alexander or any second-rate warlord in this part of the world would do."

"Come on, Dan. I came here like everyone else. I wanted to do my part and fill the square."

"Then don't change, and you'll ace the course. First thing's to become awards and decs officer. That way you can write yourself up for any medal you choose. As many as you like. Then you'll need to find a cushy staff job in Seventh Air Force Headquarters. Command Post's good duty: safe, anonymous."

"I don't deserve that, Dan."

"I know you don't." He took a long drag on his cigar. "I tend to go off the deep end more often lately. I'm short, and this debacle is getting to me. Sacrificing all this treasure, all these people."

"Is it really so bad?"

"Really so bad? Thank God I can still keep my feelings from the enlisted troops. But its more difficult controlling the officers. Sometimes I don't have the energy to slap down men who go eyeball to eyeball with the enemy."

"FACs have a tough job."

"Take Scooter. He's becoming a drunk, but I need him. At least my guys haven't cut a parody tape like *What the Captain Really Means* that's been circulated all over Southeast Asia."

"What's the answer?"

"May not be an answer. Time's running out. A man comes to learn a war and stays to play the game. He lets his replacement sweat the problems he didn't have the balls to handle."

"You're saying what my Ops Officer's too reticent to say. He calls it the 'Vietnam Civil War.'"

"He might be right. Surely you knew what you were getting into. Didn't you wonder what motivated Ho Chi Minh? What did you teach your students?

"Truth is, I didn't probe beneath the surface. Facts aren't clear from a distance of ten-thousand miles. Maybe under those circumstances it's easier to risk your life than stand against the institution that's put food on your table for fifteen years."

"Let's drop this sorry subject, Alex. It's late, and you haven't told me anything about the wife and kiddies and what's happening at Colorado Springs."

"Merrilane's got a job in the athletic department. The Academy's settled down now that the second cheating incident's resolved."

"I told you they didn't get everyone involved in the first scandal. That cancer was bound to grow again. You can't tolerate deviates in our profession. It's like war; half measures won't work."

"Let's not get on that again," Alex said. "Besides, I want to ask you about some of the people Merrilane works with. Do you know Colonel Tucker very well?"

"Old Harvey Tucker," Dan chuckled. "He's an organizational genius. If she can please Harvey, she can please anyone."

"That's nice to know since she briefed him today."

"I stand by my statement. If she got out of Harvey's office with that sexy hairdo unruffled, she's a natural-born administrator."

"What do you know about Rodney Pike, the colonel's assistant?"

Dan rocked back in his chair as he laughed. "Now there's a character. Knows Academy sports and athletic programs inside out. Sharp competitor; wins all the bets. Golf was invented to be played with people like Rod. In sum, a great guy."

Alex hesitated, but then spoke in a voice more stable than he believed it would be. "That's what I've heard. Do you know anything about his personal life?"

Dan's brow furrowed. "It's fairly common knowledge he's a jet-setter. Bachelor. Always has a late-model convertible, usually with a new dolly in it. That's why the cadets are drawn to him. He's living the fantasies of twenty-eight hundred young studs. He's so smooth—manners, dress, dancing—you name it. It's like . . . like . . . he's the kind of guy you'd have a drink with, even if you knew he'd just seduced your wife. Why all the interest in Rod Pike?"

"He's Merrilane's boss," Alex murmured.

CHAPTER SEVEN

ACCEPTING THE BROADMOOR INVITATION allowed Merrilane to indulge herself for the first time since her husband had left. Waiting just inside the hotel's entrance for Rod to return from parking the Corvette, she admired her reflected image. *Quite a transformation*, she thought, *after a harried day drawing all the details together*. Kim had helped by pressing her taffeta skirt while she showered. Afterwards, working quickly in front of the steamed mirror, she dabbed the foundation, brushed gold shadow on her upper lids, added eyeliner, and finished with two swipes of blush across her cheek bones. Pleased with what she saw, she applied plenty of lipstick in case she later decided to leave her trademark.

Rod had arrived with the convertible top thoughtfully raised, so her sprayed bouffant had survived. The long-sleeved, high-necked velvet jacket provided a satisfying backdrop for two strands of pearls. Adjusting the jeweled rosette and its pendant dangling from her left earlobe, she hoped her incessant babbling during the drive had not spoiled the effect of carefree sophistication she had cultivated. If it had, the shameful manner in which she greeted the elderly doorman—flashing a revealing collage of lacy red slip and sheer hose—had surely restored it. Although she might excuse her devilish mood as a reaction to having finished the planning phase, she knew better. She was starved for attention—primed for a night on the town with no one counting the cost or keeping score.

Sensing her need, Iris had insisted the children sleep over. "You deserve an evening with nothing to disturb your pleasure," she had said. "Enjoy yourself and memorize the details because I want a play-by-play."

She smiled to her reflection, thinking of the transparency of the self-assured colonel's lady who loved nothing better than passing juicy bits of gossip. Iris's penchant for all things red, along with her recent emphasis on diet and exercise, suggested her own yearnings were flaring like a supernova before its inevitable cooling.

Appalled by the pettiness of her thoughts, she tried to will them out of her mind. But they bounced back, this time clustering around the husky athlete whose image was now framed in the glass of the doorway like one of the items of memorabilia lining his office shelves. Handsome and experienced, he was too dangerous a specimen to cultivate within the transparent and straight-laced military community. For Merrilane the Academy had become more a goldfish bowl than the zoo to which the cadets compared it. And plenty of sleek cats were watching the swimming fish.

Rod strode into the lobby, hooked an arm behind her waist, and swept her along with him to the upstairs dining room. "Good evening, Charles," he boomed. "Have you saved my table?"

"But of course, Mr. Pike." The maitre d' greeted Rod with an enthusiasm unfamiliar to Merrilane. Bowing slightly to acknowledge the lady, Charles led them to a table all starchy white, glistening silver, and tall glasses. He seated her with the sweep of a father swinging a favorite child, then eased the cork from a bottle that had been chilling in a silver urn. She had anticipated the waiting refreshment but was surprised by the deep red of the liquid Rod swirled in his glass.

"Exquisite," he murmured staring through the poised crystal and directly into her eyes. Reanimated by a nod of affirmation, Charles stepped to Merrilane's side, filled her glass, moved back to replenish Rod's, then disappeared.

"To the most amazing performance by a previously unknown and unappreciated lady."

"Why thank you, boss," she added his title to remind him of their circumstance. "But I am appreciated; the children rarely forget a Mother's Day."

They both laughed as they touched glasses, but Merrilane's titter became a spontaneous outcry causing heads to turn at nearby tables. "Cold Duck! How did you know it's my favorite?"

"Elementary, my dear Watson," Rod affected his Holmesian accent. "I simply asked Lady Harbinger. But I must say, old girl, I was quite unprepared for all the tidbits she gave me."

"Ah, get on w' you," she was Eliza Doolittle before the transformation. "A girl can 'ave no secrets."

After laughing over the events of the day capped by Harvey Tucker's frustration at being unable to fault her briefing, they agreed not to discuss further the athletic department, the Academy, or the Air Force. Channeled by their exclusionary pact into talking mostly about themselves, she soon felt as if they were speaking in tongues, resorting to superficialities—past schools, travel, hobbies—to mask any real clues regarding character traits and proclivities.

Without visible cue, their waiter substituted a Manhattan for Rod's wine, and Merrilane—head beginning to twirl and speech rising a fraction of an octave—realized someone had coached the staff explicitly and she would be called upon to make no decisions. She was being pampered. More than that, intuition told her she was also being courted by a charming gentleman, as opposed to being bird-dogged by some besotted aviator at a sleazy party. A burst of tinkling laughter escaped her at the thought. It flowed across the table, burbled around Rod's handsome features, and caused him again to lift his glass to her.

She had been courted only once before—over greasy hamburgers and sweating cokes. Entertainment since had been mostly at smoky squadron beer busts or ultra-traditional wives' club dances where she always knew with whom she would be leaving. She tried a sultry female smile, looking through lowered eyelashes at the man whose hand she patted to acknowledge the gesture.

Charles materialized in time to keep her from shattering their pact. She had somehow drifted from the thought of squadron parties into a graphic recollection of how terrified she had felt during the Cuban Missile Crisis when Alex had deployed, leaving her and the children within the prime target zone of a Strategic Air Command base. Charles was accompanied by an assistant and a cart loaded with materials—romaine, cubed French bread, Parmesan, additional condiments, trimmings, and dressings she did not immediately recognize—that allowed him to concoct a spectacular Caesar Salad. After completing his performance, accepting their compliments, and serving them, he whisked himself back to the dusty bottle she was sure existed just out of sight behind the palms.

"I should stop eating now," she said after finishing her salad. "But I can't." She laughed at her confession then lustily broke a hard roll sending crisp fragments spattering across the table. "How clumsy of me," she said. "But good!"

His laugh told her he was familiar with the story Alex had passed to her following some otherwise-forgotten deployment to Morocco. Not to worry. A busboy was already brushing away the crusts. Spotting the waiter closing in on her right, she placed her hand over the rim of her glass, thought better of it, and allowed him to "top 'er off."

While her attention was distracted, Charles reappeared to display a masterful arrangement of steamed vegetables and whipped potatoes surrounding a sizzling Chateaubriand.

"You know what I like most about being with you, boss?" She hushed his reply. "You don't ask me to make choices. Alex— bless his heart—dear, departed Alex always has to know what I want to do. Sometimes, when you're tired of kids pestering you all day, you'd just like for someone else to call the plays." She again patted his hand. "You know what I mean?"

For a long while they ate in silence: she savoring each morsel, eating slowly so as to capture the exact nuance of taste for her report to Iris, he mechanically carving and consuming only the meat.

"Thank you for appreciating the arrangements I've made," he finally said. She started to reply, but a twitch of his hand restrained her. "I'm sorry your husband's name came up because I'd wanted tonight to be totally yours. You still don't understand what you've pulled off. You're a natural for detailed planning; maybe it's your mothering instinct. Whatever it is, it's a scarce commodity these days."

His sincerity injected a seriousness she thought they had outdistanced on their mad ride to the hotel. "You've still got challenges," he continued, "but they'll bring out talents you never knew you had. This separation's going to make a new woman of you."

"Thank you," she was speaking to the wine glass, swirling it, hoping to find in its vortex grains of success and happiness. "I suppose I needed kind words more than the Chateaubriand and Cold Duck."

"Just one thing more. I brought you here, and I'll get you home untouched by human hands. In fact, you've been pushing too hard. Take the weekend off. Come back rested Monday so we can crank up your plan."

She put down her glass and stared at the flickering candle. "That's kind of you. I'm a bit fragile tonight. Not cut out for celibate living."

"Few of us are."

"What if he should be killed? What would I have? Two children, a mortgage, a middle-aged body." She raised her gaze, focusing it just below his eyes. "No one's more vulnerable than a flyer's wife. She may be able to balance the checkbook and fix the car, but uncertainty shadows her. It's like tip-toeing around someone with cancer. Never knowing when he'll be taken."

She picked at one of the carrots. "Don't get me wrong. Sometimes life's as romantic as a vintage movie, but he's around so seldom. Always TDY somewhere, or flying, or preparing some briefing or other. But worse of all is realizing nobody cares that my husband's fighting for our country in Vietnam."

She stabbed a carrot, impaling it on her fork, then mashing it to pulp. "Do you think anyone in this room knows where

Vietnam is, much less that men are dying there right now? Perhaps even my husband, . . . tonight."

Charles' approach broke the wine's spell; Rod dismissed him with curt assurances.

"I needed to get that out," she said, "but you didn't need to hear it. Now let's do justice to this beautiful meal and to whatever else you've planned." She hesitated slightly, then smiled like a nervous little girl who had just made a decision. "And, if it makes you feel any less apprehensive about escorting another man's wife, forget it. I'd rather be here with you at this moment than with anyone else anywhere in the world."

CHAPTER EIGHT

ALEX AWOKE with his face mashed against the bare mattress. His mouth reeked of Vietnam: moldering vegetation, sour dirt, the tang of Agent Orange. He rolled onto his back gasping for breath, sucking long gulps of stale air. Beyond the partition, sing-song gibberish accompanied the mamasans' shoe polishing. *Must be late*, he thought, *shoes are their final task*.

The coagulated odor of burnt electrical wiring plugged his nostrils and accentuated the rancidity of stale beer tainted by crystals of fire extinguishing foam that clogged his throat. Foul as the concoction tasted, it was preferable to the bile of instant panic it had replaced.

Sitting up in bed—a damp sheet across his mid-section, hair disheveled and itching—the images and sensations began to coalesce. He had drunk little, two Black Labels chug-a-lugged in quick succession, but he felt like a hung-over undergraduate who had awakened to find someone had brought him home, undressed him, and tucked him safely into bed.

Unwinding from the sheet, he replaced it with a towel, groped for his toilet kit, and shuffled barefoot through the swinging door into the lounge. Gingerly stepping between the squatting mamasans, he ignored their playful and probably lewd remarks as he lurched for the bathhouse.

The tepid shower refreshed him. He attacked the grime and odors that tarnished his body, finishing by lathering and rinsing his hair three times. He rubbed himself down with the coarse washcloth, removing most of the water and noticing how bleached and unhealthy the skin appeared. Pinching himself around the waist, he estimated he had lost fifteen pounds since leaving home. His belly was flat and his chest, hairless except for scattered blond strands on his sternum, was leaner than it had been since high school.

Wrapping the towel back around his waist, he walked slowly to the basin where he had left his shaving materials. Lifting his eyes to the mirror, he saw a haggard face peering grimly back, its forehead mutilated by a bullet hole. Muttering expletives he realized some perverted jester had placed three decals in a string across the mirror, devilishly achieving the illusion of bullet-shattered glass. He slid his kit sideways to occupy the adjacent basin.

"I hear you guys almost bought the farm." It was Bill Wolfe's whining voice.

Leave it to Wolfe, he thought, *to make insensitive comments and sophomoric attempts at humor*. Wolfe, the navigator who normally flew with Swenson, had hung the life-size foldout of an oriental beaver in the Spook House lounge. The mamasans seemed not to notice, nor did any of the other men. But, to Alex's sense of decorum, it was outrageously inappropriate, and Wolfe was forever incapable of understanding why. Undoubtedly it was he who had defaced the mirror.

"Yeah, I guess so." Alex moved to leave, but Wolfe blocked his way. Boyish looking, with severely cropped hair and rolls of fat tumbling over the waistband of his boxer shorts, he pranced with childish insistence.

"Well, what happened?" he demanded as Alex slipped past him toward the screen door.

"Mid-air with the forward air controller in an OV-10. Crash landed on the runway." Alex was gone before he could ask for more.

Dressed in a clean set of fatigues, he found a table in a corner of the officers' club and stared at the blank tablet before him. He had the night off and wanted to compose his thoughts before the investigation into the loss of the high-performance OV-10, which was programmed to replace the puddle-jumpers now directing tactical air strikes. Last night's collision had destroyed the prototype brought in-country for combat evaluation. Its destruction, along with the loss of two test pilots, was a cruel setback. No one seemed concerned about the Gooney Bird's damage or Archer's superb airmanship.

Remembrances, like probing tracers streaking and ricocheting through the night landscape, crisscrossed his mind: a peculiar greenish-yellow hue from the sputtering flares, not light, just the absence of darkness; a single searchlight popping on near Long Bien, sweeping the sky once, then switching off; Archer's jaw keeping the beat of the droning engines as he chewed his gum; dying embers of napalm stirred by the impacts of two 750-pound bombs as Icon Two Four slanted upward glistening like a leaping trout.

"Spooky Seven One . . . we've been hit . . . I think we're going in." He recalled the curiously dispassionate way he had transmitted those words immediately after the neck-snapping jolt that skidded the aircraft sideways, threatening to roll it inverted. After a long moment, he withdrew a pen from his right leg pocket and began to write:

Bien Hoa Air Base
12 May 1968
Dear Colonel Harbinger,
Since this is only my second letter, I'm not doing well as your man in Vietnam. Last night I was almost no one's man anywhere. Lt. Col. Archer and I had scrambled to flare for a fighter strike just east of Nui Ba Dinh, the Black Virgin Mountain.

When we arrived, two forward air controllers flying a combat evaluation of a twin-engined OV-10 were working a flight of F-100s. They assigned us an east-west orbit planning to run the fighters north-south so as to avoid the mountain. After arranging the choreography, describing the target hedgerow, and firing two marking rockets into it, the FACs cleared each fighter in turn for napalm followed by bombs.

We had the area lighted like night skiing at the Broadmoor with two flares at a time in the air. Everything was routine: napalm right on the money, bombs in the nape. Then the OV-10 dropped down to evaluate the damage.

We were turning over the target when he zoomed up and sliced his left propeller through our rear fuselage, severing the rudder cables, jamming the elevators, and almost throwing our flare kickers out the open cargo door. He rolled over and went straight in.

We knew landing would be tricky, but we had both engines, elevator trim, and normal aileron control. At touchdown the right strut collapsed and the old girl swept off the side of the runway and caught fire. We scrambled out amid dust, chemical foam, and the flickering red light of flames.

Forgive my rambling, but they say writing's therapeutic, and I don't want to lay this on Merrilane. I've had some disturbing thoughts lately. Someone said the worth of a man's life is judged by the sort of children he raises. What if I don't come back? Who'd raise Kim and Jeffrey?

When I heard of Alvin Connors' death, I recalled Merrilane telling me of watching Kim playing with his little girl and the daughter of Dick Kraus, who's now at Da Nang. She said she realized one or more of those children could soon lose her Daddy. Alvin's already gone.

Enough of that. Take care of yourself and pass my love to Iris.
Cheers,

He glanced at his watch. Seeing it was almost closing time for the base's dining hall, he hastily addressed an envelope, folded the pages of his letter, and stuffed them into it. He promised himself to write Merrilane later in the evening.

Leaving by the back door beside the club's kitchen, he found his way blocked by a wall of heat emanating from a bank of fire-blackened fifty-five-gallon drums which had been forged into charcoal grills and now resembled the burned-out fuselage of a shattered Spooky. Attempting to pass, he shielded his face with the thin letter. Once again the taste of bile puckered his mouth and triggered a vision of a gaunt, ashen-faced Al Conners emerging from a wall of flame and beckoning to Kim and Jeffrey. Tears penetrated his tightly closed eyelids causing him to feel his features blistering, dissolving, sacrificing themselves to the purifying fire. He stumbled back, wadded the letter, and threw it at the apparition before retreating to the protection of the building's sandbagged wall.

CHAPTER NINE

MERRILANE HAD SLEPT until the sun overheated her body and infiltrated her eyelids. She blinked rapidly, unaccustomed to the brightness of her bedroom at midmorning. Then she stretched like a pampered cat free to spend the whole day purring and grooming herself. Rising from the tumbled mass of top sheet and comforter, she appraised her image in the mirrored closet doors, massaging her flat stomach, measuring the amount of tissue she could pinch between her thumb and forefinger. *Not bad for two children.*

Without bothering to slip into her leotard, she crossed her legs at the ankles and dropped to the floor, steadying herself with her fingertips as she straightened her legs and leaned forward in the first of her yoga postures. Often she had detected Alex pretending sleep but watching mesmerized like some fifteen-year-old Peeping Tom, his eyes darting from her smooth appearance in the mirror to the reality of her undulating body on the carpet.

She rocked back, drew her knees close to her chest, dropped her arms between her legs to grasp the insides of her heels, and slowly extended her legs in a wide vee as she balanced on her coccyx. She had opened herself to the sun, offering her body as casually as she would rotate the potted geraniums in the greenhouse. The sun merely observed, but the posture itself spoke in delicious strains of muscle tension, minute quivering for balance, and tingling gooseflesh causing the delicate hairs on her arms to look like droplets of sun-burnished ocean spray. *Mirror, Mirror on the wall . . . can I balance or will I fall?* She was holding the posture longer than the requisite ten seconds. Under stress her arms began to tremble. With no upper arm flab, her image looked good—youthful. She inspected her breasts, fearful of detecting a sag, then smiled to see unbiased confirmation of their continued symmetry. Glare and natural coloring spoiled proper definition of her areolas, but the engorged nipples thrust themselves out, showing deep center dimples. Her effort to maintain the hip stand until she finished cataloguing her charms caused a sympathetic vibration within the mirror's image. Its epicenter was the trembling patch of dark pubic hair guarding the bright exclamation mark of her neglected labia. Spasms dashed through her body, shattering her concentration and causing her to topple backward. She lay stretched full length thinking how it might be to have a demon lover—a secret spirit, yes, a genie like Charles to visit her on demand, to service her frayed nerves, and know just when to withdraw.

She closed her eyes tightly, creating a shimmering white screen on which to project Charles' features. She had paid little attention to his face, yet his image began slowly to materialize. Full head of dark hair combed straight back and receding high on the temples giving the affect of a monk's cowl that masked the deep-set eyes. Prominent nose, with flaring nostrils blending into parenthesis-shaped furrows encompassing a mouth that broke wide in smile when he greeted Rod, then receded to a nonjudgmental slit as he acknowledged the lady. She would have found it hard to clothe her portrait in anything but the tuxedo he had worn. A demon lover should be tuxedo-clad, with pleated shirt, pearl studs, wing collar, black tie, and perhaps a red sash sinister across his chest.

She wondered if hot blood flowed behind those colorless lips, or if they served only to sheathe sharp incisors. Shivering, she reached for the comforter and pulled it down upon her. Frequently, if the children were still asleep and he did not have to report to the squadron immediately, Alex had slid down beside her after the final lotus. She accepted his self-classification as a world-class lover, yet sometimes after overhearing snatches of woman-to-woman conversation or reading particularly steamy sections of a current novel, she felt cheated that she had no appreciation of the competition. A series of time-consuming jobs throughout her high school and college years, necessitated by her father's abandonment, had seemingly pre-ordained Alex to be her first lover, and then only on her wedding night.

Her husband's ardor confirmed the passion of their courtship, and she reveled in the comforting belief she had been his first. That was God's plan: cavorting like young rabbits, learning together. She had treasured their story of self denial and wanted to share it later with their children, but rampant pre-marital and extra-curricular sex now made her tender story sound naive. Square.

As if to convince herself otherwise, she conjured up memories: "I can tell the way he's taxiing you'd better brace yourself young lady," the Operations Officer had called to her. The bullet-like B-47 heeled over, drastically compressing its left outrigger strut as Alex aligned himself with the small group of overdressed crew wives, shy children, and bored ground crewmen. She could see his helmeted head, pivoting white in the cockpit, oxygen mask flapping alongside his left cheek. Then he was tall beside the ladder, crewcut hair plastered wet, red welt across the bridge of his nose, words lost against rasping power cart, arms reaching, cracked lips rutting, tongue dueling tongue. Later, children entrusted to some forgotten Samaritan, she ran breathless among Jekyll Island's deserted dunes feeling his laughter on her shoulders. "Tell me you love me," he shouted into the chilling October wind. "I love you, love you, love you," she cried as he pulled her down into the sharp sand. "Tell me again you love me." But his lips brushed her eyelids and inhaled her words as she exposed her soft throat to him.

She backed away from the intensity of recall, lapsing instead into analysis. She had stood up relatively well to the strain. They endured by looking to the future, a time when the separations would be less frequent, a time when the family could accompany him to exciting foreign locations. Joining the faculty at the Air Force Academy had been the future, worth the intensive study to acquire a graduate degree. Although still required to fly, the irritants of SAC duty were gone. Twenty-eight-day overseas Reflex deployments and seven-day isolated Home Alert tours were replaced by camping in the Rockies, fall afternoons at Falcon Stadium, and all the social and intellectual trappings of a serious academic community. Still frightfully busy, the time Alex devoted to classroom preparation was often spent in front of a fire with the incentives of a late-night snack, a drink, and sleep uninterrupted by a jangling telephone.

Thoughts of Alex—his strength, his integrity, his good humor—tumbled within her mind. Everything in the room was connected in some way with him. Yet, when she threw off the comforter, repositioned her body, and closed her eyes in a meditation posture, unconscious thoughts darted to troubling remembrances of Rod Pike's courtliness: his eyes probing hers through the wine glass, his lips breathing the single word "exquisite."

He's making a play for me, and I don't know how to handle it because it's been so long since anyone's done it. John Horning at the squadron party when Alex was away. Pretending he'd had too much, slipping his hand lower as we danced, then pawing like a randy teenager as we walked back to the table. Mimi sitting right there, stuffed into that gold lame´ sheath, hanging out at the top, rumored to be pretty hot. Why wasn't she enough?

Alex thinks no bluesuiter would do that to his wife . . . because he wouldn't do it to theirs. What about Ed Nipper when he pinned me against the washing machine? Rod's different. Right out of the old movies . . . a man in complete control. Savoir faire of Cary Grant less the superficiality. More Clark Gable as Rhett Butler. And if I play Scarlett, he'll not give a damn.

This is crazy. Like teenage fantasizing over Mr. Tomlinson. Scribbling diary secrets, bumping into him by the teachers' lounge, interviewing him after every swim meet. He tolerated me like an indulgent uncle. But, toward the end, he seemed to wait for me.

Can't afford involvement. Not any. No one. Not fair to Alex or the kids . . . or to me. Poof—no career in athletics. Or maybe a big boost. Why charm a married woman? I'm clean; that means something these days. And getting horny.

Hold it, old girl, she commanded her reflection. *Stick to your knitting.*

Not on your life! her eyes winked back. *He went off to battle leaving me boxed in by young warriors.*

She shivered so violently that she pulled her legs in tight, wrapped her arms around them, then squeezed with all her strength, seeking physically to pull herself together. She got up, went to the window, and jerked on the thin chain rotating the vertical blinds perpendicular to the pane. She stood naked, sun streaming upon her, contemplating the woodland setting through the bars of her cage.

After awhile the thoughts receded into darkness like the twinkling lights of departing bombers seen through the opaqueness of tears. Looking at her bedside clock, she realized Iris would soon be over, drawn by the lure of coffee and the need to pry. Quickly she showered, toweled, brushed her tangled hair, then pulled on a pair of white toreador pants. She searched her closet for the crimson sweater she often wore with them, then on impulse ignored the sheer bra she had pulled from her lingerie drawer and slipped the sweater over her head. As she stepped into her penny loafers, she heard the sound of Iris's footsteps on the gravel path.

"Here are the children's clothes," Iris said as she offered a crumpled grocery bag. "I'm sorry I haven't washed them. "

"You've already done more than enough. How heavenly to sleep late without a care in the world."

Taking the bag, she was struck by Iris's drab appearance:face without makeup, wispy hair stuffed under a faded peasant scarf, unpressed blouse showing stains on the left breast. She had expected her to come bounding into the house with sparkling eyes, leering grin, and a demand for intimate details.

"I just this moment got dressed," she said, "and haven't even brewed coffee. It'll take just a sec. "

"Don't fix any for me; it seems that's all I've had since yesterday. "

"Don't tell me the kids strung you out that much. "

"No. It wasn't the children; I wish it had been. " She began to weep, reaching out to clutch Merrilane who awkwardly patted her back while absorbing the expanding sobs. She led her into the greenhouse, seated her on the wicker settee, then settled beside her still cradling both of her hands.

"Oh, my God! What is it?"

Her face showing every blemish, every wrinkle, Iris looked furtively around the room, stopping momentarily to gaze at her favorite pillow. Wiping her eyes with a twisted handkerchief already damp, she sniffled twice and fought for composure. "Frank heard from the tests yesterday. He has a malignancy. They're air-evacing him to San Antonio this afternoon. I'm going with him. "

"No, Iris," she instinctively drew back her head, "not Frank. He's as fit as any man I know. "

"Appearance doesn't have anything to do with it. They didn't even let him come home. I spent the night at the hospital worried out of my mind. Lori Wurtsmith stayed with the children and took them to her house this morning. I didn't want to interfere with your evening. "

"What can I do?"

"There's nothing anyone can do right now. It's serious or they wouldn't be taking him to Wilford Hall. They said I can stay in guest quarters. "

"How does Frank feel?"

"You know Frank. He's trying to make light of it. The Dean was in to see him last night, and the Superintendent called. Frank told them both it's a 'classic case of Air Force overreaction.' But he's concerned."

"I don't know what to say. "Merrilane brushed the tears from her eyes with a forgotten napkin that had been lying on the coffee table.

"There's not much to say. "Iris had composed herself. "We'll have to wait and see. "She brightened a bit and patted Merrilane's hand. "What's your situation?"

"I'm fine. Slept till ten thirty, did yoga, and had a quick shower. Dinner with Rod was absolutely scrumptious. He's a wonderful host—perfect gentleman. "

"I didn't mean that. I wondered if you'd heard from your husband. "

Dropping her eyes, Merrilane noticed the bright red lacquer had chipped from the nail of her ring finger. "I don't know how he is. I haven't heard from him since that crazy, mixed up MARS call. "

"That's the problem," Iris said. "Not knowing how they are."

CHAPTER TEN

ALEX BEGAN HIS JOURNAL upon leaving California, but he became seriously involved only after arriving at Bien Hoa. On mornings when fatigue caused him to drop lifelessly into bed, he subsequently placed the journal at the top of his priority list, sometimes sacrificing meals to catch up. Even a two-day absence from its pages allowed his memory to blur.

He wrote remembering Erwin Rommel's difficulty recreating the lessons of his first war imperfectly lodged only in memory. In writing, he came to realize he was better prepared to discuss warfare intellectually than as yet to command a gunship. His reading of *The Red Badge of Courage* had warned that combat would test his resolve. *All Quiet on the Western Front* taught him to expect privation and to realize he might not survive. Clausewitz's *On War* had shown the absurdity of trying to win by military means alone. Aware of the clash between military and political viewpoints concerning Vietnam, he wondered if he would ultimately record that no successful strategy was agreed before time ran out.

The enemy's intelligence and tenacity impressed him. Their ability to attack without warning implied the tacit support of the populace. Realizing this, and knowing his country was using weapons designed to inflict indiscriminate pain—napalm, cluster bombs, flechettes—caused him to reflect upon the war's morality or, at the least, its fairness.

Having brought his journal up to date on a rare night off, he leafed through its pages while listening to rain drumming on the roof, gushing off the eaves, and spattering into the drainage ditches. He appreciated not having to preflight an aircraft in the deluge, thereby avoiding for a time the feel of clammy metal, green mold, and wet feet. He had skipped dinner in hopes the rain would abate so he could eat midnight breakfast. He was a night person now, a vampire rising to fly into the darkness, then scurrying back before first light.

Sunday, 5 May 1968

Two sorties totaling 9.2 hours with Peter Pan (Panatelli); 106 hours so far. Scrambled to 260 radial, 25 miles from the Bien Hoa tacan. Lighted for air strike; hosed down area afterwards. Several secondary explosions; left a good-size fire burning. Later fired to protect troops trying to recover a machine gun.

Ordered to suspected mortar position south of Saigon. No forward air controller. Couldn't pinpoint the particular intersection of a canal and the Saigon River. Short rounds are the bugaboo. Peter says villagers hide in bunkers dug inside their hooches. Archer says not to worry; they're all VC anyway.

Decided not to shoot. Having Peter, Hubbard, or Archer in the right seat reduces the stress. The instructor gets hung if anything goes wrong. Soon the decisions will be all mine.

Peter says South Vietnamese (ARVIN) units always want us to spray indiscriminately to their front regardless of the populated areas. Large US forces often want only illumination flares. They're comfortable just knowing we're overhead. Long range patrols or ambush teams don't want their positions compromised by our flares. That's the toughest firing: trying to see their tiny strobe beacons in the blackness and then gauging range and bearing to the bad guys. I'm not looking forward to it; a Spooky's short rounds could decimate them.

Monday 6 May 1968

Big night: three sorties and a rocket attack. Total 8.5 hours. Charlie's got something going. First concerted action since Tet. Scrambled to support a strike on a town west of Saigon by F-100s out of Bien Hoa loaded with napalm and bombs. Nape came first, two canisters at a time, and then the bombs. They left the village an inferno. The FAC then committed them for strafing on a second ville two kilometers north. The impacts of their cannon shells walking up the main street looked like a child's sparkler thrown in the dirt.

Dropping flares is such a passive undertaking one can't help feeling like a disinterested bystander, some frivolous god looking down on the follies of man. Flares cast a greenish-yellow wash, distorting the landscape with flickering shadows. Outside the circle of contami-

nated illumination, the earth is a velvety black cloth ominously dark toward Cambodia, pierced by light in only a few places to the south, but flooded to the east by the millions of blips making up the Saigon-Cholon-Tan Son Nhut complex. Overhead billions of stars prick the dome of the night sky in a spectacle almost as awesome as the twinkling bursts that had preceded the fighters.

Got deathly ill about 0400 and had to unstow and use the aircraft's potty. A humbling experience. Pilots want everyone to think we're above such mundane functions. We've certainly convinced aircraft designers, as the facilities are always primitive. The unwritten law is "Clean it if you use it." That's one job the poor crew chief doesn't get stuck with.

After landing and cleaning the bucket, I was sitting in the crew truck when four rockets hit near the fuel dump. We had on our flak vests and helmets. Mother Hubbard had seen to that. The rounds could just as well have landed on our portion of the flight line.

Friday 10 May 1968

Most productive night yet! Two sorties with Peter Pan totaling 9.1 hours. Lighted for two fighter strikes. I've got the hang of flaring; firing's another matter.

Ate midnight chow after landing then scrambled with Peter in the left seat for a South Vietnamese fort on the Cambodian Border.

In clouds the whole way. Finally popped out to see mortar blasts illuminating the outpost. No one answered my calls, so we circled while our Vietnamese interpreter worked his own frequencies.

Finally I raised a round-eye at Tay Ninh who knew the frequency of a Special Forces camp that had a land line connection with the guys who needed us. Since he didn't want to give the frequency in the clear, he told me to "go up 2.4 from Jack Benny's age." Every VC radio operator must surely know Jack Benny's 39, but I didn't care who might be listening.

"Wildwood Pumpkin" answered saying the enemy was overrunning the camp, had already occupied one bunker, and were pouring through the wire on the southwest side. The ARVIN commander wanted us to hit the southwest point of his pentagon-shaped fort and do it quick.

Peter rolled in with three guns on fast fire. I saw five secondaries, probably satchel charges carried by the sappers. We had blacked out and pulled our props off sync. But our flares silhouetted us against the cloud base, and our tracers pinpointed our flight path.

Answering green tracers filled the air; most arched behind us, so Peter and I could ignore them. But our gunners and loadmaster had to look. Learned later our engineer had crawled inside the armored flare box. He experienced only the pictures his mind produced. I think the rest of us preferred the tracers.

Pumpkin radioed that the enemy was pulling back, abandoning their dead and wounded. Peter hosed their route of retreat then shifted northwest to engage a .50 caliber machine gun.

There's not much anti-aircraft fire this far south. But it's well planned. They offset their guns from the attack or escape routes and never fire unless we're beginning to hurt their main force.

I tend to think of "Charlie," the little guy in black pajamas. But we're increasingly meeting the North Vietnamese Army, the NVA. I've argued with Archer that this proves the North is invading the South. He's not impressed; it's still a civil war to him with us on the losing side.

His eyelids drooped. Outside the rain still pelted down. He thought of the grunts in the field, holes filling with water, feet soaked, rain streaming off their helmets and down the backs of their ponchos. He thought of their apprehension, knowing weather had grounded all air support. They could forget the friendly light, the comforting drone of Spooky overhead, the helicopter gunships, and the lifesaving Dust Off.

He was grateful not to be a grunt in the field, or a Thud jock waiting to be called to go North before ever dropping off to sleep, or a Jolly Green rescue pilot facing another day hovering inside the cauldron. He began his nightly prayers by asking the Lord to be with each of those men, with all of the US and the ARVIN; then he prayed for the souls of his enemy. He dropped off to sleep still holding his journal and thinking about all the people he was glad he was not.

CHAPTER ELEVEN

ALEX GAINED PROMOTION to gunship commander in mid-June: two months, ten firing missions, and 250 hours in the aircraft following his arrival at Bien Hoa. Afterwards he fell into a cycle of flying, sleeping, and eating. From time to time bland letters arrived from home. Merrilane, in an almost unrecognizable scrawl, wrote their children were enjoying the recreation program, she was losing weight "running my legs off," and Rod was priming her for a "great new job with fantastic possibilities."

He answered in kind with innocuous notes telling about the base facilities, the weather, and the patrols, as if that were all his job entailed. Sometimes, rereading what he had written, he wondered why he should feel disheartened. The food was plentiful and good. He nightly gained experience that could lead to high-visibility assignments. All he had to do was put in his time, fill the squares, and play the game.

Would George Patton, Billy Mitchell, or Curt LeMay have played this game? He had trained for war all his life, even as a little boy maneuvering tin soldiers in the black dirt of his yard. He knew how and when to apply air power; he had read Clauswitz, Caesar, Thucydides; he could organize and motivate. But he refused to play a game that sacrificed men, ignored the storehouse of history, and seemed to have no defined goal.

Why, he mused, *continue circling air bases knowing the army's counter-battery radar and artillery can now defend against rocket and mortar attacks? Why not move closer to the action on the Cambodian border? When will a tactics manual be published to standardize procedures for flare dropping, operating with FACs, and working with helicopter gunships?* The lack of answers to these questions exacerbated his professional frustration. *Maybe*, he thought, *I need to talk directly to the tactics office in Saigon.*

Ultimately he mitigated the aggravation by becoming Mother Hubbard's executive officer, responsible for complying with the multitude of peacetime regulations still in effect. Soon he found himself frequently thinking less like a soldier and more like a bureaucrat. Billy Mitchell had rebelled against that in1925, and they cut his heart out. *Was that why*, he wondered, *modern generals were submissive to foolishness?*

His days merged into an unremitting grind of flying, napping, and working at the trailer. Soon his efforts bore dividends: file cabinets bulged, reports went out on time, and the floor sparkled. Even the haggard look around Hubbard's eyes began to fade. For his reward he received a ration of aircrew banter, including some that crossed the border into jealous grousing.

Sometimes, as he plied his course around the patrol envelope, he reflected on what motivated fellow officers to harass him. Was there even one person he could consider a confidant? Where in the Spookies could he find the sense of belonging and comradeship he had felt in SAC? Then, one night as he listened to the hypnotic drone of the engines, he realized his unit was just a bunch of strangers thrown together for a short time, never again to meet after finishing their tours. And his confidant? Only the mother of his children, who seemed to be slipping further away than the ten thousand miles physically separating them.

Think only of flying, he commanded himself. *Ignore the pressure building in your loins; hang on a few more months before daring to think about seeing Merrilane.*

Desperate to see his children, Bill Pritchard told him he planned to meet the whole family, twin babies and all. "Screw the cost," he said. "Gotta make sure the kids touch my face, so they'll remember how I looked, how my whiskers dug into their little bellies, and how my arms lifted them above the waves. Time for Momma after lights out," he said. "Strip the bank account, sell the mutual fund, borrow from the credit union, but get to Hawaii and live like a king."

But before Hawaii in the seventh month, Alex thought, *will come places like Lai Kay in the fourth, Duc Lap in the fifth, and Katum in the sixth. After that, what strange name, what set of coordinates awaits in the game of Filling the Vietnam Square? Outside his own little family, who cares?* Listening to the drumming of the engines and watching the twinkling stars, he had finally answered the question others smarter than he had figured out the first week, or some like Archer had known long before they came. Nobody cares.

CHAPTER TWELVE

MERRILANE LAY ON HER BED surrounded by reports. A thick candle cast a soft glow over the room. In times past its aromatic scent had both soothed and aroused her as she lay close to Alex. Not tonight. The giddy day of triumph in Harvey Tucker's conference room had long past, replaced by the seemingly endless task of pulling details together. Congratulatory smiles from associates quickly dissolved into furrowed brows and shabby excuses whenever she broached yet another requirement. Still, she launched the activities on schedule. Little thanks to Rod Pike who abandoned her after their evening at the Broadmoor.

Desperate, she had called General Safire, the Commandant, appealing for assistance from among the available pool of cadets. She knew upperclassmen were handling the basic training of freshmen in Jack's Valley and hoped Safire would detail one or two to help her.

She remembered the nervousness she felt waiting for the general to come on the line. "Merrilane!" his cheerful voice had boomed. "Congratulations on the job you're doing with those kids. The Superintendent told me they looked better than my cadets."

Safire was quite a charmer. Some said those two MiG-21s he blasted from the sky just dropped their gear and flaps and waited for his missiles to run up their tailpipes. But he sounded sincere. In any case, she knew a cadet's time would be a cheap price to pay if it not only guaranteed a reciprocal favor from the athletic department but also allowed the Commandant to share in the reflected glow from her project.

"I'll get back to you," he said. "I think I have just the gentleman you need."

The general's secretary called within thirty minutes to say Cadet First Class J. D. Pinski would report after the noon meal. Shortly after one o'clock, as she figured bus schedules for the girls' water ballet team, she heard a clumping sound that became more distinct as the clicking typewriters in the outer office fell silent. Looking up she saw limping toward her a toothy grin, a T-shirt stretched over a huge torso, and a worn cast protruding from the slit right leg of otherwise skin-tight fatigue trousers.

"Afternoon, Ma'am," a voice boomed like an offensive television commercial. "I'm Jack Daniels Pinski. The Comm said you wanted me to kill somebody."

Merrilane heard the snickers from the main office where the typewriters were still silent. "That's not exactly right," she said. "All I need is some scheduling help. Are you sure you're up to it?"

She tingled even now remembering how his eyes had coveted her as she rose from her desk. They roved leisurely, seemingly intrigued by the wispy swirls of her hair, maybe a little amused at her perfectly applied cosmetics, but obviously impressed by her white blouse with the stand-up collar and narrow epaulets. She remembered her cheeks warming as if she were standing alone on the market block while some heathen prince casually shopped for an addition to his harem. When he finally answered, he couched his reply in the formal argot cadets seemed to believe made whatever they said acceptable.

"Yes, Ma'am," he said with twinkling eyes, "you can rest assured, Ma'am. Jack Daniels can satisfy your every need."

She ignored his remark and his injury. Offering him a chair beside hers at the cluttered desk, she explained her project and the administrative workload that prevented her from getting out of the office to spot potential conflicts. Pinski asked a few terse questions, then shifted his leg dramatically, winked at her, and said, "Your troubles are over, Ma'am."

She smiled recalling her feeling of perverse pleasure as she rose from her desk, brushed the eraser crumbs from the front of her skirt, and adjusted the waistband that covered her flat stomach. Prancing out the office door, she had called over her shoulder, "You're on your own, Mr. Pinski. I'll see you at four-thirty."

Fluffing up her pillows and shifting her position in bed, she realized she had thoroughly enjoyed defusing Jack Pinski. His behavior characterized that of a small number of senior cadets whose proclivities, when coupled with military training, imparted an arrogance men sometimes called laudatory but most women found insufferable. Having been in a bitchy mood all morning, she had relished the opportunity to stifle the young man's ego while simultaneously stoking his interest in her.

Surprisingly, Pinski evolved into her white knight. By the time she returned to the office that first day, the bus schedule was typed for her signature, and he had introduced himself to the office staff as "Miz Cannard's scheduling officer." In that capacity, he had also designed a wall chart to display the names of the teams, their play dates, game locations, coach's name, and won-loss record.

Dropping her veil of antagonism, she had signed the schedule without reading it and quickly approved his design. Insisting she leave the details to him, he had the chart made, installed, and filled with data within two days. As "Mr. Inside," he did most of the scheduling, posted the results, and extinguished the fires that flared from time to time. Watching him work, she could almost hear the details clicking into place. Having the services of an aide like Pinski allowed her freedom of movement. She met the coaches, observed the clinics, made sure first aid packs were available, coordinated the use of playing fields, and extended the concept of an Academy-only program to one that next year would encompass the Black Forest and the Palmer Lake school districts.

Kept on the run during normal duty hours, the only time she found to confer with her assistant was after five. That gave her almost an hour to review the details of the day and forecast what was on the horizon. She realized she was conducting what Alex and his SAC friends would call a "stand-up briefing." But it was limited to the two of them, and they did not stand; they sat huddled together in the deserted office, often with heads almost touching as they worked.

Breaking off her reminiscences to rummage inside the drawer of her bedside table, she extracted a tablet and ballpoint. She had neglected writing Alex for four days, or was it five? But how could she explain today's events? Things had started innocently enough: she and Jack poring over his charts for two hours putting the finishing touches on the playoffs in soccer, field hockey, and softball.

Thinking back, she could not say she had been unaware of the breakdown in formality and the feelings of easy familiarity that had evolved between them. Despite Alex's warnings regarding the necessity of walking a narrow line whenever cadets were present, she had thought their situation was different. It was professional, job-oriented, a relationship where rank and authority had little need to intrude. Being heavily burdened with the responsibility of making the decisions and running all the coordination, surely she could not be blamed for missing the danger signs. To her, Pinski's continual attempts to move into areas more her own prerogative, his offers to miss dinner or to come back later to work, even his insistence he drop off plans at her home on the weekends, were only the outgrowth of an enthusiasm and dedication equal to her own.

But today she had learned differently, had seen the nature of the beast coiled inside young Mister Pinski. She had returned at ten minutes after five, breathless after rushing in from Colorado Springs, and apologetic for keeping him waiting. As he automatically did each time she entered, he had risen to greet her. But this time he was less clumsy.

"You're out of your cast!" she remembered shouting. "Let me look at you."

She rushed around the desk instinctively placing her hands on his shoulders to hold him at arms' length. It was the first time they had touched, and she felt an involuntary shutter. Like a superbly trained wrestler moving to exploit an improperly executed hold, he brought his own hands up to clamp each of her arms and pull her body tight against his. "I want you, lady," he said distinctly before stifling her reply with his lips.

Stunned, her mind flashed back to the time she had skidded on ice and was spinning toward the thin cables marking the precipice. One moment she had been comfortably unconcerned; the next found her totally out of control and sliding toward oblivion. Popping back into focus like a slide reacting to the projector's heat, her mind riffled the rape scenarios she had imagined during countless lonely vigils. She struggled to disengage, to pull away from the hot marble of his encroaching body. But her defense was as brief and ineffective as that of a rabbit caught by a pouncing hound. Like the rabbit, she was terrified any movement would cause her captor to snap her slender neck. As panic immobilized her, he released her arms, sliding both his hands up alongside her face and into her hair. At the same time his harsh tongue penetrated her lips.

As his stubby fingers shredded and tangled her bouffant, ego muffled her confused emotions and banished passivity. She slipped out of his grasp and retreated to the doorway clasping her arms tightly across her breast. He moved to follow but stopped, transfixed by her expression of consternation even before hearing her soft whimper.

Neither spoke. He dropped into his chair breathing deeply and reaching for a handkerchief to rub the lipstick from his mouth. He extended it to her when he saw the tears streaming down her face. She accepted the folded square of cloth and began to dab at her eyes. Afterwards she retrieved her purse from the floor, found her comb, and walked to the mirror on the wall. Deftly she arranged the strands of hair, swirling them into an approximation of her usual design. Then she applied a few strokes of make-up and a thin strip of lipstick. After arranging her blouse which had pulled from her skirt, she turned to face him.

"I'm sorry that happened, Jack," she said. "Perhaps I led you on in some manner, but that was not my intent."

"Don't apologize," he said. "I've wanted it to happen, fantasized about it, plotted it. But I didn't plan it for today because a lot's been going on that I needed to tell you about. It just happened. I guess it's bigger than the both of us." He tried to grin with the last cliché, but the effort surrendered to a quizzical look, with his eyes darting around the room as he fretted over her next move.

Their exchange had given her time to reorganize her thoughts. Once again she was the detached executive, a role she had grown to relish. "Jack," she said as he avoided her eyes, "you've been a great help to me. But I'm a wife and mother as well as a working woman, and I can't afford any more distractions."

Why had she chosen those words? Why didn't she make it clear she would not tolerate any further advances? The precise circumstances were hazy in her mind now as she tried to remember exactly what else she had said to him. She knew he had seemed to understand, had gone on to brief her, and had discussed the next day's activities before leaving.

One detail she recalled too vividly, moaning audibly as she relived the incident. She remembered feeling almost a mother's compassion when she saw his downcast eyes and slumped shoulders as he rose and moved awkwardly toward the door. But that twinge had changed to rank desire as her eyes traced the muscle structure across his back and shoulders.

CHAPTER THIRTEEN

YOU HAD YOUR CHANCE, mister, and blew it. Let her get away after she made the first move. Sliding those cool hands on your arms making the hairs stand up and tingle. She was yours: a trout ready to roll belly up. Belly up, belly up, heaving and moaning, belly up. Eyes wide, lips quivering, voice a whimper. And you, dry-mouthed and shaking, slacked off the line. Oh, Daddy! Is she worth it? You always had a good eye. You told me so.

"Biggest problem you've got to face, son, is what to do about women." Hiram Pinski had brushed a wayward coal back into the fire. "If you take after me, the juices are flowing hot and heavy. If you take after your mother, you may not have a problem at all."

"I've got a problem, Dad."

"Wondering about your performance, are you?"

"Responsibilities, too."

"Responsibilities is it?" Pinski leaned back chuckling and pulled two dripping bottles from the cooler. "Don't take yourself so damn seriously. Look what it got your mother."

"You're telling me I don't have any responsibilities."

"I'm saying you're not *solely* liable. When a woman plays along, she shares the obligation. They want equality? I say 'fine.' But let 'em go in with their eyes open, like a man.

"Don't get me wrong. Life's not pure indulgence. The idea's to find a balance that allows a man to take life as it comes. He's got to learn to treat women as people, not goddesses."

"They might as well be goddesses. They're so remote."

"You're talking girls. I'm talking women."

"Come on, Dad. That kind of thinking will get me in the penitentiary."

"Thinking like that will remove all the romantic claptrap and let you put sex in perspective. It's ultimate communication: intercourse between friends. Don't complicate it."

"But Dad . . ."

"Look, I know I'm asking a lot. I just don't want you to put yourself through unnecessary heartache. The best sex partner is a woman who accepts it as naturally as you do. Don't allow the fucking taboos to mess up your life." He had laughed at his little pun, adding an exclamation point with his up-ended bottle.

And you, poor little fella, couldn't wait to net her. Couldn't wait for an invitation. It would have come. You've seen it before. Acting so prim while knowing all along she's been abandoned. Soon she'd have said "what the hell" and begged you for it. Afterwards she'd wonder if it wasn't her idea from the start. You knew that, and still you couldn't wait. Afraid time would run out for you like it did for him.

If you'd played her along, taken it easy, flattered her, you'd be doing it right now. Doing it like dogs on the carpet: rolling and tearing and biting, both of you making plans for the next time. Like dogs, that's good. You're hung up on her. And she's Air Force property; that makes it all the better.

As he began the steep climb leading to the dormitories, a sharp pain shooting up from his ankle broke his trance. The bone was still weak; but without the cast, the leg felt as light as his head which seemed to be floating toward the jagged crest of Pike's Peak like a radiosonde dangling beneath a weather balloon.

What if I meet an officer? Falcon Code number Forty-nine: "Pardon me, sir, but you have me confused with someone who gives a shit."

He rubbed the back of his hand across his mouth wondering if he had removed all the lipstick. He realized he should have relieved himself and checked his reflection in a mirror. That's what women are for, he mumbled almost aloud, to be man's relief valve. Miz Alexander Cannard, USAF, just one more pit stop on Black Jack Pinski's road of life.

Merrilane would have been surprised, shocked really, if she had gained access to her cadet's personal logbook with the nine carefully lettered names and inscribed stars. But what might be surprising and shocking to a sheltered housewife could be considered admirable from a certain masculine perspective. His most recent dalliance was "Sally," awarded a miserly two stars. She had been preceded apparently by sisters: "Julie" listed first (two stars), then "Carrie" (three!). Curious, she would have squinted to read the amplification printed in tiny letters within precise brackets following Carrie's name: "Mrs. Oliver J. Fischer ('Mamabear')."

You sure made a nice recovery. Gotta admire that in a woman. Standing there afterwards, all back together, and beginning to lecture. Not knowing I'd heard it all before from Julie Fischer's mother. I'd seen ol' Mamabear sizing me up all the while she was pushing Julie at me. Not knowing we were already making it in Papabear's Beetle. What a nice guy. Who'd hump such a nice guy's fifteen-year-old daughter?

She'd been so happy I'd dropped by. Julie wasn't home, and the Buick wouldn't start. And her with so much shopping she just had to do that very afternoon.

Then we walked into the garage with her trailing so close behind that the smell of the booze overpowered her overpowering perfume. Popped the hood. Knees beginning to shake, goose bumps springing out on my arms, breath coming fast as I leaned in to check the battery.

And Mamabear sliding her coarse hands up under my shirt, "Oh, Jackie, honey," then folding her arms tight across my chest and arching her shivering body over my back, "Light my fire, Baby." Attaching herself like a leach. "Love me, Jackie Baby. Love me."

Horny married women, can't beat 'em. Earning three stars easy, maybe four, with their stock of experience and pent up frustration. Trying to prove they're still alive, just like the soap opera queens they watch all day. Poor neglected Mamabears. Born thirty years too soon. Nothing to do but sit home all day, takin' a little nip from time to time, watchin' the tube, livin' their fantasies through their daughters, an' hoping Sis won't get stuck with a loser like they did. Wonder what Mamabear was thinking as she hung on me whispering all those gutter words and fumbling with the zipper on my Levis? Did she ever really care any more about me than I cared about her? What was in her head when she started rubbing me up? Same as in mine as I turned to face her? Relief, pure and simple. Just our inalienable right to relief.

But what if I'd been some kid . . . some boy just beginning to come out of his shell? She could have ruined me, if I hadn't already started ruining myself. And all the things she screamed that last night after I told her she'd better get some lessons from Julie. Imagine saying those things to me after all I'd done for her. Haven't thought of Mamabear for a long time. She was good. Like stretching out in the sunlight on the warm bow of an anchored boat and being gently lifted and dropped by each incoming swell. Oh, Mamabear, more power to you! I take back all those nasty things I said. But Mamabear, you got a right to know: Goldilocks is gonna sleep in your bed.

She'll make me a Double Ace when she goes down. The Boss-lady's number ten. Number ten on a ten-point scale. Funny. She's probably number one on the Major's list. By now he's thinking like a gook. "My sistar Num-bar One, GI." Wonder how many pit stops he made before settling on her? How many since? Merrilane, Merrilane, my little chickadee; fly with me to the garden of earthly delights . . .

He gained the entrance to his dormitory without encountering anyone. He had missed the dinner formation, but that had become routine lately. Smiling at his reflection in the glass doors, he saluted himself, taking confidence from his appearance. No bed check or roll call; time to play commando again. First came support for his ankle. Jump boots did the trick. Next he pulled out his field jacket. Then the knitted watch cap, friend of a hundred adventures: skiing at Vail, stalking the weary doolies, slipping through the forbidden corridors of Fairchild Hall after lights out. He was all set, ready to reenter the lists, but this time he would have a plan.

Once outside he considered diverting to the gym, showering with water hot as live steam, then letting the sauna's vapor sanitize his congested brain as purifying sweat oozed from his body. He wondered how long it would take to soak away his impurities, the worst a cadet could have.

No, he thought. *Gotta visit Barbie doll. Seize the moment! Ride to the sound of the guns.* He jogged easily to the cadet parking lot and began to strip away the canvas cocoon shrouding his new Corvette. *First Classman's car if there ever was one.* He planned to drive toward Castle Rock until the light began to fade, then double back toward the Black Forest.

Clouds were whipping across the mountains, promising spectacular thermals for the glider pilot gutsy enough to reach for them. The threat of rain only added to the sense of adventure. They had endured three days of almost solid rain, he recalled, after he and his father had flown to Maine for his sixteenth birthday. The Colonel wanted to go somewhere far from the command post. He also needed a break from Mom, his son had thought at the time. She could be a tremendous pain without even trying; nothing was ever good enough.

The Corvette flashed through the north gate accelerating to gain the interstate. Its driver, however, was straining the red Navion through swirling clouds, windshield stippled with beaded crystals, wings an opaque slab of rime ice. He had pulled the seat all the way forward so that he hunched over the wheel, intently scanning the flight instruments, and casting anxious glances at the manifold pressure gauge. His father lit a cigar, expelled a huge cloud of smoke bringing the obscuration inside the cockpit, and thumped him on the thigh.

"Loosen up, son, and enjoy it. Don't let the bird know a little weather bothers you."

Releasing the seat catch and sliding backward, he trimmed off the control pressures and sneaked his father a sideways grin. Ahead he saw a lightening of the veil, then an aureole shimmering with the colors of the visible spectrum. They popped through the circular rainbow into sparkling sunshine.

"Attaboy! Couldn't have done better myself."

After a refueling stop at Cleveland where he broke a five-hundred-foot ceiling in light rain, he descended smiling through thick clouds into Lewiston, Maine, for his second instrument approach of the day.

"Field in sight, Capt'n," his father sang out fifty feet above ILS minimums. This time he thumped him on the back.

Remember how we huddled under a tarp I rigged to protect the campfire, sipping on a couple of Coors, beginning to dry out but feeling a letdown after the hunter's high? I can see you, Dad, leaning against a log nursing that beer, staring into the fire, unfurling your true colors with no embarrassment.

You really were a great Dad. I don't think I ever told you. Wish I had. Treated me like a grownup even when I was a little kid. Remember how you always gave me beer when we stayed up late to tie flies? Drove Mom up the wall. You talked about he-man things. Later, when I was all-everything at high school, you knew I was screwing my eyeballs out, but that was okay because you were still trying to teach me about women, not girls.

"A man wants a woman who doesn't smother him, who doesn't move in so tight."

"What's a woman want?"

"The good ones want the same thing."

"If you know so much about women, what happened between you and Mom?"

"You're learning, Son. Learning to ask the penetrating question. Problem is there's lots of slippage between theory and practice. Most of the time, you don't figure out good theory till your practice is in shambles."

"We don't have to talk about it . . ."

"No, it's time we did. God knows your mother and I never do any more. She was seven years younger than me. I'd been pretty wild in England during the war, never knowing if the next mission would be my last. That was an excuse of course, but a damn good one. Not that you needed an excuse. An English lass is special, a natural woman. Anyway, all that was past when I met your mother, and yet it wasn't past. She saw me as Prince Charming awakening Sleeping Beauty. But, as she awoke to her womanhood, she seemed to ignore her own life and start living mine, wanting to share my job, my thoughts, my fantasies—even crowding me in bed at night. I reverted back to my wartime style, lots of one-night stands, leaving little clues so she'd know and then back off. When you and your sister came, she tried to live through you until there wasn't much of her left except a nagging woman who needed to be aware of every single happening. I sometimes think my kiss turned a fun-loving college girl into a shrew . . . and me into a frog." He laughed a dry little laugh and wet it with his Coors.

"You still love her, though . . . "

"How can you love something that tries to bore into your head like some alien in a sci-fi flick? I love my job because I'm judged solely on results. I love you kids because you don't crowd me or refuse to talk to me. But I sometimes wonder what I'll do when they make me retire and when you kids are on your own."

"What'll she do?

"I don't know. Maybe we'll be stuck with each other. Maybe out of boredom we'll try to grow back together. Stranger things have happened.

"I wish you would. I think you need each other."

"Marriage doesn't come with a guarantee. You can sleep with a woman before you marry and think you're compatible as mink, but I'll be damned if I know how you can forecast whether she'll continue to develop as a whole person."

"I always hated it when you two argued. I thought somehow it was my fault."   •

"Well, it wasn't. We've never had any complaints about you or your sister. Both better than we deserve."

I wish you were here with me, Dad. We'd continue on up to Denver and have a big steak, and some beers, and talk flying and stuff women will never know about no matter how hard they try to get inside our heads. I think about you all the time. About what they did to you. I feel your touch even now when I'm so hyper I can hardly feel anything but the blood pounding in my temples. When you left you put your arm around my shoulder like you always did. But instead of just hugging me, you kissed me on my forehead. And I can still see your eyes glistening as you told me you didn't care what I did with my life as long as I didn't drift. You wanted me to do something worth doing, and be good at it, so that when it's over there wouldn't be any regrets.

Oh, Daddy, you promised me nothing would happen to you!

Coming in from the east where no houses existed, he eased the car over graveled ruts, then parked among the pines. He circled the Frenchman's place on foot, forgetting his weak ankle. Landfall was the enclave of three houses clustered at the top of the road.

Colonel Harbinger's next door to Barbie Doll. Rumor says he's got the big C. Tough luck; nice guy; good lookin' wife. Hard rain, no moon, pitch black. Glistening greenhouse bulging like a jungle insect's eye. Just a simple stroll to her back door. Wonder how the Viet Cong's making out? No sentries, no trip flares, no mines. No guardian angel circling overhead.

CHAPTER FOURTEEN

"MUST BE WINNING THE WAR," Alex said. "Monthly Commander's Call just like stateside."

Peter Pan opened one eye, closed it again, slid lower in his seat, and pulled his fatigue cap down until only his moustache and chin showed. "We're starting standardization checks next month," he muttered. "More paperwork for the instructors."

"Then they'll bring in a team for a compliance inspection," Alex said as he also slid lower in his seat.

The theater was stifling despite the open side doors and two pedestal fans struggling to circulate fetid air. Hubbard and Archer huddled near the podium debating how to replace their advertized speaker.

"What time's the four o'clock meeting?" someone heckled from behind Alex. Laughter ceased as the rear door crashed back on its hinges, upsetting a butt can and sending it clattering across the concrete floor. Striding into the room was a real, honest-to-God infantry officer who bounded down the aisle and onto the stage.

"I'm Major George Holman," the apparition boomed. "Sorry for the delay." White perspiration stains mottled his green fatigue blouse, and four fragmentation grenades bobbled from the webbing crisscrossing his chest. His right hand brandished an automatic rifle as if it were a pointer in an illustrated lecture. What caught Alex's eye, however, was the long, decidedly non-regulation knife strapped to his right thigh.

"Some of you know me as 'Jungle Watcher.' My job's to shore up the Vietnamese District Chief by teaching him how to coordinate the efforts of the Territorial Forces, the ARVIN, and United States units. To keep from going nuts, I sometimes run my own search and destroy missions."

Holman balanced on the edge of the stage, sweeping his torso left and right making devastating eye-contact with the air crews and their maintenance counterparts. "We swept into Tri An at first light this morning and caught Charlie fast asleep. Wasted six VC as they *dideed* out of their hooches. Found eleven 122mm rockets and a system of caves with a primary entrance from the river bank. If you're into camouflage and engineering, I invite you to spend the night with me and tour the *ville* tomorrow when we go back to blow the tunnels."

"That's for me," Alex whispered. "I'm not flying tonight; it's a chance to see how we can work better with the grunts."

"It's also a perfect way to get your ass blown off," Panatelli said. "What do you know about playing soldier?"

"That's the point. Westmoreland talks about getting to know the enemy; we don't even know our own people!"

Alex realized the magnitude of his mistake some two hours later when he and the major drove out the north gate. "You take the right side," Holman said, "and I'll watch the left."

The setting sun cast long shadows making it difficult to discern illusion from what might be black-clad figures. "That's quite a knife," Alex said without taking his eyes off the tree line. "I've never seen any with a guard in front of the handle."

"One of a kind. Had it made special in Korea."

"How come? There's plenty of fighting knives."

"Not like this baby," Holman thumped the sheath. "None of the others protect you from a sword."

"You putting me on? This isn't France under Louis Fourteenth."

"One rainy night," Holman spoke as if reciting a familiar script, "my patrol blundered into a North Korean squad. Their officer had a sword that looked six feet long in the lightning. We went hand-to-hand, and I had only an issue knife."

"What happened?" Alex's eyes left the road to probe his companion's face.

"See these?" Holman extended his right hand from the wheel, so that Alex could view the thin white scars radiating from the vee where thumb and forefinger met. "That's what happens when a man with a knife fights a swordsman."

"How did it end?"

"His sword's hanging over my mantle back home."

"What a story! Will I have one to match it after my visit?"

"Never can tell. Few of you zoomies accept my invitation. Just you and Lieutenant Kidd so far. He takes this Civic Action stuff to heart—even goes into the villages by himself."

"Mother Hubbard's told him he'll return in a box if he doesn't cut it out."

As the Jeep rounded a sharp turn in the road, Holman indicated the complex of hooches and bunkers clustered on the high ground. "Here's home," he said.

The jungle had been defoliated around the perimeter, giving the occupants clear fields of fire into which they had strung a web of concertina wire impregnated by trip wires, flares, Claymores, and land mines. Holman pulled his vehicle into a revetment and motioned for Alex to follow as he headed toward his headquarters bunker. Inside, he introduced his fellow Americans who were clustered around a table cleaning weapons. Later he showed his guest the tent where he would sleep and the dugout that would shelter him in case of attack.

"Memorize your way to the bunker," he said. "More than one new guy has, to his sorrow, run the wrong way during a mortar barrage. Drop your gear and let's take the grand tour."

Holman led the way, obviously proud of his fortress and happy to show it. To Alex it was a throwback to the rosebushes: to the meticulously constructed fortifications he had erected in his father's garden for his tin soldiers. Of course the wire had been absent. A little boy knows nothing of barbed wire. But the trenches, dugouts, machine gun nests, even the flag poles, were standard features he had built long ago. Back then he also had defended against an unseen opponent, an all-powerful enemy who attacked with dirt clods and a Red Ryder BB gun.

"See that generator?" Holman indicated a sand-bagged mass percolating noisily. "I'm authorized one, and I got three. Those fifty-caliber machine guns? Authorized two; have six. The refrigerator in the main office? Authorized none; got two. Jeeps? Authorized two; got five in working order and rebuilding two more. If you're going to do the job in Vietnam, especially in a backwater like this, you've got to be a scrounger, or you'll live like a pig and die like a gopher.

"I got myself and the six other round-eyes you met. The rest are Puffs—popular forces. Something like our national guard, but they get the dregs as far as weapons and equipment are concerned. If I didn't scrounge for 'em, their combat effectiveness would be zero."

Alex wondered if he could fill Holman's boots. How would he organize this mass of humanity—men, women, and children belonging to a primitive society and loyal to God-knows-who. If he were Holman, of course, he would have had infantry training and combat experience. But would that be enough?

"Good God!" Alex said as he crested the hill and gazed into a shanty town inhabited by a race of people far different in appearance from the lightly bronzed Vietnamese. The figures, squatting around their cooking fires, were much darker and appeared related to aborigines he had seen peering from old copies of *National Geographic*. The men, dressed in loin cloths, stared at him. "Who are these people?"

"Look, but don't touch," Holman whispered. "They're my special forces."

"Special forces?"

"Part of Project Phoenix, our belated attempt to eradicate the Viet Cong infrastructure. Pretty complex program on paper. Suspect has to be fingered by three separate sources before any action's taken."

"I've heard we'd started such things, but I didn't connect it with this."

"What did you expect, a lottery to get the VC to claim their prizes?"

"No, no, I didn't expect that. I guess I never gave it much thought."

Holman shook his head. "My friend, if it wasn't getting dark, I'd take you right back to Bien Hoa before you see anything else that opens your eyes. You're like ninety percent of the general officers, most of the good folks at home, and all the goddamned politicians. You just never give it much thought."

"You're hitting below the belt, George. If I didn't want to learn, I'd be back at the club soaking up Black Labels."

Only the night creatures and the strained droning of Spooky 73 climbing to the rocket belt broke the silence. Alex could sympathize with Holman, a dynamic officer locked into a thankless job far from those who could reward him. But frustration with his lot, and disdain for his guest, was no excuse for gauche behavior.

"I'm sorry for the put down, Alex, and for the invitation to visit. Now you'll forever remember men we've adulterated. They weren't natural assassins before we imported, trained, and set them loose. After World War Two, we were revered as liberators in this part of the world. Now we'll be damned for siding with the French and adopting tactics of our communist enemy."

"Who controls them?"

"The CIA ostensibly; nobody probably. A dead body is a dead VC. Severed ears are VC ears. But it may be working. If you kill enough suspects, you're bound to get a share of the ones you really want. They're only slopes. Right?"

Alex was surprised at the lavish meal Holman's staff had put together on short notice: barbecued chicken, rice, canned peas, and chilled rose´ wine. Over coffee they discussed the day's operation, next morning's expedition to blow the tunnels, and the military situation in general. Sergeant Wallingford, a hefty non-commissioned officer who had soldiered with Holman in the past, dominated the conversation with anecdotes from his career and a comparison of the stifling Vietnamese climate with the bone-chilling cold of Korea. Then he went into his "short" routine.

"I'm so short," he said, "that I have to reach up to tie my boot laces. Three hundred and sixty days on this tour, and tomorrow I'm blowing tunnels when every VC in the district knows that's what I'm gonna be doin'. Major, I don't know why you're doin' this to me."

"Because, Andre, I can't go, and I want my best man looking after our visitor. If you get in a bind, Major Cannard can call in a B-Fifty-two strike."

"Hey, don't bring me into this," Alex said. "I'd rather inspect your district from the front seat of a Cobra gunship."

"You're my kind of man, Major," Wallingford said, "but we're lucky to see a slick once a week, much less a gunship for the things we do. But I'll gladly settle for one of your bomber strikes on them tunnels. Then we could stay here and watch reruns on AFVN Television until I rotate home."

"Sounds like you're finally showing your true colors, Andre," Holman said. "You're not really scared to go tomorrow are you?"

"You bet your sweet ass I'm scared. If it's not an ambush, they'll be wall-to-wall booby traps. Charlie don't appreciate what we done today, and I'll lay odds he'll be out to settle the score."

"Well, I think you can handle it," Holman said as he rose from the table. Noticing Alex starting to arrange the dishes, he stayed his hand. "That's Mamasan's rice bowl. She'll scavenge enough food to last herself, her man, and her babysans for three days. You'd better get some sleep. It'll be an interesting day for you tomorrow."

Lying on his back in the darkness, Alex thought about the next day's activity. Sergeant Wallingford was right. The VC would be expecting them. How stupid to be taken out by a booby trap, a device symbolized by a conical dunce's hat. He had no need to be going tomorrow. Merrilane would say he had no right. His superiors at Nha Trang would agree. Losing one of their pilots to a booby trap or sniper's bullet when he was on an unauthorized junket would be hard to explain.

But he was strangely composed. Military history was his specialty; and for the first time, he was going to walk into the unknown like countless soldiers before him. The majority of military history was just that, walking into battle, not slipping underneath in a submarine, or dashing overhead in a jet. He would go in concerned not to have an assigned task. But he would also experience the entire range of emotions others had felt since before the time of Alexander the Great.

Mosquitoes had found him and swirled about his head angrily conspiring to penetrate the netting. Their ineffectual buzzing was no threat, but a feeling of deep apprehension descended upon him. An animal sixth sense convinced him someone was watching from the darkness. Then a face appeared within his mind's eye. The features were those of the assassins he had seen at the cook fires. He rolled onto his left side, drawing his knees up and cupping his hands to protect his manhood. He wished for a knife like Holman's.

CHAPTER FIFTEEN

AT 0830 THE CONVOY HEADED for Tri An with Captain Moore, looking studious in black-framed glasses, in the lead Jeep. Sergeant Wallingford and Alex followed in another. Both vehicles carried mounted .50-caliber machine guns. Behind them struggled three trucks belonging to an engineer unit out of Long Bien.

"Is this the way you always travel, Sergeant?" Alex asked as he scanned his side of the road. "We don't seem to be keeping any kind of interval."

"Relax, Major, we're in a pacified area. Besides, all this civilian traffic proves everything's copacetic."

"I thought you told me you'd killed six Viet Cong here yesterday."

"Young kids, not hardcore cadre or NVA regulars. No sweat till we get to Tri An itself. Glad I'm not the tunnel rat who's going to crawl inside them holes."

Alex did not reply but noticed Wallingford stopped tailgating the captain's Jeep, and his eyes began to sweep his side of the road. *He must have realized how short he was*, Alex thought.

The day would be hot; sweat stains already ringed his fatigue cap. He had molded the bill to coil tightly about the upper rim of his sunglasses. Despite the heat, he wore his flak jacket zipped in deference to Mother Hubbard's orders. A .38-caliber revolver, hanging low on a web belt, a canteen, and his M-16 made up his total equipment. He had neglected to bring his steel pot. The grunts surely considered him just another rear echelon sightseer, but that did not concern him as he began to envision taking a walk in the sun.

What did arouse him more than he wanted to acknowledge were the exquisitely shaped young women clad in flowing *Al*

Dais who jogged alongside the road balancing their loads on long poles. He must remember to buy the costume for Merrilane, but that whim faded as the leader pulled off the road, and Wallingford swung in beside him.

They had driven for less than half an hour, and he was becoming increasingly more disillusioned at the lack of precision he had expected. The engineers climbed absent-mindedly down from their trucks, dropped the tail gates, and started rummaging to find the dynamite and fuses they would need. The operation so far resembled something less professional than the highway department crew he joined the summer before his senior year. At least his old gang deployed road guards to slow approaching traffic.

He could discern the *ville* through the palms about twenty-five meters off the road. Only scattered underbrush grew between the tall trees. Beyond the cluster of ten or twelve hooches, he could make out reflections from the sluggish Dong Nai. The Americans sauntered toward the village, more a gaggle than any type of military formation. Holman had instructed him to "stick close to Wallingford," and he intended to do so. Approaching the shelters, Alex noticed a stranger greeting the captain. The gaunt figure was dressed in khaki trousers, white shirt with sleeves rolled up two turns, and a narrow-brim straw hat pulled low over his eyes. He was smoking a Marlboro, the brand name on the package filtering through the thin material of his shirt pocket. Mirrored sunglasses completed his attire, giving him the sinister appearance of one of Haitian President-for-Life Francois Duvalier's *Tontons Macoute*. Reinforcing the chill this apparition cast was an unearthly rising and falling wail emanating from the village.

"Who's that?" Alex raised the muzzle of his M-16 slightly to indicate the man in the white shirt.

"Informer, secret police, CIA, who knows?" Wallingford said. "Be careful how you look at the SOB, or you might find yourself part of the body count."

"What's that noise?" Alex once more raised the muzzle of his weapon, this time moving it in a small circle.

"That's the Vietnamese funeral, or at least the wake. Better get used to it; you'll hear it the whole time we're here."

None of the populace had come out to meet the troops. The place appeared deserted except for the unnerving chant that seemed to come from all directions. The white-shirted man went off by himself, entering the hooches as if he were the landlord, and drawing out the occupants for interrogation. Twice he struck his victims roughly beside the head, once knocking a thin woman to the ground. Alex's finger inched from the guard to rest on the trigger of his rifle. Wallingford saw the movement, slid close to him, and whispered a hushed, "Steady, Major."

The performance was evidently routine and probably expected by the peasants. *We won't be winning any hearts and minds today*, Alex thought. *They must have known about the tunnels. Probably helped dig them . . . voluntarily, even joyfully? At gunpoint? Or, after all these years, do they just fall out like oxen to be harnessed and worked by whoever happens to be passing through?*

He followed the engineers who drifted down to the riverbank to look over the entrance to the system. A sampan could be guided into the steep bank and its cargo off-loaded in a matter of minutes. Nothing at ground level would indicate anything unusual had taken place. After milling around for ten minutes, the soldiers chucked two smoke grenades into the opening, then sealed it with a shelter half. Within thirty seconds, telltale wisps of smoke began seeping from ventilation shafts in a number of places leading toward the village. More grenades down the shafts generated a mustard-colored fog that hung over a clump of bamboo growing at the end of the path connecting river and village.

Probing with a bayonet, Wallingford detected metal beneath the vegetation. As he continued, more smoke issued from the disturbed sand etching a circular outline around the tangled grass. Satisfied he was not working with a mine, he lifted the clump exposing a battered wash basin camouflaging the tunnel's entrance. "Where's my Rat," he shouted.

The party shuffled around, smoking and harassing each other, for another twenty minutes waiting for the smoke to clear. Striped to his waist, the Rat bounced forward hitching up his baggy trousers like a bantamweight prize fighter. In place of ten-ounce gloves, he held in his left hand a five-cell flashlight, and in his right a cocked .45-caliber pistol. To Alex he looked scarcely older than Jeffrey. A filthy blue bandanna encircled his forehead, and a shock of blond hair hung in shards over the headband and cowlicked in back.

"Tie that there rope 'round my boot," he said in an eastern Kentucky twang. "And pull like hail if'n ah jerk twict."

Without another word, he slid headfirst down the shaft and crawled off into the blackness.

My God, thought Alex, *was I ever that dumb? His accent suggested an experienced woodsman. How many times had he plunged through darkness searching for frogs? Creeping forward, with flashlight in left hand and sharpened gig in right, to mesmerize the big green bulls, and then plunge the gig squarely into their fat bellies. Did their piercing, child-like scream ever bother him?*

Better get a grip, he thought. *Someone needs to be thinking about where the hell we are.* He walked closer to the river, peering into uncontested VC-land. Remembering the death of Union General John Sedgwick, shot off his horse by a sharpshooter's bullet, he kept from exposing himself. Finding nothing of further interest, he ambled past the activity at the tunnel's entrance and picked his way toward the village.

Great place for booby traps, he thought. *But maybe the VC didn't have time to rig them.* As he walked, he scanned the ground for trip wires and the trees for dead falls. Beside one of the hooches lay a woven mat, looking as if it had been dropped during the previous day's activity. *Strange, everything else looks ready for inspection.*

Moving closer he noticed a bulge in middle of the mat indicating something poised beneath it. With the edge of his boot, he cautiously lifted one side, then carefully lowered it.Wallingford, noticing his charge was not around the tunnel entrance, had come looking for him. "Whatcha got there, Major?"

"Don't know," Alex replied without taking his eyes off the mat. "Maybe a snake. But I've got booby traps on my mind, so I'm leaving it for the experts."

"I guess you're talking about me then." The sergeant strolled over to the hooch, grasped the end of a protruding roof pole, and jerked it free. Returning, he inserted one end beneath the mat, flicked it to the side, and exposed a filthy GI canteen cover. "Don't move, Major. There's something inside."

"Leave it alone, Sergeant; it's got booby trap written all over it." Alex's voice was something between panic and command, but Wallingford ignored him.

Hearing the alarm in Alex's voice, two passing engineers altered their path and approached the kneeling sergeant. "Hey, Major, I think you just got yourself a souvenir. Two homemade VC grenades!"

"Grenade!" One of the soldiers shouted, as he and his buddy flopped onto the ground.

"You chickenshits," yelled Wallingford. "Nothing to get uptight about. Just two homebuilts some papasan dropped on his way out last night. See?"

He up-ended the pouch holding his left hand to receive the bounty. Nothing happened. He shook the case, and two apple-green spheres dropped into his palm where they immediately exploded.

As he rolled from side to side on the ground, blood spurted from his shattered forearms and his screams drowned the funeral lament.

"Medic! Medic! Oh Shit, Medic!" Alex yelled. Ripping the battle dressings from their helmets, the two engineers sprinted to the thrashing man.

"Oh God, I can't see!"

Alex stood like an impotent observer, struck deaf by the concussion and dumb by the realization his discovery had resulted in this carnage. His ears rang, his head ached, splotches of blood and flesh covered his face and the front of his uniform. No medic had accompanied the force detailed only to destroy a tunnel in a pacified area. Off to one side, the captain knelt talking into his radio as he squinted to determine map coordinates.

By the time the engineers had plunged their ampules of morphine into Wallingford, Alex was beginning to function. Shivering violently, he removed his belt and gave it to the men who worked to stem the flow of blood from the left stump. Wallingford's right hand hung by the tendons, gone for all practical purposes. Someone took Alex by the arm and started to lead him away. It was the Rat: filthy, sweat covered, and completely under control. His mouth seemed to be moving, but Alex could not make out the words. Then the boy spat, and he realized he had been chewing a gigantic cud of tobacco. His eyes and gentle, guiding hands talked for him.

He sat his charge against a tree, doused the blue bandanna with water from Alex's canteen, and began to wipe blood from his face. Then he retrieved his M-16, released the magazine, checked the chamber, and slid the full clip into his lower blouse pocket before returning the weapon. He unzipped Alex's flak vest, pulled aside his fatigue blouse and tee shirt, and poured the remaining water onto his pounding chest. Now he was talking and pointing overhead to where a helicopter was dropping onto the road. The boy wanted him to get up and join the others who were carrying Wallingford in a litter made from a shelter half and the pole he had used to lift the grass mat.

As the chopper settled onto its skids, Alex recognized the Bien Hoa crash alert bird. As they loaded the comatose sergeant, Alex surveyed the soldiers, their sleeves rolled above their elbows, gathered around Jeeps with mounted machines guns. It was a photograph of French Legionnaires from the pages of Bernard Fall's *Street Without Joy*. He had seen it all before.

When Captain Moore clutched his arm, he realized he, too, was being evacuated. After brief resistence, he found himself lying beside the sergeant as twin rotors whirled faster, sucking dirt, grass, and sand into the open compartment. Before lift-off, someone tossed beside him Wallingford's severed left hand, fingers curled, tendons trailing, a bright wedding band sparkling in the sunshine.

CHAPTER SIXTEEN

THE RINGING IN ALEX'S EARS SUBSIDED on the dash for Saigon, and he could only watch the medic attend to Wallingford. Soon the jungle gave way to cultivated paddies, hooches, shacks, and finally, buildings. Swinging into the wind, the pilot dropped precipitously toward a huge red cross painted on the macadam beside the evacuation hospital. With uplifted faces and outstretched arms, a team of corpsmen and nurses waited to remove Wallingford and rush him into the operating suite.

Alex clutched the aluminum brace of the canvas seat as they reached for him. "I'm all right. I'm not hurt! Not at all." Still they clamored and motioned for him to come quietly. Searching for something to pacify them, he grabbed Wallingford's severed hand and thrust it forward. They wavered, like wheat under the rotors' downdraft, then scattered as the pilot increased throttle, pulled the craft into a hover, and clattered away toward Bien Hoa.

Hubbard waited as the rotors spooled down then moved forward to help him dismount. "Christ," he said. "You're a mess."

"I'm okay, but I could use a shower."

Hubbard dropped him near the Spook House, then returned to the flight line to lock up his weapons. In the deserted bathhouse, he took a stray towel, found a bar of soap, and walked into a stall. After standing motionless in the hot water for a time, he stripped, lathered, and scoured himself with the gritty soap.

Long, his mamasan, had seen him arrive and was waiting with his clogs, underwear, and a fresh flying suit when he emerged, towel-wrapped, carrying the dripping mound of clothes. "You take," she said placing the clean items on the ledge made by the sandbags, "Long wash."

He stepped into the baggy coveralls ignoring the sour odor associated with even freshly washed clothing. The smell of seared flesh that permeated his fatigues had been so much worse. Slipping into the clogs, he started for the Spook House door but stopped when he saw Hubbard returning. He joined him, easing himself into the vehicle's passenger's seat and propping his right foot on the door fairing.

"I should have taken Peter's advice and stayed home."

"Hindsight's twenty-twenty," Hubbard said.

"You'll have to talk a little louder, sir. I still have some ringing in my ears."

"You'd better have the flight surgeon check you out," Hubbard said a bit louder and more slowly.

"I'd rather not, if that's okay with you. I'd like to get some sleep before tonight's mission."

"Suit yourself, but I've taken you off the schedule. You've already had a full day. Holman called and told me as much as he knew. He feels bad about putting you in jeopardy."

"He feels bad? What about me? Knowing I caused a man to lose his hands? He may even be blinded."

"Breaks of the game. You've had a tough experience, but you're blameless. The guy I sympathize with is the poor bastard out of Da Nang's Spooky flight—got a short round supporting a Marine sweep. He's grounded and it looks like the DO's planning to hang him."

"Oh, my God," Alex whispered. His thoughts darted to the pilot, another victim of the fortunes of war. But his concern, like a smoothly thrown boomerang, quickly returned to his own situation. "At least he wasn't right there spattered by innocent blood and seeing the effects of his mistake."

"Don't go prima donna on me. Holman said you found a booby trap, and the sergeant's own stupidity got him wounded. He was experienced; he should have handled it."

"If I hadn't found the grenades, it wouldn't have happened."

"That's absurd and you know it, Major. If you hadn't found them, someone else would. You're a big boy playing hardball. You found the booby trap. The sergeant should have known how to deal with it. You became the innocent bystander, and he almost got you killed. Think about that.

"I see your point; it's just that . . ."

"I think we've debated enough. I've changed my mind. Get some sleep because you're back on the schedule flying with that new guy, Featherstone. He needs a lot of watching."

Five hours later, even before the formal briefing, he was dispatched to map coordinates X-ray Tango 418 442—the 35-mile point on the 303 radial of the Bien Hoa tacan—scrambled in daylight to assist troops in contact. Before Blackie Charmoli had plotted the position, Alex recognized the implications. X-ray Tango meant War Zone D, the Viet Cong's long-time stronghold.

A recent graduate of flying training who had been primed for jet fighters, Tommy Featherstone was the usual new Gooney Bird co-pilot: slow, tentative, and miles behind because of the confusing arrangement of radio and interphone switches. During engine start Alex had found himself rushing ahead of the checklist, repeating the very actions that so unnerved him as a neophyte. "I'm in a hurry," he said as he cranked the right engine. "You clean up after me."

"I haven't seen any action," Featherstone shouted as the engine caught, hiccupped, then roared into life. "I don't know how much help I'll be."

"Don't sweat it," Alex yelled. "I'll tell you what to do."

After takeoff Blackie came forward, squinting into the sun to search for landmarks. Ten miles from the target, Alex cleared off the traffic control frequency and called the forward air controller. No joy. Switching to the Fox Mike radio, he tried the army ground commander.

"Angry Hornet Six, this is Spooky Seven One with twenty-eight thousand rounds and sixteen illumination flares. Over."

"Spooky Seven One, Angry Hornet. Standby."

As the numeral "five" joined its companion "three" in the lower half of his tacan instrument, he dipped the left wing and saw a panorama reminiscent of the Little Big Horn. In a clearing just north of an east-west road, armored personnel carriers hunkered like circled pioneer wagons. Tracers crisscrossed their perimeter as four helicopter gunships darted to and fro along the treeline south of the road. Billowing smoke from their rockets vied for his attention along with impacts of mortar shells within the circle. From the west, trailing a long dust plume, a relief force of three tanks charged into contention.

Covered by helicopters and reinforced by tanks, Angry Hornet began his breakout. Using his black grease pencil, Alex diagramed the battle area on the pane of his sliding window. The limited number of illumination flares concerned him if the battle stretched long into the night. As the helicopters pulled off the target and regrouped for home, he rotated his selector switch to brief the cabin crew.

"We've got a bunch of APCs starting to move east with three tanks following. Choppers have expended. No FAC on the scene. These guys are in deep serious, and I don't think their Six's ever heard of a Spooky."

Switching back to the Fox Mike radio, Alex made his second transmission to the ground commander. "Angry Hornet Six, this is Spooky Seven One. Could you use our load of seven point six two ammunition?"

"Ahhhh . . . Spooky Seven One, are you a gunship?"

"Roger on the gunship."

"Spooky Seven One, can you hit the treeline southeast?"

"Roger, Roger. Rolling in now."

"Co-pilot," Alex called on interphone, "check external lights off; master gun switch on. Loadmaster, I'll mark the target with a ground-burning flare. Standby for my call. Gunners, give me number one on slow fire."

On the ground the vehicles trundled east to where the road made a ninety-degree turn to the north skirting the western edge of a good-size *ville*. Alex rolled into the familiar thirty-degree left bank, aiming east of where the choppers had worked. As he eased his thumb onto the firing button, the area within his gunsight illuminated with muzzle flashes and tracers stabbing toward the convoy.

"All guns fast fire," he commanded as he jabbed the button. Instantaneously the deep-throated moan and the acrid stench of gunpowder filled the cabin and cockpit. Spooky's red tracers descended in a trailing arc burning out a thousand feet above the target. Mentally extending their path, he judged the bullets to be slamming into the ground just where he wanted them. He ceased firing after four seconds, noting as he circled through a northwesterly heading that the rearmost tank was burning.

"Loadmaster, standby on the marker flare . . . ready, ready . . . NOW!" He underscored his command by flashing the green drop light mounted in the cabin above the cockpit entrance. On the ground darkness obscured his target, but sunlight still transformed the aged transport into a glistening moth lazily flying a predictable pattern.

"Featherstone," he shouted across the cockpit, "keep an eye out for that flare. It'll be a twinkling point of light."

Again he poured a red stream that fell like flaming oil dumped from ancient battlements. The invisible enemy fought back, arching tracers like flights of fiery arrows seeking the rampaging dragonship.

"Watch yourself, Spooky," Angry Hornet's voice was steady but high pitched. "You're taking heavy fire from south of the road."

Appraising the threat, Alex knew guns shooting at him posed no threat to troopers aiding comrades escaping the blazing tank. Steepening his bank, he noticed the faint glimmer of his marker flare immediately next to the dark scar of the treeline. Sighting on the pinpoint of light, he unleashed the dragon's breath just as a sparkling whip of green tracers probed upward.

CHAPTER SEVENTEEN

LYING ON THE BED inhaling the candle's cinnamon fragrance and hearing steady rain, Merrilane was still too agitated to begin the letter she owed her husband. Physically exhausted, emotionally confused, and sexually adrift, she prayed for the serenity she believed existed in the lives of those answering a higher calling. *What would it be like*, she wondered, *to be Mother Superior?* Not only to have control of one's own passions, but also to have created an environment of order and peace? But it need not be that extreme. What miracles could she perform if she were treated simply as a fellow human being not expected to be either a homemaker or a Superwoman? *Why is everything thought of as a game with winners and losers?* she asked herself.

Couldn't life be a team sport rather than a quick-draw contest? Alex Cannard, what's your game? Your duty's here, with me, raising your children. That's what I bargained for. Instead you abandoned me in a den of hungry wolves. Rod Pike, what's your game? You've no more sense of commitment than Alex. Just that Rock Hudson charm. That's not enough. At least not yet. Jack Pinski, I know your game. I'm to be your disposable woman. Tossed aside later like a worn toothbrush. But you've sworn to be honorable. Would you break your vow for me? Could I be more than a fascination until the next centerfold arrives?

She gave up her questioning and began to write:

July 15, 1968
Dear Alex,
The candle flickers, the rain falls, the bed is cold. It's daylight where you are and already tomorrow. I find it hard to deal with the fact you are not only gone, but you're living a day ahead of me (in the future) while I struggle here in the past tormented by memories of

*women like me whose lives have been destroyed by quirks of fate, or—
God forbid—by the inattention of their own husbands.*

*It's almost four months since last you gave the room life with
your deep and measured breathing. Often in times past, lying awake
close to you, I've been consumed by fear you'd be taken from me. I
put those thoughts out of my mind by stroking your strong back or
slipping my hand ever so lightly to grip your manhood. But now in
the quiet of night, I find all those banished fears crashing in on me.*

*I know you fly at night, and I find myself dreading each sunset.
I've come to feel so vulnerable to darkness. At times I think maybe
the Viet Cong is out there, slipping quietly through the fir trees, crawling across the open lawn, ready to assault me as I lie unprotected in
my bed. I know it's foolish. But I'm beginning to think there'll always be a dark figure out there somewhere as long as you're away
from me.*

*Daytime is all right because I'm busy. Then I come home, fix sup-
per, and try to listen to what the children say, knowing I'm more
interested in feedback on the Youth Program than I am in how their
lives are developing. Finally I retire to an empty bed I cover with
paperwork in a vain attempt to keep from thinking of us.*

*I think of the time we drove to Jeckle Island, just the two of us,
after you returned from North Africa. Or I think of going to
Breckenridge and getting snowbound in Sam and Dee's condo. I remember the family camping trips to Yosemite: especially when the
kids were asleep, and we sat locked together before the fire planning
our lives and sharing our innermost thoughts.*

*We don't confide anymore. I've re-read your letters searching to
find some spark. But nothing's there. It's as if a censor had taken out
all the life, leaving only descriptions of the weather, the food, the administrative routine.*

*I wish I had someone to unload on. Marriage is meant to be a
sharing. I'm not made to live by myself. When we're together,
everything's fine. I have no fears; I look forward to the night. You've
told me it's the same for you. But you haven't told me lately. I need
something to get me through until Hawaii. When will it be?*

*I'm lying here getting mad at you for being away, for putting me
through this. I'm becoming aroused, and you're not here. What am I
to do? What do you do? Or does the flying and the administrative job
keep your mind focused? What if I told you a cadet assaulted me this*

afternoon? Taking me by surprise, crushing me into his massive chest, bending me back, pushing his hard tongue into my mouth? What if I told you my hungry body responded instinctively, grinding my pelvis into his before I regained control?

Would you steal a plane and fly home to kill the son of a bitch? Would you write a memo to the Commandant asking the cadet be put on restriction? Or would you slap me for leading the young gentleman on?

Breaking from the trance in which she had been writing, she became conscious of a sound different from the splashing rain water—a persistent tapping coming from the rear of the house.

"Forgot to close the damn vent." She flung back the quilt, scattering her papers, and swung her legs down to the white rug. Rushing into the kitchen, she flipped the wall switch and peered, back lighted in a babydoll negligee, into the sparkling cascades rolling down the transparent roof of the greenhouse.

"It's me, Miz Cannard."

Startled, she drew back, turned obliquely, and covered her breast with crossed arms.

"It's me, Jackie. I didn't mean to scare you."

"Jack Pinski!" she shouted. "What are you doing here at this time of night?"

The storm cell rampaged in full maturity directly over the Cannard home. Lightning lit the night, danced crazily on the glass, and illuminated the cadet's soaked and shaking figure. She moved close to the screen door, oblivious of her state of undress, intent on seeing if the latch was secured.

You'll catch your death of cold . . ." a sharp crack and rolling thunder interrupted her, "if you're not struck by lightning first."

Looking hastily over his shoulder then back at her, he flashed a sheepish grin. "That just occurred to me. Please let me in."

Another crack of lightning and simultaneous thunder turned the greenhouse into an incandescent carrousel. Three intense explosions of light and sound transformed the carrousel into a strobe-lighted disco stage. A soaked, deformed hulk and a petite fairy princess practiced their roles, each trying to upstage the other. So entranced were the players, they did not notice the little boy who had emerged from his room to stand in the corridor sleepy-eyed and frightened.

"Let me come in, Merrilane. For God's sake."

"All right. But just until the storm passes." Her fingers slid open the latch. "You can come in and explain yourself, but no funny stuff."

He stood in a pool of water shedding his jacket and watch cap, hair and face glistening with raindrops. His trousers were soaked through, and he shivered like a dog that had just pulled itself from an ice-filled pond. She tossed him a large beach towel that had covered the chaise lounge.

Scrubbing his face and hair, he reveled in the woman's essence permeating the towel's fibers. The power of the storm had banked his ardor, but the smell of her fragrance reinvigorated him. He smiled at the spectacle he must be presenting, as he stood with water still dripping from his boots onto the redwood flooring.

"All right, Mister Pinski, I'm waiting to hear why you turned up on my doorstep like a drowned puppy. The storm's passing; you'll be able to leave in a few more minutes."

"I'm sorry, Ma'am . . ."

"Knock off the humble cadet routine, Mister."

"I'm serious," he examined his muddy boots as if too bashful to look at her negligee. "I've felt so bad about what happened this afternoon . . . so ashamed, you being an officer's wife and all . . . that I went on a run out the north gate, and I just ended up here . . . and it started storming . . . and my ankle hurts something awful. I guess psychologically I was just drawn . . ."

"Don't con me, Jack. You wanted a piece of ass, and you thought this was the place to get it. Right?"

"Right." He lifted his eyes scanning and measuring her as a missile's tracking radar evaluates its target before locking on for the kill.

"I'm impressed. They really do teach you to tell the truth don't they?" He realized he had made his second mistake of the day. On her home turf now, she was not the scared rabbit she had been in the deserted office. She was not Julie's mother craving every bit of affection she could extract.

"Well, Mister Pinski, have you ever considered what I might think about it? Don't you have any common humanity, or do they train that out of you?" He tried to interrupt, even held up his hand like a first grader wanting to be excused. She ignored his hand and overran his words.

"I have a tremendously tough job to do, two children to raise, and a husband who's flying in circles every night over Vietnam. I don't have to put up with a cadet in heat who makes me the brunt of his erotic fantasies. You ought to be ashamed of yourself. Now get out of my house and don't come back! You're off the project. When you think of this scene forty years from now, you can label me the one that got away. And you can label yourself as an insensitive bastard who's as far from being the ideal cadet as . . . as . . . Elmer Fudd!"

He moved toward her. She stood her ground, eyes blazing, hands on hips, nipples erect and punching out of the thin covering of the night dress. "You're in my space, Mister," she hissed. "Back off!"

He hesitated, then retreated, stooping to pick up his jacket and cap, before letting himself out.

Shaking with anger, she slammed and locked the kitchen door, switched off the light, and walked up the dark hallway to stumble over the small form sleeping on the carpet outside her room. *How much had he seen? What will he remember? Who will he tell?* Weeping, she stooped to pick up her son and carried him into her bed placing him gently on his father's side. Before blowing out the candle, she paused long enough to tear to shreds the letter she had written.

CHAPTER EIGHTEEN

"**TODDY ONE ZERO,** Toddy One Zero, do you read Spooky Seven One? Come in please . . . Toddy One Zero . . . "

Alex flicked the UHF toggle switch on his interphone panel leaving Featherstone to babble without overriding his own clipped words with Angry Hornet. Behind him, hunched over his navigational chart, Blackie Charmoli used the VHF radio to beg Saigon for air support: fighters, choppers, a forward air controller. Working the target alone, Alex computed wind drift to keep his flares over the battle, searched for muzzle flashes, and calculated how best to stretch his remaining munitions. Thin scud, like a fisherman's gossamer net, settled onto Spooky's orbit, veiling from time to time the spectacle below and jolting the aircraft with fingers of turbulence grasping from a line of approaching thunderstorms.

A determined enemy, encroaching weather, and demoralized friendlies forged an ominous situation, but he began to feel the sense of elation that always seemed to strengthen him when the odds lengthened. He had first experienced it in multi-engine pilot training. Just he and another student in an obsolete B-25 being drawn inexorably down into ice-laden clouds by a windmilling propeller on a dead engine. He had nailed the inbound course to Will Rogers airport at the outer marker and broke out at two hundred feet with the runway stretching to receive them.

Often in the B-47 simulator, he seemed most alive when the fire-warning lights flashed and the fuel panel blinked solid red. But that was all play-acting and perhaps did not count. No question it was real that night off Bermuda with flames engulfing the navigator's compartment and smoke obscuring his view of the tanker.

Soothing confidence now flooded his body, outpacing the surging blood and spurting adrenalin. Angry Hornet Six, perhaps responding to a new tone in Alex's voice, badgered his subordinates into abandoning the burning tank and continuing their dash eastward. Approaching the point where the road jinked north, the vehicles slowed and bunched together. A torrent of red and green tracers, punctuated by the splashy orange impacts of rocket-propelled grenades and mortar shells, lashed out from the village sited east of the junction and from the jungle south of the road.

Anticipating a second ambush, Alex had descended five hundred feet to stay clear of the clouds and was perfectly aligned to rake the southern-most enemy position. Once again the dragon roared.

"Good shooting, Spooky!" Angry Hornet called. "I requested immediate artillery on X-ray Tango four six two, four four two. Keep clear."

"Alex," Blackie called, "that arty's coming out of Fire Base Sally. Continue working south of the road."

From his firing circle, he saw four simultaneous explosions erupt in the center of the village, followed by a single star shell curving upward from the structures.

"Ooooh shit!" Alex said loud enough to be heard by Featherstone who was still trying every thirty seconds to contact the non-existent forward air controller.

"Angry Hornet, this is Spooky. Did you see that red signal?"

"That proves they're in there, Spooky. Now we pour it on."

As the village disintegrated under the pounding of 105mm howitzer shells, the column completed its turn and moved up the road only to spring another ambush where a bridge spanned a diagonal canal.

"Major Cannard, sir," the forgotten Featherstone called over interphone. "I've got an Apache Four One calling our FAC on the UHF radio. He's a flight of two with napalm and high-drag bombs."

"I'll talk to him," Alex signaled the loadmaster to toss another flare then switched radios to greet the fighters. "Apache, . . .Spooky's got a convoy under heavy pressure and no FAC on scene. Hold on the Bien Hoa tacan three-zero-three radial, thirty miles, till we sort this out."

"Roger, Spooky, what's the story?"

"Blackie, come up on UHF and brief Apache Four One."

"Angry Hornet, Spooky has two fighters overhead with napalm and bombs . . . " Breaking his transmission, Alex banked left to engage the new ambush site.

"You're on target boss," the loadmaster called, "but the lead vehicle's broadside and burning on the bridge."

"Angry Hornet Six . . . Come up, Angry Hornet!"

"Spooky, this is Apache. That front's moving in fast and we're guzzling fuel. What's the story?"

"Standby; I'm working one up for you."

"Pilot from Navigator. We're down to four thousand rounds and nine flares. Get those fast movers in, or we can kiss the whole bunch goodby."

"Wait, Blackie. I'm hitting the dike now." He pressed the firing button sending dollops of orange tracers curving to splatter along two-thirds of the embankment. Then the roaring harmonic ceased as the final bullets cleared their spinning barrels.

Simultaneously a continuous stream of red tracers whipped back and forth across the windscreen so close that animal instinct triggered a collision-avoidance impulse. Alex wrenched the control wheel hard right, booted full rudder, chopped power, and sucked the yoke into his gut, virtually stopping the aircraft in mid-air and forcing it onto the cusp of a stall. A shattering crash just behind his seat dispatched reverberations of fear to his brain and bowels. Featherstone, unrestrained by seatbelt, slammed back in his seat then shot upward to ricochet off the overhead console.

Spooky poised on her right wing, shaking like a dog on its hind legs, shaking, shaking, threatening to snap inverted, then dropping precipitously. Somewhere aft of her tail, a dying flare sputtered twice then burned into darkness leaving behind sluggish controls, a plunging dead weight, and a pilot sure of only one thing. Truth existed, but not in the books in which he had sought it.

Frantic yells and screams of panic from the cabin gradually muted as returning air flow again shrieked outside the craft. Was he inverted? Spinning? His instrument panel emitted only blackness.

"Dear God, give me light."

Immediately a huge storm cell, racing across from Cambodia and towering to forty-thousand feet, illuminated long enough to provide a horizon line and a directional reference. Easing in the power as he breathed a silent *Thank you, Lord*, he heard and felt the churning Pratt & Whitney engines respond. Airflow burbled, whistled, then finally streamed.

Featherstone revived enough to shine his red-lensed flashlight on Alex's instrument panel allowing him to complete his recovery to level flight and then to a modest climb. The altimeter indicated eight hundred feet. "Anybody hurt back there?"

"Nothing serious, major, but go easy on the barrel rolls."

"Anybody pinpoint that gun?"

"Roger, pilot. He's in the northwest corner of the big paddy where the slopes have their skirmish line. But I vote to stay away from the little fucker."

"Nav, I need you forward to look at Featherstone and check for damage behind my seat." Blackie appeared at his elbow shining a flashlight on the groggy co-pilot. "Don't worry, Alex," he shouted against the straining engines. "It's only a nosebleed, and your battle damage was the water bottle hitting the deck. As for me, I'm transferring to the motor pool. I'm too old for this shit."

Continuing his climb to the base of the clouds, Alex leveled at twenty-four hundred feet then toggled the overhead switch signaling the loadmaster to expend another flare.

"Angry Hornet Six, answer Spooky Seven One." The lead APC still blazed furiously.

"Spooky, this is Apache Lead. We've got to dump this stuff quick or lug it home. You havin' any luck?"

"Roger Lead. Your target's an ambush line on a dike west of the north-south road out of the village that's still smoldering. About a klick north of the village is a burning APC. The dinks have a fifty-cal in the north-west corner of the rice paddy directly west of the vehicle. Make your runs south to north on the line of ambush breaking hard right to avoid the gun. Base of the broken cloud layer is twenty-four hundred feet. I'm running at that altitude east and west with left turns. Got the picture?"

"Roger, got the picture." The laconic voice, muffled by a clammy mask and straining against the oxygen's pressure, sounded as if it came from a mechanical man. "I also got the book. Rules of Engagement forbid dropping without a certified forward air controller."

"Look, pal, if we don't get this together quick, the only book those troopers will get is the one the Chaplain reads at Arlington."

"Spooky, I need a FAC."

"You got me, Apache. I'm a SAC."

"Say again. Are you a Forward Air Controller?"

"Better than that. SAC, Sierra Alpha Coco, Strategic Air Command. Don't tell me you TAC jocks are going legal on me. You're cleared in hot."

"Negative, Negative. I'm not dropping without a Forward Air Controller."

"Standby, Apache. I got a call on Fox Mike."

Hitting the switch for another flare, Alex dipped his left wing and surveyed the battlefield. A second vehicle burned. Blocked at the rear of the column, the tanks sat unable to bring their heavy cannon to bear.

"Hello Apache Lead, our problem's solved. I'm talking with an army controller in a Jeep at the head of the column. The situation's as I briefed. He wants you to hit straight up the embankment with twenty mike-mike. Give him a good strafing pass, and he'll clear you first with nape, then with high drags. One hitch. I've got five flares left. That's fifteen minutes max light. We gotta do it quick like a bunny."

The heavy-breathing, suspicious-sounding voice of the flight leader came back after a long pause. "Just for the record, what's the controller's call sign?"

"Catch Two Two . . .You're cleared hot for a twenty mike-mike run south to north on the dike west of the road where the APCs are sitting. Break hard right after your run."

"Roger. Lead rolling in; guns hot."

Alex settled into an elongated orbit heading into the target as the fighter walked his cannon impacts across the top of the dike.

"Apache Two, . . . Catch Twenty-two clears you hot. Put it where your leader did. Break, break . . . Apache Lead, Catch Two Two sends you a 'well done.' You'll be cleared for a nape drop on your next pass. He wants it right where you began your strafing."

"Apache Two off the target, breaking right. I got that fifty-cal marked. Request clearance on the gun with napalm."

"Apache Lead rolling in hot with nape."

"Roger, Lead, make it quick. Two more flares and it's gonna get awful dark. Break, Break. Apache Two, Catch Twenty-two clears you on the gun with napalm."

"Apache Lead off the target."

"Apache Two in with nape."

"Pilot this is Loadmaster. APCs are fording the stream like a herd of turtles. Tanks moving up. I'm fixin' to toss our last flare."

"Apache Lead cleared for high drags on the dike. Salvo your load into your napalm fire."

"Apache Lead off the target breaking right climbing to angels two five."

"Apache Two rolling in with high drags on the fifty-caliber."

"Roger, Two. Be advised you have forty-five seconds of light."

Alex rolled out on a westerly heading just in time to see the second F-100 glistening in the reflected light of the dying flare. Four flashes marked the impact of his bombs, their subsequent shock wave rocking the low-flying gunship and confirming their potency.

"Two off the target, breaking right, climbing to angels two five."

"Roger, Roger," Alex called. "Catch Twenty-two sends his compliments. Sorry he can't provide damage assessment, but somebody turned out the lights."

"Spooky, . . . Apache Lead. Thanks for the flares and the radio relay. I never did care for landing with ordnance. Break, break. Two, . . . let's go Paris Control for vector to home plate."

"Roger, Lead. Break, break. Spooky, if you ever see Catch Twenty-two, tell him he does okay for a SAC weenie. Two out."

As Alex settled onto a south-easterly heading for Bien Hoa, Featherstone leaned over to tap him on the shoulder.

"Sorry I wasn't much help, Major. I guess it's best to stay belted all the time, but I couldn't see anything from my seat."

"Don't sweat the small stuff, Tommy. I rarely strapped in when I rode co-pilot. Your flashlight was there when I needed it. Any permanent damage?"

"Naw, just blood all over my flying suit. Nose is all crusted inside, and my head feels like it's about to split. I'm ready for a good, long nap.

"Don't mention sleep. Think you're up to flying her home? My arms and shoulders feel like I've been lifting weights. Better get the pitot heat on; we're running into solid cloud, and that lightning's getting closer. Flying the late CAP tonight's not gonna be a picnic."

Alex got little rest on the homeward leg. Featherstone had much to learn about the moods and characteristics of the propeller-driven Goon. Making the radio calls, running the descent and landing checklists, and watching Featherstone's every move required his complete attention. Yet his mind would not forget Angry Hornet. Had he only lost his radio, or was he thrashing with bloodied limbs as Wallingford had done some nine hours previously? More likely he was a charred carcass lying inside the simmering vehicle.

He talked Featherstone through the landing like a father teaching his son to ride a bicycle. The copilot rounded out high, then sat watching as the airspeed dissipated. Alex nudged the yoke forward, eased in some power, and added a measure of left rudder to keep the old girl tracking the runway's centerline. All the while he conducted a running commentary in a soothing tone leaving Featherstone with the impression he had recognized the problems, fed in the corrections, and made the graceful touchdown all by himself.

Switching to ground control after landing, he learned he was to refuel, rearm, and scramble for troops in contact south of Saigon.

CHAPTER NINETEEN

THIRTY MINUTES LATER Alex lifted Spooky Seven One off and racked the aircraft into a climbing left turn to intercept the 225 radial outbound from the Bien Hoa tacan.

"You got it co-pilot. Track outbound on the radial and level at thirty-five hundred feet."

Wouldn't hurt my feelings if they called this one off. Heavy lightning toward the target. Or maybe arty. Solid clouds now. Who else's out here?.

"Paris Control, Spooky Seven One climbing to thirty five hundred, twelve miles out the Bien Hoa two-two-five radial. Do you have us on your radar?"

"No joy, Spooky. Our weapon's bent."

That figures. "Paris control, do you have the cloud base in the local area and a forecast for Bien Hoa for zero two hundred?"

"Negative Spooky. Our circuits to Bien Hoa and the Tan Son Nhut weather station are out. Try Tan Son Nhut tower on VHF."

"No time, Paris. Spooky out."

Sweat landing weather later. Rough turbulence. Kid's got his hands full. Probably never been in serious weather at low altitude. Pitot heat's on. Keep rotating beacon on for awhile. No telling who's blundering around in the soup.

"Spooky Seven Two, this is Seven One requesting weather in the Saigon envelope. Spooky Seven Two? . . . Any aircraft this freq, give Spooky Seven One a call."

Everyone must have gone home. Rough as a cob.

"Hold it in the road, co-pilot. Stay on the gauges and watch your altitude." *Right engine running hot; crack the cowl flaps. Oil pressure's high. Keep an eye on it. Here it comes. Nothing like heavy rain for a wake up. She's a leaker. Coming in the side windows and the overhead hatch. Left leg soaked already. Wonder who's out there? ARVIN with some poor US advisor most likely. God, I'm tired. Must be getting close. Right engine still hot. Pressure high but holding. Dial in the Fox Mike and see what we have.*

". . . rockets on the berm, Two. Watch out for that mother in the treeline. Almost zapped me on my last pass."

Target's hot, but they've got help. Must be a Cobra Light Fire Team.

"Rowdy Rover, this is Spooky Seven One with forty thou- sand rounds and twenty-three flares, over."

"Oooooh Shit, Lead. I'm hit bad. Watch that sonofabitch."

"I'm on him with rockets. Pull off to the north by the canal, and I'll be right with you."

"Cowboy Lead, can you hit that berm to our front?"

"Negative, Rover. I'm dry, and I got to get my wingman home. I think I heard Spooky calling you this freq."

"Cowboy Lead, this is Spooky. What's the base of the clouds? Go ahead."

"Ragged cloud base at fifteen hundred feet. Lots of rain and lightning. We've been working underneath. I think I clobbered the thirty-caliber that got my Number Two. Rover needs you bad."

"Spooky, this is Rover. Do you read me?"

"Roger, Roger. Spooky Seven One in solid clouds at our normal firing altitude. What's your situation? Over."

"Started with twelve ARVIN Rangers. We're up against a canal in two bomb craters. Got three men with me. One suck-ing chest wound. No contact with the other hole. Bad guys squeezing hard. You're my last hope, buddy."

"Hang on Rover. Tell me when you see my rotating bea-con."

"Co-pilot, start a five-hundred-foot-per-minute descent. Hold her on the radial . . . Nav, come up here and help us search . . . crew, we've got a round eye and ARVIN rangers in a mess. Loadmaster, get two ground-burning flares ready . . . Gunners,

I'll take number one on slow fire . . . copilot, start breaking your glide to level at fifteen hundred feet and give me a hundred and twenty knots airspeed. Concentrate on your instruments; we'll do the looking."

"Spooky, you popped out about two klicks southwest."

"Co-pilot, give me a standard-rate left turn to a heading of north."

"Rover, I've doused our external lights. Flash your strobe beacon for me."

"Roger, Spooky . . . Spooky, I hear noise to my front. Give me a flare. God, I need light."

Sure you do. Light to paint me like the sitting duck I am. Easy shot for a thirty-caliber. Duck soup if they have a fifty. "Roger, Roger. Two million candlepower coming on." *Light may do it. Scare 'em off with light. Fire a burst to let 'em know we're a gunship.*

"Crew, watch close for ground fire."

"Alex, you gonna stay this low?"

"What's the alternative, Blackie? . . . Loadmaster, stand by to drop both marking flares."

"There's his strobe, Alex! Eleven o'clock beside the canal."

"Good eyes, Blackie. Call Three DASC and tell 'em we gotta have choppers."

"Loadmaster, standby the markers . . . co-pilot, steer ten degrees left. Loadmaster . . . ready . . . ready . . . NOW!"

"Spooky, they're probing us. Hit directly east my position two-five meters."

"I got the aircraft, co-pilot. Master gun switch on."

"Rover, I can't shoot that close."

"I gotta have it now! They're coming."

Stick with me, Lord. Gunsight re-set. Settle down old girl. Airspeed good, altitude good. Damn the rain. Got the markers. There's his strobe. Hold the bank. HOLD THE BANK. Hold it. Short burst. Two seconds.

"Rover, did you see my fire?"

"Roger, Spooky. Azimuth's good, but bring it in and stop the flares. We're taking RPG and AK-Forty-seven fire. Bring it in Spooky. For God's sake, man, shoot."

Damn scud. Damn lightning. Rain again. Lost his strobe. There's the markers . . . I think. Hold the bank . . . hold the bank. Stop the rain. Back off, God! Steady, . . . trim off the pressure.

"Spooky, they're here. Fire for Christ's sake!"

Short bursts. Short bursts. Hold the bank. Hundred meters south of the markers, abeam the strobe. Short bursts.

"Damn it, Alex, you've run us into a thunderstorm!"

"Rover, what's your situation? . . . hello Rover . . . Rover come in. Rowdy Rover."

"Anybody see muzzle flashes? Loadmaster, you read me?"

"Can't make out nothin'. Everybody's sick back here. Bouncing like a bronco."

"Rover, do you read Spooky . . ."

"Spooky Seven One . . . aaaaah . . . This is Cowboy Five Four . . . inbound with gunships and a reaction team. Can you fire to mark the target?"

"I've fired enough tonight, Five Four. No contact with Rover. My two ground markers are burning a hundred meters north of his position and seventy-five west. He's in two craters on the edge of the canal."

"Roger, Roger. Got your markers in sight. How 'bout popping a flare."

"Flare's out."

"Good flare, Spooky . . . Holy Mother of God! Looks like hand-to-hand at the end. Sure hate losing that round eye."

"Sorry about your round eye. He was my buddy, too.

CHAPTER TWENTY

WHAT WAS THAT HE KEPT CALLING ME? Friend . . . pal . . . buddy? That's it: Buddy. He called me Buddy. You're my last hope, Buddy. That's what he said. Immersed in darkness, surrounded by aliens, buffeted by nature, he placed his faith in a stranger's voice and a weapon with the precision of a cheap can of spray paint.

I needed a "Spectre" gunship. A smooth flying Lockheed AC-One Thirty with a computerized fire-control system, radar and infra-red sensors to find the enemy, and 40mm Gatling cannons to kill him!

So they hated to lose the round-eye. What about the slant-eyes? The wiry little ARVIN strikers swaggering like boys playing war in their too-big helmets and form-fitting tiger suits. Lots of mourning down in the delta today: wailing, crying, screaming. Grieving for little guys blown away by the dragon's breath.

And back in the world, anguish hovering like it did in that Mickey Rooney movie. What's the name? "The Human Comedy?" Where he pedaled his bike around delivering the notification telegrams. No messenger boy now. Two officers carrying the carefully typed letter, hunting through the housing areas or searching the country lanes till they find the place. To break the news that was already broken the moment the big car stopped in front and they got out self-consciously straightening their ties and brushing the creases out of their uniforms. Each trying to maneuver the other into going first. The thin wife will sob on the chest of the man with the letter. Abandoned on the floor, the baby will crawl to the man's legs and try to pull himself up to see what's caused his mommy to cry. Say he's only wounded, she'll plead. Say it's a mistake. Tell me it could be someone else. Such a common name . . . Buddy.

And the Dust Off will lift you out, stiff and anonymous in your green bag. Maybe you're already in Saigon. In the long, white building at Tan Son Nhut. Getting hosed down for the second time. But now it doesn't hurt. Nothing hurts anymore, except for your bud-

dies. How long will the memory last? Will the pain be triggered by a sudden rainstorm, or twinkling lights on the ground, or maybe even a nostalgic song—nights are long since you went away . . . .

You played the game just like me. Took your chances and lost. You'll get the medals you came for. Purple Heart, Silver Star. The Vietnamese'll give you a Cross of Gallantry made from the cheap metal and faded cloth you'd expect in a ravished land. It'll look tacky alongside the sleek, burnished US medals. But it sounds good: Cross of Gallantry. You'll go home in a box, but it'll look nice with the flag draped over it. And later the flag'll look forever tragic when folded into a cocked hat of white stars spangled on a sky of dark blue. Maybe you'll be buried in Arlington, escorted this time not by scrawny little foreigners but by immaculately groomed, six-foot giants of the Old Guard, the "President's Own." We're all the president's own; his own pawns to piss away on the global chess board.

More likely you'll be entrusted to some ragtag bunch of weekend warriors who'll drop you in a red clay patch while cows stand unconcerned off in the pasture, bunched under a tree and looking with big uncomprehending eyes matching those of the thin woman who's still crying even though filled with Valium.

As uncomprehending as the cows, your family will most likely never learn the circumstances. They'll just know something precious has been sacrificed, and they'll grieve each time they see the careworn face of their checkmated president.

But as irreplaceable as you are to them, you're just a routine transaction to the army, a flick of the computer key. Just one of some twenty thousand already blown away since we've been here. Small potatoes. Over twice that number get wasted on the highways each year. No harm done to anyone who really counts. You weren't the quarterback, just some backwoods lineman. The politicians will continue to smile benignly on camera as they mouth platitudes concerning our obligations, only to revert quickly enough to military jargon in their underground war room, spitting out the acronyms as if they knew what they meant, sprinkling in gratuitous profanity to impress the hard-charging generals who'll smile and nod in vigorous agreement. Then on they'll go with manipulating the policies, obscuring the costs, and hiding behind the flag in the belief there'll never be a reckoning.

"Hello killer," Mother Hubbard was smiling as Alex pulled the door shut against the trailer's internal vacuum. "Just had two calls about your escapade with the Big Red One last night. Flight leader from Phan Rang said you showed 'superior initiative and skill.'" Hubbard gave the words the sarcastic tone he reserved for clichés passed routinely between units.

"Then just now some major called from Dau Tieng babbling about you pulling 'em out of a crack. Said they lost their Six—roasted in an APC. Lost their Fox Mike radio and RTO. Big-time casualties: sixteen Kilos and twenty-four Whiskeys. Said they'd have lost the whole bunch if it hadn't been for you. Said you ought to get the Silver Star . . . You wanna write it up?"

"No, I just want to forget it."

"It's a cinch Blackie Charmoli won't write it up. How about the new guy? What's his name . . . Featherstone?"

"He's all right," Alex said, removing the wet rain suit and hanging it to drip into the wastebasket. "But he's got a lot to learn."

"Yeah, they all do. But I mean can he write the justification and the citation? Remember, if you get a Silver Star, the rest of the crew gets DFC's."

"Forget it, Mother. They're passing out DFC's like Cracker Jack prizes. Now I guess they'll start on the Silver Star. Let's leave something for the guys going home in boxes."

"My, aren't we the jaundiced one today."

"Did you hear anything from down south this morning?"

"Down south?"

"Near Binh Thuy. Second mission last night. ARVIN ranger patrol wasted while I was composing the citation for my Silver Star."

"Excuse me, Colonel," the clerk yelled from the far end of the trailer, "telephone for you."

"Don't run off," Hubbard said as he picked up the receiver.

"Yeah, that's right . . . Say again? . . . Hubbard, Lieutenant Colonel . . . Yeah, I'm talking to the pilot now. He's right here. You wanna speak to him? I already talked to one of your majors this morning . . . Binh Thuy province? Okay, I'm with you now."

Alex leaned forward, watching the perplexed look on Hubbard's face harden.

"I see . . . Yes . . . Yes . . . I'm sorry to hear that . . . All of them? . . . Can you be sure? . . . Yeah, I guess you're right. Would have been a matter of time anyway. What can I do? . . . Yeah . . . Yeah. I see. No, I agree. Nothing to be gained from that . . . Yeah, I'm glad you did . . . I'll check his training records just to be sure . . . Okay . . . Thanks . . . Yeah, I appreciate that . . . Okay, so long."

"Short round?"

"Appears to be. I'm sorry, Alex. Breaks of the game."

"Aw, Mother, . . . it's no game."

"Don't let it grab you. Balance it against the convoy you saved. Those guys in the delta didn't have a chance. Intelligence had no idea North Vietnamese regulars were that far south. He gave you twenty-six KBA."

"Twenty-six killed by air," Alex lowered his head and cradled it with both hands, "does that include our people too?"

"Damn it, Alex. Don't talk like that. I know how you feel, . . . believe me. We all do. There's not a pilot in the detachment who hasn't come back one time or another and waited for the phone to ring. It's messy business."

"He said I was his last chance. Calling me in close, knowing I was his only hope. I'd have pulled it off except for the turbulence . . . and the rain. The tracers were burning all the way to the ground. I had his strobe and my two marker flares. I'd reset the gunsight and was compensating for the wind. I . . . I called on the Lord."

Hubbard pulled his chair next to Alex and bent over, as if huddling during the Big Game. "Don't overreact. They can't be sure of anything. The bodies were all mixed up together. Most probably the friendlies were already wasted when your . . . "

"What happens now, Mother? Investigation? Hanging?"

"Nothing."

"What do you mean, 'nothing.' This is a short round! The kind of thing politicians get vindictive about."

"You're wrong on one count, my friend. It's a *possible* short round. We have more important things to do than investigate possibilities."

"What happens to me?"

"Nothing you don't want to happen. Stop taking all this shit to heart."

"I can't fight my nature. It tears me up knowing I killed our guys."

"Dammit, I told you once, and I'm not going to tell you again. You don't know you killed anyone but the sons of bitches who overran the friendlies. Now hide it somewhere so dark you'll never think of it again! I'm the commander here, and I'm satisfied. You're flying with me tonight, and I guarantee you we'll be firing. Now get out of here."

He left the trailer dragging his rain gear in the mud as he lurched up the rutted alley leading to the Spook House. The mamasans laughed as he entered, but Long ran to get him a towel. She undressed him down to his jockey shorts accompanied by the shy glances and laughter of the others. He shuffled off to his room with the towel draped around his waist.

As he entered his cubicle, he saw a solitary letter lying on his bed. He picked it up studying the sloppy, block-printed address and the Colorado Springs postmark. Absentmindedly he slit one end of the envelope with his survival knife and pulled out the contents. Sitting down, he looked at a crudely designed, haphazardly executed newsletter: *The Falcon Code.* Puzzled, he scanned the front page. Slanderous articles about Air Force Academy people and policies. *So the underground newspaper phenomenon finally hits the Academy.*

Filling the top quarter of the second page was a crude tracing of the familiar rip-off caricature of "Lucy," one of the gang from the *Peanuts* comic strip, appearing very much pregnant. In place of the cartoon's head was a superimposed photograph of poor quality. To Alex, however, the characteristic hairdo, patrician features, and dazzling smile were unmistakably Merrilane's.

CHAPTER TWENTY-ONE

"WHAT ARE YOU DOING HERE?" Merrilane demanded as she entered her office.

"Don't go getting upset, Miz Cannard," Pinski leaped to his feet as if surprised by an inspecting officer. He grabbed a white legal-size envelope from among his charts and extended it to her. "If you kick me off this project, the Commandant will hang me. Besides, no one else can understand my system."

"Mister Pinski, I fired you last night, and I meant it."

"I know you did, and I deserve everything you plan to do to me. Yesterday was not one of my better days." He smiled a country-bumpkin kind of turned-down grin. "In fact it was the worst day since I forgot to order evening chow for Jack's Valley, and eight-hundred doolies went to bed without any supper."

The absurdity of his analogy—attempting to equate a sexual assault with a failure to order hot dogs and beans—transformed her expression from that of vindictive prosecutor to amused juror. "It wasn't one of my better days either."

"I didn't sleep all night. And the run back in the mud really did a job on my ankle."

"Serves you right."

"Kind of God's punishment, I guess. I thought a lot about that last night . . . and about Major Cannard . . . and what you said about me remembering this forty years from now. I don't want to think about it that way even now. I want to remember you and Major Cannard as having been my friends, people who really cared about what happened to me. What you said about me being so far from the ideal cadet . . . that really hurt."

"I'm sorry, but I was angry and distraught, and maybe feeling even a little bit guilty."

"That's all right, Miz Cannard, you didn't do anything. You were right about it being a cadet fantasy. It's hard living here. Like a monastery. I try to be a good cadet, but I know I've fallen short. I'm clumsy and insensitive."

"Don't get down on yourself. An officer has to be confident." She had dropped her hands from her hips and now began arranging the record folders she had meant to put away the day before. "It's just that I believe it's best for you to get back into the cadet wing. Among people your own age. I'll fix it with General Safire. He's been more than kind to allow you to stay this long."

"You don't understand, Miz Cannard. If you take me off now, my job won't be finished. The Comm'll know. And I'll know . . . worse, I'll still know forty years from now. That's an awful thing to remember. Please give me another chance."

Throughout his conversation Pinski kept waving the envelope like a novice fencer trying to mount a proper defense but deathly afraid to go on the attack. Now he thrust the letter straight forward, placed it in her hand, and recovered to a defensive stance.

She looked at the sealed envelope, bare except for the typed name: Mrs. Alexander Cannard. "What in the world is this?"

"It's your insurance policy. Inside's my resignation letter addressed to the Comm and undated. It's yours to use any way you wish. I didn't commit an honor violation yesterday, at least by the Code's legal definition. But I stained my honor by trying to compromise yours."

"Jack, you don't need to do this."

"Yes I do. I hadn't planned what happened yesterday. I admit I've fantasized a lot about you. Maybe to the point where I misinterpreted little things you did . . . I'm not too swift when it comes to women. But last night when I came to your house, I was really upset. I wanted to apologize, to make it all right between us. Then you came on so strong and asked me that question right out. And I just gave you the answer you expected. Now that I think about it, maybe it was a lie technically. I'm getting confused again. Don't keep me dangling any longer. You've got my career in that envelope."

"This is silly. I don't want your resignation. I just want . . ."

"Don't you see what I'm trying to do? I'm giving you something concrete so you can be sure of me. The Air Force's going to be my home and my family. It would break Dad's heart if he knew I hadn't made it through this place. That letter's a contract between you and me. It's for the completion of this project and no 'funny stuff,' as you called it."

He was finished, like a stuffed mechanical bear that had done its little dance and run down its spring, so the last movements, the last syllables of its voice, were almost lost to its audience.

"What can I say?" She heard some of the office staff walking down the corridor. "Maybe I was wrong when I called you insensitive. I guess I should be flattered over your attentions, but I'm not. So if this is a charade on your part, don't think I'm above forcing your resignation."

The others were coming in now. "My, aren't we the early birds," Wendi Emerson called as she swung by the door.

"Just going over the plans for the play-offs; they'll be here before we know it."

Wendi continued her rounds, plugging in the coffee pot she had cleaned and set up the previous afternoon and arranging Rod Pike's desk so perhaps he would coordinate on the final inspection plans for the new field house. She stopped by the duplication room where Lilly McCauley struggled with the first of a pile of mimeograph masters representing the department's fall teaching schedule.

"You're doing that all wrong, Lilly."

"You got that right," Lilly acknowledged, rubbing the side of her nose and leaving a long smear of black ink. "I should have Mr. Touchdown helping me." She rolled her blue eyes in anticipated glee.

"No chance of that. Barbie Doll's beating your time. They're together when we get here and together when we leave. Will Ken return to find a new Papa Doll has taken his place?"

"Not likely. Barbie's too sharp for that. She knows her public's got their eyes on her." Lilly had temporarily abandoned the flimsy sheet. Being the wife of a staff sergeant, and therefore considering herself deprived of living with the intensity of the opposite caste, she would rather speculate on the carryings-on of the officer corps than settle for the black and white certainty that would flow from the machine.

"If you want to know what I think," Wendi said, "Alex Cannard had better fly back here quick, or he may find himself changed into another kind of bird."

Lilly's expressive face screwed itself into a picture of feminine bewilderment. "I don't get it; you think his bird's going to fly the coop?"

"That's not exactly what I had in mind, but who's to say your analogy's any less appropriate than mine?" Wendi stifled her laughter, then let it burst out, not knowing if she were laughing at Lilly's plebeian education or at Merrilane who had borne the brunt of office gossip since her night at the Broadmoor.

"Well I'll tell you one thing, Mister Jack Pinski can put those well-shined shoes of his under my bed anytime he wants to."

"Easy, Lilly, that's how rumors get started. You know our cadets have an honor code to guide them."

"Sure, everybody knows that, and some are stupid enough to believe they all follow it. Besides, it doesn't cover that kind of cheating, just the important kind: cheating on tests. I surely wouldn't ask him any questions, so he'd have no reason to lie. And there's nothing in my house worth stealing. So I'd be the perfect woman for him. Willard wouldn't even care. In fact he'd be kinda proud, Jack being a First Classman an' all. And it'd give him a lot more time for fishing."

"No wonder you like working in this little cubby hole. If you stay here with the duplicating fluid long enough, you probably can't detect the fishy smell when you get home."

"You know, I never thought of that," Lilly showed deep concentration, eyes glazed over, lips pursed. "Maybe you're right. Maybe I should quit complaining about the lack of ventilation and start considering it a fringe benefit."

"Hello ladies, passing the time with a little girl talk?" Rod's voice filled the small room, bounding off the walls like approaching thunder.

"Oh, Mister Pike, I didn't expect you so early." Wendi blushed wondering how long he had been standing at the doorway.

"That's evident," Rod played with his secretary, then let her off the hook. "Otherwise you'd have my coffee ready."

"I'll have it in no time," she said as she slipped by him and hurried toward the small urn whose red eye was now glowing.

"Make it two cups. I want to catch Mrs. Cannard before she gets on the merry-go-round."

Striding to the entrance to Merrilane's office, Rod boomed a greeting and an invitation for her to join him. Getting up from an unusually productive planning session with Pinski, she grabbed her notepad and followed her boss.

"Come in my dear." Rod was still performing for Wendi's benefit. "How lovely you look."

Wendi had often heard that line, as had most of the women in the academy community. Like them, she had relegated it to the Rod Pike cliché file.

"Let's have our coffee in the sunlight," he nodded toward the sofa.

"Thank you, but I prefer a straight chair. What do you wish to know? I have a ten-thirty appointment."

"Can you give me a rundown on the play-offs and the field-day schedule? I think I can get the Supe to give out the awards."

Wendi placed a small tray on the coffee table and left the room pulling the door closed behind her. Merrilane ignored the coffee as she launched into a succinct briefing. Her discussion with Pinski had provided all the material she needed and more if Rod should wish to thrash out details. As she talked, she realized how invaluable Jack had become. Losing him would have been a catastrophe. Instead, she now had an able assistant on a short leash. The thought of having absolute control over a man's destiny gave her a feeling of unaccustomed superiority.

Rod listened attentively, sipping his coffee from time to time. He asked few questions, and she perceived he wanted to tell her something.

"When are you going to meet Alex in Hawaii?" he asked when she had finished.

"Sometime after field-day and the awards banquet," she answered. "Why do you ask."

"No particular reason."

"Don't play with me, Rod. I know you don't ask questions or call for private briefings for no reason. Out with it."

"It's just that talk's developing about you and your cadet."

"You're kidding. Who's doing the talking?

"Wendi for one. I overheard her this morning gossiping with Lilly."

"I'm surprised you're a rumormonger, considering you're probably the subject of more tales than anyone I know."

"I can handle it. To tell the truth, I enjoy doing things I wouldn't do otherwise just to live up to expectations."

"Things like taking me to the Peppercorn Inn and the Broadmoor?"

"That's not fair. The Broadmoor was the payoff of a legitimate bet. A very pleasant evening I might add, but still a payoff. The Peppercorn was a convenience. Again very pleasant but still a convenience. There was talk about that, I'm sure. That's why I decided to let our relationship cool."

"Come now, boss. I've grown up a lot since Alex left. I'm more inquisitive now, and maybe even a little smarter in the ways of the world. You dropped me because you were sure I could run the program without you and because you were too busy doing the Colonel's work while he was on leave. Maybe you also thought you wouldn't be able to add me to your string, so I wasn't worth the investment."

"That's a horrible thing to say. Their isn't any string."

Rod's rejoinder was so unexpected, so objectively stated she knew it must be true. "My God. What are you saying?"

He sat upright in his chair, maybe a little surprised himself by the admission. "It's a simple story," he said in a monotone something like a prisoner would use after being broken by many hours of interrogation. "Not as romantic as Jake Barnes, but then Hemingway always did a better job than life. Not a war wound. Didn't you ever wonder why I had no combat record? I've spent my life hanging around real men, listening to their stories of derring-do and seeking to match them with stale sports anecdotes. Looking for companionship, I've taken out practically every eligible woman between Pueblo and Denver. Going with most of them only until they learned I couldn't finish the job. Would you believe it? Gymnastics accident. One second young, virile, stretched out and arching perfectly overhead; the next coming down on the bars slightly off kilter."

"Oh, God, don't . . ."

"The worse part is not being able to satisfy the women you really feel close to. Going so far—going so well—getting rave reviews up to the finale. And then not being able to finish the performance. Aborting the mission, the cadets would say. Tough. Tougher on my companions than on me because I always knew what to expect."

"Rod, I'm so sorry."

"Strange how they react. I don't know how many times I've spun this tale for the benefit of some wide-eyed woman who'd earned the right to an explanation. Most are really understanding. Especially those with a past that didn't include much intimacy. They're happy with just the tenderness and the flourishes. Surprising how many women friends I really have. Women who, for me, have shut off their two principal needs, complete fulfillment and the opportunity to talk about it.

"I've been able to maintain some long-term relationships purely on a Platonic basis. Some, believe it or not, have proposed marriage. Can you beat that? I've considered it. Lots of other males, who are less a man than I, have accepted that accommodation. I haven't as yet."

Listening in shocked and then sympathetic silence, she realized for the second time this morning she had heard a virile man confess innermost secrets and then run down as if all the energy had drained out. "I don't know what to say. It's difficult to comprehend."

His lips parted in a half-smile. "That's what I hoped you'd say. Nothing."

"Of course. I wouldn't think of discussing it. With anyone."

"So now you know the deep secret of why I have so many women. Because I can't have so many women. There's humor there somewhere. But I've spent my adult life reflecting on it, and I haven't found it . . . or the justice. Job and I, continually asking, 'Why me, Lord.'"

"I wish I knew what to say."

"You're a very sweet person, Merrilane. Believe me, if things were different, I'd be trying to live up to my reputation as far as you're concerned. There's something fragile about you that interests a man. Maybe even—forgive me for saying it—maybe there's a code, a secret beacon you're beginning to transmit as you gain confidence. Maybe you're inviting investigation."

"That's a shameful thing to say."

"Please let me finish," he said reaching out to touch her hand. "Believe me, whatever spark that's flickering in you, men will respond to it. You've been protected in the home. But once in the man's world, you're fair game. And there're plenty of hunters thinking only and always of conquest and domination. You'd be amazed at the stories women have told me while I held them as I'd hold a baby and patted their backs. Tales of atrocity as horrifying as any that come out of the war zone. Tales of giving birth on the kitchen floor because the husband was out boozing with the boys. Tales of pictures found in wallets, of perfume-soaked letters in the backs of bureau drawers, of bank accounts cleaned out because a husband chose to live a secret life. Does that shock you? Then you're not ready for the tales of physical abuse—enforced bondage, required swinging; you simply can't imagine it. Maybe what the world needs is a few more of us Lord Chatterleys just to listen and pat women's shoulders."

"Rod, you dear, dear man."

"Enough of the sad talk. I'm usually better company than this. I admit I enjoy myself a lot more when I'm wearing the mask. But I want you to listen to me. Watch yourself carefully. Start thinking of Hawaii with your husband, and don't let the thought fade. Start planning for the return of your man and the role you'll assume then. And remember, if you want the masculine point of view without any of the risk, Uncle Rod's ready if not able."

"Thank you for the offer and for the confidence."

"Just be careful, my dear, of your young cadet. I don't like his looks. He's one of the few they get here who's playing a game all the way. He's a taker. He'll take the education, he'll take the glory, he'll take whatever he can get. And, unless I'm dead wrong—and I've never been—you've got something he wants. And he's going to try to possess it anyway he can."

"I hope you're wrong about Jack. But if you're right, I still have something to keep him in line."

"I sincerely hope so. But I'm afraid what you need to fend off Pinski is chasing around Vietnam on a fool's errand."

CHAPTER TWENTY-TWO

HUBBARD SIPPED from the steaming mug. "Hot. That's what I wanted. Hot target to get you over your funk. Bad guys never cooperate." The two pilots sat in the deserted operations trailer, having chosen not to compound the boredom of an unproductive patrol with the sure monotony of midnight breakfast. Hubbard drank from the last survivor of two cases of ceramic cups some forgotten predecessor had ordered from Thailand. The black mugs with the squadron's ghost emblem had become collector's items, disappearing one by one as their users rotated back to the world. Alex slumped in a folding chair, oblivious of the swaying floor and chattering windows that danced to the rumble of distant explosions.

"Another Arc Light going in," Hubbard said. "They're working those B-Fifty-twos overtime." He rose to top-off his cup. "Dammit, Alex, your long face is getting on my nerves. What's it take to get you back up to speed?"

"Send me home."

"You and a half-million other round eyes. What would the rest of the world think?"

"Who cares?"

"Obviously the President, the generals, and all the war contractors."

"Who cares who counts?"

"Honestly, Alex, you certainly don't talk like a college professor."

"That's because I wasn't. I was an instructor at the US Air Force Academy."

"There's a difference?"

"We cared about our students."

"Professors elsewhere don't?"

"Not in the same way. We got to know them outside the classroom: invited them home, fed them . . . trusted them."

"So you're pretty high on the Academy?"

"Have been. By and large they turn out a good product."

"You want to go back?"

"No. You get out of the mainstream if you stay too long, and teaching burns you out. It's time for us to go back to SAC. But right now I've got to get home for a few days."

"You know the only way you get back early is in a box. What's eating you?"

"I can't tell you, Mother."

"I'm sorry, Alex, but there ain't no way."

"I've got to do something that can only be done on the scene. Now we gotta make it happen."

"What's this 'we' stuff? You got a mouse in your pocket?"

"This is serious. My wife's in danger. I need some time home. It can't wait until R and R. What about a medical excuse . . . a headshrinker?"

"Seeing a shrink will shoot down your career faster than a VC gunner."

"But the regulations say . . ."

"I don't care what they say. You know what happens in SAC when someone gets hung up in the Human Reliability regs. They take him off a crew, and he finds himself shuffling papers in the backwaters of the Pentagon. Same thing here. No commander's gonna take chances with a guy who may have psychological problems."

"I've got to get home."

"And I gotta have more than your fervent desire before I try anything. What's the problem, another man?"

"Maybe. Maybe worse. Someone's sent me a copy of an underground Academy newsletter with a picture of my wife's face on a cartoon of a pregnant woman."

"Why your wife?"

"I don't know. Perhaps coincidence, but I can't take a chance. Maybe they just clipped her picture out of a Wives' Club paper. Or they could be targeting her specifically. Maybe one of the cadets we sponsored, or even one of my students who thinks I gave him a raw deal."

"Excuse me for asking, but are you sure she's not . . . involved . . . with someone?"

"What do you think's been going through my head? My mind's been in overdrive thinking of possibilities."

"Any luck?"

"We've both had plenty of opportunities. But we didn't . . . I didn't . . . " He looked up at Hubbard, then quickly dropped his eyes again. "She's always been active on the base: wives' club, Family Services, swimming, tennis, horseback riding. Model Air Force wife. She's gone out of her way to entertain the cadets. Particularly the doolies—the freshmen. We've adopted five or six every year. Having them to dinner, putting up their dates for the dances, going to their games."

"Alex, I know this is sickening, but you can't allow some anonymous bastard to get to you."

"He has, Mother. Coming on top of everything else. You just start imagining things you'd never think about otherwise. Pretty soon you're doubting yourself, asking what you've not done that you should have been doing. Then you reason nothing would be wrong if only you were with her. That leads you to questioning why you're here and comparing all the high-sounding justifications with what you've seen in wasted resources and mindless destruction. Pretty soon your wife's a whore, you're less than a man, the world is going to hell, and everyone is a son of a bitch. All because of a piece of trash you got in the mail."

Another Arc Light bombing rumbled in the distance, setting up a harmonic vibration that shook all the windows and caused the trailer again to sway.

"Alex, I know you're tired, and you've been under a hell of a strain, but you've got to get this in perspective. If you've never doubted your wife in the past, surely there's no reason to suspect her now."

"Things are different. She's out on her own. Working in the athletic department. She's not tied down with the kids like when we were in SAC. I don't know how she's reacting to it. She used to write every day, but now I'm lucky to get a scribbled note once a week. She's meeting a lot of guys who're on the fast track downtown. They're bird-dogging her if they're normal; no doubt about that."

"You ought to be happy she's in a responsible job. Ought to feel proud they're bird-dogging her. If my Catherine would lose forty pounds, maybe they'd bird-dog her too. That's good for a woman's morale. Stop jumping at conclusions. You don't feather an engine just because of fluctuating oil pressure. Hell, when you get something concrete, like a 'Dear John,' then you can start getting up-tight."

"I am proud of her. I'm not one of those Neanderthal Men. I'm really happy for her. But damn it, I know there's frustration in her job. And where there's frustration, there'll be a friendly shoulder to cry on."

"I'm disappointed in you, Alex. You're not giving her much credit. If she's married to you, she must be pretty good merchandise to start with. And if she's raised two children, there's been frustration. And if your marriage survived a tour in B-Forty-sevens, as much as you guys were gone, she must know how to handle propositions. Once you get some sleep, you'll see things a lot clearer."

"Maybe you're right, Mother."

"Mother's always right, don't you know. Now that we've cleared that up, would you mind going through that pile in my basket and telling me what needs to be done first?"

"It could be one of those arrogant First Classmen. Some of my friends won't let them in their houses. The system seems to turn certain personalities into dominating, inconsiderate snobs. Especially around women. They think they're objects to be used only for pleasure. Some of those guys are more than capable of doing this to Merrilane and me."

"Why suspect a First Classman? I'd think after four years they'd all have the party line."

"Actually three years. They become seniors after their predecessors graduate in June. The class of 'Sixty-nine is unusual. They were freshmen when the first cheating scandal broke. We're not just talking cribbing on tests. A mafia-like organization existed with extortion schemes and death threats. It's possible a few were infected back then but weren't identified. Some believe the investigation was concluded when dismissals reached a hundred and politics dictated we'd had enough bad press."

"You're telling me PR decided the extent of the investigation?"

"That was the dominant rumor. If it's true, and if some of those who were spared also survived the second scandal two years later, we could have a few really hardcore deviants."

"Damn, Alex, don't destroy all my illusions. You mean some bad apples may have stayed in the barrel?"

"Figure it out for yourself. If they did, they'd be Firsties now. And First Classmen oversee the basic cadet indoctrination. In fact, other than some small number of First Classmen and all the incoming class, few other cadets are on campus during the summer. The doolies couldn't possibly publish an underground newspaper. Who does that leave? Now's the last chance to root the bastards out before they get their commissions."

"It's a crazy story, Alex. If the Academy's as sensitive to media attention as you say, they'll give only lip service to your complaint, and you'll prolong your wife's embarrassment. My policy on bad press is to ignore it. Most people don't read even the legitimate media closely, and those who do can't remember two days later what they read. Any time you respond to something relatively minor, you'll find you just shot off your own foot."

"You mean you won't help me?"

"I didn't say I wouldn't help you; I said I couldn't help you. But that was my first reaction. I always like to see how creative I can be when the situation requires it. We may need to send a pilot to ferry a replacement Goon over here from the States. Or maybe it's time we sent someone back to confer with the training people. Or perhaps Fairchild-Hiller at St. Augustine could use a consultant on their AC-One Nineteen gunship conversion. You could have a week's delay-en-route on your way to Florida. I'll see what I can do."

"I'd appreciate it, Mother. I'm beginning to think I have the Reverse-Midas touch. I'm not half way through the tour, and I've crash-landed once, had a booby trap go off in my face, caused a short round, and now I have wife trouble."

"Listen to me, and listen good. I won't stand for that kind of talk. Self deprecation and superstition will ruin an outfit, and I'm not going to permit it in my unit. So knock it off. In your self pity you conveniently forgot getting recommended for the Silver Star by an army officer whose unit you saved from certain massacre."

"I'm sorry, Sir."

"You certainly are," Hubbard's eyes blazed. "You impressed me as one of the best officers I'd seen. You've supported my policies when the others laughed. You've got the detachment's administration in better order than most stateside units. Now, damn it, get your head out of your ass. Worse case, if your woman's catting around, she won't be the first. And it doesn't matter a ratz to me except it affects one of my pilots. So get your shit straight. Write her a letter, call her from Saigon, get your R and R paperwork going . . . whatever you have to do to straighten it out so it's not my problem! Do you read me, Major?"

Visibly stunned by the fury of Hubbard's attack, Alex stood almost in a brace. He had forgotten who he was talking to. For a while he had thought of Hubbard as just another pilot, a friend. He resolved never to make that mistake again.

"I apologize for my conduct, Colonel. Will you be needing me anymore tonight?"

"No. If they haven't scrambled us by now, they're not going to."

"In that case, I think I'll head up to the Spook House. You going?"

"No. I want to finish the rest of the coffee and write a few reports before the second shift lands."

Alex picked up his flak vest and slipped it over his flight suit. He was opening the door to leave when Hubbard called.

"I forgot to tell you. Seventh Air Force rang up before briefing last night. They've got an emergency opening for a Major to work with the SAC office in Saigon coordinating B-Fifty-two strikes. Your name's in the pot."

CHAPTER TWENTY-THREE

EARLY THE MORNING after Halloween, along with all the witches, goblins, and vampires who were also going to ground, Alex wheeled Spooky 74 into its revetment. Hubbard awaited him. Three hours later he was on the shuttle bus to Tan Son Nhut airbase, adjacent to Saigon, wondering what a combat tactics officer did and what had happened to the SAC job he had expected.

The Combat Tactics office was on the second floor of a clapboard building located across the street from the main complex housing Seventh Air Force Headquarters and half a block from the officers' club. Glenn Mahan, a happy-faced major who looked as if he should be sleeping somewhere under a shamrock, welcomed him with the news that their boss, Lieutenant Colonel Adam Wootan, was visiting Cam Rhan Bay, Alex's predecessor had already rotated, and he had no idea what projects he'd been working.

"As the Sabre pilots said to their replacements in Korea," Mahan paused a beat, "K MAG YO YO–Kiss My Ass, George. You're On Your Own."

Before dawn on his second day, he climbed the swaying staircase seemingly tacked as an afterthought to the outside of the building, strained to see the faded numbers on the combination lock, and finally succeeded in opening the office door. From the clerk's desk drawer, he took paper then settled himself to write:

Tan Son Nhut Air Base
3 November 1968
Dear Colonel Harbinger,

Congratulations on what Merrilane calls a miraculous recovery. Just don't go back to work before you're up to speed. Rachel can watch the store a few days more. You'll be pleased to know your program to write contemporary history is on schedule, and the first group of scholars should arrive before I return from R&R on the tenth. In fact, they'll occupy part of our building. First thing they'll have to devise is an acronym for their office address. What about "Operation Search and Document" (O-SAD)?

My transfer to Seventh Air Force Headquarters surprised me. I'm in the Directorate of Combat Tactics, responsible for all C-47 operations. I feel guilty leaving the detachment just as I was getting proficient, but I can make Spooky's life less frustrating by clarifying their Rules of Engagement and getting their orbit patterns moved closer to the Cambodian border. Writing a tactics manual is also a priority.

There's much for me to learn. After R&R, I'll start visiting bases where Gooney Bird detachments are located. Merrilane and I have a lot of catching up to do. She's working so hard, it's difficult for her to find time to scribble more than a position report. In my case, some things have happened I'd rather she not be burdened with. So we both need to strike that spark again.

Once I get into the new job, the remaining four months should pass in a twinkling. I'll evaluate the tactics and standardization of all Spookies and EC-47s (the electronic reconnaissance birds that criss-cross the country pin-pointing enemy radio transmitters) and look in on the logistics support C-47s (trash haulers).

A trash hauler killed Bert Yenowine, the captain who used to coach football at the Prep School. Lost an engine in the soup south of Da Nang; prop wouldn't feather and dragged him into a mountain. I've often flown with Bert in Goons out of Denver before the Academy moved its flight operations to Colorado Springs. He was a fighter pilot at heart. God, how he hated the Goon.

His pen slowed, then stopped as his mind skipped back to the final approach into Lowry Field with Bert wrestling the controls, props slinging chunks of ice against the fuselage, the astringent smell of ethylene glycol so strong it tingled the nostrils, the Goon's left wing knifed into a snow squall gusting at the maximum landing crosswind component. *What superb fly-*

ing skill; what a shining personality sacrificed because of a burned-out feathering motor. Not a thing he could have done to save her, except maybe detouring down the coast rather than crossing the mountains. He could have made it in a jet.

As he reflected on whatever lessons could be learned from his friend's death, he realized he should not have written such depressing news to Frank who was still climbing out of the valley and across the mountains. He was glad he had just started a fresh page, so he could easily eliminate Bert Yenowine's epitaph. Beginning to write again, he heard someone clumping up the stairs.

"Hello Al. Who're you trying to impress coming to work before anyone else?" Stan Fox, the hyperactive F-105 tactics officer stood grinning in the doorway.

"Good morning, Stan. After the rocket attack woke me, I thought I'd get some personal correspondence out of the way before I work on General Emery's end-of-tour report."

"Don't try to shit me, Al. You're probably writing a novel about finally meeting the world's greatest fighter pilot. Make sure you spell my name right." Fox sat on the corner of Alex's desk leaning over to see what he had written. "DEAR COLONEL HARBINGER! Wow! I knew you SAC weenies were organized, but I didn't know you wrote your sponsors every morning before breakfast."

"Nothing like that, Stan. Colonel Harbinger's my old boss at the Academy and also my next-door neighbor. He's just had a cancerous lung removed."

"Kiss him goodby for me. Once that shit gets you, its like taking flak in the hydraulic system. You're goin' nowhere but down. By the way, knock off the 'Stan.' I only answer to my call sign: 'SugarFox.' Surely you've read about me in *The Stars and Stripes* or *Newsweek*."

"Afraid not, Sugar. Since we're getting names straight, you can drop the 'Al' and use my call sign . . . 'Major.'"

"Funny, funny, Maj. You gotta be shittin' me." The captain's watery eyes twinkled from dark tunnels drilled beneath curly brown eyebrows.

Alex laughed at the frenetic playfulness of the young pilot whose appearance was of a wraith reincarnated once too often. "Yes, I'm shittin' you as you so articulately put it. But most everybody calls me 'Alex.'"

"But I'm not everybody, Al. I'm The World's Greatest Fighter Pilot! Hey, man, ALL RIGHT!" Sugar had grabbed the frame containing the snapshot of Merrilane lying on the beach at Hilton Head. "What a number; I'd like to thunk my probe in her receptacle."

"Do you manage to alienate all your associates by calling them by names they detest and then insulting their wives?"

"Insulting! Who's insulting? Jeez, man, that's the highest compliment a fighter pilot can give a husband."

"You've a peculiar sense of decorum, Sug. I bet you say that about all the women you meet."

"Naw, you got me all wrong, Maj. Only the good lookin' ones. Take that one over there, for example. Trash hauler's broad. Fat, slack jawed. I wouldn't touch her with Ho Chi Minh's dick."

"Oh, I see. I guess I'll have to write Merrilane and tell her she has an admirer."

"MERRY LANE! This gets better all the time. Why don't you just finish the letter to your sponsor, and I'll write Merry Lane. Better still, buy the farm right quick, and I'll escort you back and comfort the widow." Sugar moved off the desk and lost himself in a crude pantomime, bowing low, straightening up to roll his eyes, patting down the wiry curls that seemed to be vibrating in anticipation. "Ah yes," his voice slipped into an impersonation of W.C. Fields. "My little chickadee, I knew Al well. Flew his wing down Tu Do street, keeping him clear of the White Mice. Poor man, got run down by a Honda, . . . finished off by a pedicab. Ah, yes, imagine that. Another major loss. Now let's you and me take a little stroll." Sugar crashed back to earth, looking at Alex and gesturing like a trained seal for applause.

"You gotta be shittin' me."

SugarFox stood dejectedly in the center of the office, unfastened his metal belt buckle, unzipped his trousers, and dropped them to just above his knees as he adjusted his uniform shirt into a tight cadet tuck on either side. Then he pulled up his trousers, covering the white drawers with the bright red hearts, drew the belt tight, and yanked up the zipper.

"I take back what I said about decorum. Do you always drop your pants in the middle of the office?"

"Take 'em down anywhere I can, Maj. Anywhere I can. An officer has to keep up appearances. He can't have his shirttail loose."

"Is that what you fighter jocks mean when you talk about letting it all hang out."

"Not the shirttail, Maj. Not the shirttail. We hung our behinds out every time we went downtown. I shit you not."

"What's the story on the bombing up North, Sug? Is it really tough, or is that just fighter pilot propaganda?"

"Take everything you've heard, multiply it by a thousand, and that's half as bad as it is." SugarFox's facial muscles tightened. He had stopped the prancing and voice imitations. "Tactics suck, targets suck, strategy sucks. Try putting that in General Emery's end-of-tour report. Of course it'll be removed before the ink's dry. The general's got too much invested to start rocking the boat now. Two stars so far and a combat tour. He can see that third star just ready to pop over the horizon. Maybe another after that if he can keep from getting drawn back here before the shit finally hits the fan."

"Well LBJ's stopped the bombing anyway," Alex said evenly, hoping Sug would rise to the bait. "You won't have to go back there anymore."

"What the hell you been smoking, Maj? Don't they teach you anything at Staff College? Don't you know any military history? Don't you know fuckin' politicians?"

"What are you squids hollering about?" shouted "Tiny" Temple, the A-1 tactics officer, as he entered the office accompanied by "Phantom" Phelps, the F-4 pilot who had joined the office two weeks previously. "You've already made two mistakes, Al. First you came to work early; then you tried to discuss something rationally with this skirt chaser."

"Who asked you to join our formation, Shorty?"

"Look, Hotrock, just stay out of my way today. I'm gonna be hurling my pink body at the trail tonight, and I don't want to expend any energy putting your lights out."

"Oh, that explains the baggy flight suit. I thought you'd forgot to wash your khakis last night. Everyone knows you're too tight to hire a mamasan."

"Why don't you knock it off about mamasans? You don't hire 'em just to do your shorts with the red hearts."

"Gentlemen . . ."

"That's your third mistake, Major. You called Cro-Magnon here a gentleman."

"Isn't there anything you two agree on? Or does this routine run perpetually?"

"Yeah, Maj," Sugar answered. "We're together on what I just told you about strategy. And even our Phantom of the Opera will drink to that. I don't know how it is with you fly-by-nighters, but for the real studs operating up north or in Laos, the whole scenario stinks."

"Roger that," Temple echoed.

Phelps nodded blankly, as if he had participated in six thousand similar conversations, and continued sorting through the morning's message traffic he had picked up at the Comm Center. "Well, guys, the Great Cowboy's stopped Rolling Thunder. North Vietnam's completely off limits. Now Uncle Ho can get back on his feet while we stooge around in ever-decreasing concentric circles till we finally fly up our collective asshole."

"Just what we were saying when you came in," Sugar said. "Screw around some more while the dinks bring in tons of SAMs, Triple A, MiG-21s, all that shit. Then, when Numbnuts decides to crank up the bombing again, the shit-hot crews will have rotated, and we'll have to send up a bunch of amateurs and pay the price for increasing their learning curves. I can't fuckin' believe it!"

"Let's change the subject to something vitally important," Alex had enough of strategic planning for the moment. "My R and R starts in two days. What's there to do in Hawaii?"

Pandemonium broke out among the three fighter pilots just as the rest of the office staff arrived to wonder what all the noise was about.

"Are you kidding, Al," Phelps said. "You really are spooky. You meeting your wife?"

"What difference does it make," yelled SugarFox. "Procedure's the same on any R and R . . . screw your eyeballs out!"

"You takin' your kids?" Temple had moved in close to Alex so the others could not hear.

"No. They're in school, and I honestly can't afford it."

"You got your priorities mixed up, Al." The bantam-weight pilot looked up into Alex's eyes. His mouth was a rigid line scarcely broken as he repeated, "You got your fuckin' priorities mixed up."

The others drifted off to check the text of Johnson's latest gambit or to prepare for their day's activity.

"Yeah, I know what you're saying. One of my friends at Bien Hoa said the same thing."

"Fuckin' A. I had my four kids along in Hawaii. And if I can swing a second R and R, I'll have the little buggers there, too."

"You see," Alex said quietly, "there's something that's built up between my wife and me. I wanted us to be alone so we could pull it together before it goes any further."

"Sorry to hear that, Al. But no matter. The kids need their Daddy more than Mama does. Not all of us is gonna make it. We're not in sync like jocks on the unit level. Our sleep cycle's always off. It affects our timing. We're more at risk than the guys who do it every day. It's a sporty course, so take my advice. Bring the kids even if it means borrowing the fuckin' money. I did, and I don't regret a penny of it. You gotta get your priorities right, Pal. None of us knows how much time we got left."

CHAPTER TWENTY-FOUR

BACK-LIGHTED BY A FULL MOON and obliquely facing Diamond Head, Merrilane Cannard heard the soft brushing of the carpet as the door yielded to Alex's touch. She had posed herself on the low couch, sheathed in an indigo muumuu, hair loose on her bare shoulders, a white gardenia above her left ear. Only her eyelids moved, fluttering to keep incipient tears from spoiling the illusion of timelessness. His vision blurred as he stepped to her side then dropped on one knee as Arthur to Guinevere. She turned to him, eyes wide like a surrendered creature of the forest. He buried his face in the folds of her dress, inhaling her fragrance, feeling his rough fingers catching the threads of her garment.

Beginning to lose control, he disengaged, closed his eyes, and envisioned the dark water of Lake Tahoe seen on a somber November dawn as he climbed eastward out of Sacramento, heavily loaded and straining to clear the snow-dusted peaks. He opened his eyes to the surprise of finding her still there, but now watching him intently. He saw his hands, calloused from gripping the control wheel and throttle knobs, gently begin to stroke her face as the second hand of the watch on his left wrist jumped with increasing rapidity from pip to pip around the dial's circumference.

She woke first, shivering under the slight breeze. He looked so thin, she thought, and bleached. She had so much to tell him, so many possibilities upon which to get his advice. Shifting slightly to retrieve a filmy scarf she had meant to introduce into their lovemaking, she wrapped it loosely around her hand and began to skim it across his face, brushing his lips and tweaking the tiny hairs that protruded from his nostrils. He began to stir, stretching and luxuriating in the sensation of emerging leisurely from sleep.

"Hi, pretty lady."

"Hello, handsome man."

They showered together, dressed, and went out to stroll Honolulu's wide avenues hand-in-hand. He fired questions about the health and activities of the children, relatives, and friends. At a pancake house incongruously decorated like a Swiss chalet, they ate waffles piled with strawberries and whipped cream, drank black coffee, and laughed over a trove of photographs she had brought.

Then they returned to the hotel to don swim suits and lie in the sun beside the deserted pool. The water was cold, but it provided an excuse to huddle close together wrapped in a single beach towel. Neither seemed ready for serious talk, content instead to comment on the hotel's architecture, the friendliness of the people, and a possible itinerary for the next few days. After a while they sat like two strangers who had met and formed a passionate liaison, but whose minds were now separately and increasingly searching for ties of commonality. She noticed in him an unusual and distracting inability to meet her eyes and a disquieting quirk of beginning to frame a question then abandoning the attempt as if he were distracted or perhaps unsure of how to proceed.

By mutual but unspoken agreement, they abandoned their efforts to confer as being premature. Instead they gathered their few possessions, wrapped themselves in towels, and with hanging heads walked slowly from the lovely garden. Once inside their room, they squared off as if to settle by combat whose fault it was that they were in the stale-smelling cubicle rather than the sunny paradise beside the pool. Alex, the instigator with a well-flicked wet towel, was not prepared for the hostility of Merrilane's answering slashes, chops, and scratches. Looking like an unhorsed Apache warrior, she circled him counterclockwise, bent at the waist, arms spread for balance, pupils flashing. Not taking his eyes away from her, he appraised the athlete who was his adversary. She would easily pass for a woman in her late twenties, flat stomach belying her matronly status. Her ample bosom hung barely restrained by the thin halter of a string Bikini that seven months ago she would not have dared to wear outside her own dressing room. Only the barest triangle of white slashed between her legs. Her tan was immaculate. How had she achieved it, if she worked the schedule she said? How many pairs of masculine eyes had ravished her as she lay at pool side cultivating that tan? Were there cadet eyes also? Did one pair belong to the roving reporter from *The Falcon Code*?

She continued to circle, now reversing into a clockwise pattern. She scooped up a heavy pillow, heaved it at him, and began licking her lips as she goaded him to attack her. The sharp sounds of slaps on taunt flesh, audible gasps for breath, thumps of padded furniture slammed against paper thin walls—any of these, in rational times, would have driven them into obedience, silence, and embarrassed apology. Smarting from the sting of the pillow and bleeding from a deep scratch half-way down his right arm, he stepped out of his wet trunks and slung them at her midriff. Bending low and circling with both hands extended and gesturing for position, he caught their images in the narrow mirror—a stark reflection of pre-historic confrontation fit only for the shadowed wall of some hidden cave.

Determined to end the potentially tragic charade, he feinted low to the left, saw her shift to counter, then lunged upward, going for her hair. He demolished the arrangement she had protected so jealously at the pool, exploding the petals of the white flower as he grasped her right arm, shifted his weight, and rolled her onto the hard-tufted carpet. Straddling her stomach, he pinned her arms, then went for her throat. Sniffling hard to stifle tears, she turned her head to keep his lips from finding her mouth. Embarrassed into relaxing his hold, he was unprepared for her renewal of the fight. Suddenly he found their positions reversed: himself on the bottom with a throbbing head and she riding high on his chest flashing the toothy smile he had seen in pictures of victorious Viet Cong.

153

Infuriated, he returned to the attack, ripping the small patch of cloth from her crotch, throwing her on her back, and penetrating her as she tried to wiggle out from under him. He held her slim buttocks so tightly he imagined the tissue rupturing into bruises that would mark his conquest for days. Neither uttered a word, just guttural breaths almost lost in the thrashing of liquid-cooled bodies. Later, coiled tightly together, they slept until the sun had started its long slide into the Pacific.

During the next day, they lost themselves in infinite variations of animal pleasures: plunging through the pounding surf, stuffing down fat hot dogs slippery with spicy mustard, slapping each other with great quantities of suntan lotion, touching, kissing, fondling. They adopted strange but acceptable ground rules forbidding the raising of any topic that might develop into a significant conversation. Emphasizing sexual abandon, they came to resembled nothing so much as a carefree soldier and his strumpet. Then a flare-up of cystitis suspended the sexual marathon, smashing them to earth with the simultaneous realization their communication lines were not simply tangled, but quite possibly ripped out entirely.

Attending a luau on the evening of the second day, she recognized Jean Wainwright, a Fort Carson army wife she had met through her activities in Colorado Springs. Jean was escorted by her husband, a tanned infantry captain who had arrived on the same flight as Alex. The two couples became a foursome sitting cross-legged across the low table from each other eating the exotic food and laughing at thinly-veiled innuendos concerning their recreational activities. Walt Wainwright, who had recently moved with his unit to guard the Newport bridge northeast of Saigon, smiled broadly and extended his hand a second time when Merrilane mentioned Alex flew Spookies.

"You guys are number one in my book," Walt sputtered with his mouth full of roast pig. "Whenever Spooky's working, we just sit back, light up, and watch the show. You ever fly Spooky Seven Two?"

"I've been at Seventh Air Force headquarters for almost two weeks," Alex replied. "But it seems like I flew Seven Two or one of the other call signs every night for almost eight months. Seven Two's one of the birds we keep over the Tan Son Nhut rocket belt. Not much exciting ever happens."

"Maybe not for you. But the dinks would give a main force battalion to blow that bridge, and nighttime usually gets a little hairy. Any chance you flew about three weeks ago on a Sunday night?"

"Yeah, I think maybe so. That would have been one of my last missions at Bien Hoa. We just dropped illumination flares as I remember. Sheer boredom"

"Maybe from your perspective, Major, but we had VC frogmen coming at us all night. They're the best; they've even sunk freighters unloading at the Saigon docks. Without your light, they'd have blown us and the whole shebang sky high."

"Nice to hear from a satisfied customer. We seldom get any feedback." Alex whacked off another huge hunk of meat and passed it to Wainwright. "Good pig. Let's eat him while he's hot."

His attempt to change the subject did not work. Tongue loosened by beer, the captain resumed the conversation talking across the pig and raising his voice unnecessarily loud. Others were beginning to listen.

"Good God Almighty, if you're lacking feedback let me ease your mind. Next to beer and mail from home, Spooky's the best friend a grunt could have. You couldn't get me up in that bucket of bolts tooling around the Fish Hook and the Parrot's Beak and inviting every slope in seven provinces to take a pot shot at me. Man, give me the good earth and some honest sandbags between me and the black hats."

"Every man to his own devices," Alex mumbled while trying with his eyes to signal Wainwright to turn it off.

"First part of my tour, I spent at Kontum. You know Kontum? Sure, everybody knows Kontum. Spooky's there every night hosing down the dinks. Drawing fire from three or four fifty-caliber positions at a time. Never pulling off. Just blasting away. I saw that one out of Pleiku go down. Wrapped in fire all the way. Most brilliant flame I ever saw. Pilot's voice just as calm as could be calling the next Spooky down from the stack, so we could have constant protection. Blew apart when they hit the ground. Lit the whole countryside like daylight . . . Awesome."

Merrilane studied Alex's face in the pulsing light from the flickering torches.

After returning to their room, they lay on the couch propped by huge pillows, sipping champagne Alex had bought during his flight's refueling stop in Guam. Out the open balcony door, they could see Diamond Head dark against the moonlit sky: for her, Bali Hi; for him, Nui Ba Dinh.

Choosing her words carefully, she returned to the subject of Spooky's mission as if she were hoping to crack the lid of Pandora's box just a tiny bit. "Sweetheart, what Walt said, and what you've led me to believe are entirely different. Are you playing straight with me?"

"I guess not completely," he sipped his wine. "How about you?"

"What do you mean, how about me?"

"Just that. Your letters have been so sketchy except for the gushy descriptions of Rod, Jack, and every other male in Colorado Springs who's capable of picking up a badminton racquet."

"Now wait a minute. That's a cheap shot."

"See, you're even learning the language."

"Alex, honestly! What do you expect me to do while you're off on the great crusade? Sit home and knit?

"Penelope did."

"Oh, Alex, do you have to go literary on me? Times have changed. We women are finally beginning to get our act together!" In disgust she leaned over the side of the couch and rummaged in her purse. He heard a metallic click like the safety being thrown on an M-16, then recoiled as flame spurted a foot in front of his nose. In the circle of light, he saw her face—frowning brow, cheeks hollowed—as she ignited the tip of a cigarette.

"You've come a long way, baby."

"Alex, you can be such a prude when you put yourself to it. Smoking settles my nerves, gives me something to hang on to when the going gets rough."

"You used to hang on to me."

"Alex, let's not let this go any further before we both say things we'll regret. And don't you go into the hurt-little-boy routine." She exhaled a cloud of smoke through her nostrils coughing slightly and spoiling the effect. "You said you hadn't been completely honest with me. If you think you're sparing my feelings, you're just being condescending."

Refilling his glass, he contemplated the angry red button that was the tip of her cigarette. Then he started talking so softly she drew nearer and strained to catch his words.

"I fly an obsolete, uncomfortable, poorly lighted, underpowered transport whose design is almost as old as I am. The newest model we have was made in nineteen forty-four when I was thirteen. I launch so heavily loaded with eight men, three side-firing Gatling guns, forty-thousand rounds of ammunition, forty-eight flares, and a full fuel load it's problematical whether it'll stay airborne if we lose an engine. I drop magnesium flares, in some cases dating from World War Two, knowing we're all dead if one ignites in the cabin. I work with people on the ground, like Walt Wainwright, who have absolute trust in my ability to bring them salvation regardless of fatigue, weather, darkness, ground fire, or inoperative equipment.

"Sometimes I duel with fifty-caliber machine guns that could open us up like a sardine tin. To make it easier for them to hit us, I'm forced to fly a predictable circle around the target afraid of breaking out of the pattern and losing what few visual references I may have. To complicate matters, I work with forward air controllers, fighters, army Mohawks, and helicopter gunships, any of which can be expected at sometime or other to fly through my altitude or blunder into the path of my bullets. The good news is I won't be doing this practically every night now that I've been moved to Seventh Air Force. I'll just get to do it from time to time in order to keep my sanity when I'm fighting with some headquarters ego-maniac who has anything more than a gold leaf on his collar."

Her cigarette smoldered. After a while she snuffed it on the Formica top of the bedside table.

"I didn't tell you," he continued, "because I didn't want to worry you unnecessarily. I never lied. Many of the missions are boring and unproductive. I just didn't tell you about the ones that were unusual. I figured you didn't have a need to know."

His mind raced backward through his store of memories, stopping, reviewing, and rejecting. He remembered the grinding, lurching ground loop when the damaged gear folded, and the urgent rush to pull Blackie loose as the flickering red light pulsed through the dust-filled cabin. He recalled flying through turbulent clouds filtering miraculously between two dimly-lighted army choppers. He felt the downwash of the beating rotors as he lifted off with the delirious Wallingford convulsing beside him. He shuttered at how close he had come to trusting the inept Vietnamese tower operator who cleared him for take-off despite landing traffic flaring for touchdown. He found, skipped, then returned again and again—as a phonograph needle jumps at a record's flaw—to the delta and the plaintive voice telling him he was his only chance.

She lay mute, as if stripped of vocabulary. Sometime later her muffled sobs broke the stillness. But by then, he was lost in fitful sleep.

CHAPTER TWENTY-FIVE

LATE THE NEXT MORNING, they strolled to Fort DeRussey to rent the red Fiat convertible he had reserved. Their destination remained his secret, but he confided it was a special place he had read about.

"Sounds like a tourist trap to me," she groused.

"How can anything named the 'Crouching Lion' be a tourist trap?" He had awakened refreshed, had perfect weather, had his woman. She felt better, if not quite good. Cystitis had awakened her four times, but after forcing herself to consume great quantities of water, the cramping had abated. As they walked she clung to his upper arm, unconsciously massaging his biceps. When she caught herself, she spontaneously laughed and pulled him close. A passing sailor stared at her from behind mirrored sunglasses. She pushed away from her husband, allowing his arm to drop free. He slid it low around her waist and pulled her back, so they walked as if closely hitched, thighs touching.

He wore a red and yellow Hawaiian shirt, white slacks with swim briefs underneath, and tan canvas shoes with crepe soles. In a black-and-white snapshot, he would have made a passable *haole*. But in color, his pallid skin marked him as an alien, and his close-cropped hair and wanton companion proved he was just another parolee from Vietnam.

Whipping onto route 61 heading northeast toward the mountains and accelerating through the gears, he dropped his right hand onto her wraparound skirt, fumbled to find its opening, and slid his fingers to cup her inner thigh. "That's got to be the smoothest skin ever," he yelled against the slipstream.

"Oh, I don't know, sweetheart," she laughed moistening her dry lips with deft swipes of her tongue. "Last night it seemed to have stubby whiskers on it."

"Come on, honey, slip out of your skirt and give me and the truckers a break."

She had suspected for years his secret fantasy was to turn her into an exhibitionist. *Well, why not?* She untied the cloth belt, pulled the skirt from beneath her, and folded it carefully before placing it behind her seat.

"Good God, Merrilane, what are you doing?"

"I'm doing what you asked, sweetheart," she shouted as she pulled off her halter.

"But I thought you were wearing your bikini. You're as naked as a jaybird!"

"I am aren't I," she said as she looked down at herself then started arranging a towel to absorb the heat from the vinyl-covered seat. "This is such a lovely idea you've had." She removed the kerchief from her head, allowing her hair to whip in the wind.

He braked hard, pulled out of the passing lane, and dropped behind a laboring refrigerated van with a Jolly Green Giant leering from the rear cargo doors.

"Come on, sweetheart. Put something on before we get arrested."

"Silly," she said in a normal tone now that they had slowed behind the puffing giant. "Who's going to report me? Certainly not those nice men in the big trucks. And the Giant's lips are sealed." She lowered the back of her seat and extended her arms behind her head. "I'm really glad you slowed, dearheart." She flicked her tongue again around her pursed mouth. "The wind was drying my lips something awful."

Checking his rearview mirror, he saw another trucker coming up fast. Soon he would find himself boxed in.

"Come on Merrilane," he pleaded. "You've made your point. Now put something on before Lady Godiva becomes famous on every CB radio in Hawaii."

"Oh, all right," she pouted as she pulled a beach jacket over her shoulders. "But I wish you'd make up your mind. Don't you want to give those drivers a break anymore?"

He ignored her as he flipped on his signal and moved out to pass the Giant. As they pulled abeam of the cab, she stood up in her seat, whipped off her jacket, and twirled it like an Aqua Ballerina at Cypress Gardens.

"Oh . . . shit," Alex groaned as he saw the trucker's astonished look and heard the trumpeting of the diesel's tattling air horn. "What possessed you to do that?" he shouted. "I told you to cover up."

"I gave it some thought," she yelled in his ear as she dangled over his shoulder and nuzzled his sideburn. "But then I remembered I don't let men tell me what do anymore. What's wrong? You ashamed of my bod?"

"No, nothing like that. I did want this to be a day we'd remember."

He drove seventy, but news of a flashing beaver in a red Spyder traveled at the speed of sound and triggered a cacophony of horns, whistles, and shouts. For her part, she took no notice but lay nude working on her tan. He chuckled remembering the look of the first driver, face framed between his wife's jiggling bosom. SugarFox would have appreciated it. When at last he sneaked onto the coastal road for the final run to his destination, he knew the day's highlight was behind him.

At 11:29 he whipped the roadster into the sweeping turn that would finally divulge the Crouching Lion. "Close your eyes," he commanded. She placed her hands over her face but, true to her new code, peeked between her fingers.

"You can open now," he said as he turned into the parking lot. Above them, set back in a grove of palm trees, loomed the long veranda, pitched roof, and massive chimney of the Crouching Lion Inn. "What do you think?"

"Looks like a tourist trap to me." She hopped out of her seat swirling the skirt around her waist. Kneeling beside the door mirror, she fitted her halter and passed slender fingers through her hair. Then she ran around to hug him. "This will be what I remember, dearest," she said as she kissed his thin face.

"There's a legend," he said. "The lion, Kauhi, was an alien god chained on the cliff you see there as a watchman—the watchtower of Heaven is what his name means. Unhappy with his fate, he didn't move until the beautiful goddess, Hiiaka, came by singing a song which aroused him. He wanted to go with her, but she continued blithely along. As his passion and strength ebbed, he gradually turned to stone."

Their food arrived, served by a beautiful Hawaiian girl whose downcast brown eyes and glistening black hair reminded him of Long. At this time of day, she was most probably scrubbing oil-stained flying suits or flailing away at fatigue blouses. He had never really thought of her as a woman, but simply as a device for keeping him relatively presentable.

"What's wrong, honey? Aren't you hungry?"

"What? . . . oh, sorry. I was just thinking of something."

"Penny for your thoughts."

"No. It's nothing to talk about."

"Something I don't have a need to know?"

"Nothing like that. It's just that I have a different perception now. Good things sometimes make me think of bad things. I'm trying to learn to freeze the good moments to blot out disagreeable times later."

She stared at her food, examining the folds of ham surrounding the fresh shoots of asparagus.

"Please eat," he murmured. "I don't want to spoil this."

She speared one of the chunks of pineapple, raised it to her lips, then hesitated. "My point of view's also changed. The handicapped youngsters I placed into the athletic program for example. Their appearance and speech patterns intimidated me, but they just required my getting to know them."

"Our problem—yours and mine—is we want life always to be fair for everyone. Your program builds people up, whereas I'm trapped in a situation of having to blow them away."

"Is 'trapped' the way you feel?"

"It's the way a lot of us feel at one time or another."

"But aren't you accomplishing something?"

"On occasion . . . breaking up an attack. Talking with the guy on the ground, you hear the increasing pitch of his voice, and you both know your being there is the difference."

The waitress approached but, seeing Alex talking low over his scarcely touched meal, veered off.

"Archer—remember he talked to you on the MARS call—thinks it's all a civil war. Says we'll lose like the French, be hated more, and detest ourselves for decades. At first I thought he was just a malcontent, but now I'm beginning to think he's right."

He paused, hoping she would extricate him, then picked at the watermelon. "I feel trapped because the little guys on both sides are getting ground up, and the honchos don't give a ratz. I'm playing a game of Russian roulette doing what I've sworn to do, yet living for the day when I can reclaim my life."

Again he paused, but she remained silent. "I feel trapped because the enemy will beat us, and they'll deserve the victory. We've screwed around so long the country's mind set is defeatist. That's what's against Nixon. We're beginning to see ourselves as the bad guys . . . the bullies."

He stopped, again expecting a comment. Then he realized he had lost his audience. "Please excuse me. I didn't mean to get on this tangent. I wanted this place to be special, somewhere we'd always remember."

"I'll remember the Crouching Lion and so will you. I'm sorry Vietnam affects you so deeply. I've been so absorbed in my own development, I didn't realize your values and ambitions might be changing too."

As the waitress cleared the dishes and presented the dessert menu, Alex asked her to pack a picnic meal while he and

Merrilane had coffee. Talk shifted to the children, really for the first time since they had been together.

"Do they resent my being away?"

"It's hard to get much out of them," she answered, feeling unsure of her ability to summarize what passed for family life. "Now that they're in school again, I don't see much of them. Iris is making Kim a budding Cordon Bleu, and Frank's a second father to Jeffrey. When I'm away on weekends, he takes him to the cadet parades, or out to the glider port in the Black Forest."

"I didn't realize you were having to work weekends."

"Just occasionally. I thought I wrote you."

Trained to detect cover stories and half-truths, he felt the red flags pop up. The server's arrival with a picnic basket terminated what was beginning to be less a talk and more an interrogation.

"Think you can beat me to the car?" he asked as they skipped down the front steps. Grateful for a change of pace, she slipped out of her sandals and stooped to pick them up.

"You bet I do! And if you just happen to win, I'll be your slave tonight."

"You got a deal, lady. You carry this!" Laughing, he thrust the parcel into her hands and sprinted down the path stiff-arming imaginary tacklers. Taking a direct line to the car and ignoring the tropical plants that tore at her legs, she dashed for the convertible, arriving there breathless but still ten yards ahead of her husband.

She flung open the door, tipped the seatback into position, whipped off her skirt, and slammed the door before he could lay a hand on her. "Too bad, Tarzan. Didn't they teach you never to take the trail in the jungle? Now be a dear and run back to fetch our food."

Not acknowledging the humor, he turned to retrieve their dinner. "What matter, Great White Hunter?" she shouted as she wiggled into her bikini, "Sheena upset Slave Trade?"

After stowing the basket, he headed out the road searching for a secluded beach. She lay back in her seat, eyes closed, humming a catchy but unfamiliar tune with a rock beat. Spotting an access road and dazzling white sand beyond the intervening palms, he turned into an area that seemed created for nature lovers. After stripping to his trunks, he took her hand and led her far up the beach, not talking but concentrating on the gritty feel of the damp sand on his toes and reveling in the simple act of walking into the freshening breeze. They rested in the shade of palms, both measuring the passage of time by the pounding of incoming waves. After a while they napped, lying on their backs with only their hands touching.

They awoke simultaneously, not knowing how long they had slept. The sun was once again sinking and promising a spectacular display behind a bank of purple clouds signaling a squall's approach. He brushed the sand from her upper torso, kissing her shoulders when the task was complete. She felt the first pangs of returning cystitis, began to feel its spasms corroding her mood. Strolling just at the edge of the incoming tide, feeling their footsteps eroding under their feet even as they walked, they made their way back to the car.

He set out the food: paté, hard rolls, Italian salami, slaw, cheese, and fruit. She kissed his cheek when he displayed the familiar oval-shaped bottle of sparkling Mateus Rosé but secretly wished for water—maximum fluid to flush her bladder before the infection overpowered her.

"Tell me about your job," he said surprising her as she munched the hard crust of a roll.

"It's a simple job now that summer's over. I might be let go soon." She eyed storm clouds now much nearer. "Working's been a God-send. I was really antsy after you left."

She swung her head suddenly, riveting her eyes on him, aiming the lash of her words. "You don't know how I've hated being just a copilot all these years. Always deferring to your decisions, changing locations when your career demanded, volunteering my talents when I could have had a life outside the perimeter fence."

"Easy, Honey. We've lived comfortably . . ."

"Don't tell me about comfort!" The sudden pain in her groin caused her almost to cry out. "I've met people our age in Colorado Springs who could buy and sell you a thousand times over."

"I'm not for sale."

"You know what I mean. Powerful people who defer to nobody."

"People? You mean men? Are those the ones you spend your weekends with?"

"Is that what's in your craw? I can't believe you have no more faith in me than that! What if I'd accused you of trifling on me when you had the run of Europe and North Africa?"

"That kind of life never appealed to me."

"Well it never appealed to me either before now." She grappled in her bag, found, and lighted a cigarette against the stiff breeze. "But I'll tell you honestly. As I grow older, my sex needs are easily the equal of any man's."

"Calm down, Merrilane."

"Grow older! Does that ring any bells? I'm growing older, and I haven't accomplished anything on my own. Not until Rod Pike gave me a chance and now has primed me for a project in the Springs. I'm at the right place at the right time to put together something really worthwhile. That means more to me than blowing up some stupid bridge in Hanoi or propping up a bunch of hoods who call themselves the Saigon government."

"The rain's coming." Caught by the wind, his voice sounded a long way off. "Let's get our things in the car."

"I certainly will." She flipped the cigarette with amazing strength against the gale that now stung their bodies with sand pellets. "If your idea of romance included the beach scene in *From Here to Eternity*, you can get yourself another co-star.

"That was my plan." The wind whipped his words away; so to her he looked like a stupid camel, chewing his cud in the midst of a sandstorm.

Sporadic rain drops—huge, hot, hurting—pelted their bodies as they reached the roadster. He tossed the gritty towels and basket in the jumpseat, pulled up the black canvas top, and crawled behind the wheel. She made no attempt to help secure the latches even though the wind rocked the vehicle and threatened to rip its top away. Torrential rain beat a drum roll on stretched canvas. Lightning etched psychedelic patterns across the steamed windshield while crashing thunder seemed bent on splitting the thin veil still protecting them.

She sat rigid, mind churning the events of the last few minutes. Even at his first approach, she had detected a new and vulnerable—maybe even cowardly—seed in her husband's character that had caused to germinate a previously dormant, highly vindictive strain in herself. Now, seething with anger and suffering intense burning and recurring spasms of pain, she quivered at the far boundary of self-control. The storm's rising fury triggered the image of Pinski on her doorstep, sharpened her feelings of abandonment, stoked her passions of outrage and rebellion.

He slid his hand tentatively over her wet thigh. She slapped it away.

"I'm afraid, Merrilane . . ." he said. The rest of his sentence was lost to the storm's fury.

CHAPTER TWENTY-SIX

MERRILANE'S VIEW from thirty-one thousand feet stretched for hundreds of miles, but nothing materialized against the ocean's reflective brilliance; no other aircraft, not even a cloud, challenged the trackless sky. Spasms of cystitis gnawed at her bladder from time to time accentuating feelings of despair and frustration that had replaced those of hope and anticipation she carried on arrival. She punched the button controlling her seatback and rotated the cushion as far as it would go. She was relieved the aircraft was less than half full and the seats surrounding her were vacant. She needed time to talk to herself.

Where'd it go wrong, dearie? You came for a good time. No deadlines, no crises, no screw-ups. Good first scene: silent movie, nothing spoken, no script. But he never made the transition to talkies. Intimidated by the sound track and the spotlight. Trying to bluff his way through. Up-staging, scene stealing, muffing your cues. Playing to the audience, acting the clown. Mumbled monologues, sense lost in translation. Coming on like a starved dog.

But why pretend you hated the service? Would life have been better with a doctor or lawyer? Quit kidding. Where'd you have met them? Fraternity dances you never attended? Who besides Alex saw you'd fit his career plan? Remember the goose you were before the efficient commanders' wives got your attention?

Would any professional be home more? Help raise kids? What about faithfulness? Get serious. Stream's overstocked with wiggling suckers. Is that what Alex sees? Does he think you're in the rapids, dashing toward that pool of loose women?

What's after Vietnam if you stick with him? Colonel's wife? Good chance. With graduate degree and tickets punched, he'll attract sponsors for a shot at General. Can you cut it as Mrs. General? Iris could. But Frank flamed out, and she never even met the promotion board.

*So your destiny's tied to Alex, and you'll never be more than second
fiddle without a chance to be lead violin.*

*You're crazy. You know? Most women would trade places with
you instantly. Clawing to get your house, your clothes, your car . . .
your man. Some would even want the kids. Who'd want your job?
Fuck the hours, they'd say. And the hassle. Then why should you?
What about in fifteen years? Age fifty-one. Still young. Making what?
Forty to fifty thou? Independent. Kids on their own. And a job. Some-
thing to do each day. A niche carved out all by your lonesome.
Lonesome? Who's lonesome if you're nationally known? Picture on
magazine covers. "Time" trumps some base newspaper in the North
Dakota snow fields.*

*What's really bothering him? Not your being away from the chil-
dren. He knows you need an outlet. But he's afraid. Said so himself.
Afraid of the powerful men. Afraid you'll become damaged goods.
How quaint. Terrified of the gossip. What else is he afraid of?*

"You're awfully pensive returning from Paradise." The man
was bending over her, left elbow braced on the seatback in front,
dark red tie hanging straight down and almost brushing her
face. "They're about to serve dinner, and I detest eating alone.
May I?"

He was already settling himself next to her as she blinked
her eyes sleepily. "Well, I'm not prone to argue," she found
herself saying as she pressed the button restoring her seat to its
upright position.

His laugh showed strong teeth, brilliantly white against a
surfer's tan. "I'm Chick Jaeger," he leaned into her conspirato-
rially. "Flying in from Bangkok and just beginning to get my
second wind." She marveled at his striking resemblance to Rod.
Same general size, same look of confidence, same hair curling
over his collar. A virile Rod who already had his limit of pre-
dinner cocktails. "And you're a Vietnam grass widow sneaking
home after a five-day, round-the-clock orgy."

"Aren't you being a bit presumptuous?"

"A whole lot presumptuous, my dear. That's what's got me where I am today."

"And where are you?"

"Trying to get to first base with a beautiful woman who obviously needs cheering up."

"But if your supposition about the orgy's true," she flicked her tongue around her lips, "I've already been cheered up."

"That's where the challenge comes in," he lowered the folding tray from the seat in front of him and reached to do the same for her.

"What challenge is that?"

"To see if I can score all the way from first base." He laughed quickly as if to sanitize the words.

"What if I . . ." The stewardess was reaching across him placing the plastic tray in front of her, "said I don't play baseball?"

"I'm flexible," he hesitated, making an elaborate gesture of nibbling the soft dinner roll. "I can play any game you propose . . . any position."

She smiled broadly as she slid her left hand across his rumpled trousers and squeezed. "Night baseball might be fun now that you've brought it up."

He choked momentarily, returned the roll quickly to his plate, and took a long drink directly from the milk carton. "You must have spent some time in Bangkok."

"No, but I've read the book."

"What book's that?"

She was cutting a small slice from her Polynesian chicken and appeared not to hear.

He leaned close, lips almost touching her hair. "What book?"

She turned her face to his, slowly chewing her food. "*Karma Sutra*, of course. I assume you've read it."

The attendant was back, this time pouring white wine in the squat plastic glasses nestled within the compartmentalized tray.

Jaeger raised his glass. "Never read it, but studied the pictures."

They spent a pleasant twenty minutes conversing as they finished their meals. He talked extensively about himself, his business as a contractor extending the runway at SAC's Utapao bomber base in northern Thailand, and his affection for Bangkok. "War can go on forever as far as I'm concerned."

Without consulting his seatmate, he asked the attendant for a wine refill rather than after-dinner coffee. She requested a large glass of water. "I'm doing all the talking," he said as he stowed his collapsible tray and lifted the armrest between their seats. "You're just sitting there like the Mona Lisa . . . haven't even told me your name."

"Margaret."

"Margaret what?"

"The young people today use only their first names. Pertains to world brotherhood, spontaneity, something like that."

"Well, I'm forty-six years old, and I like to know who's in the line-up when I play hardball."

"Margaret Whiting."

"The singer?

"No. Not that one. I'm just a little fish in the pool."

He reached up and snapped off the overhead lights. Flying eastward into the night, the sky was almost full black with stars beginning to appear. "Whatta ya do?

"I'm a dancer in Vegas."

"I thought you looked flashy . . . like you ought to be in show biz. What casino?"

"Stardust."

"I been there. Maybe I could come by and see you around Christmas." He raised his leg onto the seat, knee resting on her thigh. "Gets pretty lonely around Christmas. You got kids?"

"Don't want any."

"Sometimes you get surprised."

"I'm never surprised."

"Husband a fighter pilot?"

"Supply officer. Afraid of flying."

The cabin was dark now. And quiet. Attendants slumped in first class, shoes off, feet up. He slid his hand behind the small of her back and drew her close to whisper in her ear. "I wouldn't be afraid of flying with you, honey."

She turned her head, kissing him full face, rolling her lips on his, feeling the surrounding stubble rasp like coarse sandpaper.

"Holy Christ, Maggie!" He was trying to shake open the ebony blanket the attendant had distributed.

"Time for you to slither back to your tree, Mister Hunter. You've had your dinner and a goodnight kiss."

"What's wrong, Sweetheart? You can't just dance away!"

"Oh, but I must! My contract limits me only to striptease."

CHAPTER TWENTY-SEVEN

"LOOK WHO'S HERE, GANG. The old Spook himself. How's your wife, Alex?"

"Better than nothing." He had dreaded facing their innuendoes, detested returning to sun-bleached sandbags, mind-altering heat, and high-decibel noise. Camelot to Dogpatch in the words of a nameless grunt. "Where's Tiny and SugarFox?"

"Both left yesterday on the morning Skatback courier. Tiny to Naked Fanny and SugarFox to Takhli." Mahan answered while continuing to rummage through a manila folder.

"What the hell's happened to this place?" Alex surveyed a line of wall lockers that had advanced fifteen feet during his absence to gobble up the space where a rank of three desks had previously stood.

"It's your historian friends from the States."

"I thought they were supposed to move in downstairs. Where's the Colonel?"

"Over at Seventh. If he'd spent more time politicking before they moved in, we might not be living on top of each other. Chief historian's female. Almost too pretty to look at, but as tough as the Paul Doumer bridge. She locked those bedroom eyes of hers on Wootan, and he volunteered us to move the furniture. I think he's in love."

"You're shittin' me. You mean we rolled over when they grabbed our space?"

"Temple blew in from a trip the day after they arrived and hears all this fighter-pilot jargon floating over the lockers: canisters, nape, Willie Pete, flak suppression, high angle dive bombing, the whole smear. Like a convention of the Red River Rats. So he climbs up expecting to see Robin Olds holding forth. Here's this circle of four-eyed civilians and fuzzy-cheeked graduate assistants. He goes ballistic. 'You Apple Knockers,' he yells, 'not one of you bastards is wearing wings.' Then he shinnies over the top of the lockers and berates them for forty-five minutes until Monique rings up Wootan to call off his pit bull."

Alex smiled at the thought of Tiny leaping like Snoopy off the top of his doghouse. The Air Force needed such men on the trail to hurl themselves through the uncharted mountain peaks and into the black holes bubbling with red tracers. More than that, they needed them in the headquarters to keep the planners and policy makers honest.

"Sounds like I missed a lot while I was gone."

"You didn't miss a thing. It's all a constant re-run. Tiny'll come back to badger the DO into putting fast movers over the trail to protect the Spads. SugarFox'll get kicked out of Korat again for wearing his tree suit instead of regulation flying clothing. Memos will circulate, recriminations will carom like billiard balls, the dust will finally settle with nothing accomplished except another day crossed off everybody's calendar."

"Today's different." Airman Woziniac's voice broke as he hung up the telephone. "Major Temple's airplane exploded last night near Tschpone, and Captain Fox was hit this morning just after releasing on some trucks.

Early that evening, fighting jet lag, fatigue, and grief, Alex gathered Major Edward F. Temple's personal effects. Wootan had cautioned him to make certain nothing embarrassing or incriminating—photographs, address books, letters, condoms, other items of a man's private life—was included in the package that would go to his wife. Glenn helped inventory the few possessions in the small cubicle. Alex knew they would find nothing to confiscate. Temple was a family man, the kind who skimped on his discretionary spending to bring his children on R and R. Tiny Temple was no SugarFox.

"That's about it, Glenn. We'll have to check his wallet when they send it over. He wouldn't have taken it on a combat mission."

"Yeah, you're right. But it'll be clean. The little guy was a straight arrow."

"Straight arrow." Alex rolled the words softly off his tongue knowing they were the epitaph of a good man, a good father. "I used to think that was enough."

Glenn watched him seal the brown envelope. *There's something on his mind*, he thought. *A preoccupation that'll get him killed.* He wondered what he would find in his friend's personal effects.

Alex yawned uncontrollably. "I don't suppose there's any chance of delaying Sugar's stuff until tomorrow? I left Honolulu at midnight, flew all night and half the day, and worked since getting back."

"Wootan wants it done, but I can handle it myself. I've called a vehicle to run me downtown."

"No, we're a team. I'll be all right after we get outside."

Not knowing Saigon, Alex had wanted to experience the drive to the legendary villa operated by pilots from the reconnaissance squadron. But he fell asleep just after they cleared the main gate.

"Buddy. Buddy. Come on Spooky."

Alex scrambled upright once the words penetrated. "Oh . . . Glenn . . . I thought I heard Buddy calling."

"Who do you think I am? I'm your buddy."

Alex stared at him. "You're not Buddy. He got chewed to pieces by seven point six twos."

"Come on, Alex. Let's get this over with."

They walked to the sandbagged machine gun position protecting the iron gate, flashed their ID cards at the lethargic Vietnamese guards, then made their way up the flagstone path toward bright lights and throbbing music.

"We're from Seventh Combat Tactics," Mahan shouted at the grinning man in the Philippine wedding shirt who met them at the door. "Captain Fox bought it, and we have to get his effects."

"Yeah, we got the word," the man shouted back. "I'm Louie Pasternak. We're holding his wake. How about a Mai-Tai? Sugar's favorite drink."

"Thanks, but we've got to get back. Besides, my friend's out on his feet. Hasn't slept in forty-eight hours."

"Man I got what he needs." Looking quickly behind him, Pasternak pulled from the swirling mass of dancing bodies a beautiful Eurasian girl, resplendent in a skin-tight dress of shimmering blue Thai silk. He spun her toward Alex. "Here's one of ol' Sug's favorite girls. She's distraught as you can see."

"Look, Pal," Mahan was in his face, "cut the shit and take us to Sugar's room."

"Sure, Mac. Ya don't have to get belligerent."

Alex and Glenn, like pilgrims at Vanity Fair, followed their guide through the crush of gyrating men and women. They gained the stairwell and plodded up three flights to the penthouse apartment where a spectacular view of the city awaited them. Alex paused by the balcony noticing the smoke trails and sepia-toned illumination of two drifting parachute flares. When Pasternak switched on the dim ceiling light, he knew they stood in SugarFox's lair. Beaver shots covered the walls: posters, centerfolds, glossy professional photographs, amateur Polaroids. Soiled clothes hung from doorknobs, light fixtures, and the open panels of an antique armoire. Aviation magazines littered the floor. The only organized area was a bar stocked with bright rows of scotch, whiskey, gin, and vodka bottles. The focal point was the brass bed and the gigantic stereo speakers flanking it.

"Good God! It'll take a truck to get all this stuff out of here."

"Not really, old chap." Pasternak snatched a scrap of paper from where it was taped on the dresser's mirror. "According to Sugar's will, legally witnessed by two fellow officers, he's left this room, the Honda motorcycle, and all his clothes, to the winner of a lottery to be held among members of this household three days after his purported demise. The three days, he always insisted, will give someone with his Christ-like characteristics time to return."

Glenn scanned the homemade will, then extended it to Alex. "What do you think?"

"Looks legit to me. At least as legal as anything else in Saigon. What say we go through the drawers, collect any stray money, rings, and such, and then respect Sugar's wishes."

"Sounds good. There's a certain perfection in this room. It'd be a shame to tear it apart. I don't know where Sugar is now, but he's used to living in fighter pilots' heaven."

Returning after midnight to Tan Son Nhut with the small bundle they had salvaged, Alex and Glenn saw a light in the Tactics office. They discharged the driver and trudged up the outside stairs to find Wootan sitting at the clerk's typewriter.

He looked up as they entered. "Good morning, gentlemen. Finishing up the inventory?"

"Yes, sir," Glenn replied. "We just got Captain Fox's effects. Any more details?"

"Bunch of Sandies and a Nail FAC looked for Tiny at first light. Couldn't find the wreckage. He'd got to NKP in the afternoon and put himself on the schedule right away. Sugar partied a bit after getting to Takhli, but was ready for the midmorning launch. Nobody saw a chute, and another beeper was already garbaging up the emergency frequency."

"I know Sugar," Glenn said. "He's probably got the presidential suite at the Hanoi Hilton and a mamasan to help pass the time."

"Don't count on it. We're talking a minimum altitude, high-speed bailout from an uncontrollable aircraft. You don't beat those odds."

"I'm with Glenn, boss. Sugar's a legend."

"Wishful thinking, guys. But I hope you're right."

As the two officers prepared to leave, Wootan asked Alex to stay. "Sit down for a minute and tell me about Hawaii."

"Hawaii was fine, sir. Ideal temperature. Lots of tour packages."

"That's not exactly what I meant. Jim Hubbard stopped in the other day and told me you had a problem at home. Suggested I ask for an attitude check once you returned."

"Everything's fine, sir."

"You're sure? With our double tragedy, I could send an officer back to visit the bereaved. Tiny's from Denver."

"I appreciate the offer, sir. But that would put you even more shorthanded. I've a lot of things I need to do in the tactics area. Seems like my predecessor ignored that aspect of the job."

"A light colonel by the name of Nick Gaffney up at Nha Trang intimidated him. You need to tell me how you propose to handle that clown."

"Yesterday's events pretty well decided that, sir."

"How's that?"

"I think I'd better become your resident madman."

CHAPTER TWENTY-EIGHT

THREE DAYS AFTER THE SACRIFICE of SugarFox and Tiny Temple, their wallets and luggage arrived on the afternoon courier. A custom hang-up bag with large pilot's wings and his name embroidered in sparkling white thread on the blue nylon contained Sugar's clothes. Tiny's were in a canvas Base Exchange special. Alex and Glenn added these items to the things previously inventoried, sealed the cartons to be sent to the next of kin, and arranged for shipment. Then they tried to expunge their memories by attacking the accumulated work.

The following morning Wootan stood in the doorway separating his cubicle from the rest of the office and observed them completely absorbed in their duties. They were, he thought, similar in many ways. Each was conscientious, each was a perfectionist, each had an instinct for knowing what needed to be done. They seemed unaware they had arrived during one of the periodic crackdowns on inflated effectiveness ratings. No matter how much they accomplished, only one could gain the top rating. Wootan realized they would not care even if they knew. Tiny and Sugar had been like that.

He turned to face the stack of papers needing his attention. Staff work was as mundane in Saigon as it had been at TAC headquarters or at the Fighter Weapons School at Nellis. He reflected on the monstrous administrative and logistics tail supporting half a million men. Maybe ten percent of that strength belonged to combat units. Perhaps five thousand individuals might actually be fighting at any given time.

Wootan knew he was fortunate to head a directorate. Officers of rank comparable to his stood on each other's shoulders in some of the flying outfits. He had told General Emory it was criminal to place senior officers into the kinds of jobs they had performed as lieutenants and captains twenty years previously. Not to mention costly.

Cost seemed not to be part of the equation. Lack of funds rarely constrained plans for building the infrastructure, maintaining the exotic equipment, or transporting through a ten-thousand-mile pipeline the traditional stuff of war—beans and bullets—not to mention all the pogey bait sold at the Exchanges. And the rock bands. Does a C-130 fly anywhere in South Vietnam or Thailand, he wondered, without carrying a rock band destined to entertain the troops?

What was McNamara's speciality at Ford? Cost effectiveness? Upon appointment as SecDef, he replaced flight line snack-bar cooks with vending machines to save a minuscule buck, thereby depriving pilots of a hot breakfast. Now he pours billions down the Vietnam rathole because his calculations trump our generals' experience.

How do the North Vietnamese do it? Give their men a rice ball or two and send them down the trail. No jungle boots, no French-style fatigues, no flak vests, no steel pots, and no frigging rock bands.

Shouting in the outside office penetrated his reverie. He could see Airman Woziniac sitting ramrod straight, mouth gaping, eyes wide open like Howdy Doody. He got up, went to the doorway, and saw Alex yelling into the phone.

"You say you can hear me five? Five what? . . . Oh, FINE. Yes sir, fine. I'm fine, too. But all I hear from your end is garbage . . . That's some better. But still far off. Like you're having trouble understanding what your higher headquarters is telling you. You got my message about the tactics conference? . . . Yes sir, I thought you'd like the way we set it up at your place so as not to pull your men away from their jobs any longer than necessary . . . Three afternoons. THREE! TANGO, HOTEL, ROMEO, ECHO, ECHO. THREE afternoons only. That way they can do their regular staff jobs in the morning while I'm editing the copy and getting ready for the afternoon meeting . . . No time? That's the beauty part about it. In no time we'll have a tactics manual like the regulations call for . . . We're glad to help you do your job before PACAF steps in and burns us both . . . COORDINATE? Yes sir, we'll coordinate it just as soon as it's finished . . . What are you saying? Speak slower, Colonel . . . . That's better . . . INSUBORDINATE? Oh no, sir. PACAF can't be insubordinate to us. See, they're above both of us as far as all this administrative stuff is concerned. I know it's complicated. I'll explain it all to you when I come up."

"Holy Mother of God," Wootan muttered under his breath. "Sounds like SugarFox one minute and Tiny Temple the next."

Alex shouted louder; all other office work had stopped.

"What's that? . . . Your guys are too busy to meet with me? . . . I know they're working seven days a week. They complained to me when I was up from Bien Hoa last month. I really had a great time, playing volleyball and frying steaks on the beach with your staff both Saturday and Sunday afternoons . . . I'm sorry you feel that way, sir . . . Yes, I know Colonel Trilling and you are tight. It's nice you want to protect him . . . He certainly is a thousand-pound gorilla. But we've got some gorillas down here, too. Ours wear stars, and they like to rattle the cages of smaller gorillas who don't write tactics manuals . . . Just a little humor, sir . . . Oh, yes sir, now that you've explained it so rationally . . . We certainly will change our plans. I'll send a revised message under the DO's signature if that meets with your approval, sir. Of course I can easily get the Chief of Staff to sign if you wish . . . Oh, yes sir. Now that I understand where you're coming from. Certainly."

He lowered his voice to its normal volume compensating by enunciating each syllable.

"We're ordering four officers from your staff, by name, to be in this headquarters at zero nine hundred hours, Monday, twenty-five November, for five days of temporary duty to compose, edit, and coordinate a tactics manual to be published the first week in December. I will make quarters reservations. You will bear the transportation and per diem costs. You'll have a hard copy of the message by noon tomorrow. Goodby, Colonel. It's always a pleasure working with people like you."

Alex slammed down the receiver, picked up a pencil, and started writing. Thirty seconds later, the phone shrilled.

Woziniac, still shaken, answered then yelled to Wootan. "It's for you, sir. Colonel Gaffney, and he sounds mad."

Wooten picked up the phone as deliberately as he would position an F-4's arming switches.

"Lieutenant Colonel Wootan . . .Yes, Colonel Gaffney."

Wootan began to shout into the receiver.

"Say again, sir. Horrible connection . . . I didn't get your title . . . Assistant DO. And you're a full colonel, of course . . . Oh, "telephone colonel." Now that we understand each other, what may I do for you? . . . You think so? I was right here, and I thought he gave you the courtesy you deserve . . . I sympathize with your workload. That's why we tried to make it easy for you, but you forced us to go to plan B . . . Sorry you feel that way. If I may correct one thing you said, however, it's not Major Cannard or Lieutenant Colonel Wootan you're dealing with. We represent the Commander of Seventh Air Force of which you are a subordinate element. Now if I hear any more of your carping, I'll sic the Inspector General on you and your thousand-pound gorilla so fast it'll make you hypoxic. Now you get those four officers in to us on time, or you can explain it to the Chief!"

The office erupted in cheers, laughter, and clapping as Wootan slammed down the receiver. He came to the doorway to acknowledge his people's applause and found them standing.

"Don't you have anything more important to do than listen to private conversations? I must admit, Alex, I enjoyed putting a sidewinder up his tailpipe. But watch that guy. You crossed him, and I know how those kinds of people operate."

Later that afternoon as Alex was putting the finishing touches on his message to Nha Trang, Wootan stopped by his desk. "How about joining me and my guest for dinner tonight at the club? Make it about seven thirty."

Alex stepped into the dining room precisely on time, grateful that the band had taken a break. He spotted Wootan seated across from a stunning brunette at a table next to the wall and as far as possible from the bandstand.

"Good evening, Colonel . . . Ma'am."

"Monique, may I present Alex Cannard. Alex . . . Professor Monique Delepierre, chief historian for Project CONTEMP."

"Happy to meet you, Professor. I'd promised Colonel Harbinger I'd help get you folks settled. But you arrived while I was on R and R, and . . ."

"Don't apologize, Mister Cannard. The move was really quite painless." She smiled at Wootan. "At least after we resolved the question of office space."

"Sit down, Alex, while I explain the system of military rank to Monique once again. You see, my dear, it's not Mister Cannard; it's Major Cannard. His gold leaf denotes Major; my silver leaf signifies General Selectee."

She lowered her eyes as if memorizing the distinction. "I see," she said, "that's why they call you Colonel."

Wootan smiled. "That'll teach me to fast-talk an academician."

"You mean as you tried that first evening?"

"Touché. Score one for the Prof." Wootan made an imaginary mark in the air. "But I was trying to teach you about fighter pilots before some unscrupulous member of the fraternity tried to get his name in the history books."

"So you see, Alex," she laughed as she patted Wootan's hand, "Adam has taken quite good care of me. But I'm eager to know how you, a military history scholar, react to what you're seeing."

"That's a hard one," he answered slowly as if unsure of his conclusions or hesitant to enunciate them in front of his superior. "I can say for certain reading military history's safer than living it. It's clearer, too. Once I had illusions of sending a series of monographs back to Colonel Harbinger. I actually wrote him only one letter from Bien Hoa. I was a gunship pilot, you see and . . . "

"Yes, Adam's told me quite a bit about you and, of course, there was today's telephone call."

He looked over his shoulder uneasily. "You know about that, huh?"

"After all, my desk is just across the row of wall lockers from yours. And you were speaking quite loudly. In fact, I'd guess everyone south of the flight line heard your conversation."

"I'll have to be careful about discussing classified information."

"Please don't; we historians need all the information we can get."

"Let's change the subject to something we all can talk about," Alex said. "Something intellectual. Something stimulating. Tell me," he drew closer to his academic colleague, "what's a nice girl like you doing in a place like this?"

They laughed and she nodded to Wootan. "As I explained to Adam when he posed the same question, Frank Harbinger's a silver-tongued devil. We'd studied for our doctorates together, and he knew I had the administrative talent to set up the office and supervise a group of historians." She paused, playing with the thin straw in her drink, then continued. "He also thought perhaps a woman's point of view could provide an additional degree of objectivity." She raised her eyes from her glass, surprised neither officer took umbrage at Frank Harbinger's conclusion.

"What's the story with campus unrest and the anti-war movement?" Alex asked.

"It's hard to judge. Campus intellectuals castigate their colleagues who've become point men for the government. Students are pulled from all sides. They listen to emotional appeals from activists on campus, they see the police gassing and clubbing war protestors at the Democrat Convention, and they watch fire fights on the evening news. Individually they don't want to have anything to do with the fighting. Self interest seems the prevalent attitude at home. But who am I to disparage it? I see Vietnam as the biggest historical benchmark since World War Two, and I couldn't refuse an offer to see it up close."

"Not an encouraging picture, Professor."

"Our society's going through changes—racial, economic, sexual—and it's too fragile to stand much more stress without major consequences. I can't do anything about prosecuting the war or healing dissension, but this project will help scholars evaluate what happens here. That's why it has to be done with complete candor. Any suggestions on research topics?"

"I've a suggestion," Wootan interjected. "Let's order before a rocket puts the kitchen out of business."

The band, a collection of Filipino noisemakers, resumed their antics and four couples began their sweaty gyrations on the dance floor. Serious conversation gave way to shouted small talk. The food arrived, plentiful and well prepared, with no suggestion it was supplied by a sea and airlift which, in that respect at least, made Saigon resemble not Paris so much as West Berlin during the blockade. By the time they had finished eating, the rock had imploded into a less strident imitation jazz allowing them to discuss favorite recipes and special restaurants throughout the world. Over coffee, as the band drifted out for another break, Monique turned the conversation back to research subjects Alex might propose.

"I'm too close for impartial analysis, but I think if I were a scholar, I'd want to know why we lost."

She stopped her coffee cup in mid-arc, then slowly replaced it on her saucer. She looked at Wootan, anticipating his reprimand. Instead he nodded his head almost imperceptibly as if Alex had simply complimented her dress.

"I must say, Major, I didn't expect such a straightforward remark. Are you shocked at what he said, Adam?"

"Not really, Monique. Major Cannard's a savvy officer who's seen plenty of action. He's entitled to his opinion as long as he expresses it with discretion and continues doing his job. He probably sees your people as our best hope history evolves from a foundation of facts. If you accept uncritically the slick briefings with the patriotic operations names, you might as well have done your writing in Washington."

Until this dinner Alex had insufficient opportunity to observe and try to categorize his superior. Wootan sat with forearms braced on the table as if he were weighted down by eventualities seldom conceived by mortals. Back lighted, his shadowed eyes exuded an almost visible force that drew his companions forward, so that they, too, appeared to be sharing his load. Alex had known Wootan was precise; he was surprised, however, to find him so articulate and so liberal. But Wootan was talking to a woman, a woman so desirable she had been subjected to undisguised stares all throughout their meal. So he could be excused, perhaps, for telling a beautiful woman what she wanted to hear.

"If you were that future scholar, Alex, what data and analysis would you want?"

"Our goals and strategy would be first on the list. Then the chain of command and how it was justified. What political limitations were placed on commanders. Give me troop strength, not just in-country but also in Thailand, Laos, and on the air bases in the Philippines, Okinawa, and Guam. Publish everything possible on enemy order of battle. I'd want hard numbers on our helicopter and aircraft losses—operational and accidental. Provide the argument for defoliation of the jungle and cite any ecological studies made before authorizing its use. Trace the effect of the bombing pauses on enemy resupply to the south. I'd like to know the cost effectiveness of trying to stop individual supply trucks on the Ho Chin Minh trail. No, scrub that. I already know.

"Although it may be outside your scope, I'd like an examination of what the hell the CIA was doing, where they were doing it, and to whom. What's happened to the aid we poured into the Saigon government? What about plans to train the South Vietnamese to take over the war?"

Monique had been scribbling madly trying to record his flood of questions. She sighed when he finally ran down. "When you start, you're hard to turn off. I'm beginning to think your adversary at Nha Trang has run into a buzz saw!"

"Harry Truman's advice was to stay out of the kitchen if you couldn't stand the heat. Alex Cannard says if you can't handle the answers, don't ask the questions."

"As a woman, I've been fighting to get out of the kitchen for twenty years, and it's not because I can't stand the heat."

"Ouch, that's a hot one," Wootan said to lighten a belligerent tone his officer had injected into the conversation.

"Alex, you've given me some interesting ideas. How can I repay you?"

"There's one thing . . ."

"If it's what I think, you can forget it." Monique's quick smile wrinkled her nostrils.

All three chuckled, the men exchanging glances like naughty little boys whose teacher had read their minds.

"No, nothing like that," Alex replied. "Although, now that I think about it, my query regards the matter of sexual attraction bubbling beneath the surface relationships of male and female business associates."

"This may be out of my field. You know how we academics are compartmentalized."

"If Frank Harbinger put you on this project, your field is humanity with a specialization in womanhood. You see, my wife recently entered a male-dominated field. I'm having difficulty coping with it. What obstacles is she finding? What's she looking for? How can I . . . how can I help her?"

So that's the problem, Wootan thought. *Thinks his wife's sleeping her way to the top.*

Monique hesitated before beginning to answer. Alex noticed the smoke settling on the room's occupants making them appear fuzzily out of focus. "So you've saved the hardest question for last," she finally said. "You're asking for a seminar on the Movement, and I'm not qualified to present it. But since you gave me an honest answer to my question, I'll try to do the same because you're asking what you can do to help, not how you can get her back where she belongs.

"As for obstacles, envy from her fellow women is probably the hardest to overcome. Then there's disdain from her male colleagues who think she's mentally, emotionally, and physically incapable of doing whatever it is they're doing. She'll get disrespect from those she supervises who fail to acknowledge her expertise. Of course there'll be all shades of harassment— sexual or otherwise—from men who overestimate their own ability, position, and prerogatives.

"And don't underestimate the demoralizing effect of sexual harassment. In time it may drain a woman of her individuality, the self-confidence and spontaneous creativity that makes her a unique human being. The put-downs she'll hear over and over reinforce her classification as an object, a convenience, an appliance. I'm referring to the kinds of things said when I went to the rest room earlier this evening. Obscene, stupid comments only a deaf person would not have heard. Accompanied by acquiescent laughter from companions who were too gentlemanly to join in, but not man enough to protest. It's disgusting . . . and demoralizing no matter how often you've heard it and how liberated and callous you think you've become."

She paused to gauge the impact of her comments on two unusually candid men who—most amazingly—wore military uniforms. Seeing no trace of smugness, no unseemly attempt to dispute or embroider, she continued.

"As for your real question, Alex, I think you know what she's looking for. At this stage of her life, when children don't require constant supervision, she's probably trying to win her own wings. I suspect she's attempting to grow in new areas where she feels her talents lie. To put it in language you can understand, Frank Harbinger once told me he returned for his PhD because he had flown past the Mach, and he wanted to see what else he could do. If I can be honest, let me say if your hidden desire really is to find out whether she's out to have a fling, I'd say that's the furthest thought in her mind unless she becomes so embittered she capitulates and throws herself away in desperation. If that happens, then God help you because you've failed her when she needed you most. She's looking to you for acknowledgment that she's on the right trail and you're there to help her if she calls."

Alex sat mute. Wootan had withdrawn to some promontory observing the interplay between his officer and this perceptive woman.

"Do I make any sense, Alex, or should I stick to my own discipline?"

"You're making more sense than anything I've heard lately. Thanks for talking to me. If you and the Colonel will excuse me, I have a few things to do before turning in."

CHAPTER TWENTY-NINE

MERRILANE CONTEMPLATED THE STACK of paper she had worked through since bundling the children off to Iris's just after breakfast. She had completely cleared the bulging folder containing over a week's accumulated "Must Do" work and had put a large dent in the "Read File." Getting the children off for the weekend was a God-send, not only for her but also for Frank and Iris who seemed intent on reliving all of their early child-raising adventures now that Frank seemed to have won a new lease on life.

She had become drowsy in mid-afternoon as the sun warmed the greenhouse to a sensuous coziness. Thinking perhaps a strong cup of coffee would break the spell, she rose from her work table and went to fetch the electric percolator. Returning with the loaded pot, her favorite cup—the one with the grinning clown stretching to reach the trapeze—and two chocolate chip cookies, she felt reinvigorated and ready to tackle the remainder. After plugging in the pot, she once more immersed herself in Rod Pike's intriguing proposal. Presently the harmonious sound of spattering perks and the coffee's pungent aroma triggered her taste buds and destroyed her concentration. As she poured herself a cup, a cloud abducted the sun's warmth and drew her attention to the snow squall capping the Rampart Range. She shivered involuntarily.

As she raised the cup, she heard heavy tires harshly crunching the gravel driveway. The throaty grumbling of a Corvette's engine suddenly revved then died. "Oh damn." She instinctively patted the hair over her temples. *Rod's so inconsiderate*, she thought. *Never thinks to phone ahead.* She rose to get a second cup when the grinning face of Jack Pinski popped around the corner of the house.

"Hi," he shouted through the glass. "I thought I'd find you out here. Mind if I come in?" He was on the stoop opening the storm door before she could react. "I heard you'd been in Hawaii."

"Hello, Jack," she answered sharply. "I thought your car was Rod Pike's. He said he'd drop over about now."

"I'd like to see Mr. Pike. Get a chance to razz him for driving around in a First Classman's bomb."

Pinski was dressed like a cowpuncher. Rancher's fleece-lined coat, red and black plaid shirt, faded jeans, wide leather belt, massive silver buckle, and black boots with sharply pointed toes.

"Where's Jeffrey? Hey, Jeff," he shouted down the dark hallway, "come see what I've got." Without a response, he turned again to Merrilane. "Where're the kids, Miz Cannard? Don't tell me I missed 'em."

"Sad to say you have. But the Harbinger's ought to be dropping them off before long."

"I might be able to come back. I really wanted to show them my new thirty-five millimeter camera and get some pictures of you all." Unslinging the leather gadget bag from his shoulder, he snapped open its lid exposing a shiny Cannon body, regular and telephoto lens, flash attachment, and the usual glut of film canisters and accessories newly smitten photographers buy. "Hey, that coffee sure smells good. Got enough for me?"

"I suppose," she said. "I can make more for Rod."

"Okay if I dump this here?" He had already peeled off his coat and dropped it beside the love seat as she returned with a cup. "Black's fine for me. You know, it's getting nippy out there. Storm's coming in faster than predicted. With any luck, you'll be snowed in tomorrow and won't have to put in your usual Sunday overtime."

She sat down at the table, resigned to taking a break with the young man who had made such a fool of himself when he had last visited. She had heard little of him since the fall term began, yet his conspiratorial grin and deep voice flicked often into her mind. Where Jack had been concerned, she had not proven the all-knowing mommy her young children used to believe possessed supernatural perceptive powers.

"I really don't mind going to work, Jack, even on weekends. In fact I enjoy it tremendously."

"I don't understand women, Miz Cannard. I'd think you'd be happy as a clam with this nice house, and the kids, and cooking, and all the things women like to do."

"Oh Jack, how right you are. You don't know anything about women."

Pinski's skin flushed; he toyed with his cup, swirling coffee dangerously near the rim. "You zinged me on that, for sure. I guess I know less about women than any cadet at the Zoo."

"Don't get defensive; I didn't mean it personally. Few men know much about what goes on inside a woman's mind. But you're only twenty-one. Perhaps there's still hope you'll gain sensitivity along the way, not just experience."

"Try telling that to my AOC, ma'am. He says to forget the nuances. They just muddy up the decision-making process."

"That's so stupid. Everything can't be made black or white. Why do military men have to be so stubborn? No . . . I take that back. Since I've been working, I've found insensitivity isn't exclusively a military trait. If I continue to develop, maybe I'll find it's not a purely masculine characteristic either.

"I don't know that I'm following you," he said.

"The point is few men enter a relationship on a sharing, reinforcing basis. They go in to win—just as they do in competitive sports, in the courtroom, or in war. Even if they think they honestly love the woman, most are still ingrained with the idea of dominating her."

Pinski nodded, but his dull eyes told her he was not listening.

"Let me put it in military terms since that's all you Zoomies seem to understand. Nations become allies because they need each other. Marriage is like an alliance by allies with different strengths and deficiencies but with common goals. Yet, most of the time, neither partner understands they should be coordinating their activities with each other. Finally, toward the end of their life spans, they say 'I should have . . . ' or 'we should have . . . .' By then it's too fucking late."

"Miz Cannard!" his incredulous expression gave Merrilane her first real laugh since returning from R and R. "I didn't think you had it in you."

"We've all got it in us, Jack. You don't realize I was sexually active before you were in Little League. Where did you get the idea a woman's feelings were basically different from your own? You want sexual satisfaction; we want sexual satisfaction. We just differ on the definition. Ours is more inclusive and more long-term."

"You know, Miz Cannard, you're the first woman I've ever had talk to me as if I were an adult."

"I'm not surprised. We've been out of the closet for only a few years. Alex used to lecture about Generals Patton and Rommel. Patton had to get inside Rommel's head in order to understand him and counter his plans. He did that by reading Rommel's book. A man has to do the same thing to understand a woman's psychology. And knowing something of her physiology wouldn't hurt either. If he's going to satisfy her, he has to get inside her head and see the relationship in terms of what she wants out of it. Do you follow any of what I'm saying, or are you still concentrating on trying to satisfy your short-range urges? If that's the case, you'd be better off masturbating in the shower. That way, nobody gets hurt."

Pinski didn't answer, but the deep red tinge flooding his face told Merrilane her words had registered.

"Jack, I like you a lot. I doubt anybody can resist liking you initially. But there's something about you that doesn't ring true. Something's causing you to live superficially."

"I think I see what you're getting at, Merrilane. My father said the best advisor a young man could have was an older woman."

"Your father was wrong!" She so quickly countered the inference she thought he was drawing she failed to notice his use of her given name. "What he should have said was 'old woman' not 'older woman.' An old woman is a detached, yet astute observer. I'm an older woman; I'm still in the game. But what I told you previously is true. I don't have room in my life for you. But I'm only human. I've pressures that sometimes drive me in search of an outlet. You're close by; you're attracted to me; I could teach you to satisfy me; and I could allow you to ruin all our lives."

"Merrilane, I . . . "

"Let me finish. And for our transgression, I would be held solely responsible because I'm supposed to be the rational one. For your information, Alex and I are not swingers. I don't know what kind of person you are, but my instincts tell me not to trust you, to keep you away from me, and to hold on to that letter of resignation."

As she finished, she rose to her feet, towering over the morose young man who remained seated on the floor. As he continued to sit, apparently reflecting on what she had said, she fumbled in her purse, found her cigarettes, and flipped the lighter.

"You want one?"

"I've got my own." He found the Marlboros in the large pocket of his jacket and lighted one from the smoldering tip of her Virginia Slim. He inhaled deeply, eyes scanning outside and picking out the flecks of white just beginning to be driven horizontally by the wind.

"I mentioned my father. You knew he was killed in Vietnam?"

"No," Merrilane said as she eased herself onto the chair again. "I'm sorry."

"What a man he was. He could charm women. If he were here at your feet, you'd soon slip down beside him. He and my mother must have had an accommodation. She never let on like she was anything but the contented Air Force wife. And I guess in a way she was. She had everything she wanted outside of his faithfulness. The Air Force killed him."

"I'm so sorry. So many of our men have been sacrificed over there."

"You weren't listening! I said the Air Force *killed* him! Three Canberra bombers painted all black, taxiing out on the ramp at Bien Hoa. Your husband's probably passed over that very spot a hundred times not knowing my Daddy's there. Taxiing out loaded with chemically-fused bombs left over from World War Two. World War Two for Christ's sake! Taxiing out when one of the fuses cooked off, and a plane just disappeared in a cloud of smoke. And a moment later another one evaporated. And—are you still with me—another moment and the third went up. They thought at first it was a mortar attack. Then they realized the corroded fuses just let go.

"What do you think it was like, Merrilane?" Big tears coursed down his up-turned face. "What do you think it was like for my Daddy to sit there with his planes blowing up around him? He was sharp. He knew immediately what was happening. Was he on the brakes, dribbling in the pressure and praying for a smooth stop? Was he yelling for his navigator to get out? Did he know he didn't have a chance and was about to meet his maker? Or, God how I hope, was his the first plane to go? Did he leave with the sensation in his brain of parading past the troops on the flight line, leading his men to attack the enemy? Bless his heart; I hope so."

"Oh, Jack," she stroked his face, drying his tears with the touch of her fingertips. "I'm so sorry you live with that image. But you can't blame the Air Force. They fight with what they have. Alex is flying an airplane that's older than you are."

"You're wrong! The Air Force accepted the mission. They all knew it was the wrong war. Hell, even I know that, and I'm just a cadet. But they accepted it, allowing the arrogant Pentagon whiz kids to rub their noses in it. They accepted it just as my stupid classmates do: 'because it's the only war we got.' And wars are what get allocations and promotions. Not one general had the balls to say 'This is all wrong.' Not one senior officer fell on his sword when he saw all the principles of war violated. Who says defense is a principle of war? Or attrition? We got monks in Vietnam and protesters in the US, for Christ's sake, burning themselves up for matters of principle. But all our generals are lined up kissing LBJ's ass! And my Daddy over there flying obsolete airplanes, using bombs that should have been condemned, trying to do the impossible job he'd sworn to do."

"Jack, get a hold of yourself. You shouldn't talk like that."

"Why not, Merrilane? What does it matter what one cadet says or thinks? All that matters is what he does. And I've done plenty to fuck the system. And I'll do more. My Dad primed me for the Academy. I'd just finished my doolie year when they killed him. He thought the Zoo was so great. The finest thing I could do with my life. Learn how to take care of the men, he told me. Keep 'em from getting chewed up by a system they're too trusting to question. I'll tell you what really counts, and it runs counter to all the feminist bullshit you were feeding me. It's revenge! Pure and simple; an eye for an eye. An Academy for my Daddy!"

"Jack, listen to me," her voice flared. "You can't talk this way. You can't go around carrying such a load. You've got to share this with a professional."

"What are you smoking, lady? No Air Force shrink's going to listen to what I have to say. In about three minutes, he'd have the OSI in his office. We're talking lying, cheating, stealing, extortion, drugs. Everything the Code says we won't do."

"You're talking nonsense! Your father's death is a fact. All the rest is fantasy. Now let's break this mood and get you out of here before it snows any more."

"I don't want to go anywhere," he rolled over on his chest and looked up at her like Brutus used to do when he wanted to be fed. "I'm hungry. Besides, I might as well wait for Jeff and Kim to come back, so I can get some pictures."

"It'll be late. I can't be sure what time they'll be in with the roads getting slick."

Pinski rose cat-like to his feet, standing immediately in front of her chair and smirking. "I'll tell you what I think, sweet thing. I think they're away for the night."

CHAPTER THIRTY

MATTRESS BUTTONS CUT THROUGH the thin sheet and into Alex's chest causing him to shift positions for what seemed like the hundredth time. From a nearby hooch a Winchester cracked, its bullet ricocheting off desert rock. In their twenty-five-year-old movies, watched night after night by a goodly number of off-duty Americans, cowboys flushed Indians on Armed Forces Television. Meanwhile, their Viet Cong and NVA counterparts, lacking a television network, spend their nights humping supplies, cleaning weapons, or filtering through the jungle with rockets on their backs.

Alex tumbled and tossed, unable to sleep despite all his tricks of deep breathing, relaxation, and mind control. How many times, he wondered, had he lain awake as the hours before takeoff dragged listlessly by? In what different settings? In Savannah with the roaring air conditioner trying to cope with mid-day humidity, in transient officers' quarters all over the United States, in overseas enclaves from Morocco to the Republic of Vietnam. Tomorrow, however, he would not be piloting the aircraft. He had only to process through the passenger terminal for a seat on the spindly-legged C-7 "Caribou" transport that looked more like a starving flamingo than its rugged namesake.

The cause of his insomnia—the unfinished business he needed to discuss with Merrilane—outweighed anything to be seen on television or awaiting him in the Central Highlands. After leaving the club, he had cursed his luck upon finding all commercial circuits down and the local MARS station closed for maintenance. In desperation he tried sweet talking the military operators, getting as far as The Presidio in California before a priority call knocked him off the line. He had finally settled on writing, although he knew overdue words needed to be expressed immediately.

What would he do if Merrilane were beside him? The thought recalled long periods of foreplay, tender caresses, and exquisite afterglow in Hawaii. Still it had been deficient—lovemaking with the sound track turned off. After all the years of complete disclosure, he had stopped short of confessing his deficiency. Six words would have started it: *I killed some of our people . . . machine gunned them while trying to save them.* Would she still have caressed and kissed him? Knowing his mind and having experienced his brooding over small mistakes and omissions, she could have handled anything he confessed and given him absolution. Anything except another woman.

Confession had not worked with Hubbard. One could not be ordered to forget murder. Dan Strait had already rotated. Who else could he trust? He needed a woman's patience and wisdom. Other than Long, Monique was the only female he knew by name. But what right did he have to expose her to the crudeness of what passed for modern warfare? What would be his real motive? How much was bruised ego urging him to mate with a woman who would not end up screaming at him? What man could live with the image of his wife's contorted face ridiculing his clumsy attempts at reconciliation? Who could endure in this stifling environment when his wife's last words had been recriminations? "You spoiled everything," she had shrieked at him, "You make me sick!"

He had been in deep slumber dreaming about something he instantly forgot when the alarm clock awoke him. He figured he must have drifted off about three. Later he dozed on the Caribou, which turned out to be flying non-stop rather than making a series of bumps and jumps into and out of Special Forces camps.

Dave Lenardo, a long-time friend, met him at Pleiku, got him a cot in one of the hooches, and pointed out the nearest underground shelter. Then Alex met Stanton Montclair Rockefeller, the courtly lieutenant colonel in charge of the three

C-47s that hauled cargo for the base. He had assumed a man with such a million-dollar name would consider trash hauling beneath his dignity. He was wrong. A charming host, Rockefeller gave unhurried access to his proficiency and scheduling records then invited him to meet the officers and enlisted persons who were involved in what, in essence, was a well-managed short-haul airline.

As he prepared to leave, Rockefeller mentioned his own pet project: the marketing of artifacts made by Montagnard tribes. "Do you know Montagnard history?" he asked. "It's quite fascinating."

"Only that they guard our border outposts."

"The French termed them Montagnards meaning 'mountain people'; the Vietnamese call them '*Moi*'—savages—and have pushed them into the mountains where they've led an aborigine-like existence. We've arranged to sell their cross bows, arrows, and native cloth with proceeds going back to the tribe. If we stay here long enough, we may drag them into the twentieth century."

"Why would you want to do that?" Alex asked.

That night, thoroughly worn out, he joined the crew of a gunship launched to assist a Long Range Reconnaissance Patrol surrounded by elements of the North Vietnamese Army. Finding them was hit or miss, a matter of tracking outbound from Pleiku and setting up a search pattern. Even though the pilot established voice contact, he was unable to get a precise fix on the "Lurp" team huddling under triple-canopy jungle. Knowing few men performed creatively under the steady gaze and perfect second guessing of an unfamiliar inspector, Alex retired to the rear cabin, lay down on the cold metal floor, and went instantly to sleep.

The crew stayed over the area all night, dropping an occasional flare and depending upon the drone of their engines to reassure the team and keep the enemy from engaging. At dawn they departed knowing the patrol was exfiltrating to their helicopter pick-up point. He remembered the flight as one to which he contributed nothing except, perhaps, a sense of implied confidence in the crew's ability to do whatever was expected.

After landing he napped until noon, showered, ate some canned peaches he found in the hooch, then called Lieutenant Colonel Greg Saunders, a friend who commanded an army helicopter unit stationed a short distance away.

"Great to hear from you, Alex. How about coming over to my place for supper? I'll pick you up in forty-five minutes."

Within the hour a smiling Greg Saunders welcomed Alex into his tiny "Loach," lifted off, and settled onto a heading for Camp Holloway. The Light Observation Helicopter was just skin and bones compared to the giant CH-47 "Chinook," the army's standard cargo carrier, whose sling could lift an artillery piece or damaged chopper as easily as Alex had once picked up toy girders with the crane of his Erector Set. Its bulbous canopy resembled a swollen lens covering the eye of a mutant dragonfly. Whatever the two occupants observed from inside the lens was vulnerable within minutes to an artillery barrage summoned from a nearby fire support base.

"You always fly this low?" Alex asked as the dull brown tones of the defoliated base perimeter gave way to a verdant blur whipping just beneath the plexiglass.

"Ya can't see what's going on from three thousand feet," Saunders shouted above the whine of the engine and the whistling slipstream. "Besides, if I'm low they don't have so much advance warning."

"You ever hear of the 'Golden BB?'"

"Sure. Secret's not to run into it."

Alex recalled thrilling B-47 low level training, skipping above the waves in a pre-dawn air defense exercise, jinking around freighters outward bound from Delaware Bay before popping up for a simulated nuclear strike. But those bygone flights were plotted the day before and flown as dictated by the SAC master plan. This helicopter jaunt was a grab-ass taxi flight designed to impress the man from the junior service.

Once on the ground, Saunders introduced him to a group pre-flighting their mounts, two Cobra gunships and a Huey "slick" with mini-guns positioned at its open side doors. "You're in luck, pal. These gents are fixing to practice for an air show. You wanna ride in one of the Cobras?"

"You bet! But what do you mean by 'air show'?"

"The brass wants us to demonstrate extracting a lurp team from a hot landing zone for some congressional squids. So tomorrow the monkeys will jump. If we jump high enough and gracefully enough, we might be rewarded with an extra appropriation."

Minutes later Alex stuffed himself into a Cobra's front cockpit then started checking radio switches and flight instruments. From the back seat, Warrant Officer Taggart called to announce engine start. The pilot brought the turbine up to speed, checked in with the tower, and called his two companions. He lifted into a hover, snaked out of the revetment, down the taxiway, and onto the runway for departure. The formation leaped off smartly, climbing in trail in a wide arc which led them to a fortified hamlet near a small clearing which would serve as the site of the next day's fireworks. As they shunted back and forth burning off fuel so their maneuvers would be more spectacular, Taggart gave instruction on flying the machine.

"Nothing to it, Major. If you can masturbate, you can fly a helicopter. The collective stick on the left controls your up and down movement. Use the twist grip on the end of the stick to add throttle as you raise the collective, back off as you lower it. The stick between your legs allows you to tilt the disk formed by the rotor blades. The disk tilts and the helicopter follows. The pedals control the pitch of the tail rotor blades which offset torque from the main rotor and allow you to move the nose left or right. The bad news is you've got to coordinate all the inputs. The good news is you learn how to do it after a while.

"For today's exercise, we'll be running on north-south headings reversing course after each pass. While we're working the north-south axis, our mate'll be cris-crossing perpendicular to us. The idea is to have one of us in position to support the slick at all times. The pilot of the Huey has to be aware of our patterns, the sources of any ground fire, and the smoke from the pick-up team. He decides when to make his run in. Tomorrow we'll be shooting live ammo—rockets, grenade launchers, and mini-guns."

"Quite an arsenal, Mister Taggart. You'd think it would be enough to make any bad guys throw down their guns and hide."

"Charlie don't pay it no mind. He stands and shoots back. Sometimes you get so close you see the hate streaming out of his little black eyes. Like that poster of the eagle screaming down ready to grab a mouse with his talons. And the mouse standin' his ground givin' the eagle the finger. You ever seen that poster, Major?"

"Yeah," Alex said, "I guess everyone pulls for the mouse."

"Not me." Taggart's voice was tinny, like an old Victrola, as it came through the earphones. "I've seen the mouse zap too many of my buddies. But everybody's different. I even had a wingman pull off a target one time. We'd popped over some trees and caught three Charlies humpin' along the top of a dike big as you please. Black pajamas, straw hats, and carbines slung across their backs. Musta been kids new to the game. I got two and cleared my wingman on the survivor. His mini-guns pulverized the terrain right up to this kid who had shouldered that little gun and was bangin' away. Would you believe it? My idiot wingman just stopped firin', went into a hover, slipped broadside, and let the kid take his licks. Then he pulled off."

"Powerful story," Alex looked for expression in the rearview mirror, but saw only an ant-like head encased in a green helmet with the dark visor lowered all the way. "What happened to the VC?"

"I dipped down, threw him a salute, and wasted him with the grenade launcher."

The formation beat up the area for twenty minutes then rejoined for the flight home. Saunders was waiting in a Jeep when

Alex, grinning and drenched with sweat, climbed out of the cockpit.

"Absolutely tip-top! I've got to include a section on helicopter gunships in the tactics manual I'm putting together. We don't have a clue how you guys operate."

"Glad you liked your ride." Saunders extended a Black Label. "Let's get back and clean up before supper."

"My God, how I wished I'd brought my camera."

"Why didn't you?"

"I didn't want to look like an amateur in front of you and your people."

"That's where you made your mistake. Unless you're carrying at least two cameras out here, you don't look like a professional."

CHAPTER THIRTY-ONE

MORNING SUNLIGHT STREAMING THROUGH slits in the vertical blinds bathed the Cannard bedroom in alternate strips of light and dark. The comforter lay in a mound on the floor. An odor of stale smoke, sticky sweet and foreign, seemed to have settled on the furniture and on scattered items of clothing lying where they had been discarded. Merrilane sat in the middle of the bed, blinking against the sun. She cradled her head, feeling cautiously the matted strands of hair clustered about her eyes. Her temples throbbed. She had difficulty breathing through the stuffiness clogging her nose. Her left arm lacked feeling. She avoided looking at her reflection in the mirrored closet doors, trying instead to conjure mental images to explain her condition.

Long ago she had been on a perfect beach, frozen in time, then someone began to pry into feelings bruised by workplace sniping and antagonism within the household. Who was that nervous stranger, she asked herself. What right did he have to infiltrate her mind? Suddenly chilled she retrieved the comforter, tucked it around her trembling shoulders, then pulled it over her head.

Like water seeping through canvas, remembrance first stained, then flooded her mind spreading awareness so fresh and so painful she flung the tangled bedclothes away. Leaning tentatively on her left arm, she rummaged in the drawer of her bedside table, found the envelope stashed within the pages of her Confirmation Bible, and ripped open its flap. Hands trembling she withdraw the single sheet, unfolded it, and saw nothing written there.

Scarcely breathing she sank backward and gazed at the white ceiling descending upon her. From the dresser the dictatorial clock mindlessly winked its red eye in perpetual celebration of an overnight power failure.

Some indeterminate time later, she crawled from her disheveled cocoon, stood nude and cold on the white carpet, and began mechanically stripping the sheets, pillow cases, and mattress pad. Once she stopped, hastily consulted her planning calendar, made quick calculations on her fingers, then gathered up the bedclothes and hurried them to the washer. As the scalding water poured into the tub, she heaped cup after cup of gritty detergent on top of the linen then added all that remained in the large container of bleach. After closing the lid, she limped up the hallway feeling along the wall for support. She switched on the bank of lights over the bathroom mirror but avoided her reflection. Closing the door, she locked it, then turned the shower full hot, flooding the room with clammy vapor. Foraging in the basin cabinet, she found the chilled bottle of astringent white vinegar, methodically prepared her douche, and purged herself. Afterward she entered the shower and stood obediently under the steaming water until she sensed red welts rising on her shoulders. Rotating the temperature regulator, she subjected her body to the spasms of an ice-cold rinse.

Shaking like an abandoned and terrified puppy, she adjusted the water to a moderate temperature and began flagellating herself with a long-handled scrub brush. Afterward she filled the tub to its upper drain and slumped into the water spilling the excess in one huge wave onto the floor. She hesitated before picking up the safety razor lying in the soap tray. Appraising her waterlogged fingers and toes, she found them shriveled like those of a wicked witch who had fallen into her own caldron. Lifting the razor she noticed, really for the first time, how heavy it felt. She unscrewed the handle from the head and pulled the thin blade from its resting place. After inspecting both cutting edges, she methodically pushed the blade into the back of its dispenser, removed a new one, studied it meticulously before finally inserted it into place, and reassembled the parts.

Now moving quickly, she lathered her left leg with aerosol foam, skimmed the blade swiftly over the smooth skin, and repeated the performance on her right leg. As she twisted to finish the back of her calf, she noticed vivid blue bruises on her upper thigh. Ignoring them she lathered under each arm, then skimmed off the foam. Next she pulled herself unsteadily to her feet, drained the tub, soaped her entire body again, and rinsed under the showerhead. After turning off the water, she stood for a moment with arms raised above her head, as if for final inspection, her flank having been graded already.

On impulse she reached again for the razor, unscrewed the handle, and removed the blade. Again she ran warm water into the tub, settled into it, began splashing the liquid over her left wrist, then paused as if contemplating the exact sequence. Sometime later she pulled a thick red towel from the wall rack and folded it to make a pad to cover the tub's rim. Moving the disassembled razor to rest on the towel, she selected a new blade and inspected each edge, turning the sliver of steel over and over, entranced by its insignificance. Reluctantly she inserted the blade and reassembled the device. Seating herself on the padded edge of the tub, she applied foam to her genital area then meticulously shaved until she believed all the mystery had been removed. After showering once again, she dried herself then stepped to the washbasin.

Swirling an end of her towel across the obscured mirror, she studied the face that emerged. Puffy skin around her eyes gave her a battered visage, mercifully soon veiled by condensing vapor. Spotting her worn toothbrush, she became aware of the musky almond taste contaminating her mouth. Using great gobs of paste, she scrubbed her teeth, her tongue, and the roof of her mouth, then finished with three applications of antiseptic mouthwash.

Picking up the long-bladed scissors she used for snipping errant strands, she began pulling, hacking, and cutting the wet hair trailing in twisted disarray behind her neck. It fell in bunches, littering the floor around her, and sticking to her toes. She sobbed huge tears as she continued whacking blindly at what had been her trademark, her Barbie persona. Once her passion subsided, she entered the shower a third time, rinsing the strange shape of her head and massaging her left arm.

Without toweling she limped into the bedroom, jerked open the blinds, and stood naked, squinting against the snow's glare. As her eyes adjusted, she discerned her body's reflection in the double-glazed windows. An albino harlequin stared back at her, tan washed out by the glare, wet hair chopped into uneven spikes weaving like the snakes of Medusa. She studied the grotesquery that drifted in and out of focus between the legs of the apparition. Moving her long fingers to caress her taut stomach muscles, she pushed them further down into the pasty white void which had once hosted her perfectly groomed triangle of pubic hair. She jerked her fingers back, repelled by the unnaturalness of the feeling. *A plucked chicken. Fine!*

Slipping into a maroon robe that clung to her body but contributed little warmth, she hobbled into the kitchen searching for something to ease the churning in her stomach. She found an apple, polished red, and devoured it feeling the juice overflowing around the corners of her mouth. Then she limped back to the laundry and started the wash cycle all over again.

Shuffling back to the bedroom, she slid the closet doors apart on their silent nylon casters, and started shifting boxes on the top shelf until she located the two wig cases. Exhausted, she drew the blinds tightly, lay down on the stripped bed, and pulled the comforter over her. She tried once again to recreate the events of the night. But the mattress buttons punched through the rayon housecoat, forcing her to shift positions each time she was about to fit the pieces together. Finally she drifted into sleep.

She awoke to the persistent ringing of the telephone. Thinking of the children and the snow-covered roads from Breckenridge, she grabbed the instrument and shouted a breathless "Hello!"

The line was open but silent.

"Hello, who is this? Speak to me, damn you!"

"Hello Merrilane. Are you entertaining visitors this beautiful morning?"

"Jack Pinski, you bastard. You've a nerve calling me."

"I need to see you. Something's developed that's sure to cement our relationship."

"All I want from you is a real letter of resignation in the Superintendent's hands by tomorrow morning. The moment I see your car, I'll call the sheriff. Mark my words!"

"I've already taken your mark, dear lady. I'll be seeing you." The line went dead; its sarcastic voice stilled as if the strength of her right hand choking the receiver had been enough to break the connection.

The crunch of tires in the driveway, the thumping of car doors, and joyous shouts snapped her back to reality. "Oh Christ," she whispered. Stumbling into the bathroom, she wrapped a towel around her head and skipped to open the back door just as Jeffrey raced into view with Kim on his heels. Frank trailed close behind, looking fit and clutching the children's overnight bags.

Spreading her arms wide, she leaned far out, holding the door so Frank could enter without dropping the luggage. Eddies of dislodged snow swirled about her. As the children bushed by, the loosely twisted belt parted and her garment opened to reveal her nakedness. Frank averted his eyes, rotated his shoulders to catch the door, and allowed her to cover herself.

"You . . . you caught me off guard," she stammered. "I'd just come out of the shower."

"No apologizes necessary. We're earlier than planned." He did not look back but continued up the corridor depositing the bags in each child's room. Returning, he noticed Merrilane's jumbled bed and her room's disarray. He also sniffed an unusual, vaguely familiar odor that seemed to hang in the hallway.

"Say, neighbor," he spoke briskly as he emerged, "why not let the kids come over to our place till you're ready for them? I know Iris would love to pop corn and have some cider. You're welcome too, of course."

"Bless you, Frank. You're the one man I can always depend on."

"Hey, kids," he shouted. "Don't take off your coats. We're going over to my house for beer and pigs' feet!"

He stomped out the door followed by Kim and Jeffrey, who paused momentarily to kiss their mother. At the corner of the house, Frank turned to pick up Iris's Ford as the children raced each other through the drifts and across the yard. He stopped a moment to examine some fresh deer tracks, then continued walking to the car, where he noticed only a dusting of blown snow covering his parking spot.

Merrilane latched the storm door and crossed to the laundry where she transferred the bedclothes to the dryer, spun the dial, then stood listening to the swirling rumble hoping by some metaphysical transfer to get the tangled patterns in her mind synchronized. After awhile she limped into the bathroom to gather up the hair littering the floor. Moving into the bedroom, she replaced the wig cases and the pile of shoe boxes she had disturbed.

Hesitating momentarily at the bedside table, she fished the remains of four closely smoked cigarettes from the ash tray and took them to flush down the toilet.

Back in the bedroom, she bent to retrieve the comforter. As she scooped it up, she heard a peculiar sound, something like Christmas ornaments tinkling together. Looking closely she saw the milky-colored flash bulbs—six of them—and a crumpled yellow box.

CHAPTER THIRTY-TWO

HE WAITED UNTIL HE COULD HEAR HER steady breathing filtering down from the bedroom. Then he switched off the reading lamp, picked up his jacket and flashlight, and tiptoed to the patio door. Easing the glass panel open just enough to accommodate his thin frame, he listened for any change in the measured cadence, then slipped outside.

Frank deplored the excuses he had offered over the last several evenings for not joining Iris when she retired. Yet she appeared to have accepted them, although he imagined her eyes following his shadowy form as he picked his way across the yard. He had always known he would have made a poor foot soldier; he lacked a sureness of step and sense of direction. Nor could he have been a cat burglar even though he felt like one as he reached the treeline and began veering to a position where he could observe Merrilane's lighted window. She had begun keeping late hours, her restlessness betrayed by the sudden illumination of lights in odd parts of the house. The main entrance lantern burned all night, its low-wattage bulbs casting a puny half-circle of radiance around her front door. In the rear she now habitually burned all the lights inside the greenhouse. But their combined brightness seemed only to define the target.

Since the incident Sunday afternoon, he had also observed a bizarre change in her appearance. First she affected obvious wigs. Then yesterday she returned home sporting a severe pixie cut, a fad of the late fifties he had absolutely forbidden his wife to follow. He tried pumping Iris for gossip, but backed off when she asked him outright why he was so interested in Merrilane's affairs.

Shortly after dark again this evening, he noticed the Sheriff's patrol cruise down the gravel road flashing its spotlight into the woods. He eased himself down on a familiar log, shifting his position to observe the lighted bedroom window as well as any illumination that might come from his own house. The crisp temperature and steady wind caused him to turn up the collar of his jacket and wish he had remembered his gloves.

As he waited, his mind dredged up memories of previous associations with the Cannards. Alex, wearing his sincerity like a shimmering coverall, had impressed him during his interview for a faculty position as few others had. He was bright enough, but it was his attitude that stood out; he projected an optimistic point of view that would prove infectious in the classroom. Frank had taken for granted such a man would have selected a wife who complemented his own personality. Merrilane fulfilled his expectations. But, almost from their first meeting, he had detected something within her wanting expression, some basic dissatisfaction. Her meteoric rise in the athletic department had not surprised him.

After an hour of bone-chilling waiting, he freed his imagination to warm itself behind those tightly closed blinds. Was she sifting through volumes of business paper? Searching her husband's letters for inspiration? Breathing deep-throated sounds into the telephone? Or, could she be tossing in fitful slumber having left the bedside light illuminated for security?

What would he do if he were magically transported into her fragrant bedroom? What if he glanced in the mirrored doors and saw nothing staring back? What if a mischievous devil had granted him invisibility to arouse his most erotic fantasies? How exquisite the anticipation of crawling, ice-cold from the forest, into his young protege's place.

What stupidity huddling on a damp log, assaulted by bristling night winds, dishonoring my own trusting mate, wasting whatever time I have left. What draws me here? Perversion? Do I wait for the light to blink an invitation? For her to snap open the blinds exposing herself again? For Lady Chatterly to come seeking her John Thomas? Why do you entice me, Circe?

He shifted his position, quietly stomping among the pine needles to restore circulation. *I could almost be her father. What father conjures himself inside his daughter's boudoir? Only a dirty old man, shivering with cold, blocking thoughts of the grave by lusting like a mangy dog pulled by a bitch in heat. What's next? Luring little girls with offers of candy?*

You're on dangerous ground, Old Boy. Maybe it's the chemotherapy. Want a go with her? Certainly. Would you if you could? No. Enjoy thinking about it? Yes. Why? Exciting. Forbidden. Keeps me warm in a cold forest. Overpowering? No. Just a fantasy. A fantasy I could understand if I observed it in others. A sin? Probably not. If it stays under control. What would God think? Don't know. God, what do you make of all this? We've come through a lot together. Two wars, raising a son, academic frustration, that time Iris kicked up her heels, the operation. Why this? Why let her gown fall open? Why show me the mystery? Why put that image continually before me? Are you using me? Is that why I'm here? Or is there really a devil somewhere who's pulling strings even You can't reach? I don't believe that. Why won't you answer me, Lord? Send me a sign.

Stupid, stupid, stupid. Sitting on a wet log after midnight trying to raise God. Make Him an accessory. Funny. It won't be long now anyway. I'll soon have the answer . . . come up on His frequency. Or won't have it. And won't know it. And just won't.

A dry branch snapped sharply. Something big close by was moving slowly but carelessly. He picked up the shape as it separated from the treeline. It walked to the house, attempted to peer through the bedroom blinds, then moved arrogantly into the bright light streaming from inside the greenhouse. Testing the flimsy latch of the aluminum door, the figure seemed intent on forcing the lock. Rising from his log, Frank realized—despite all the time he had been given to think—he did not have a plan.

"Freeze," he yelled as he hit the figure with the beam of his five-cell torch. Expecting his quarry to stand like a startled doe, eyes shimmering in the intense light, he was unprepared as the black-clad intruder charged him.

"Halt or I'll shoot." The figure leaped headlong for the protection of the trees as Frank ran stiffly to intercept him. "I see you," he spoke sternly. "Come out of there. I've got men all over these woods."

He moved closer, probing the underbrush, his light magnifying each branch's quiver. "I know you're there, and I know you can hear me." He spoke steadily as if he were lecturing in the main auditorium. "You're playing a dangerous game. It'll disgrace you or get you killed." He raised his voice, now ritually exorcizing a demon as he inched forward trolling the light back and forth. "You're going to leave this woman alone. Get out of her life forever."

"Who's out there?" Merrilane's high-pitched voice shouted. Bits of falling bark alerted him to disaster moments before two hundred pounds smashed him to earth. His assailant snatched the light from his hand, tossed it still burning end over end deep into the forest, then darted away. Frank scrambled to his feet, but his left knee twisted, and he fell back against a tree. Then she was there blinding him momentarily with her flashlight and waving a .32-caliber automatic pistol in his face.

"Oh, my God, Frank. What did he do to you?" She crouched barefoot in the snow beside him, laying the gun on the ground and reaching an arm behind his back to help him rise.

"I'll kill that son of a bitch if he ever comes back," he said as if he were taking an oath on a stage with flags behind him and journalists taking notes. She stooped to pick up the gun then led him to the house.

"Is that thing loaded?"

"Yes. I'm surprised you haven't heard me practicing the last several days."

"What has he done to you?" he asked as he eased himself down on a kitchen stool beside the counter where the children usually had their morning orange juice and cereal.

"I'm not sure," she answered without looking up. "But he's bothering me, and I'm afraid of him."

"Who is it?" He had taken both her hands, spinning her around and forcing her to look at him.

"I can't tell you." Her eyes flooded. "Frank, I've felt so alone. No one to talk to, afraid even to confide in Iris." She put her arms around his neck, buried her face in his chest, and sobbed. He began to stroke her back with his left hand, starting high up near the shoulders but stopping abruptly as he felt the inward curve of her spine.

"Now, now. It's all right. Nothing's going to hurt you. Dad will take care of you."

She disengaged finally, dabbing at her eyes with a tissue. "I'm sorry to be such a weak sister. I guess I just needed to hold on to a man who didn't represent a threat."

"I don't know if I consider that a compliment."

"It's a compliment, believe me. But why were you out back?"

"I've been there the last several nights. Ever since the pieces fell together."

"What do you mean?"

"Your leaving the lights on, the Sheriff cruising the road when he's never done it before, a shadow I saw when I was getting a drink in the bathroom the other night."

"I didn't think anyone was watching over me any more. Not even the Lord."

"Merrilane, you've got to tell me who it is, so we can wrap this thing up."

"I can't. I think he'll stop coming around now that he knows you're watching. I can handle the other things." He raised his eyebrows. "The late night phone calls, the crude newsletter. I'll handle them like I'm learning to handle all the routine harassment we women have to put up with on the job."

"I assume he's a cadet. I want his name. We can't let someone like that graduate."

"Frank, please for God's sake respect my wishes. He just needs to get over this hangup he has for me. Maybe I've led him on without knowing it. Maybe I send out signals I'm not aware of. If he continues to bother me, I'll give you his name."

"I don't like it at all. You know what the honor code demands of the cadets. Harassment of a woman, assault on an officer. That's a lot more serious than your run-of-the-mill ly-ing, cheating, or stealing. If I'm aware of deviant conduct and tolerate it, then I'm compromising my own responsibility as an officer. May I use your phone?"

"Please don't pursue this, Frank. Don't even tell Iris. I know she means well, but she just can't keep from talking."

"I'm sorry. But I've got to make a call. I can do it here, or I can go next door." Without waiting for a response, he dialed the Academy operator.

"Please give me the security police desk."

He watched as she walked down the hall to check the chil-dren. *Poor child*, he thought, *she does send out signals. Better if she had remained at home where she was safe.*

"Good morning, Sergeant. This is Colonel Frank Harbinger of the history department. Would you be so kind as to ask the guards at each of the gates to note the license numbers of any incoming cadet automobiles between now and zero-eight-hun-dred? . . . I'd rather not say at present . . . That's kind of you. I'll call in the morning to see if you turn up anything . . . Thank you, Sergeant."

He broke the connection, looked inside the cover of the phone book, and dialed the sheriff's number.

"Good Morning, Deputy, this is Frank Harbinger on Stage-coach Road in the Black Forest. I saw someone prowling around my garage about ten minutes ago. When I yelled at him, he ran into the woods headed south. Would you ask one of your units to take a swing around the area? . . . Thank you; I appreciate it."

She returned wearing her slippers and stood running a comb through her hair. "I feel guilty, not taking you into my confi-dence."

"That's all right, my dear. I have a good idea who our prowler is, but I'll need more than suspicion if I expect to do anything about it."

"Dear God. Don't tell me it's base-wide knowledge!"

"No. I'm sure it's not. But, I remember Iris telling me some-time ago you had a handsome First Classman helping you. So at least I know where to start looking. And if he hasn't covered his tracks, our prowler may have something big fall on him."

"I beg you! Let it be."

"A man must do what he has to do."

"Don't speak to me in clichés, Frank. I admire you too much."

"I'm sorry. The real reason is the big bastard got the better of me tonight, and I've got a score to settle."

They both smiled somewhat self-consciously.

"I guess we'd better get to bed," Merrilane said.

He walked to the storm door, then turned to look at her once more. "You know, of course, you're very desirable. Even with short hair and no make-up."

"I suppose so," she replied.

Frank made his way across the snow-covered lawn step-ping in crusted footprints previously made. He let himself into the darkened house, not hearing Iris scurry back to their bed.

CHAPTER THIRTY-THREE

"Hi, Hotshot," Glenn smiled from a desk littered with papers. "How'd your first trip go?"

"Not bad considering." Alex slid his canvas aviator's kit across the green tiles to come to rest in a crumpled heap beside his desk. "You been here all night?"

"Is it morning already?" Glenn scratched the bristles covering his chin and pudgy cheeks.

"Any mail for me?"

"Lots of it. Some you're not gonna like."

"What do you mean?" Alex rummaged through his in-basket ignoring the smudgy carbons of official messages looking for the red, white, and blue-bordered envelopes that meant something from home.

"I picked up your traffic and scanned it in case anything was hot. That lieutenant colonel you locked horns with at Nha Trang protested the conference you called."

"I suspected he would. Now I guess I have to fight that battle all over again."

"You obviously don't know the man you work for. When he saw the TWX, Wootan waltzed across the street to the Chief of Staff, and the next day Nha Trang wired us to 'forget all after hello.'"

"I don't understand it. You try to make it easy on 'em, and they fight you tooth and nail."

"Nothing to understand," Glenn slid his chair back, tossed his stubby pencil into the overflowing wastepaper basket, and lifted his feet onto the top of his desk. "It's just human nature to want to run your own show, to resent anything coming out of headquarters as being a distraction that keeps you from getting the real work done."

"I can appreciate that, but . . . "

"No, Alex, you can't. You're dealing with frustrated fighter pilots, and you don't understand their psychology."

"Oh, come on Glenn, I've been around . . . "

"Let me finish. You're branded as a SAC-weenie and these guys are fighter jocks—extroverts with egos radar can't measure. They don't like mission folders, higher headquarters directives, tactics manuals, and all the rest of the minutiae that gets in their way."

"Are you saying I should do nothing but give standardization checks like my predecessor and ignore the whole area of tactics for close air support? We'll end up with a series of mid-air collisions or short rounds!"

"Don't get excited, buddy."

"Don't call me 'buddy.' The last guy who did went home in a box. Those sons of bitches are dragging their feet, and it's gonna get somebody killed."

"All right, all right," Glenn swung his feet to the floor. "I'm trying to say you're in a bigger fight than you realize. Wootan's gone to bat for you and got the Chief to back him. But it cost him some green stamps, and it may have given you some visibility you'd just as soon live without. You've crossed swords with the fighter pilot mafia that thinks Vietnam's their war. They're tired of having pulled hind tit to Strategic Air Command for the last twenty years. They aim to get in the driver's seat, grab the lion's share of congressional appropriations, and restore some flexibility into the force."

"Why pick on me? I'm one of them. I've flown their decrepit gunship."

"You're not listening, Alex. You're not one of them. Hell, neither am I. I'm a Naval Academy grad who's been in Research and Development for the last ten years. They don't care about gunships. And they don't care about forward air controllers. Those are both chickenshit jobs to fighter pilots. They don't give a damn about close support for the army. They believe battles are won by strangling the enemy's re-supply. But that comes after they gain control of the air—dogfights just like the Red Baron. They know you don't make Ace by dropping nape or shooting up hooches."

"What am I supposed to do? I thought our job was to give our aircrews a direct voice into this headquarters."

"That's precisely our job, and we've got to do it regardless. I just want you to know what you're up against. This isn't the Round Table. The Viet Cong aren't the only ones who don't play according to the book. Those guys at Nha Trang will emasculate you if they can. You understand? They'll cut your balls off."

Alex shrugged his shoulders and began searching again for a letter from Merrilane. "Where's Wootan?" he asked.

"Up at Cam Ran for the next four days."

"Is he still dating Monique Delepierre?"

"Don't know," Glenn tossed his head toward the row of lockers separating their space from the area occupied by PROJECT CONTEMP.

"Sorry 'bout that," Alex said, glancing at his watch. "Fat chance anyone will be over there this early."

Settling into his chair, he attacked the paper work starting first with a short report covering his trip to Pleiku, then concurring on a request to increase the maximum takeoff weight for C-47 trash haulers, and finally beginning preparations for the tactics conference. In the afternoon he scurried about the base arranging quarters, transportation, meeting places, typing support, and all the other details. Returning just before five, he found Airman Woziniac manning the telephone and looking bored.

"Hi, Major Cannard," the clerk greeted him as he walked into the office. "I thought you'd already hit the club."

"I've got a bit more to do, so I'll cover the phone if you want to bug out."

"Thanks a lot, Major Cannard." The young man was already on his feet, shuffling papers and looking for his cap. "I picked up the mail, and you have a bunch of letters and a tape recording. I'll leave the office's machine with you in case you want to play it here."

"That's good of you, Woz. Thanks."

Woziniac placed the player on Alex's desk, plugged it into the wall outlet, and said his good night.

Alex began to sort through the stack of letters before opening the tape canister. *Nothing that can't wait*, he thought. Then he saw the plain envelope postmarked Colorado Springs. Ripping the envelope open and pulling out its contents, he saw it was another issue of *The Falcon Code*. Flushing red and muttering under his breath, he shoved the whole packet into the wastebasket beside his desk.

Taking a moment to calm himself, he noticed the postmark on the plastic case was the sixteenth, which indicated a delay somewhere in the system. All the others had taken the usual five days. He slit the package's bindings, removed the three-inch reel, and threaded its tape. After flipping the power switch, he waited a moment, then pressed the "play" button:

Hello Alex, I'm recording this in my new office in Colorado Springs. I'm just beginning to get settled after moving in yesterday.

Merrilane's seductive voice sounded more husky than usual.

This recording will give me a chance to have my say without interruption, a courtesy I was not afforded in Hawaii.

She laughed nervously. He leaned forward to increase the volume, then steeled himself, elbows on knees, head in hands, eyes closed. He felt as if he were blindfolded and awaiting a sharp volley.

This is the great opportunity I hinted about in Hawaii. I thought an announcement might be premature. You also didn't seem to want to discuss anything more than superficialities. Excuse me for being bitchy. I've had cystitis ever since I've been home. But I guess your personal body count gave you something to brag to the boys about. I'm sorry. That was unkind.

On the return flight, I did a lot of thinking about being a military wife. I know we've accomplished a great deal so far, but it's been with you taking the lead. You plotting your career and me filling in where you placed me. You don't know about the obscene calls when you were in Africa or Spain. You don't know about the notes stuck under my windshield wipers. At parties you never heard the double entendres.

Savagely he lashed out, disconnecting the machine's plug. He rocked back and forth in his chair twisting the ends of the cord about his hands and testing the loop. The overloaded air conditioner cycled, its changing tempo seemingly synchronized with the blood he could feel throbbing in his temples. Meekly releasing the cord, he inserted one end into the player and plugged the other back into the outlet. The tape came to life presenting at first a mechanical, and then an accurate distortion of the way he remembered Merrilane's voice sounding. Resuming his pose, he listened for the nuances.

Doing the volunteer work while raising two children with you so often away has taken its toll. I'm fed up with it. I'm throwing in the towel before I get relegated to some snowbound airstrip on the northern tier. When you come back, we can either make a clean break or keep a marriage of convenience. This should really come as a relief. You'll be able to work twenty-four hours a day without any pangs of conscience. Naturally I'll keep the children.

"Oh, Jesus, Merrilane," he mumbled. "What in Hell's got into you?"

In case your pride's hurt, it's not another man. That would only compound my problems. If I were superstitious, I'd say the planets are aligned in a way they'll never be again in my lifetime. Colorado Springs is going to be the Olympic training capitol of the United States, and I'm going to be one of the founding fathers. Maybe I was the macho one all along.

Alex wept.

Forgive me for doing this so mechanically. I wish we'd gotten serious in Hawaii. God bless you, Alex. You deserve better than this. You deserve a more obedient servant.

The tape continued running, but the player produced only a muted roar like the crowd in the old newsreels of Adolf Hitler's speeches. Eventually the tape's loose end flapped noisily. No voice had reprieved him, had laughingly shouted it was all a joke like the ones he had so often played on her. He turned off the machine and wiped his eyes.

The sound of the telephone startled him. He decided to ignore it. But duty overcame judgment, and he lifted the receiver on the third ring.

Monique's voice was soft, feminine, everything the recording was not:

"Alex, I'm calling from my desk just across the lockers. I couldn't help overhearing your tape . . . . Hello, Alex, did you hear me? When I realized you'd come back to the office, I was going to call and ask if you wanted to share dinner. Then you started playing the recording, and I didn't know what to do . . . . Alex are you listening?"

"Yes. I'm listening. I didn't think anyone was over there."

"I've been on the job since early morning. I was here when you spoke with Major Mehan about politics in the Air Force. Perhaps I should have made some noise then, but you were giving me information I needed to know. What can I do to help?"

"I don't know what to say, Monique. I keep thinking I'm dreaming and will wake up back home. Merrilane will have muffins for breakfast, and she'll be wearing an apron. Oh, God, I'm sorry you heard that tape. Sorry you heard me."

"Listen, Alex. You can't keep this inside you. Give me ten minutes to tidy up, then meet me in front of the building. We'll take a walk. It hasn't been a good day for me either, and Adam's away. Okay?"

"Okay."

After replacing the receiver, he could hear her moving just a few feet away. He put the machine and his unclassified working papers in his top, right-hand drawer. Before locking the desk, he threw the tape in the bottom drawer among his shoeshine materials. Then he sorted through the wastebasket to be sure no classified material had become mixed with routine trash. Unconsciously he retrieved and opened *The Falcon Code*. The front page featured three grainy photographs of a nicely shaped, well endowed nude sprawled across a tousled bed. The woman was his wife.

CHAPTER THIRTY-FOUR

ALEX FLIPPED OFF THE LIGHTS before stepping outside. Closing the door behind him, he placed the rusty lock in the hasp, snapped it together, and spun the dial. He paused on the narrow landing feeling for a breeze and scanning the horizon for flares. Sometimes the Vietnamese Air Force AC-47 "Fire Dragons" were up before dusk dropping flares as if to see how many they could expend in an evening. Horizontal banks of purple and orange clouds—dying orange, not the vibrant hue that sparkled the leading edge of his wings at sunrise—discolored the western sky. The moon would be full this night, a Viet Cong moon lighting their trails, exposing their targets, and silhouetting the orbiting Spooky.

The first shift at Bien Hoa would be starting engines, he thought, or maybe were already taxiing past the loading Freedom Bird, each crewmember wishing he were in line for passage to the world. Vietnam had now become his only reality; an escape no longer existed. His internal world had been lost not to an instantaneous flash and consuming fireball but to a collapse triggered by the rising expectations of his own wife. He needed to talk to her face to face, probe her eyes as she spoke, watch her hands, listen for undistorted catches in her voice. He needed to determine exactly where he had gone wrong, so he could backtrack and maybe find a different path. He had to get home, maybe to shadow the house to see who had taken his place, who was shooting the pictures. *The pictures. The goddamn pictures.*

He saw Monique walking briskly around the side of the building and descended to meet her.

"Hello, Alex."

"Hello, Monique." He wished he could hold her. Just hang on not saying anything while she breathed against him. That was impossible with passing airmen smirking and winking. Why was it, he wondered, that events always conspired to keep people from holding each other? He wanted at least to take her hand. But uniformed officers did not stroll hand-in-hand with women any more than they carried umbrellas or ate ice cream cones.

She fell into step; he shifted to walk on the curb side. A single Jeep with a defective muffler rumbled past. Much of Tan Son Nhut's off-duty population was hunkered down for the night in various watering holes. They walked south, past the long rows of glass-fronted boxes at the consolidated mail room and the posters outside the Stars and Stripes Bookstore, drawn toward the large field near the main gate where they could see the moon rise. He veered away from the narrow, sour-smelling ditch that cut diagonally across the field ruining it for any useful purpose. Its stench permeated the night but could not pollute the moon's pristine serenity.

Dusk had turned quickly to dark. The breeze freshened, no mosquitoes trailed their steps. Neither had spoken since the initial greeting. His thoughts were ten thousand miles away. She was just there walking beside him. As they approached the gate with its barricades, guardian tank, and lounging Vietnamese sentries, he grasped her hand, squeezing it so tightly she winced.

"I'm not very good company, tonight," he said.

"I'm enjoying the walk."

"I don't know what to do except walk. I couldn't find words to describe how I feel, even if I knew. Wallingford must have felt this way when he looked at his hands, except he was blind and couldn't see what wasn't there. Maybe I should take you back to the club before the dining room closes."

"I shouldn't have called you," she said. "I should have left my desk when I realized I was intruding on your privacy."

"Why didn't you?"

She seemed not to hear. They were near the ditch again. The stench was Vietnam: sour, decaying, uncivilized.

"You ask hard questions, Alexander Cannard. Why didn't I leave? I believe I was curious to know what a wife says to her husband when she thinks no one else is listening. Never having been married, and being sensitive about it, I guess I wanted to eavesdrop on two long-term lovers. I apologize."

An image flashed in his mind. North Africa. Early 1962. Just before the Wing stopped reflexing there. One of the navigators and a teacher from the base school. Walking slowly hand-in-hand. He: married with new-born child. She: single, living overseas, searching. Two decent people who had met by happenstance. Walking for the last time.

"Your motives were pure or you wouldn't have called me," he said.

Flares stained the sky leaving their drifting smoke trails like silver tracks of snails seen in morning's dim light. Perhaps the VC were again trying to blow the Newport bridge. Maybe an ambush team had observed movement. Or an outpost had sighted a sampan gliding down the river.

Will my life be like this forever, he wondered. *Seeing suspicious lights or smelling strange odors that throw me back to this time and place. Am I sentenced always to remember, never to expunge?*

They approached the officers' club, heard the cacophony filtering through the walls, saw the tattered sandbags offering little more than visual protection. She pulled him to a stop.

"I've some cheese in my room. And crackers. And red wine. We could talk there. Would you like that?"

"Yes."

She led the way, hurrying as if afraid of being observed. They climbed the outside stairs to the second level of the frame dormitory and tip-toed along the covered porch leading to her doorway. Inside her room, a steel cot, wall locker, chest of drawers, straight chair, and Sanyo refrigerator left scarcely enough space for two people to stand. Wooden louvers covered the screened window and door, providing privacy while allowing air to circulate.

"Please take the chair," she said in scarcely more than a whisper. "I'll arrange the crackers and cheese while you open the wine."

Finishing her duties, she settled herself on the bed, tucking her legs in tightly and propping her back against the unpainted plasterboard wall with her pillow. He performed a perfunctory wine ceremony, filled her glass, then topped off his own.

"To better days," he said avoiding her eyes.

The wine's astringency neutralized the bitterness that had filled his mouth for the past hour. He sliced a bit of cheese, placed it on a cracker, and handed it to her. She waited until he had prepared one for himself.

They had finished the cheese and were on their second glass of wine when he pulled his chair closer. Having heard no other sounds from the adjacent rooms, he believed they were unoccupied. Still, when he spoke, he muted his voice.

"Something peculiar's going on at home, Monique. It started shortly after I got in-country. Merrilane wanted to stay busy while I was gone, so she took a job in the athletic department working on a summer program for children. I was happy for her, and tried to sound supportive in my letters. So as not to burden her, I led her to believe I was flying milkruns. I never confided my fears, the disenchantment I was feeling, the options I was beginning to consider for a life outside. Maybe if I'd have told her, things would be different now."

She sat watching him, nodding with animal understanding whenever he looked up from the floor seeking encouragement to continue.

"But maybe, even if I'd alluded to our leaving the service, she'd have missed my clues. Where my letters were long, daily, and superficial, hers were short, infrequent, and filled with an almost religious fervor about what she was doing. They were also full of Rod—Rodney Pike, her boss and a notorious skirt chaser."

She nodded; he continued.

"Then one day, I received a copy of an underground newspaper circulated at the Academy. The usual protest stuff about uncaring hierarchy, immoral war, all the rest of it. And vicious gossip about academy people: mostly sexual, mostly perverse. And cartoons. The cartoon on the back page was a gross representation of a pregnant woman. Her head was a photograph. And, the photograph, . . . it was my wife."

He had been mumbling to her left shower clog, which projected from beneath her cot. Expecting a reaction, he raised his eyes and realized she had not changed her position. Nothing moved except the single tear that trickled its silver trail like a dying flare down her left cheek.

"You're sure?" she asked.

"The photograph was grainy and her features were shadowed, but she has a characteristic hairdo. I'm positive."

"Can you account for how someone could have acquired her photograph?"

"I couldn't at the time, but each new letter contained some fact that ticked away in my subconscious like a terrorist's bomb. She wrote of the exciting coaches she worked with, of movers and shakers in the Springs, and—yes—even the solicitous cadets she met.

"I'd never considered her at risk before. Adultery happened to other men married to lesser women. I was too embarrassed, maybe even afraid, to raise the subject on R and R. But I managed to antagonize her with innuendo."

"Are you and your wife . . . sexually compatible?"

"From the start we never questioned our basic drives and our caring for each other. Sex has been the high point of our life together. For me at least.

"I thought she also treasured our love games, but now I suspect she's seen something different. Something where she calls the tune. Everything's turned upside down."

"What do you mean?"

He hesitated. She thought at first he was considering her question. But she realized from the way he cocked one ear that his concentration had been broken. She listened too, but heard only the usual nighttime sounds: a helicopter beating overhead, the peculiar whistling of a taxiing Hercules transport, two fighters lighting their afterburners on the take-off roll. He glanced at his watch, then continued.

"I used to think it was us against the world. All we had when we got married was our education and the promise of an air force job. Back then we talked all the time: how many children, what style of furniture, which car. Later, in SAC, we discussed career decisions and squadron politics—even infidelity and divorce which was epidemic. We thought we were immune.

"I shared my fears about not mastering the refueling technique. Even cried on her breast one night as the pressure of aborted tankers, impossible weather, and ever-changing instructors conspired against me. I deployed overseas often, but came home always to a honeymoon: candlelight dinners after the kids were down and Mateus Rosé—the sparkling kind you can hardly find anymore—ice cold from the bomb bay. So we got through the rough spots. A team they couldn't break up."

She nodded and took a slow sip from her glass.

"Then the war came. The longest we'd ever been apart was six weeks, and now we faced a year's separation. And the danger. It had been there before, but that was mostly mechanical. Something I could handle. And then, right before I left, Steinhoff from the chemistry department got killed on a night bombing run over the trail. His wife seemed to go completely mad. Seeing her like that, we both realized the dice were loaded against us. That's when I decided not to share Vietnam with Merrilane. What colossal stupidity . . . "

The shock wave punched the door off its hinges before the deafening sound and choking smoke enveloped them. Lights blinked out an instant later, but not before he saw terror in her eyes. He heard her whimpers, felt her brush beside him as she groped for the doorframe. Two more of the 122mm rockets exploded as the alert sirens warbled.

"Stay down!" he shouted. Grabbing blindly, he hooked his arm around her waist and pulled her into him as he would a child who had fallen off a boat dock. She fought like a rabid wildcat, slashing and snapping. He pinned her arms, managed to kick her feet sideways, and fell bodily on her. More rockets detonated close by. Concussions ripped through the narrow corridors compressing his nostrils and causing a high-pitched ringing in his ears. Screams and shouts answered each incoming round, yet missing were real shrieks of agony such as he heard from Wallingford.

Covering her trembling body, he began reassuring her in the dispassionate tone of a final controller guiding an anxious pilot. "Steady, steady. It's almost over. I'm here. They can't hurt you. Easy, easy. Nothing to fear. They're moving away. It's almost over. They won't come back. I'm here. I've got you, Merrilane. They can't get you."

She seemed to relax, actually to go limp beneath him. But her breathing remained rapid, and he could feel the furious beating of her heart.

"See, it's over now." The yelling had stopped. Then the hollow booms of artillery assaulted their ears, and she turned beneath him to clutch his body. "That's outgoing. It's all over now."

Still she clung, squirming and grappling until she felt his involuntary spasms and shoved him away. They shifted positions, so they leaned against the side of the bed. She moved closer to him, clasped her arm across his chest and tucked her head into his shoulder. He stroked her hair, inhaling her perfume, and realizing she was just a scared little girl all alone in the world.

Through the open doorway, he could see firemen in rubberized coats, floppy boots, and luminous helmets making their way along the littered porch, pounding on doors and checking for casualties. One poked his light into the room. "Anyone hurt," he yelled.

"No, thank you," Alex said as he shielded the light from her eyes.

"We were lucky this time," the man replied. "Have a nice evening."

"I'm sorry I was such a crybaby," she said in a child's voice without making an attempt to disengage. "I guess I was in a panic."

"You were fine. In fact, you were better than me. I just wanted someone to hold on to."

They both laughed, and he thought he felt the light brush of a little girl's lips on his cheek. "That was your baptism of fire, Monique."

"Do you really think they're gone?"

"I believe so. They usually hit and run."

"Will they be back tomorrow?"

"I doubt it. We've got ambush patrols all over. They're just trying to keep us off balance."

"They succeeded in my case."

"If you can hold out a few more days, Wootan'll be back to take care of you."

"There's nothing between us."

"I'm sorry," he said. "He's a good man. Wife died several years ago."

"He's bright and a gentleman. We're just good friends." He started to speak, but felt her fingers seal his lips.

"Please just listen. I fought you so violently because I'm not comfortable in a man's grasp. It goes a long way back. I don't know why I continue sitting with you this way. I guess because I'm still frightened; maybe because I don't consider you a threat. I feel comfortable with Adam for the same reason. He respects my wishes without asking questions." She lowered her hand.

"Vietnam has taught me, Monique, that threats come from the most unexpected directions."

CHAPTER THIRTY-FIVE

"**THANK YOU FOR SEEING ME,** General Safire."

"I'm always happy to see someone from the other side of the terrazzo, Frank. You're looking well."

"Thank you, General. I feel good. Even started running again." Safire advanced to shake hands and guide Harbinger to a chair beside an oval coffee table. Frank waited until the Commandant started to sit, then settled himself.

"May I offer you coffee?"

"No thank you, General. I'm trying to cut down. Can you imagine that after all these years?"

Safire laughed, running his fingers through his thick hair, a mannerism left over from his youth no amount of charm school could dispel. "Yes, I can. Don't broadcast it, but I'm doing the same. Quit cold turkey about two months ago, but the temptation after dinner's sometimes too great to resist."

The pleasantries over, Frank leaned closer to the boy-general, the role model brought in to impress the cadets with his youth, his rank, and his string of kills. Safire, unlike the model aircraft lining his bookcases, was full scale. He had been plucked from the Thud Wing at Korat to shore up the place after the second cheating scandal a year and a half past. Out of his element, he nevertheless learned quickly and was blessed with knowing his position was but an interim step on the ladder. He had grasped the value of team play during the air war in the north, depending on all supporting elements of the strike force to allow his boys to slip in with some chance of getting the job done. Arriving at the Academy, he had immediately tried to bridge the "terrazzo gap" by inviting the academic instructors into a closer relationship with the military training officers who worked for him. His plan for integrating faculty members into the cadet squadrons as "mentors" was working surprisingly well.

"General," Frank began tentatively, "how sure are you the cadet corps is clean?"

"Good God, Frank, don't tell me you know something I don't."

"I'm not sure of anything, and I haven't discussed this with anyone, not even the Dean."

"I appreciate that, Frank. If there's something brewing again, I'd like first crack at it. Is it cheating?"

"No, General, it's blatant sexual harassment."

"Does it involve your neighbor, Merrilane Cannard?"

"You're aware she's had harassing phone calls and prowlers at night?"

"No, Frank, but that eases my mind."

"Eases your mind! How can the harassment of the wife of an officer flying in Vietnam ease your mind?"

"Take it easy, Frank. Obviously you haven't seen our underground scandal sheet."

"I didn't know we had one."

Safire lifted his wiry frame from his chair, motioning for Frank to remain seated. "I keep them locked in my desk; I don't want the office staff to know I'm tracking this thing."

Returning to his seat with a manila folder, Safire spread two amateurish newsletters on the coffee table. "These are my private copies, enclosed in the classic plain brown wrapper and slipped under my door. Check the photographs."

"Oh, Christ, not Merrilane."

"Yes, I'm afraid so. The three in the most recent issue couldn't be more explicit, but it looks like her eyes are closed. Either asleep or drugged."

Frank rocked back and forth in his seat, supporting his sagging body by bracing his elbows on the arms of the chair. "Sweet Jesus, how could anyone print such trash? This would kill Alex."

"You don't think he knows? I'd bet the mind that concocted this filth was perverted enough to send him copies."

"Oh, Jesus. I can't believe our cadets would do such a thing. Especially to Alex. He loved them. Invited them to his house, played lacrosse with them, gave more after-hours help than anyone else in the department."

"Perverted, Frank. Someone's perverted. I mean real sick."

"What have you done about this, General?"

"If it were a SAM site, I'd put a package together and take it out. That's my line. But this is outside my experience, and it's potentially a lot more dangerous to the future of the Air Force than the whole Vietnam fiasco. If our cadets renounce the military virtues, we might as well contract our air force out to Lockheed. But I don't have to tell you that."

"No, you don't. This thing's a cancer more devastating to me than the one they cut from my chest. It'll metastasize and infect the entire corps if we don't get it."

"Finding the defective cell is the problem. We've got an insurgency right here in our own academy, and everybody wears the same uniform."

"How many do you think are involved?"

"Maybe just one. The summer issue, appearing when the cadet population was mostly freshmen trainees, suggests a First Classmen instructor may be the deviant. Probably someone missed during the previous cheating scandals."

"I assume the Superintendent's in the loop. Who else?"

"Dean, chief of security police, JAG, my deputy, and the liaison officers to both the cadet Honor and Ethics committees. That's all, except for undercover OSI agents."

"I'm relieved to know I'm not the only one concerned with this, General."

"Yes, it's a small club right now, and I hope it stays that way. We're working against time. If a First Classman's involved, we've got to nail him before he's commissioned in June. This is the Supe's absolute top priority. But you haven't told me how you got involved."

"As you know, Alex was a member of my department. He and Merrilane built a lovely house next to ours about two years ago. It's pretty isolated out there in the Black Forest, only three houses on the road. My wife cared for the Cannard children while Merrilane worked until recently with the athletic department."

"Yes, she did a splendid job. I even detailed a cadet or two to help out when she was in a bind."

"All I can think is someone was attracted to her and has set out systematically to harass her. She confided she's getting calls at all hours, and she's heard noises next to her bedroom window. She started burning lights all night and asked the Sheriff to patrol the road. Several nights ago, I thought I saw someone outside, so I've staked out the back yard since Sunday. Early this morning I accosted a prowler—big guy dressed all in black. When I yelled for him to freeze, he sat me on my rear—hard."

"I don't suppose you recognized him."

"No, but I've got a score to settle. I called security and asked them to note any incoming vehicles with cadet stickers until eight this morning. No luck."

"What you're telling me complicates the situation. A lewd underground newspaper is one thing; physical assault is another." Safire hesitated, running his hand through his hair. "Do you think there's any chance she's been entertaining cadets?"

"I wish I could take umbrage, General, but I'm losing my old-school notions regarding the collective virtue of women. In this case, however, I'd rule it out primarily because she's simply too busy working a new job in the Springs. In fact I sometimes feel Iris and I have inherited a second family."

"The head on that cartoon could have come from a number of available sources, but those three bedroom shots are another thing. Is Cannard the kind of man who'd be likely to take nude pictures of his wife that could have been found or stolen?"

"Let's face it, General, any man with an attractive wife would be tempted to record her beauty. But if these had been taken from the Cannard family archives, they would have been more tasteful. And if Alex had taken them, I guarantee they would have been artistically perfect. When you come right down to it, with the grainy affect and the harsh shadows, we can't be absolutely certain the woman is Merrilane. I think we have to give her the benefit of the doubt."

"I take your point, Frank. I'm just groping for leads." Safire glanced at his watch and started to rise. "Time's got away from us. I'm glad you brought this to me. I'll pass your information along to the OSI and keep you posted. Is there anything else I should know?"

"One thing, General." Frank paused at the door. "She's got a pistol, and I think she knows how to use it."

It wasn't until he entered the wide plaza separating the Commandant's domain from the academic building that Frank realized classes were changing. Surrounded by a swirling mass of cadets, looking like medieval monks in their hooded jackets, he wondered if secretly he envied them their youth. No, he realized, it would break his heart to graduate from this pinnacle only to come face to face with the apathy, lack of understanding, downright hate of at least fifty percent of the populace he'd sworn to protect.

Dejected, he wheeled the tiny Corvair out of the garage beneath Fairchild Hall and headed for the Officers' Club. Twisting around the sweeping curves and breathing the sparkling mountain air caused him to begin humming a tuneless fragment that transformed itself into the opening bars of *Itazuke Tower*. By the time he whipped into the Club's parking lot, he was singing the words and anticipating a leisurely European-length, two-hour meal. Unbuckling his seatbelt, an accessory recently mandated for private vehicles operated on military stations, he heard the throaty rumbling of a real sports car downshifting into the slot beside him. No mistaking Rod Pike's car or his driving style—frustrated fighter pilot.

"Hello, Rod," he shouted. "How's the old hammer hanging?"

"Never better, Frank. You dining alone?"

"Not any more."

Being slightly ahead of the luncheon crowd, Frank chose his favorite table overlooking the foothills of the Rampart Range. They discussed the Academy's disappointing basketball team, quarterback talent for next fall, and the dedication ceremony of the new field house.

The arrival of their entrees reminded Rod that subjects more important than sports prospects existed. Later, after overpowering Frank's weak resistance, Rod ordered coffee for both of them. Finally, leaning on his elbows and lowering his voice, he shifted their talk to women. "Ya gotta come down to the office, Frank. I want you to see the new crop of secretaries—talk about hunt 'n peckers."

"Sounds like fun; but with just one lung, I'm not interested in meeting anyone who might take my breath away."

"You sly old fox," Rod chuckled, "I don't know if I want you prowling around my hen house. No use giving myself competition. Speaking of competition, what's happening with that pretty little neighbor lady of yours? I haven't seen much of her since she hooked up with that bunch downtown."

"I was hoping you'd tell me. We rarely see her except when she's checking with Iris about the kids. She's working at least as hard as she worked for you, but now she's also got the commute."

"I made a big mistake letting her go, but I didn't have a lock on funding for her position, and I wouldn't have kept her from the chance of a lifetime even if I had."

"Is she as competent as the newspapers made her out to be?"

"I can honestly say that she's the finest manager I've seen in the last five years. Hands down. I told Helton—that's the guy she's working for—I told him she's got the instinct. She just takes a project and babies it like an ol' mother duck. Believe me, she always has her ducklings in line. I know colonels on the Air Staff who can't brief as well."

"I'm impressed to hear you talk that way about a woman. If you'll forgive me, you're usually recounting the sexual preferences of half the female population of Colorado Springs and Denver. Who knows, when you're in one of those towns, you're probably recounting your successes with air force wives."

"Come on, Frank. You know better than to listen to idle gossip. But I'll admit, somebody has to liven up this place. You fly boys have been known to chase a skirt from time to time. But around these cadets, any bluesuiter who can't keep his pants zipped gets a one-way ticket to a radar site on the arctic circle."

"You're right, Rod, and I hope it stays that way."

"To tell the truth, I put some heavy moves on her in the beginning. Evidently she was still an old-fashioned girl back then. But new meat doesn't last long when it's put it on display. Not if it's as choice as hers is reputed to be."

"Reputed to be? Who says so?"

"Jeez, Frank. Are all you academics completely out of it? She's the talk of the locker room. Coaches, AOCs, . . . even cadets."

"You're not serious. What are you saying?"

"Haven't you seen *The Falcon Code*? It's all over the campus. The cadets must be lining up to ball her."

"That can't be true. The idea's obscene! It's physically impossible with the hours she's working."

"Damn, Frank, if Shakespeare were around, he'd swear 'thou dost protest too much.' I'm just telling you what's going on under your nose. I was torqued off too when I saw the cartoon with her head pasted on. But this last issue had a photo spread on her that belonged in the pages of *Hustler*."

"Oh, that poor girl."

"Look, Frank, I may be a pig to say this since she pulled my fat out of the fire when I needed her, but I know for a fact she's changed her appearance and her operating style. Something's happened. Whatever it is, it appears to be agreeing with her. I might give her another go myself. After all, twenty-five hundred cadets can't be wrong."

"Rod, you're a big bullshitter, but I like you. Everybody likes you. But I'm telling you as God is my witness. If you lay a hand on that girl, I'll blow your fucking brains out!"

CHAPTER THIRTY-SIX

THE MORNING AFTER HIS RETURN from Pleiku, Alex represented his office at the Director of Operation's staff meeting. The DO was another tall, thin, fighter pilot almost indistinguishable from others of the breed except for the two stars on each side of his shirt collar and a forehead furrowed by frustration's bitter acid. He recited estimates of infiltration tonnage sky-rocketing since LBJ's bombing halt then punctuated his conclusions with photographs of Eastern Bloc freighters lying like bulging cornucopias in Haiphong harbor, vehicles streaming down the Ho Chi Minh trail, and missile sites mushrooming around Hanoi and Haiphong.

Almost five years separated the DO's meeting from the last intelligence briefing Alex had experienced in SAC. On occasion back then, someone would slip a girlie photo among the flow of repetitious slides as an attention getter. But he was unprepared for the attractive woman's face that flashed on the screen as the DO's finale. Nevertheless he recognized beneath her steel helmet the high cheek bones, flashing eyes, and self-conscious smile as she posed crewing the enemy's anti-aircraft gun.

Afterwards he finished his correspondence, ate a sandwich at his desk, and composed his trip report. As the afternoon sun overpowered the air conditioner, turning the office into an oven with a runaway thermostat and seemingly stagnating time, he began to speculate on the property of minutes which allowed them to speed up or slow down. Over a hot target, when integrating himself into the ballet of darting forward air controller, leaping fighters, and drifting flares, he seemed to perform outside time, to labor within an orchestrated background of radio chatter piped directly into his brain. The passage of time in those cases was documented later by a count certifying the expenditure of finite materiel—tracer rounds and flare canisters—further verified by depleted fuel gauges confirming something had indeed happened. He wondered what became of the slippage, of those unaccounted moments. Did they remain suspended in the subconscious, to surface from time to time in the future in precise and terrifying detail?

He was deep in thought when the door burst open. Startled, he rose to his feet as he recognized his nemesis, Lt. Colonel Gaffney, and the Big Gorilla himself, Colonel Trilling.

"What's this latest trick you're trying to pull, Cannard?" The colonel's voice boomed against the row of wall lockers the way concussions from B-52 strikes frequently did. Alex felt his gonads shrivel, tasted tainted meat along the roof of his mouth, and warmed to spurting adrenalin. He stepped from behind his desk to confront the intrusion.

"Yeah, Cannard," Gaffney was so close to the colonel Alex thought perhaps their arrival had inflicted him with double vision, "haven't you disrupted us enough with your damned yammering for a tactics manual? Now you're screwing with the orbit points we've lived with for a year and a half."

Ignoring Gaffney, Alex crossed to the colonel extending his hand. "Good to see you again, sir. I trust you received the draft copy of our manual. General Howerton got the other."

Wootan appeared in Alex's peripheral vision standing behind the two visitors.

"Yes, I got the manuscript. It's buried under a ton of paper."

"Too bad, sir. The general sent me an "attaboy" I've already indorsed to the Wing."

"That's good of you, Cannard. I'm so damned busy these days, I rarely have time for the niceties."

"He directed me to send the draft to our training people in the States and gave us a week's suspense to get a coordinated final to the printer. He wants personal copies for every Spooky pilot and forward air controller. Info copies for all fighter and helicopter gunship units."

"Major Hoskins told me we had a good product. Should have produced it long ago, but it fell between the cracks."

"Good help's hard to find, Colonel. That's probably why you didn't get the full story on the orbit points."

"Look, Cannard," the veins in Gaffney's neck stood out like overinflated bicycle tubes. "I've put up with enough of your fucking innuendo."

"Good afternoon, Gentlemen." Wootan's rasping whisper startled Gaffney. "We're delighted you've paid us a visit, but we share space with a group of civilians, and we try to keep our language appropriate in tone and volume."

"Colonel Trilling," Alex said, "may I present my boss, Lieutenant Colonel Wootan."

"Good to meet you, Wootan." Trilling flushed, realizing his inexcusable blunder in military protocol. "I should have spoken to you about this orbit matter first."

"No harm done, Colonel. Would you like coffee?"

"No, thank you. We don't have much time, but I'd like to know why you recommended a change in the orbit of our Saigon patrol. Maybe," he glanced at Gaffney, "I haven't been given the big picture."

"Very simple, Colonel," Wootan said. "At one time Spooky was kingpin of Saigon's rocket defense, but now computer-directed artillery's our weapon of choice. Meanwhile more frequent attacks on Cambodian border outposts urgently require Spooky's protection. Instead of diverting the Saigon patrol, however, policy dictates scrambling the alert bird out of Bien Hoa. Moving our patrol orbit north to Dau Tieng and dispatching the airborne gunship will provide air support within ten minutes—a half-hour improvement in current response time."

"Sounds plausible, Wootan. I'm flying the Saigon patrol tonight to check it out. If you'll excuse us, we'll let you get on with your work. Unless I call you tomorrow, you've got our full cooperation."

As the two visitors left, Gaffney was not quite so close in trail.

"Alex," Wootan's tone detracted from the triumph of the moment, "come in and let's chat. The rest of you get back to work."

Alex slid into the chair beside Wootan's desk. "Thanks, boss, for bailing me out, but I could've handled those fucking bastards."

"Alex," Wootan said so hushed he had to lean forward to hear. "You're losing what differentiated you, and it worries me. Few pilots manage to stay humble. We seem to train it out of them in the air and talk it out of them at the bar. But the outstanding generals I've known have been humble men. Any number of air force officers might have labeled those two as you did. But when you came to work for me five months ago, you wouldn't."

He struggled to answer.

"I should have questioned why you've grown so agitated; but after losing Tiny and SugarFox, I needed you to burn the candle at both ends. Yet each time you returned from a trip, I could see a piece of the Alex I knew had been chipped away and a chunk of the stereotype slapped in its place. I thought you were just getting short; but instead of weaning yourself, you accelerated your pace. Pressing, I've been told. Dropping under the cloud deck and into the small arms envelope."

Wooten paused.

"You're a cinch for colonel and maybe for general if you don't get crossways with a fair-haired boy like Trilling. But I'll be damned if I want to see any more insensitive misanthropes getting ahead."

Woziniac came to the door with a sheaf of messages but retreated when he saw the major sitting bent over, staring at the floor.

"Didn't Monique tell you?"

"Tell me what?"

"I got a 'Dear John.' Not your average letter, mind you, but a recording! Probably the first soldier in history to get a Dear John tape. And when I played it after hours here in the office, she was next door and heard the whole damn thing. I'm really surprised she didn't tell you. Almost restores my faith in women."

"I'm sorry, Alex, but you're not unique. It's tough and lonely for service wives. Speaking as one previously short in the understanding department, all the merit badges you pick up along the way can't match the loss of a good woman."

"I appreciate your interest, sir. I know the last few words don't come easy, but there's lots I won't understand until I'm alone with her. Maybe not even then. It's more than just another man. I've tried to put it out of my mind, but my file of things too painful to remember is getting pretty full, and I'm just holding on until someone tells me the Freedom Bird's waiting."

CHAPTER THIRTY-SEVEN

ALEX COULD NOT REFUSE to attend his own farewell party, but memories of a previous visit to the raucous club owned by Vietnamese air force officers dampened his spirits. He dreaded a replay of his introduction some five months past to a beer-guzzling clientele, insipid food, and disheveled soldiers groping perfumed women to the beat of "The Ballad of the Green Berets."

"We wanted to give you a reminder of what you've been fighting for," Arnie Bridgewater yelled over the primordial rhythm of the music. As they squeezed into the packed bar, a sweating youth grabbed with both hands the head of the girl entwined around his chest and began kissing her lips—furiously working, Alex thought, with all the tenderness of a plumber's apprentice suctioning a clogged drain.

"Thanks, pal," Alex shouted back. "I know what I've been fighting for, and it leaves tomorrow at zero nine hundred."

The sleek hostess beckoned the group, then advanced through the crowd toward a table in an alcove away from the central barroom. A one-armed man with a horribly scarred face was sweeping the glasses, butts, and cans from the table onto a tray. *Surprised they keep him around*, Alex thought, *but who looks at death when the Dragon Lady's on display?*

The hostess' slim body showcased a high-collared dress of shimmering crimson silk, skirt deeply slit on each side. Dangling jade earrings, dark fashion glasses, and thick lipstick completed her costume. She appeared to be quality merchandise, and Alex tried to imagine her face stripped of the deep layer of cosmetics. He decided he liked her style, not particularly her clothing but the confident way she handled herself. No one had attempted to fondle her as she opened a path; rather the jostling men had given way, appearing to fall as common-ers to the passage of royalty.

Excepting Glenn, who had left three days previously to fly missions out of Danang, Alex was not close to any of his mates. He had accepted their invitation for what it was, the fulfill-ment of a social obligation rather than an expression of any special esteem they might have held for him. Wootan avoided these bashes, preferring instead to invite the lucky man to meet him afterwards for dinner at the club.

"What did you learn in the last twelve months?" The ques-tion came from the newest member of the office, O. W. Mulloy, the gigantic C-123 transport pilot who seemed as uncomfort-able in the stifling environment as Alex. Not known for sparkling conversation, O. W. had, nevertheless, asked the only question that might give meaning to the event. What did he expect? Enlightenment? Or simply the veteran's technique that might protect him from tracers lacing the final approach of dis-puted jungle airstrips?

The Black Labels arrived: frosty, expected, and appropriate. Alex took a long drink, trying in his mind to form a chain of meaningful words to answer O. W.'s question. But as he re-turned his beer to the table, he discerned O.W. in deep conversation with Fishburn, the loudmouth who had replaced Tiny Temple. Wootan had not filled SugarFox's slot, saying he had no need of a Thud pilot since the bombing north had stopped. Alex suspected, however, that he still hoped the manic aviator would turn up with tales of having parachuted into a North Vietnamese bordello.

"How about a little going-away present from the boys, Alex," Bridgie was yelling again. "Pick out any of these little brown dollies, and she's yours to sneak home in your bag. Tell your wife she's a household robot that does tricks for pennies a day." Alex noticed O. W. didn't join the general laughter, re-garding instead his ebony hand clamped firmly around his drink.

Another round of Black Labels appeared. Alex still nursed his first. He intended to be alert when he dined with Wootan.

Monique would probably be included, and he wanted her to remember him as a gentleman.

"Go easy on Alex, you guys," O. W. yelled. "Can't you see he's a straight arrow to the end."

Alex sipped his beer. "And this is the end. If I never get west of San Francisco again, it'll be too soon."

"Spoken like a true SAC weenie," Bridgewater retorted. "Flying around the flag pole like a U-control model with the wires manipulated from Omaha." Alex noticed even the trash hauler joined the fighter jocks in derisive laughter. "What's your wife think of leaving God's Country and going to the Louisiana swamps?"

"Get off his back," Fishburn screamed. "Any SAC base is a woman's paradise; their men get locked in the alert quarters for seven straight days every other week and fly twenty-four-hour missions the rest of the time. So SAC ladies don't ever worry about getting chased around the bedroom day and night like true fighter pilots' wives."

"Come on, Fishy," Alex spoke so quietly the circle drew itself tighter to hear. "There's never been a true fighter pilot's wife."

The huddle exploded backward as Fishburn sputtered.

"That'll teach you to mess with 'Skyking,'" O. W. howled. "He'll zap you with one of his electronic thunderbolts, and you'll have to go back to flying by the seat of your pants."

"What's this 'Skyking' stuff? The only Skykings are fighter pilots."

"Haven't you ever heard the voice of God on the high frequencies, Bridgie? Periodically all day and night 'SKYKING, SKYKING, Do not answer! Do not answer!' And then He spouts a long string of code only the elect can understand. And He repeats it twice, so they don't forget. Then He commands 'em again not to answer. He's some dude, that SAC God. He don't fool with a Bible; He just blasts His commandments out on the airwaves whenever He takes a notion. And He don't want back talk: 'DO NOT ANSWER. DO NOT ANSWER.'"

"Man, I'm impressed." Fishburn's eyes brightened. "A real Old Testament God. Whatta I have to do to join, Alex? I'm already circumcised."

"Sorry, Fishy. When a SAC guy screws up, he's banished to live with fighter pilots. Your precious Tactical Air Command is kinda like Hell. No way can anyone in TAC be saved."

"That's intriguing religion," Fishburn said. "But you got one thing wrong. TAC's only Purgatory. Hell's right here."

"Roger that, my friend," Alex rose from his seat. "And I'm ascending to a higher ring. The colonel's meeting me at the O Club for his traditional going away dinner. Anyone leaving now?"

"Naw, we'll stay awhile and finish another round. Who knows, we might even feel lucky and decide to eat here."

"No long goodbys." Alex began shaking the outstretched hands.

"Say, man," O. W. said as he took his turn. "What goes on at that last dinner with Wootan?"

"Don't know for sure. I've heard he tells how we rate as officers, the kind of stuff generals write on confidential effectiveness reports."

"Man, I don't know that I want to hear what Wootan thinks of me. I got a feelin' he hits close to the quick."

Happy for an excuse to leave, even if it required having his soul probed by Wootan, Alex broke into a run as he fled the accursed place. Sweating profusely he paused at the entrance of the club's dining room in hopes of spotting Monique's dark hair and inviting smile. Instead he saw only Wootan sitting alone at the table where the three of them had first gathered.

"Hope I haven't kept you waiting, Colonel."

"No, Alex, I'm happy you managed to break away at all. Maybe it's not so smart to ask a man to dine with his boss the last night he's in-country. But it's my way of insuring he'll be in shape to make the morning departure—and maybe to remember me and some of the lessons I've tried to teach him."

A serious-faced youth, dressed in a white coat with sleeves too long, brought a basket of hard crusted French rolls. After offering them first to Wootan and then to Alex, he produced a bottle of Pinot Noir, 1962. Wootan examined the label, nodded, then unhurriedly went through the wine ritual.

After they had tasted the bread, Wootan raised his glass to eye level and fixed his gaze on Alex. "To your resurrection." They touched glasses and drank.

"I understand, sir, you've postponed your own rebirth by extending for six months."

"Yes, I've some unfinished business."

The waiter brought a salad of crisp lettuce and tomatoes. Fresh greens always meant the shuttle flight from Delat had arrived.

"I've found it interesting," Wootan said moving away from any consideration of the motives behind his extension, "to reflect upon how officers accept headquarters duty. Some arrive dragging their feet, complaining they were Shanghaied. A portion of those people choose to scurry back to their hooches after each day's work, cook their meals on a hot plate, and spend their evenings watching re-runs on their Sony portables. Others say, 'What the Hell, I might as well enjoy it.' And they act like schoolboys on holiday, drinking, carousing, generally reverting back to their youthful lifestyles.

"A second category come with the idea it's just another remote tour. They figure the war's out in the boondocks and the bases are reasonably secure. So they go into automatic drive, asking someone to wake them when it's over."

Alex shifted uncomfortably detecting something of his own recent behavior. But his boss didn't seem to notice.

"Still others hit the ground running toward the goal of getting their tickets punched. They've got the whole tour planned to provide maximum visibility and minimum exposure.

"Then there's some, a goodly number actually, who arrive with a dedication to the cause of Vietnamese freedom. These people also separate into groups. A few keep their dedication.

Some rotate at their scheduled time; some extend; some go home in boxes. Unfortunately more and more of the original true believers are beginning to flame out. They wise up, come to believe they've been misled into resisting the nationalistic striving of the Vietnamese people."

The waiter materialized beside the table impassively offering a huge oval plate holding a marvelous Chateaubriand surrounded by potatoes and fresh vegetables. Patrons at nearby tables stared in disbelief.

"I can't believe that tenderloin, sir." Alex raised his glass. "Can't believe you did this just for me."

"You're one of my people. Enjoy this last supper in Vietnam." They ate in silence for a long time, savoring the succulent meat and the tart accompaniment of wine.

"At the risk of shattering the illusion, Colonel, might I ask where you placed me?"

"As you know, Jim Hubbard fire walled your effectiveness report when you left the Spookies. He justified it with specifics—number of combat sorties, rounds fired, flares expended, additional duties performed. He named names, places that count to anyone who knows what's happened here. Kontum, Tay Ninh, the Parrot's Beak, the Fish Hook, Fire Base Barbara, Nui Bau Dien. He referred to the commendations you received from three FACs and the telephone calls he'd had from grunts you supported. When he told me he was sending an exceptional man, that was good enough for me."

Wootan topped off their glasses and continued. "I found you to be one of the finest officers I'd seen: spontaneous, energetic, guileless. You accepted your fellow officers as comrades and helpers, not as competitors to be cut out of the pattern. That's an unusual trait, especially among the other SAC officers I've known."

"What you're saying is flattering, Colonel, but you're putting it in the past tense."

"That's correct because that Alex is dead. He was wounded in Hawaii during the second week of November and died sometime in early January. Whether he can be resurrected is moot. His spirit's somewhere out in Limbo while his body continues to perform its military duties in a commendable, some might say, an extraordinary manner. But that spiritless, humorless, sometimes spiteful body is not the one I inherited from Jim Hubbard, and it bothers me because it happened when you were my responsibility. Lately you've adopted a calculating manner of dealing with people that allows no leeway for human interpretation. You've lost the spark, Alex, your optimistic belief in man's basic goodness. It was responsible not only for your being a hesitant killer, but also for your performance as a sensitive leader who got people to perform better than they were accustomed.

"The paradox is that when you go back into the sterile, by-the-book routine of SAC, you'll do well. You'll become their hatchet man. And you'll do it with such style that the youngsters will think that's the way to operate, the preferred way, maybe the only way. In the process you'll not only have furthered the computer-generated, mechanistic way of committing and employing military forces, but you'll also have contributed to the ruination of a generation of follow-on officers and to the loss of what makes the United States worth fighting for—a person's freedom to do any job the most efficient, most creative, most enjoyable way."

Alex toyed with a piece of carrot, unable to speak. His head drooped lifelessly, but Wootan could still see his twitching eye lids and clinched lips. "Looks like you've got a pipeline into my mind, sir. You're telling me everything I've told myself for some time now."

The youth returned with a covered pot of coffee.

"How much of this did you put in writing?"

"Only the good things. Even in your present state, you're unquestionably fit for promotion to lieutenant colonel. If I were to put all of my analysis on paper, SAC would jump you to Brigadier tomorrow."

"I wish we'd have had this conversation earlier, Colonel. The old Alex needed the encouragement. He used to get pretty despondent that his leadership style wasn't even recognized, much less appreciated."

"Tell me, when you handled Gaffney on the phone and later in the office, was that the old Alex or the new?"

"I think that was still the old Alex. He may have been a nice guy, but he wouldn't have let the toads have their way."

"That's interesting. You're suggesting it's possible for competent, nice people to eat nasty guys for breakfast?"

"You already knew that, sir. Anyway it's good that Glenn did well. He's more than competent, and he's a nice guy too."

"Maybe there's hope. Your metamorphosis isn't complete or you'd have slammed Glenn instead of complimenting him. But why bring up his name?"

Alex cast his eyes around wildly. "It's become common knowledge there's a crackdown on halo effect, so I naturally assumed he'll get your top rating."

"Assumptions can get you killed. You're a pilot; you ought to know that. But you're correct about effectiveness reports. Promotion boards can't function if everyone's rated minimum magnificent. In your case, despite the flaws in the character of the new Alex, your performance has still been superior to most staff officers I've seen."

"That's a surprise, Colonel. I hope I'm worthy of it."

"You're worthy for the time being, but I seriously recommend you get your house in order."

"I've got some pretty serious problems at home, sir. I don't even know what they are completely, who's at fault, or even who all the players are."

"Just keep your head, and follow your instincts. Don't be too judgmental or inflexible. You've seen what that's cost us over here."

"I appreciate your arranging this supper, Colonel. I'm glad it was private although I'd hoped to see Monique before I left."

"She's waiting for you in her room. I told her I wanted to see you in confidence. She knows it's 'man-talk' as she calls it, but she wants to say goodby. And I think she'd like some privacy, too."

Wootan rose from his chair and offered his hand. "Remember what I've told you. Perhaps our paths will cross someday. Let's hope in more pleasant surroundings."

Outside the club Alex turned left toward the dormitory area. He found Monique's building, climbed the outside stairway tentatively, but then walked with positive steps toward her room. He could see downcast light slanting through the louvered window. She opened the door before he could knock.

"Hello, Alex," she was back lighted, her face in shadow, hair haloed. "I hope I don't attract the rockets on your last night in Saigon.

"I wouldn't mind." They stood close to each other whispering because of the lateness of the night and the closeness of others in neighboring rooms. He leaned forward and kissed the top of her forehead. "Could we walk?" he asked.

They strolled, hand-in-hand, perhaps a hundred yards when he spotted a bench beside an encrusted barbecue grill in a small patio. They sat down, still holding hands, facing each other.

"I've missed seeing you, Monique."

"I'm glad to know that."

"I'm embarrassed. Ashamed might be a better word."

"Why ashamed, Alex?"

"Because I didn't have the strength of character to see you after the rocket attack, even though I knew you probably needed a friend just as much as I did."

"I did; still do as a matter of fact. But I read the danger signals too. So I understood why you avoided me."

"It's been the most mixed up period in my life. I think maybe at times I've had a death wish. Wootan called me on it once. Death would have been such a simple answer. Kids would have had a medal and pictures of a never-aging father. Merrilane would have been free to do as she pleased."

"Hush," she once again placed the fingers of her right hand against his lips. "That's nonsense, and I won't listen to it."

"You're right, non-sense: the sense of being non, nothing, disbursed as free atoms and molecules doing whatever atoms and molecules do without my having to worry about it or about anyone's feelings or welfare. I've thought a lot lately about the economy of taking a tracer in a fuel tank. One moment you're there, king of the hill throwing everyone else off, and the next you're just some free-spinning collection of basic elements. The only thing bad is seven men would have been spinning around me, and I didn't want that to happen. I don't want one single creature—no man, no elephant, no tiger, no snake—nothing to ever be killed in my name again."

"Alex," her head was upturned in the darkness and close, "you mustn't let yourself think like that. The world's too short of good people."

"I know, Monique. I'm an historian too. It's always been short of good people. They get ground down when they're over-extended and when the systems and codes they depended upon are depleted. What you could once put your trust in is getting stripped away. Everything's being eroded and defoliated: rice paddies, jungle, tradition, courtesy, trust—love."

"Alex, listen to me." He could feel her firm breast against his arm, the warmth of her thigh against his own. "Soon you'll be home. You can listen to Merrilane, console her, and ease her growing pains." Her words were rushing, impassioned like the summation of an enthusiastic professor after the bell had sounded. "You have the capacity to do that—and to build a new life together."

"No," he said, "it won't be like that. My training won't allow it. The historian in me will keep going back to the past probing the blank spots for meaning. My pilot side will analyze the wreckage to find out what caused the failure. My ethnic heritage simply won't let me write off an undeserved Dear John without a reckoning. Just like my soldier's nature will never accept an excuse for the way this war's been misdirected."

"Your wife's insane to throw away the future she has with you."

"That's easy for you to say since you have everything she thinks she needs: professional standing, managerial expertise, independence."

"I'd trade her in a moment, just to experience tenderness from a man who loves me so much he avoids other women who might compromise that love. And to have children call me 'Mother.' I've gained the recognition you mention because I couldn't have what my nature cried for. And, as your pilot friends say, 'it sucks.' I'd hoped this adventure would open doors for me. I'm tired of faculty committees splitting hairs as if they believed the administration would consider their deliberations. I'm tired of sending out papers to journals to be ignored for months only to come back with inane comments demanding revision. I'm tired of being alone without one single confidant I can whisper my dreams to."

"What about Wootan? It's easy to see how he feels about you."

The light from a passing truck bounded off a wall and danced in the tear tracks on her cheeks. He raised his hands to cup her face as he stroked away the moisture with his thumbs.

"Don't fret, dear man, I'm under control. I'm teary because one of the few decent men I've known is at risk." Her voice broke. "And because I have feelings of uncontrollable revulsion when another decent man touches me. Your holding me during the rocket attack was the first time I've let a man control me since I was a child?"

"Sounds like we both need professional help."

"I tried it once, just after graduate school, but didn't play fair with my therapist. As I got older, and my career fell into place, I thought maybe I was destined to live alone. You made me question that belief, and now you're leaving."

"Oh, Christ, Monique. I didn't . . ."

"Please let me finish. I feel closer to you, Alex, than any other man because you covered me with your body when rockets were falling. Afterward you held me close and stroked my hair, and then you left me. If you'd been planning a seduction—if anyone goes to the trouble of doing such an antiquated thing anymore—you couldn't have prepared it any better. You've had me lying awake at night thinking about the feel of your body on mine. And now you're leaving, and we almost missed saying goodby."

"So typical," he said. "Maybe there's only two or three people in the world we're ever fully comfortable with, and we let life separate us. Wootan doesn't. You know, of course, he's extended so he can be with you."

"Yes. But I asked him not to. I'm not committed to him."

"Unfortunately I am. To him and to Merrilane. You think I acted courageously during the rocket attack? That was instinct, male protecting female. But Wootan made a calculated decision. He's risking his life to be close to a woman he's not even sleeping with. If you can't understand what that means, you really do need a therapist. Somebody dispassionate, not a guy like me who'd be exploiting you to solve his own disconnects."

Monique stood, drawing him up with her, and led him back to her door. Once there, she kissed his hands and stepped inside.

CHAPTER THIRTY-EIGHT

SOME BEGAN CHEERING as the aircraft rotated into the take-off attitude, but Alex waited until he felt the last tremble of the gear rising cleanly from the runway. Then he added his own voice to the roar filling the cabin. The deafening noise, relieved grins, and nudges from his seatmate celebrated a phase of life dropping behind just as the details of Tan Son Nhut and the surrounding countryside merged into a gray haze. The chartered Pan American 707 had scarcely cleared the field boundaries when smiling stewardesses, their white blouses unbuttoned perhaps an extra notch or two, came rushing down the aisle dispensing linen towels so cold they had to be individually pulled from the frozen stack.

Scrubbing furiously, he scraped a layer of accumulated grime, frustration, and fear from his weathered face. He was safely away from Vietnam, never to return. On his way to the world, back to Merrilane and life just as he remembered it.

He had chosen a window seat not for the view, but to isolate himself while he tried to sort out his feelings and develop his options. *Got to put this on the front burner. No tactics manuals, no orbit patterns, no screaming for air support. Got to line up my priorities. Put Kim and Jeffrey at the top.*

His mind broke lock, running far out to where fluffs of cumulus were building on the coast near Vung Tau. He studied the billowing vapor, seeing for the first time in a year the clouds not as obstacles complicating his mission but as a significant portion of nature's beauty. He looked for shapes or signs, perhaps for smiling children with bountiful hair. Instead he visualized the voluptuous curves of a woman's body reclining indolently. With difficulty he pulled his eyes away from her massive breasts, scanned the aircraft's wing and gently swaying engine pods, then drew them back into the cabin.

For some time he analyzed the pattern of fabric on the seatback in front of him, then he began to consider his situation: *At the academy I neglected the family. Always the patient teacher at work, but only a tired and short-tempered boarder at home. Three years of opportunity produced a Commendation Medal, a battered lacrosse stick, and a collection of pornographic images printed by the same cadets I broke my back for. But this past year provided the perpetual applause of colored ribbons to document my worth: Two Distinguished Flying Crosses, a Bronze Star, Vietnamese Cross of Gallantry, Air Medal with a bunch of clusters. Yet coiled among them, like a fanciful-appearing serpent concealed by their vivid colors, lies the echo of a doomed man forever empowered to slither into my thoughts.*

What if I combine the last four years, maybe add the one in grad school, and total the ledger. What's the sum? An understanding of history, knowledge I've done my duty, awareness the meek will get beat out of their inheritance, and heartache canceling any possible gain.

Depressed by the monologue's tone, he pulled the in-flight magazine from its pouch and began riffling the right-hand corner of its pages as he had done the *Big Little Books* of his childhood, hoping to see an animated vision of his future. He flipped through the magazine twice then replaced it and went back to his musings.

Got to dope it out scientifically—jam the scraps of information, speculations, and passions into a test tube and distill the truth. Use facts, assumptions, and criteria to find a solution. But most likely it'll be wrong because its light on facts.

FACT: An Academy underground newspaper printed nude pictures of a woman who resembles my wife. FACT: Someone sent me a copy. FACT: Merrilane worked for Rod Pike, a dedicated cocksman, in the athletic department. FACT: She performed spectactularly. FACT: She's "on the ground floor" of a new sports enterprise. FACT: She wants out of the marriage. FACT: Ordered to SAC, it's too late to resign. FACT: I love my children. FACT: I love my wife . . . or is that only an assumption?

CRITERIA: A solution must satisfy the air force, protect the children, and . . . pacify my wife.

ASSUMPTION: She's the woman in the pictures. ASSUMPTION: She's unfaithful. ASSUMPTION: She's involved with cadets or men connected with her job . . . but her sins are insignificant compared to mine. Stop! Imagination's not part of the scientific method! She hasn't killed anyone . . . except perhaps me.

What's my game here? Am I ready to crucify her just to claim the moral high ground? Or am I backing off my manhood and letting some son of a bitch overrun my nest?

"Excuse me, sir," the blond stewardess stretched to offer a tray. "You must be doing some powerful thinking."

Not powerful enough. I need a handbook with emergency procedures to stabilize emotional problems. Got to find her frequency, moving up or down from Jack Benny's age till our voices meet to coordinate our defenses. Stop! Get back to the method.

POSSIBLE SOLUTION: Dangle the perks of a wing commander's wife—best quarters, top hostess, ticket into downtown society. Praise Washington's opportunities for a bright staff officer and flashy wife. Show her the carrots—a NATO tour with travel all over Europe. Then hit her with the stick. POSSIBLE SOLUTION: Same as the first, but no demands. Sell what's in it for her. She'd cut a wider swath in Washington and Europe than in Colorado Springs. POSSIBLE SOLUTION: Promise domestic help so she can go to school or start a business. POSSIBLE SOLUTION: Agree to a separation during B-Fifty-two training. Aim for reconciliation before the move to Louisiana. POSSIBLE SOLUTION: Worse case, demand a clean break—a divorce with her losing the kids. If she wants to play hardball, jam the bat down her throat.

The army lieutenant seated to his left convulsed violently against his seatbelt, eyes darting like BBs in a child's hand puzzle.

"Still back there?"

"Yeah, . . . I guess so, Major." He rummaged in the seat pocket as if to find something to read. "I've had trouble sleeping lately."

Reverting to his analysis, he did not like where the options were taking him. *All solutions would keep me out of Leavenworth. Staying together gives the children their best shot. Or is a clean break better? Anything destroying their mother's image would be catastrophic. Better they think their father a bastard than their mother a slut.*

What if I slap her face first thing and start shouting? Get serious! These aren't Vietnamese peasants being resettled. She stayed with you when other SAC wives baled out.

What if I could record all this turmoil? Straight from my mind without worrying about the grammar or sweating the logical inconsistencies. Then provide a headset and ask her to play the tape. Why not instead fashion a phone patch to let her eavesdrop directly on the percolating ideas and thoughts racing through the kinky passages inside my head?

What if, when we're close and loving in the night, we could actually merge not only our bodies but also our brains, so that we became whole again like the mythical Titans? Instead of just the raging beast with two backs, we'd become a single-minded giant, and she could gauge the depths of my love, share the experiences I can't verbalize, and neutralize the jealousy I feel when I think of her being possessed by someone else.

And in the merging process, would I find a critical defect in her chemistry that allows ambition to flood her brain wiping out her sense of duty and inflaming her passion for self-gratification?

He closed his eyes, expelling as he did so a violent, piercing groan. He pushed against his seatbelt and thrashed his head from side to side. The lieutenant was looking at him when he revived. "Still back there, Major?"

"No, buddy . . ." he regarded him blankly, then nodded his head forward. "Up there."

CHAPTER THIRTY-NINE

ALEX NEVER CHOSE a recommended action. His mind refused to focus long before they dropped into Guam for refueling. At Hawaii he waited on the airport's observation deck with a breeze washing bitter memories across his face. With a fresh crew, more fuel, beverages, food, and the nauseatingly sweet smell of disinfectant permeating the cabin, the 707 again lifted off for the final leg into Travis Air Force Base. Once on the ground, the passengers filed out, scarcely acknowledging the bright smiles and "Welcome Home" greetings from their stewardesses clustered in the doorway. They should have paid more attention; it was the only welcome they got.

An hour and ten minutes later, he was aboard a scruffy military bus, the same model that plied between Tan Son Nhut and downtown Saigon except no wire screening covered the windows to deflect grenades. They jolted into the sunset toward the San Francisco International Airport. The freeway was packed with rushing automobiles, all with their windows rolled up, most with but a single occupant staring straight ahead.

At the ticket counter, he found the earliest flight to Denver departed in the morning at zero seven thirty with a connection to Peterson Field. Disappointed at having to spend the night, he bought his ticket, checked one of his bags, and called Holiday Inn for a pickup. In his room, he stripped to the waist, turned the air conditioner full cold, and rinsed his face in order to be alert when he talked to Merrilane. Then he sat down on the bed, checked the number in his notebook, and dialed home.

"Darling," he said tenderly, "I'm in San Francisco, be home in the morning. I love you desperately." The phone rang for the fourth time. He changed his tone, trying to sound more conciliatory, and spoke the lines again. Still the phone rang. *Maybe they ducked out to get something to eat. Might be at Frank's.* "I'll give him a call," he muttered.

"Good evening, Colonel. This is your neighbor trying to locate his wife and kids! . . . San Francisco airport. Can't get out until early tomorrow . . . I'm fine. Lost my baby fat, but really feel great . . . She's where? . . . What on earth for? . . . But she knew I was coming home . . . Yes, I suppose you're right. No other alternative . . . They are? . . . May I talk to them? . . . Oh, I see . . . I appreciate Iris' doing that . . . I'm sure you're right . . . No, that's too late to call. I'll see you all tomorrow . . . Eleven Forty-eight. United. So long, sir."

Rolling back on the bed, he pulled the spread over his naked chest and closed his eyes. He didn't bother to set the alarm.

The United Airlines flight seemed to be starting an approach to Peterson Field almost as soon as it broke out of the pattern at Stapleton. He had flown this route many times in Goons out of Lowry and T-29s out of Peterson itself. Castle Rock was still there, looming out of the arid sand. The pilot descended over the Black Forest, giving him a clear view of the Academy with the great expanse of windows ringing Fairchild Hall and the thin spires of the cadet chapel brilliant in the morning sunlight.

"Thank you for bringing me home," he said as he brushed by the stewardess.

"Glad to be of service, Major. Have a Happy Easter."

"Daddy!" Jeffrey and Kim shouted together as they raced into his arms. He was glad they piled into him, thankful he could wipe his tears on their clothing without drawing attention to his emotion. Kim, especially, seemed to have grown so much; he was happy she had not held herself back shyly. He gave her an extra hug and kiss. Jeff was still short for his age, probably wouldn't begin to sprout until junior high. But Alex could feel the wiry sinews in his legs and knew he would play lacrosse.

"Come now, children," Iris was trying to disentangle them. "Let your father catch his breath."

"I haven't breathed anything as sweet in a year." He laughed as he struggled to stand up. Then he grabbed Iris around the shoulders giving her a monstrous hug ending with a kiss on the cheek. Kim had stepped back in deference to Iris, but Jeff still had his arms around his father's mid-section. Alex stooped slightly, grabbed the little boy and threw him up to dangle, head down and laughing, from his left shoulder. Simultaneously, he drew Kim close to him and started walking to where Frank stood smiling by the wire fence.

"Hello, Colonel," Alex saluted. "What do you think of these wildcats of mine?"

"We're devastated you're taking them away from us."

After dropping Alex and the children at their door, Frank and Iris excused themselves, saying they were going to the Easter brunch at the Club. Alex wanted to get out of his uniform, but he could not tear himself away from the chattering boy and girl. Jeff seemed suitably impressed with the three rows of ribbons now occupying the space between his father's left breast pocket and his wings. He cuddled up in Alex's lap, feeling from time to time the trace of stubble on his father's chin, and recounted a year's worth of unshared activities. Kim had disappeared, but the aroma of coffee cake explained her absence.

"Daddy," she yelled from the kitchen, "do you still drink your coffee black?"

"Sure do, sweetheart."

Soon she appeared carrying a carefully arranged tray containing orange juice, a steaming cake, a silver coffee pot, and stacks of cups, saucers, plates, silverware and napkins.

"That's a fine brunch, honey; looks like your mother's been teaching you to be a hostess."

"Mrs. Harbinger taught me," she said without looking up. "Mom's too busy."

Alex dismissed the slight tone of sarcasm. "She's lucky to have you to give her a hand."

After serving the cake and pouring coffee for her father and milk for herself and her brother, Kim sat on the arm of her father's chair.

"Tell me about your Mom. Is she feeling good, or is she letting the job get her down?"

"She cut her hair," Jeffrey said crinkling his nose.

"You're kidding! She wouldn't do a thing like that."

"Yes she did," Kim confirmed. "Cut it herself while we were skiing at Breckenridge one weekend back in January. Did a horrible job. Almost cut it all off. Had to wear a wig until it grew out some."

"Good thing you didn't see it, Dad." Jeff's round eyes told Alex it must have been bad.

"It's the new job, I guess," Kim took up the explanation. "She dresses like a man. Blue or grey suits, white blouses with little ties, and her man's haircut."

From the looks the children traded, Alex knew they did not approve of their mother's transformation. But he also realized they were already testing him.

"I'm sure your mother has her reasons. The Barbie style took a lot of time to arrange."

They spent the day romping through the woods, visiting the site of Brutus' grave, and throwing snowballs made from pockets of icy slush shadowed by the dense fir trees. Before nightfall they piled in the old Plymouth to go to town. The engine cranked slowly, finally caught, then ran roughly. *Needs a battery and a tune-up,* he thought, *and replacing before we start to California.* On the way they passed the exclusive Dublin Inn, surrounded by Cadillacs and Lincolns, a monument to a poor girl's dream. *We all have dreams,* Alex thought as he glanced at his children sitting close beside him. *Some even come true.*

They ate at McDonald's, relishing the cheeseburgers, fries, and shakes while he regaled his children with stories of rubber eggs, reconstituted milk, and the way Peter Pan's moustache absorbed gravy. After seeing a return engagement of *The Sound of Music*, the last movie they had seen together before his departure, they stopped for pizza near the line of motels marking the northern boundary of Colorado Springs.

They got home late. Too late for a school night, but Alex did not want to surrender the experience. He had prayed his first day home would not be spoiled, and his prayer had been granted. Someday, he thought as he got his children ready for bed, he would learn to be more specific in his prayers. The meeting with Merrilane was yet to come, and judging from what Frank had said, she probably would not be back until after midnight.

Once he had the children down, he again showered, shaved, and dabbed himself sparingly with the potent cologne he had left in the medicine cabinet a year ago. His flannel trousers fit loosely, but the beige turtleneck she had bought him in Columbus covered the uneven belt line. When he pulled out his black jodhpur boots, he was happy to see the spitshine had protected them. He made a fire in the living room and settled down with the paper to await her return.

The sound of gravel crunching in the driveway roused him. Squinting against the glare of headlights, he recognized her form rising from what appeared to be a low-slung sports car. The automobile lurched backwards out of the driveway, curving onto the road and sliding in loose gravel as its driver slammed into gear and snarled off. Swinging her luggage awkwardly, she tottered on spike heels like a mare that had become entangled in her tack. He swung the door inward stooping to grasp her bag and reaching with his free arm to encircle her waist. He tried to kiss her, but she slipped away.

"Alex, my bladder's ready to burst. I've had cystitis all weekend, and I'm about to wet my pants." She disappeared around the corner of the foyer looking in her crumpled blue suit and short skirt like a harried stewardess on some short-haul airline. He put down the bag, wiped the sleep from his eyes, and walked back to sit down in the recliner by the dying fire.

He heard her rummaging in the bathroom, running water, brushing her teeth, and gargling. When she came back, she had shed the jacket and loosened her blouse's top buttons. Standing in front of the fire, she kneaded the flesh on her backside as if to restore its circulation. She appeared to have put on weight around the waist. He had difficulty seeing in the firelight, but her short, feather-cut hair seemed bleached far lighter than he had remembered it. Still, she was a handsome woman, and he had not seen her in almost five months.

"What time did you get in?" she asked.

"About noon. Frank and Iris brought the kids out to meet me."

"They've grown, huh?"

"Kim has. She's quite a young lady. Looks just like you in some of your old photos."

"Well, what do you think of the new Merrilane?" She sucked in her stomach, lifted her arms above her head, and turned slowly counterclockwise.

"Very nice, but I never saw anything wrong with the old version." Rising from his chair, he moved on her. She twisted out of his path and headed through the wide arch separating the room from the hallway.

"Why don't you check the fire, I've got to get up early tomorrow."

"It's already tomorrow," he said as he adjusted the copper screen and turned off the reading lamp. He entered the bedroom as she was stepping out of her skirt in front of the open window blinds. She wore no slip. She bent from the waist, unfastening her bra and liberating her breasts. "Have a souvenir," she tossed the filmy mesh in his direction. It stalled halfway and fell like a streaming parachute.

"Be a dear, and toss me my gown hanging behind the bathroom door."

He fetched the long cotton night shirt and extended it to her as she pulled down her dark pantyhose. A pattern of small bruises encircled her white buttocks.

"If I'm to play the doddering professor to your Blue Angel," he said, "you'll have to let me see the script. You seem a lot more rehearsed than I am."

"What are you mumbling about?" She was already crawling beneath the covers. "Turn off the light. I've got to be out of here by seven. Since you're home, you can get the kids on the bus. They're used to the routine."

Switching off the light, he closed the door and rotated the pin in the knob. He could feel blood pounding in his temples, his breath came in snatches. He undressed in darkness with only the glow of his watch hinting the Master had returned. Its luminescence disappeared as he slipped it into his right boot. She rolled onto her stomach as he lifted the blanket and sat down beside her.

"Merrilane, I've waited too long to talk to you, and I'm not waiting a second longer. I'd hoped to discuss this face to face, but I can talk in the dark to your behind if that's what you want." As he spoke he laid his hand on her buttocks and squeezed hard.

"You're hurting me!"

"From the bruises I saw when you did your striptease, I'd say I'm not the only person to have played grab-ass with you recently.

"What do you mean?" She had pulled forward, twisting out of his grasp to turn on the bedside lamp. She sat rigid, her back tight against the headboard, knees tucked under her chin, long fingers clutching the bedclothes around her body.

"Check six," he said evenly. "What, or should I say who, has gotten into you? What possessed you to send me that goddamn tape and to think you could give me the idiot treatment now? What in the goddamn hell have I done to justify your acting like a tramp and treating me like dirt?"

"Doing what to you? Did I put you in cold storage, expecting you to spend the rest of your life doing piddling things as an on-call volunteer? Did I run out, leaving you to fight off the wolves? Was I the one who pounded your body in Hawaii like it was a hunk of meat?"

"You're saying I did all of that?"

"You most certainly did. But times have changed; the worm's turned into a butterfly, and believe me, Buster, this butterfly isn't afraid of flying." He leaned forward placing his hand on her leg. She slapped it away, starring at him with blood-shot eyes.

"Are you on dope?"

She reached to snap off the lamp, but he caught her hand and pulled her toward him seeking to place her face in the light.

"I asked you a question. I've seen that look before, but never in my own home." She tried to pull back, but he had both wrists. "I asked you if you're on drugs, God damn it!"

"Keep your voice down. You've no right to shout at me or question my actions. I'm my own person!"

"You sure as hell looked better when you were my person. Acted a lot better too. What the hell's happening to my marriage?"

"It was my marriage too, and a damn sorry one at that! I told you, I'm my own person. I won't hold myself to the fine print on a contract I signed when I didn't know what life was all about."

"And I guess now you think you know," he still held her wrists. "What the fuck's your life turned into? Running in the fast lane, letting the neighbors raise our children, smoking dope or whatever it is, and taking on the entire cadet wing!"

"What are you talking about?" She spat the words: cold, penetrating, barbed like punji sticks. "Are you worried about your precious career, your spotless reputation?"

"I don't have a reputation any more, and neither do you."

"What do you mean by that remark?"

He released her wrists, got up, and walked to his wardrobe. Pulling out the top drawer, he withdrew a brown envelope and threw it down beside her. "Try explaining these, Madam Butterfly."

She unfolded *The Falcon Code* and glanced at the pictures. Then she wadded the pages, threw them across the room, and snapped out the light. He moved back to her side of the bed, leaned down and began to caress her thigh. She slapped blindly in the darkness, catching him across the face. "You bastard," she hissed. "You're responsible for this. You and your goddamned war."

He could feel the hot blood burbling in his nostrils and taste it in his mouth. Stripping the blanket and sheet from her body, he mounted her and penetrated despite her lunges and twists. She spat in his face just before he planted his bloody mouth on hers in a ravishing, silencing assault. Five months' worth of need and ninety days' accumulation of jealousy, anger, and hate exploded inside her as she mutilated his back with her sharp fingernails. He rolled off abruptly, visualizing as he did a blacked-out Phantom dumping its load in the dark.

"I hope," she said gagging on the blood from his nose, "you're proud of yourself."

"Not proud, Lane. Not satisfied either." He moved away and feigned sleep.

CHAPTER FORTY

"WHY MAJOR CANNARD!" Rachel turned from her file cabinet and gave Alex a crushing hug and a sisterly peck on the cheek. "Colonel Harbinger told me you were home, and I've been relishing the thought all morning of kissing a handsome war hero."

"It's good seeing you Rachel. If I'd known how passionate you were, I might not have rushed off to Southeast Asia."

"You should have known," she shot back. "I've spent most of my waking hours telling men how desirable I am. But they're all like you; they'd rather fight than switch."

"Go easy on the man, Rachel," Frank was smiling from the doorway. "He's in a weakened condition. He got home only yesterday."

"I know, Colonel," she replied with an exaggerated wink. "That's why I'm trying to exploit my advantage."

Squinting into the morning sun, Alex followed his mentor into the familiar office.

"Have a seat, Alex. I didn't expect a visit on your first morning home."

"Since Lane had to go to work, I dug the blue suit out of mothballs and thought I'd use the day to visit old friends."

"Anyone in particular besides me?"

Rachel slipped into the room carrying a small pewter tray with two cups. She served Frank what appeared to be weak tea and sat a cup of ferocious black coffee before Alex.

"I'd planned to drop by the athletic department and see Rod Pike."

Frank studied his protégé over the rim of his cup. "We've had some bad luck with former members of the faculty, so I know the dean will be glad to see you home safe and sound."

"Yes, Bert's death hit me especially hard. I'll get around to seeing the dean as soon as I get a few things sorted out. I thought I'd get a first-hand report on Lane's job proficiency. I understand she worked under Rod."

"That's correct, but I understand he more or less abandoned her to sink or swim. She told us she was sinking until she got the loan of a cadet from General Safire."

"Oh, yes, the ubiquitous Mr. Pinski. I'd like to talk to him, too."

"Tell me, Alex," Frank interrupted as if impatient to change the subject, "what's the one thing that impressed you most during your tour?"

"Leave it to you to ask the hard essay question, sir." Alex leaned back in his chair, hesitating as if simmering the broth of his experience to skim off just the essence. "It may sound like the school solution, but I'd have to say it was the bravery of the men I worked with. I had a unique perspective circling overhead, watching the comings and goings, eavesdropping on all three radio networks. No one tried to weasel out no matter how dirty the job. I'm talking about older men, some with strings of degrees, not just kids who might not have known any better.

"That's not to say they weren't scared. An A-1 pilot at Pleiku told me he thought it was just a matter of time before the weather, the mountains, or the flak would get him. 'The percentages,' he said. 'They're beyond your control no matter how good you are.' Yet he kept going out into the darkness every night."

"That's what you did wasn't it? Kept going out every night."

"I guess so, Colonel, but that was different. The odds usually were in my favor. His were always stacked against him. Or take the rescue helicopters, the 'Jolly Greens.' Once I flew in one whose pilot was completely white haired, must have been pushing sixty. Recalled for Korea and stayed in afterwards. We dropped into a hole in the jungle so tight our rotors were chopping branches off the trees and the door gunners were calling corrections in feet left or right. His life was continually linked to the fate of some stranger the NVA might be using as bait. His job was to go into the Valley of the Shadow and hover there exposed to every weapon in range. Lots of people walked or flew through that Valley, but to go there and then to hover— that takes brass balls. I remember one night, a Dust Off pilot . . ."

He stopped his monologue, sensing he was exceeding the space in the colonel's blue book. He looked out toward the playing fields. "No one ever said, 'I'm gonna abandon you while I go back and steal what's yours.'"

"You look bad, Alex. Strung out. Are you able to rest now?"

"I suppose, sir." He continued to stare out the windows. "But I suspect I'll never be able to rest completely."

He turned back toward Frank. "Lane's asked for a separation. I guess part of the problem is she's attracted to someone else."

"I'm sorry." Frank dropped his head. "These past months have taken their toll. I suspected she was going through some kind of crisis."

"Do you know the lucky man?"

"No, truthfully I don't. But I ask you not to jump to conclusions. Have you and Merrilane talked about this?"

"We've talked around it, but we haven't discussed it. That's the most frustrating part. As far as I know, we'd never had a communication problem before this past year. Now it's like I'm listening to a string of phonetic letters without having the proper code books."

"Alex, you're just back from a traumatic experience. You've got jet lag, and you've got culture shock. Everything's changed; everyone's suspicious because of the way Johnson manipulated the war. Nixon and Kissinger came in on promises, but so far they're just dancing. And all this confusion's adding fuel to the Women's Movement. They see how badly men have managed the affairs of the world, so that housewives like Merrilane are thinking they can do a better job.

"From my perspective, I think they probably can."

"Your wife's had to face this turmoil alone, knowing if anything happened to you she'd be just another untrained woman saddled with two small children. If she's stumbled, try to keep an unbiased historian's point of view. Don't jettison her because your male ego's bruised."

"You may be right, sir. But you've never had to worry about Iris's undercutting you just when the career breaks were beginning to come."

"Every married man has to face the possibility of his wife's being unfaithful. Why do you think the bedroom farce is such an enduring genre? Iris is a hot-blooded woman who sees herself as rapidly losing her charms. Make-up won't cover the lines anymore, and hair color doesn't seem to be worth the bother. She's also seeing her younger sisters having opportunities she was deprived of.

"I suspect the idea's occurred to her that if she's going to experience her own mid-life crisis, she'd better do it quickly. In short, she's human just like everyone else. And so am I, my young friend. I'll admit to having had, from time to time, feelings for other women as lustful as the next fellow's. If I should learn of my wife's infidelity, I hope I could be mature and charitable in my judgments."

Alex rose from his chair extending his hand. "Before I leave, may I ask if you're familiar with *The Falcon Code*?"

"Yes . . . I am."

"And the pictures?"

"Yes."

"Then you see this isn't just your everyday, discrete affair. Are the pictures common knowledge?"

"Iris never raised the subject, which leads me to believe they're not wives' club gossip. The Commandant has the OSI working the problem."

"Any further words of wisdom on how I should conduct myself? Just pin a metal coxcomb device on my Vietnam Service Ribbon, sort of a Distinguished Flying Double Cross."

"Try not to be bitter. They'll all be watching you, particularly the Comm who'll soon be moving on to greater things. He notices men who stand up well under pressure, and he'd make you a powerful sponsor. So don't do anything foolish; it would be beneath you."

"Thank's for your confidence, sir. But after this last year, nothing's beneath me."

He left Frank's office, grateful that Rachel was not at her desk, and took the stairs rather than risk getting trapped in the elevator with former colleagues. He cut across the terrazzo separating the academic realm from the dormitories and military training offices, walking fast, returning cadet salutes, and disregarding the envious glances directed at his ribbons. Pausing at the top of the stairs leading down to the athletic complex, he admired the dimensions of the new field house. Racing down from the foothills and ripping across the campus, the wind chilled his thin blood. *Must be turbulent at pattern altitude. Bumpy enough to warn of a wind shear on landing. Better hold a few extra knots on final approach. Good advice, remember to keep your speed up.*

"Major Cannard to see Mr. Pike," he announced to the receptionist. *God, another fat one.*

She nodded, looking him over, eyes darting from his shoulders to his name tag as if checking to see if he were really who he said he was. Then she buzzed her boss, holding the telephone's mouthpiece close to her painted lips. *Probably telling him Merrilane's cuckold's waiting but appears unarmed.*

"Alex, Welcome Home!" Rod's voice boomed across the office causing anyone who might still have been working to know the Knight Errant had returned. He bounded to Alex's side, threw a muscular arm across his shoulders and reached for his right hand. Anticipating an athlete's grip, Alex thrust his own hand tight against the thumb thereby eliminating the leverage Rod depended upon for his first intimidating gesture. *Little trick I learned from the Viet Cong, you smiling bastard. Get in tight.*

"Come on in," Rod led the way. "How about some coffee?"

"No thanks, never touch the stuff." Alex walked in and closed the door.

If Pike's surprised, he doesn't show it. A Gaffney with personality. "Thought I'd drop by to let you know I'm home now, and you can stop screwing my wife."

"Jesus, Alex," Rod stood flatfooted like a tennis novice who had gone to the net only to see a perfectly placed lob arc over his head. "I haven't touched Merrilane. Don't get me wrong; she's a damn fine looking woman, but I've got scruples."

"Forgive me, Rod. You mistook my meaning. I meant you've diddled me. You know how the system works; we're a package deal to the Air Force. They expect her to progress just like me. From what I understand, she punched her tickets under you and got squat in return."

"Now that's just not so." Alex saw the color flood back into Rod's face. "I saw she got plenty of publicity, found her the opportunity of a lifetime in the Springs, and even gave her an engraved plaque at her going-away party."

"Come on, Rod; they can't file a plaque in my personnel folder. Did you ever put your thanks in official channels? If you haven't, you're screwing both of us."

"Oh, Jesus, I see what you mean," Rod stammered. "You know what I thought you meant?" He laughed nervously. "Sure, I'll take care of it right away. A letter to the dean signed by the athletic director. It'll get to the right people."

Rod's embarrassment appeared to Alex to stem not from having to face a jealous husband, but from his inability to claim credit for a conquest. He recalled what Dan Strait had said, and realized it was true. If Pike had admitted his guilt, he would probably have accepted his offer of coffee.

"Rod," he moved closer, lowering his voice almost to a whisper, "as one man to another, are you familiar with *The Falcon Code* that circulates in the cadet wing?"

"Yes, I'm sorry to say. It's a disgrace."

"And the pictures?"

"Yes."

"Have the pictures been widely circulated?"

"Yes," Rod looked down, moving his foot to smooth out where a chair had been pulled across the carpet. "But I think only in the locker room."

"I guess everyone thinks he knows who the woman is."

"Pretty much so."

"What's the attitude of the officers; I assume the cadets are wondering where the sign-up list is."

"Actually no. The cadets seem embarrassed by the whole thing. I think if they found the publishers, there wouldn't be much left for the Honor Committee to debate. As for the officers, my guess is each one's glad his wife wasn't singled out."

"Do you have any idea who's involved?"

"If I had to choose, I'd finger Mister Pinski, the First Classman assigned to Merrilane last summer."

"Why?"

"Circumstances of being able to work into her confidence, but mostly a gut feel that's he's taking the system."

"What do you mean?"

"Some cadets are here for reasons other than Duty, Honor, Country. They manage to get out of being commissioned some way or other and walk off with a top-flight education. In the past they could resign late into their senior year or take an honor violation leading to dismissal. The supe's tightening up, but what can he do? You can't have them as officers, and you damn sure don't want them infecting the enlisted force. So usually you write 'em off like the spoiled merchandise they are."

"Does Pinski want to get out of his service obligation?"

"No, I don't think so. He's different from the usual parasite, but I still have the feeling he's sneaky. Comes across to me as being cynical beyond his years, playing with the rules, bending or breaking them and using his considerable charm to stay above suspicion. If I had a daughter, I wouldn't want her to associate with him."

"Did Lane ever go out with him socially?"

"Not that I know of."

"Well, Rod, it's been good meeting you. I hadn't looked forward to it and had no idea how it would go."

"I'm glad you came over, Alex. I've heard a lot about you, all of it good. I think the world of your wife. She's been under a strain, and I guess I was responsible for part of it. But when I woke up to what was happening, I did what little I could. I got her a job off the site and tried to keep an eye on her."

"I appreciate that."

"Tell me, Major. What would you have done if you'd decided I was the guilty party?"

"I'd have cut your balls off."

"Well, if you try to do that to Pinski, be careful. He's smart and he's tough. He's not the type to roll over and beg forgiveness. He'll fight you tooth and nail, and I'll lay odds he'll fight dirty."

CHAPTER FORTY-ONE

THE BRISK WIND HAD DROPPED the chill factor ten degrees since his morning walk to the field house, causing Alex to detour by his home, rummage through his aviators bag, and trade his uniform blouse for a faded bomber jacket with the leering "Devil's Own" insignia of the 96th Bomb Squadron. Further compromising military dress and custom, he jammed his hands in its side pockets as he strode toward the cluster of cadets preparing the long-winged Schweizer sailplane for launch off the winch.

"Mister Pinski?" he inquired as the group noticed his approach and snapped to rigid attention.

"Here, SIR!" Pinski towered over the others.

"As you were," Alex released the cadets from their frozen positions. "Mister Pinski, may I have a word with you?"

Pinski gave a few hurried instructions, then jogged easily to join him on the lee side of the operations shack. *All-American Boy: handsome, solid, and . . .*

"Cadet First Class Jack D. Pinski reporting to the Major, SIR!" He shouted in the unnecessarily loud voice cadets affected while simultaneously flashing a perfect salute: palm completely flat, thumb tucked in tight, hand inclined slightly downward.

In no hurry to relieve him from the psychological disadvantage mandated by their difference in rank, Alex inspected the young man as if he were viewing him from the dark side of the glass separating witness from suspect. He had the convict's close-cropped hair, in this case blond, eyebrows bleached almost invisible, and squinting eyes hooded by a duck-billed baseball cap. His strong nose and flaring nostrils brought to mind a high-strung stallion. His lips, sealed by four years of practice, were clinched in an inexpressive line surrounded by heavy whiskers almost unnoticeable because of their lack of coloring. Unmindful of the cold, or perhaps more interested in affectation, he wore his jacket and flying suit zipped low allowing tufts of light blond hair to spill over the neck of his white T-shirt. The rest of his body, except for its heroic dimensions, could have belonged to any cadet: government-issue physique clad in government-issue flying suit, shod in government-issue black jump boots.

"Relax, Mister Pinski," he said returning the salute with his own, smoothly and flawlessly executed. "I'm Alex Cannard."

"Yes, SIR! I know, SIR!" Pinski's exuberance caused him to wonder how many teachers, officers, and women had been conned previously by this poster-quality cadet. "I've seen your picture on Miz Cannard's desk in the athletic department, SIR."

"She's spoken of you, Mister Pinski. Says you're a natural-born manipulator."

Pinski missed the inference, or if it registered, failed to respond. He showed none of the usual cadet reticence when talking to a strange officer. "Glad to have you back, Major Cannard, SIR. I bet you've got lots of stories to tell."

"That's right, Mister Pinski, and questions to ask."

"I can imagine, SIR. Lots of things been going on while you were away. Politics, campus unrest, woman's lib. Of course we don't get any of that around here. Keep inside our shells for the four-year incubation, then pop out as a new class of fledgling falcons." *Pinski's cooking now,* Alex thought as he watched the boy bring his massive hands into the conversation, *working to take the initiative and defuse what he takes to be suspicion in my eyes.* "Hey, look Major; I'm scheduled off the winch now. Wanna take a ride?"

He looked toward the launch area, appraising the slim fuselage, long wings, and bulbous canopy of the craft. Then he reeled in his gaze, boring into the eyes of the First Classman who had so deftly maneuvered to entice him into the only environment where a cadet could be in complete control. "Sure, show me what you've got."

Leading the way to the sailplane, Pinski then introduced him to the ground crew, much to the disappointment of Third Classman Baldacci whose place the officer would be taking. Settling gingerly into the narrow rear cockpit, he snapped himself into the harness of the parachute nestling in the curved aluminum seatback and pulled the leg and chest straps tight. Little need to study the sparse panel, just the primary instruments: needle, ball, and airspeed with clock, compass, vertical speed, and altimeter thrown in to make up for the absence of oil pressure, cylinder head temperature, and manifold pressure gauges. One unfamiliar dial caught his attention: a "variometer" which Baldacci said measured exactly when the craft had entered a thermal and started to ascend.

Having completed an inspection of the craft's general condition and freedom of movement of its control surfaces, Pinski stopped to check his passenger. "We aren't equipped with an interphone, Major. Don't need one with no engine noise to overcome." Then he crawled into the front cockpit, and started strapping himself in. "She's certainly not a Phantom," he smirked over his shoulder, "but she'll fly higher than a Gooney Bird."

"That may be true, Mister," he called back, "but at least the Goon can take off under its own power."

The acceleration from the winch glued him to the seatback. Pinski established a gentle climb to a hundred feet then raised the nose sharply into a climb reminiscent of the graceful sweep of the departing U-2 he had observed on occasion in Morocco. For the first time in his experience, no thunderous sound of engines at maximum thrust and sympathetic vibration of the airframe diluted the pure thrill of flight. His aural senses recorded only the rush of air splitting past the canopy. Having reached the apogee of the launch, Pinski lowered the nose, released the tow cable, and banked gently toward the foothills north of the Academy's observatory.

"We've got maybe five minutes to find a thermal," he called, "or we'll have to put 'er back on the ground. But if we can't find one on a day like this, we don't deserve to be called aviators."

Tumbling over Pike's Peak to meet them, thick rolls of high clouds blotted out the sun and plunged the cockpit temperature to arctic values. As he adjusted the frayed knit collar of his jacket closer around his neck and checked the zipper's closure, Alex noticed Pinski's mirth-filled eyes taunting him from his rearview mirror. The frail craft began to shudder, then buffet alarmingly in the air currents swirling above the rising terrain. *We're pretty low, ground's coming up to meet us on this heading.* Relief overcame apprehension, however, as the needle on the rate of climb indicator pegged, and the stark terrain details drained away. Pinski whipped the craft into a tight turn fighting to remain within the thermal as he spiraled upward.

"We've got her now, Major. We can ride this beauty to paradise."

Despite the cold, he was intrigued by the performance of the craft and its pilot. Less than fifteen feet away, he saw an eagle taking advantage of the same cyclonic pattern while looking with detached interest at the huge blue gull pacing him.

"Thermals are a lot like women, Major; some are built for speed and some for comfort."

He delights in breaking taboos, tossing out comments like bread thrown to ducks just to see which ones you'll ping on. He knows cadets and officers don't discuss partisan politics, the Commandant's policies, or recreational sex.

"A fat one like this got me my Diamond height award. Like to have froze my patootie off. Thought I'd end up trading the family jewels for one solitary gem to put in my logbook." Again the reflected eyes twinkled.

They slipped out of the thermal heading due east at 11,500 feet. Alex shivered from the cold; the canopy was beginning to frost over; and the thin air made him light headed. But Pinski deployed the speed brakes, pitching the Schweizer into a steep descent with loudly whistling wind accompanying the spinning altimeter needle. Retracting the brakes, he whipped the craft up and over the top in a sweeping loop as flawlessly engraved on the speckled Colorado sky as the cursive script on a debutante's invitation. "Nothing like putting the old girl on her back," he yelled. Leveling at 8,000 feet, Pinski skirted the south edge of the Black Forest Glider Port. Alex was still cold, but the spasms were gone and the chill was bearable, even— like the loop—invigorating.

"Thought you might like a look at your place from up here, sir. You can see there's been quite a few housing starts this past year. Want to fly her?"

"Thought you'd never ask," Alex shouted as he gave the stick a jiggle. "I got it." He was unprepared for the aura of tingling joy surrounding the control stick. It drained immediately into his caressing hand, and from there rippled throughout his body, eliminating the chill and neutralizing for the moment the dark thoughts he harbored. How fragile and sensitive she felt now smoothing out in clear air and cruising in perfect trim.

"Got to treat her like a woman, Major. Get in her head, anticipate every notion, and she'll follow wherever you want her to go. No engine torque to worry about. No dead weight to haul around. Real flying. Too bad Orville and Wilbur had to fuck it up."

"You've got a lot of skill, Mister, like an inborn talent. You might wish, however, to include your word choice in your crosscheck." He found it unnecessary to speak loudly as they cruised in still air away from the mountain wave. "Anybody in your family ever been a flyer?"

"My Dad was the World's Greatest Fighter Pilot." Alex saw the reflected eyes locked on. "He taught me to fly a glider before he'd let me touch a light plane. Sometimes we'd fly all weekend if he could get away. Just him and me. Sometimes going for altitude, wheezing oxygen, and me freezing my buns off. He never got cold, he was a real man." Alex saw the eyes, pupils closed down to insignificance, drilling into him. "Watch your heading, Major. Gliders don't take kindly to being left alone. Like women, you can't leave 'em and come back expecting to find them on the same old course."

"You trying to tell me something, Mister? Seems like you're having a hard time keeping women from intruding on your flying instruction."

"Oh, no SIR," Pinski sat arrogantly in the front seat, arms stretched along each canopy rail, eyes glued on the mirror. "It's just that pilots always link the two subjects."

"Not all pilots, Mister Pinski."

"Sorry, SIR! I guess I've been around fighter pilots all my life, at least before I came to the Zoo."

"Do you mean the Academy, Mister?"

"Oh, yes. Sorry if I offended you, SIR! I meant the Academy."

Alex turned toward Colorado Springs placing the panorama of the institution off their right wing. He noticed Pinski dutifully sweeping the skyline for other traffic but ignoring the imposing scene he had so often conjured in his mind's eye during the last year.

"You seem highly proficient as a flyer, Mister Pinski, although it remains to be seen whether you can cut it with the Air Force. How are you making out in the other department."

"The other department? I don't understand, sir."

Realizing they were steadily drifting lower, he rolled into a curving arc to intercept the downwind leg of the airstrip's traffic pattern. "Women, Mister Pinski, women. Don't tell me you're all talk and no action."

"We don't have time to do anything more than talk. It's an unnatural way of living, if you ask me. I'll take the bird now for landing."

He felt the jiggle in the stick as Pinski took control. "You got it," he shouted. Then he watched as the cadet jockeyed the craft into the pattern, trading altitude for airspeed, and rolling out lined up with the runway markers on the sod field. Precisely on speed and glidepath, wind drift killed, Pinski's eyes no longer probed the back cockpit but scanned his airspeed indicator and altimeter while bringing the touchdown point into his cross-check.

"Do you get your kicks," Alex's voice thundered, "out of publishing dirty pictures of officers' wives?"

The eyes reappeared momentarily in the mirror, more white showing than previously. Concentration broken, Pinski allowed the nose to drop. Airspeed shot up seven knots. He deployed the speed brakes but was slow compensating and allowed the nose to rise dangerously. He forced it down, but the single wheel under the cockpit hit prematurely causing the aircraft to bound back into the air cocked awkwardly into the wind. He saved the landing from a complete washout, but barely. When they rumbled to a stop, left wing dipping onto the ground, right wing tilted high into the air, jeering members of the ground crew surrounded them.

"Jeez, Mister Pinski," Baldacci shouted, "I could have done better than that, and I haven't even soloed!" Others joined the melee, shouting, joking, obviously enjoying their opportunity to jeer the self-proclaimed "World's Greatest Glider Pilot." Pinski took the ribbing in stride, giving back as much as he got, but finally admitting, "I blew it."

"Mister Pinski," Alex called.

"SIR?"

"It's only quarter till four, let's go somewhere and debrief."

Pinski detached himself from the group and followed him to the side of the operations shack. "I really need to be getting back, sir. I have to make the evening meal formation."

"Not to worry. I called General Safire and got you a pass. Told him you were a friend of the family, and we'd like you to dine with us."

"I couldn't do that, sir. You're just back, and I know you have a lot of catching up to do."

"Nonsense. The family'd love to see you. I understand you were a regular fixture around the house for a while. Besides, we need to talk about some pictures that have been circulating."

Pinski looked at the ground as he traced circular patterns in the sand with his boot. "No, I really can't impose on you tonight. We're having some extra study time in the squadron getting ready for an electrical engineering exam. If I don't pass it with a high grade, I won't get out of here in June. I just can't spare the time."

"Well, if that's the way it is." Now Alex was the one to look at the ground as if gathering strength for his final assault. "Have it your own way. A quiet chat over coffee, or an interrogation with the OSI."

"What do you mean, the OSI? What do those guys have to do with you and me—or anybody else?" Alex saw the same pattern emerging he had often seen before—self-assurance melting as pressure built. Pinski's eyes narrowed as if he were protecting them from the direct beam of a powerful spotlight. Alex noticed a throbbing pulsation enlarging the vein near the hairline above the cadet's left temple.

"You're no doubt familiar with *The Falcon Code* circulating within the cadet wing as an underground newspaper. I also assume you know compromising photographs of my wife have been published along with obscene commentary. We'd just like to find the people responsible, and if they're cadets, keep them from having any further connection with the Air Force."

Pinski leaned back against the clapboard wall. "You're accusing me?"

"Yes," he replied. "You've been close to my wife; you've been in my home numerous times; only trusted First Classmen have the freedom to get into mischief. And, from what I understand, you charge your father's death to Air Force maliciousness. So I guess that gives a twisted mind good enough motive to embarrass the Air Force and its people any way it can."

Pinski advanced on Alex, hands closed into tight fists. "Those are serious charges, Major. Especially without a bit of proof. Haven't you heard of *The Uniform Code*? You can bet we cadets know it chapter and verse. And believe me, this isn't the way a pre-trial hearing is conducted."

"Pinski," Alex flared, talking fast and so low the wind almost overpowered his words, "this is the kind of justice they don't teach in schools. It's the kind I've learned in the last year: Viet Cong justice. I'll wipe out the whole Cadet Wing if that's what it takes to get the sick son of a bitch who's behind this. I came to size you up, and I'm not impressed. You're an egotistical, immature bastard, not God's gift to flying—much less to women!"

"Fuck you, Maj," Pinski lashed out. "You don't intimidate me. Neither does your OSI. In two more months, you can take this place and shove it!" Pinski turned away and stalked toward the parking lot.

"I'm not finished with you, Mister," Alex shouted. "I'm gonna be on your tail forever!"

CHAPTER FORTY-TWO

SOMEONE DROPPED MERRILANE at the front drive just as the six o'clock news ended. Alex and the children had made supper, Kim's special tuna casserole. They ate in the greenhouse sitting cross legged on the floor watching a public television documentary on polar bears, the children laughing at the antics of the determined female and her tumbling cubs. Merrilane had changed from the gray pinstripe suit into white toreador pants with a blue cashmere sweater. Her short, harshly bleached hair was somewhat softened in the fading light. She had little to say, being content to refer the children's questions on the mating habits of bears to their father as she had deflected much of their routine maintenance to Iris over the past year. Combining with Merrilane's detachment, the evening's chill caused Alex to turn the electric heaters on full high. Kim and Jeffrey seemed particularly clinging and obnoxious, bickering over who would clear the dishes and who would fix the dessert.

Free of the demands he had become accustomed to, Alex asked his son to bring him a second can of beer.

"You've developed into quite a boozer," Merrilane said. "I've never seen you drink more than one at a sitting."

"Got the heebie-jeebies. Must be the altitude—or the cold. What say I make a fire in the living room? We can have a snack after the kids go down."

"Suit yourself," she replied as she carried her plate toward the kitchen. "I've got work to do."

She was smoking at her desk and wearing a pair of reading glasses he had not seen before when he looked in after cleaning the kitchen. "Care to join me in front of the fire?"

"In about an hour," she said not looking up.

"That's all right, the fire's just getting started, and I promised to help Kim with her homework. She's quite interested in astronomy; but I suppose you know all about her class project and the field trip to the observatory Friday night."

She was not listening. He crossed the hall to Kim's room, where she sat at her desk surrounded by star charts and thick library books.

"What do you know about constellations, Dad?"

"Everything there's to know," he said realizing a year ago she still called him Daddy. "When you were a baby, I traveled all over the world depending on the stars to get me there and bring me back."

"Did you have your own special star? One you talked to at night?"

"Yeah, I guess I did. Leastways I had my own constellation. Cygnus—The Swan—has always been my favorite. I suppose all ugly ducklings dream of becoming swans."

"Show me Cygnus on this map of the heavens, Dad."

"Here's my friend," he said, "boxed in by the 'navigator's triangle' formed by Deneb, Vega, and Altair. Deneb is also the Swan's tail, here are his wings—these four smaller stars—and Albireo is at the end of his long neck."

"Now I see him, Dad. Will he ever break free?"

"Hard to say, sweetheart. Swans are strong flyers, so I'd say he has a chance." He looked away for a moment wishing he had picked the big dipper for his daughter's edification.

"I'd love to have a swan for a pet. They're so dignified looking. But my teacher said swans mate for life, so I guess I'd have to have two. Anyway, Cygnus needs to be free in the sky not trapped in some old triangle."

"Don't you worry about Cygnus; he's also a tough fighter. Here, let me show you how we used the stars to navigate." He sat on her bed, spread the charts and sketched a great circle course from Jacksonville to Morocco. "We'd coast-out heading east to meet our tankers south of Bermuda. Flying high, about twenty-eight thousand feet. Three B-Forty-seven bombers. If it was pitch black, you could pick out the flashing tanker lights maybe fifty miles out. You can't believe how beautiful it was to rendezvous with those tankers. Their colored beacons so intense you thought you could reach out and break off a piece of light and chew it like taffy. Christmas trees, that's what the tankers looked like. Tiny Christmas trees huddled together—blinking red, green, and white—just barely moving as you got ready to descend. Then we'd drop on 'em like Captain Ahab's longboats going after old Moby Dick because, as you got closer, you'd see those sparkling little trees had turned into a school of fat, white whales. Pretty soon you'd pull right up under one's belly, and the lights would be glowing and flashing and blinking right inside your head. And you know what?"

"What, Daddy?" Her little girl's face had returned, and her wide eyes were fixed on his.

"You'd look up and see this time the gigantic whale had his own harpoon, weaving from side to side and up and down like he was getting ready to throw it directly at your chest."

"Oh, Daddy, what would you do?"

Her childish concern touched him. "I'd just move right in and take the best shot that long harpoon could give. I knew Cygnus was watching over me, and nothing bad could happen while he was up."

"Oh, Dad," Kim giggled, "you haven't changed a bit. You sucked me in again with one of your stories."

"It's the truth, sweetheart. After the refueling, we'd climb back as high as our weight would allow and set our sights on North Africa. And Cygnus would see us there. He and the other stars were what we depended on."

"Weren't you ever afraid all by yourself out over the ocean?"

"Not really. I had my navigator and my co-pilot. We were a team. We all depended on each other and backed each other up. Remember my navigator, Pete Mandich? He brought you that big doll, the Spanish Dancer, from Madrid. He'd give the co-pilot information from star tables just like these you have here, and the co-pilot would crank the star's direction and its altitude above the horizon into his sextant to help him find it. I'd tell him when to start and stop his observation, and he'd track the star in his viewfinder for exactly a minute. Then he'd give the reading to Pete who'd plot a line on his chart. Shooting three stars would give us a `fix' like this." He drew a series of three lines intersecting to form a small triangle next to his course line and continued to explain the intricacies of celestial navigation.

"It's ten o'clock," Merrilane was speaking from the doorway. "When are you two going to give it up?"

"Mom, you ought to see what Dad's shown me. He knows all about the stars, and Cygnus is his favorite constellation."

"That's nice, but he offered me a drink, and I think I need one before turning in."

"Okay, Mom," Kim winked. "I'll share him with you now, but tomorrow night he's promised to teach me all the stars."

When Alex came into the living room carrying the tray with two fat mugs and the stoneware pot of hot spiced wine, he found Merrilane occupying one of the arm chairs rather than the sofa. He sat the tray down on the low table beside her and dropped into the chair adjoining it. "Thanks for adding another log; I didn't realize the fire would burn down so quickly."

"It's surprising how soon the flame dies." She dipped her mug toward him, "Cheers."

"Are we going to continue to talk in double-entendres?"

"Pardon me," she said, "I'll try to keep it simple for your small mind."

"I may have a small mind, Lane, but I never believed it was narrow. I'd just like to know what's happening to us. I'll be damned if I can understand how we got here. I can't even remember what set us off in Hawaii."

"Then I'll tell you." Her mouth moved slightly off synchronization as if some amateur were pulling her strings. "I'm sick and tired of being a piece of meat, ravished by you or any other bastard who can get me at a disadvantage. Power's the only thing you sons of bitches understand. And I'm going to have plenty of it."

"Power's not . . . "

"You came to Hawaii with just two goals: to catch up on your sex life and get me to sacrifice a satisfying career. That's why you never once mentioned my bringing the kids. Sharon Bailey took her children; Mildred Pomeroy even took the baby. You didn't want them in the way. Once I was there, you acted like a stranger off in another world most of the time, looking over your shoulder in crowds, tentative—not wanting to make any decisions."

"You're right about the children. We needed the time to-gether—earned the right to spend those five days just for ourselves. Christ, I didn't know if I'd ever get another five days, and I chose to spend them only with you. Doesn't that mean . . . "

"Don't make me laugh. You continually brought up the men I worked with. You showed about as much trust and faith in me as . . . as your precious Cygnus shows toward anything on this earth!"

"Lane, I'm suddenly tired. I feel like the life has been sucked out of me, like Robin Hood having his blood drained drop by drop and thinking of Marion and how it could have been. I saw a movie one night in Nha Trang when the winds from an ap-proaching typhoon kept us on the ground and the rain swept in torrents like automatic weapons fire across the exposed side of the building . . . "

"I don't care to hear any of your goddamn homilies."

"Steve McQueen in *The Sand Pebbles*. With Candice Bergen who didn't know squat about anything in the real world. And they were attracted to each other."

"I told you I'm not interested . . . "

"And they couldn't communicate because of the difference in their experience. And he ends up in a Chinese courtyard sur-rounded by invisible enemies sniping at him. And he yells, 'What went wrong? What in hell happened?' Then one sharp report reverberated around the cold stone of the coliseum he'd been thrown into. And he slumped. Goddamn it, Lane, I felt as if my brother had been shot dead."

"See, that's what I mean. I tell you I don't want to hear it, or don't want to do it, and you trample right along. Our life isn't a movie. Steve McQueen will never age. Fifty years from now he'll still be in that courtyard looking virile. You and I will be dead. Can't you see that? We're aging. The clock's running and there are no timeouts. You have your lifework. You can do it with or without me. I don't have anything I can point to and say 'it's mine.'"

"What's yours is sleeping in their bedrooms. That's your primary job right now. I'm your primary job. That's the way it is. That's the way it's always supposed to be, and men have busted their asses to make it that way. To have a home, not just a place to eat and sleep. And to have a family, not just a herd of related individuals who share a roof at night."

"Well I've got news for you. That's exploitation! And it doesn't wash anymore. You men had your chance and you muffed it. Now it's our turn."

"Does it have to be an either-or proposition?"

"As far as I'm concerned, yes."

"Are you moving with me to Louisiana, or do you intend to stick with what you said on that tape you dropped on me?"

"I meant every word. I'm not leaving everything I've worked to build in the past year. Your behavior last night only confirmed my belief I'm doing the right thing for me and the children."

"You mean taking their father away from them? Don't you know what they're going to have to go through as they grow up? This drug thing's going to explode! Peer pressure's gonna eat 'em up. Why limit their defenses?"

"That's a laugh. What are the odds you'd be home when they need you? Do you think anyone, much less your own kids, is going to confide in the big SAC man?"

"There's nothing wrong with SAC. It won't be like B-Forty-seven days. Most B-Fifty-two bombers pull their alert at home where the families can visit."

"Wonderful life. Where do you satisfy your marital obligations? In the back seat of the alert vehicle?"

"Wherever turns you on."

"Don't get cute with me, Alex. I've had enough of alert tours and of family schedules knocked cockeyed because of your flying or squadron duties."

"Barksdale's the garden spot of the Air Force. Housing's good and there's plenty to do around Shreveport and Bossier City."

"Maybe if you like paddling through the water moccasins and fishing all the time. What's there for me? Let me guess. I could get active in the Wives' Club, volunteer my time with Family Services and wear their cute little uniform, or serve doughnuts at the bloodmobile. I've done all that! What else's there to do? Lie beside the club pool drinking one martini after another until one of your friends picks me up?"

"Name one of my friends who ever made a pass at you."

"Ed Nipper, for starters. Does that surprise you? Good old Ed. Your best friend from pilot training. Stopped by when you were in North Africa ostensibly to set up a surprise birthday party. Had me backed into the washer room. If Kim hadn't come in with one of her friends, he'd have gone all the way. Don't look so shocked. How about Dick Irvin and Will Morris? At least they were gentlemen about it. They had the graciousness to proposition me outright. And that nice squadron navigator you liked so much. Beginning to hit home? Yes, dear Major DeLaney. The one whose wife was always pregnant. Suggested he could do your crew a lot of good by scheduling you on the right missions. All I had to do was 'play ball.'"

"Well, you can forget about Ed. He was blown to bits by a SAM over Haiphong."

"Serves the bastard right."

"Shut your mouth, Lane. If Ed or any others made a play, you must have enticed them. Are you sure it's not just in your mind? Is that it? Do you need some help? It's no sin. You've had a lot of pressure on you."

"I resent your . . . "

"Why didn't I see it before? That explains it all!" He spouted the words as if fervor would make up for thoughts unsaid in Hawaii.

"Save your breath. There's nothing wrong with me a therapist could fix. They're for people adrift. I've got my goals, and I've set my priorities. Now if you want to come along to bed, I'll be good to you. Give you a taste of what a marriage of convenience could be like before you make up your mind."

She rose from her seat, sidestepping quickly in front of his chair as if expecting him to lunge at her. She was almost to the archway when he spoke.

"I saw your boyfriends today."

"You did what?"

"I saw your boyfriends today," he repeated as he stood to confront her. "At least I saw two of 'em. Rod and Jack. Even went flying with Pinski, but I assume you have too."

"What are you talking about?"

"I'm going to crack this thing, Lane. I'm not giving up the only people who mean anything to me without a fight. When I told Rod to stop screwing my wife, I thought he'd wet his pants. But when he got over his dismay, he was so forthcoming maybe it really was platonic between you two."

"You've no right to confront anyone based on supposition and gossip."

"Strange. That's about what Mister Pinski said."

"What makes you think I'm involved with Jack? He's only a cadet."

"You've seen the pictures." He dropped his head not wanting to see the impact his words would have on her. When he looked up, he saw tears in her eyes.

"He damn well printed them. The question is, how did he get them? If I'd have known it was by force, I think I'd have killed him this afternoon. I've wasted better men. But with the way you've been acting, I don't know who's the aggressor. How guilty is he, Lane?" Alex towered over his wife who had wilted into a chair. "Tell me he forced you. Please, for God's sake, tell me he forced you."

"Stay away from me," she said. "And stay away from that boy!"

CHAPTER FORTY-THREE

ALEX SAT IN THE GREENHOUSE nursing his third cup of coffee. Merrilane had departed leaving him to be awakened by the children squabbling over the toothpaste. Not knowing their departure time, he had been in the shower when they went outside to await their bus. They had acclimated well to his return, beginning now to ignore him as they went about their household duties. With their departure had come the quiet. No chattering air conditioner, no ringing telephone, no muffled B-52 strikes. He had riffled through the television channels, but snatches of firefights and helicopter insertions dominated the early morning news, so he abandoned his search for an acceptable time waster and now sat trying to conjure a worthwhile day's schedule. But the sun was seductive and the coffee rich and unlimited, causing him after a while to give up the mental effort and sit passively waiting for someone or something to arrange his agenda for him.

He knew he was still disoriented by the dream, its scenario etched by repetition on his brain. The events the dream had evoked, however, had escaped him. He remembered awakening suddenly, sitting straight up, thrashing his arms, and throwing the blanket into the darkness. One moment he had been wrestling to force the wildly bucking gunship beneath the cloud base, hearing the hoarse voice urging him lower, and straining to catch the faint blink of the twinkling strobe; the following instant he sat bathed in sweat in the soft depression of the mattress sensing Merrilane's presence crouching hushed in wide-eyed terror. He recalled savagely rubbing his head, spattering the fat beads of perspiration, then purging his lungs in a plaintive sigh followed by a panicky inhalation as if he were sucking the dregs from a near-empty oxygen bottle.

"What's wrong?" she had cried. But instead of coming to his aid, he felt her retreating further away, putting one foot off the side of the bed, and raising her weight as if ready to spring from his lunge. His mind snapped back into the dream seeing his orange tracers spewing out behind while simultaneously processing the feel of the mattress, the smell of her muted lotion, and the glowing red numerals announcing 3:16. He remembered feeling blindly for his Tee-shirt beside the bed, finding it, and wiping behind his neck and across his chest. Then he realized he was still pressure breathing, probably hyperventilating. He held his breath and the dream faded— Spooky 71, out. He found the sheet, pulled it over his naked body, and eased himself down on the damp mattress. She settled her weight, but continued to sit on the edge of the bed.

He had begun to shake, chills rippling through his body causing him to pull himself into a ball as if he were trying to roll out the emergency hatch of a stricken B-47. He hugged his shin bones, pulling them tight, forcing his thighs hard into his chest. Still the spasms racked his body. He remembered her pulling the blanket over him, tucking the satin edge around his neck as his mother had done that freezing night when he awoke choking with croup. Teetering in the cold-soaked passage, fighting the mind's blasting maelstrom, he fought to roll through the hatch into the swirling emptiness. His teeth chattered uncontrollably even as he tried to lock his jaws. The slipstream would catch him, dashing his body along the length of the fuselage, but he had to escape. Too late. They were spinning, centrifugal force freezing him to the bulkhead. He would go in with the twisting plane, drilling into the center of the earth before the final explosion.

In lucid moments shivering on the bed, he had felt as if his mind and body were permanently out of synchronization, his mind racing backward in time, hanging up periodically to dash round and round tracing each of his most intimate and lasting fears, while his body had finally tumbled out the gaping hatch and was spinning away into deep space. He tasted the copper tang of panic freezing in his mouth. Split apart, he was unable

297

to harmonize, unable even to find the two phases. He lacked the wiring diagram, the oscilloscope, the tools with insulated handles. Then, as he acknowledged he had lost the game, she slipped the heat of her body into his shroud. Perversely his thoughts went to Monique on the night he had covered her as rockets fell. Monique's strong features, framed in cascading dark tresses, motioned him back, but Merrilane's lithe body reeled him in.

He remembered her kissing him hard on the mouth, as if she had suddenly realized how close he was to permanent shattering. Or was that another time? She cradled his burning head in her lap, stroking his matted hair as if to smooth the flow of thoughts burbling inside his skull. Or was that his dear mother? She began to massage him, initiating their lovemaking like the application of some regimen of prescribed therapy. Or was that hazy memory just one of the tantalizing fantasies he had designed long ago to put himself to sleep? At some time or other, he seemed to remember pulling her close and falling into deep slumber holding her bonded so tightly that he smiled knowing no one would ever again strip her from him.

Yet, when he awoke to morning sunlight, she was gone.

The tentative rattling of the back door startled him. Iris, a towel-covered basket in her hands, was peering nearsightedly in. He roused himself quickly, opened the door, and kissed her cheek.

"Talk about being in another world," she said. "I thought you'd notice me when I came around the corner. I stood at the door at least thirty seconds before I jiggled the latch."

"Sorry, neighbor. I should have smelled those blueberry muffins. I haven't had one in a year, not since the morning before I left."

"I thought maybe you could use something homemade." Iris sat the basket down. "You know," she said sliding her hand over the tablecloth, "we made this, Kim and I." She hesitated, "We've done a lot of things together. I guess the Good Lord granted my wish to have a daughter. At least for a year. And I really believe working with Jeffrey salvaged Frank's spirit."

He had taken one of the cups from a tray and was filling it for his neighbor. *What a handsome woman. Harboring a special spark: class, sophistication, self-confidence.* He recalled the fantasies she had generated the first time they met at the reception for new faculty. Sheathed in a strapless blue gown that complimented her frosted hair, she was the kind of woman he assumed Merrilane would be at the same stage in her own development.

"You're not having any goodies?"

"No. We women over forty have to watch our weight." She smiled.

"I'm glad," he said breaking open one of the warm muffins. "All the fat women I've seen since coming home have depressed me. Appearance says so much about a woman's state of mind."

"What does it tell you about me?"

Surprised, not having categorized Iris as a woman requiring second-party appraisal, he grappled for an acceptable reply. "Oh, that's asking too much of the just-returned warrior."

"Maybe that's because I expect him to give straight answers to direct questions."

"For one thing, I would expect a person who bakes this well to be a rotund man wearing a white uniform, flour-spattered apron, and high chef's hat."

"Alex, we've both been through a trying year. Both exposed to dying men. When you look at me, do you see continued life or approaching death?"

"Good God, Iris, why so serious on such a beautiful morning?"

"I'm asking, and I want your answer. It's important."

"Yes, I believe it is." He stopped toying with the remaining bits of blueberry, and looked at her as closely as he would a cadet who had presented himself for extra instruction.

"If it really matters, I find you haven't aged. Not just in the past year, but since we first met. I assume it takes you longer each morning to maintain your position, but you do it. Unless your mind betrays you, I'd imagine you'll hold the line at least into your late eighties, maybe forever." She started to interrupt. "No, let me finish. If I were a different kind of man, I believe I'd try right this moment to take advantage of your mood, to compromise you for my own benefit. But to answer your question, I see life. Lots of life."

"And you're not the kind of man to compromise me?"

"Unfortunately, no." He dropped his eyes, "I'll have to be content with another of your muffins." He smiled self-consciously as he tried to lighten the conversation.

"You're a kind and considerate man, Alex Cannard. Maybe the second kindest I've known. You always seem to know what to say to a woman, not to be condescending but to make her think you'd talk to her that same way if she were a man."

"Thank you, my friend. But I don't always know what to say to women. Maybe I used to, but I don't any more. And I'm not kind. I snap at people, particularly people I used to go out of my way to put at ease and to teach. I've been home with my children just two days, and they're already crowding me."

"That's expected. You've been away a long time. People and times have changed radically. The society's fragmenting more than anytime since our war. But after Japan surrendered, we returned to innocence for a while. After this one, there'll be no returning to the old ways. Ever."

"I suspect you're right. I know I've felt like the fifth wheel since I've been home."

"Everyone distrusts the government. As a result, men see their duty differently. Women judge the turmoil as an opportunity to make a break, to go after the brass ring on their own. The pendulum's swinging, and it's got a knife edge ready to cut down any tradition, any person, any thing that gets in its way. That big rye field has turned into a mass of red poppies, and there's no one to catch Kim and Jeffrey before they fall. Your children are at risk, Alex Cannard, and so is your wife.

Without you, their chances of finding themselves before they self-destruct will be dearly compromised."

"You paint a dismal picture, Iris." He put the second muffin back in the basket. "You've been under a strain. Are you sure you're not misreading the signals?"

"Alex, I know I'm not an intellectual. I've devoted myself to antiquated things: my child, my husband . . . my garden. But Frank's illness opened my eyes. Sitting beside his bed, I had an opportunity to read the news magazines and to put things together. The train's off the track. The engineers and conductors are all looking to the Far East trying to pound some insignificant little country into acquiescence while we're losing our own children and our civility."

He could not recall having heard her speak so forcefully. But then, not having expected insightful conversation from her, he had never really listened. "Surely it can't be that bad."

"That bad! You obviously can't believe a whole society could get such a head start toward ruin in only a year's time. Some of it's been out of your range, but lots happened right under your nose, and you still refuse to see it. You, the last healthy, decent man I know, and you can't see it." Tears streaked her mascara. He noticed in the direct sunlight her skin had a harsh, leathery glaze he had not detected before.

He extended his handkerchief. She took it, dabbed at her eyes, then knotted the cloth in her hands.

"Perhaps this is the worse possible time to tell you, Iris," he searched for words. "But Lane and I have decided I'll be going alone to California for B-Fifty-two transition and then on to Louisiana for assignment. We don't want to yank the kids out of classes and inflict two moves on them in less than six months."

"Oh, Alex, you poor man. You weren't listening to a single word I said."

CHAPTER FORTY-FOUR

AS THE AIRSPEED INDICATOR ticked off 146 knots, Alex lifted 400,000 pounds of aircrew, metal, electronics, and jet fuel from the runway at Castle Air Force Base. *Just an overgrown B-47,* he thought, *with two extra throttles and three more men to keep track of.* "Gear up," he commanded, tapping the brakes to stop the wheels' rotation as the hydraulic system pumped the outriggers and four massive dual-tired trucks upward to nest inside the outboard pods and main fuselage. "Flaps up." He concentrated on achieving his climb schedule, allowing the speed to accumulate in proportion to the degree of retraction shown on the flap indicator. Missing was the thrill, perhaps eradicated by weeks of repetitive simulator practice. For Lieutenant Colonel Alex Cannard, propelled into the sparkling California sky by eight churning, smoke-trailing J-57 engines, followed by the eyes of military personnel, farmers, and passing motorists, tracked by departure control radar, and graded by the alert instructor hunched in the co-pilot's ejection seat, the dominant emotion was boredom.

Had he run through his allotment of unique experiences, he wondered as he flicked the electric trim button. Was life to be all routine from here on, previewed by television, computers, or simulators?

"Nice takeoff, Alex," the instructor's voice punched through the intercom. "Looks like you were born to fly the BUFF."

"I hope not, Herb. Why is it I always draw big airplanes with little bitty cockpits?"

The mission settled into the routine they had spent all the previous day perfecting. His mind reverted to channels dredged by nine years of B-47 procedures. Refueling rendezvous was almost identical—same radio calls, similar speed schedule, familiar picture from the observation position immediately behind and fifty feet below the tanker. Just a bit of a change at hook-up as the boom passed overhead before thunking into the receptacle aft of the flight deck. He stabilized behind the tanker searching for reference points to tell him when he was creeping in or slipping back. Nudging only the two inboard throttles to synchronize speeds exactly, he recalled the many times when throttles jammed to their limits would not halt the inexorable slide of a heavy B-47 off the boom. Even in the rarified atmosphere almost six miles above the earth, the effort necessary to control the refueling B-52 was minuscule compared to the sloppy, sometimes unpredictable, but always physically draining contortions required to tame the B-47.

After a while, as the rhythm of aerial mating re-established itself, a sense of confidence, almost of complacency, seemed mixed with the oxygen he sucked from his mask. During the subsequent high altitude navigation leg, he discovered he was only the driver and not the coach and supervisor he had been in the less sophisticated B-47. The two navigators, separated from his view on the lower deck and further isolated within the privacy of their own interphone system, teamed under the supervision of their instructor to perform all the celestial calculations, sextant observations, and plotting of the resultant sun lines. Skip Thorpe, twenty-two years old, recently graduated from flying school, and computer-assigned as his co-pilot, swapped seats with the instructor and tried to look professional by scanning the horizon for traffic and taking fuel readings every ten minutes. Herbie Galway, the Instructor Pilot and a friend from the 96th Bomb Squadron, nodded in the jumpseat as sunlight bathed the flight deck.

To stay awake, Alex plied himself with tepid coffee, searched for and replaced tiny, burned-out instrument light bulbs, and tried to anticipate what problems might emerge during the low-level navigation and bombing phases. Weather was usually the biggest headache and most frequent antidote to pilot inattention. But the gigantic California High, dominating the charts for a thousand miles in any direction, obviated concern. *Haven't had so much fun,* he thought, *since checking standardization folders at Pleiku.*

The pace accelerated, however, as they exited polar steering and dropped into a descending teardrop pattern which reminded him of the sweeping arc into Nouasseur which always ended with a cold beer. Tonight's beer was still five hours away. Flattening out his glide and pushing up the throttles as he leveled on the first heading, he felt the familiar chop of low-level turbulence. He engaged the autopilot, flipped the altitude-hold switch, and called for the checklist to calibrate the terrain-following radar scopes glowing dumbly on both pilots' instrument panels. Most students and some veterans dropped behind at this point. Alex and Skip did not. The initial attack on the target, and the subsequent racetracks, were to him again repeats of what had become second nature long ago.

They returned at dusk, getting descent clearance passing abeam Bakersfield and receiving radar vectors to the final approach. He intercepted the ILS localizer then, engines throttled back to a whisper, captured the glide path at the outer marker. Thumbing in a bit of back trim, he crossed the fence at best flare speed, holding her off until she settled.

"Beautiful," Herbie murmured. "Let's take her around and see if that was just luck." Bringing in the power after the instructor had repositioned his flaps, air brakes, and stabilizer trim, he felt the aircraft leap off the ground assuming the curious, nose-low attitude it held at light gross weights when climbing to pattern altitude. He began to enjoy the sensations of flying once more as he exchanged his chauffeuring role for pilot's work. Not even the tightly fitting oxygen mask and the heavy plastic helmet could dilute the pleasure of demonstrating he was in complete control of the gigantic BUFF.

After the final landing, the crew followed a familiar ritual: a stop at maintenance debriefing to report the aircraft's mechanical and electronic status followed by a half-hour at the student squadron completing forms and conferring with their instructors.

He was in no rush to return to his sterile BOQ room, but the others were pushing to break away. With the exception of Alex and Skip, all had families and home-cooked meals waiting. He had hoped the prospects of a six-month vacation in the spectacular region surrounding the base would finally entice Merrilane to accompany him. She, however, rejected the trail of carrots leading ultimately to a SAC bombardment wing. When Kim had begun questioning the heated words she heard passing between her parents, he had arranged for an immediate posting to the West Coast.

When the group broke up, he invited his co-pilot to join him for dinner at the officers' club.

"Sorry, Colonel," Thorpe replied with a wink, "I gotta heavy date in Merced. Now's my time to practice touch and goes."

"Not to worry, Skip. Would you mind dropping me at the officers' quarters?"

Being without family, wheels, or initiative on a Friday night meant for Alex the start of another unproductive weekend spent confined to base. Stopping by the housing office, he pumped a handful of change into a vending machine and gained his dinner. Later, without showering, he stretched out on his cot and dozed. The roar of a J-57 being trimmed at the engine test stand awakened him. Squinting to see the luminous hands of his watch, he realized it was too late to make the movie and more depressing to hit the club bar than to stay in his room.

"Could try a call home, then do my run," he caught himself verbalizing like a senile old man.

"Hello, Lane? Hope I didn't wake you . . . Sorry. I'm feeling lonesome and thought maybe I could talk to the kids . . . Oh, I see . . . I guess so . . . Had my first Fifty-two ride today . . . No, there's little joy in it. I'd better let you go. At least it's good not to yell 'Over' every time we've finished speaking—Over . . . We used to say a lot in the five minutes they allowed us. The guy next in line was scowling and counting down the seconds. Always seemed to come down to 'I love you.' I still do, you know.

"How's the job? . . . That's great. It'll mean a lot to the town . . . I ought to let you get back to sleep. Lately I've noticed I toss and turn after once being awakened. Doubt I got three hours last night. Otherwise I'm fine. Running every day just like all the other maniacs . . . No, I hate it, but it takes up an hour I'd otherwise have to program.

"Gym's a bit small. Well managed. They try to counter the drug problem with athletic programs. Don't know how else to reach the burnouts. God knows it's not Duty, Honor, Country anymore. Well, . . . I'll let you go.

"But drugs are something we need to discuss. Kim and Jeff'll have to grapple with them. Kids out here don't see anything wrong with Marijuana . . . I'm disappointed to hear you say that, Lane. I've never even accepted your cigarettes. Madison Avenue's zeroed in on you folks. We've got more to fear from them than from Wall Street. The financiers just manipulate money; the ad people program our behavior.

"But why disparage the good life now that I'm again a member of the international jet set . . . I should get a squadron ops job after humping a crew for about six months, They're short of guys with SAC experience. Lots of us have hung it up . . . Yes, pinned 'em on Wednesday. Actually I painted them on. The base exchange was out of silver leaves, so I got some model airplane dope and painted my gold ones . . . Thank you; now they match my hair. It's turning grayer every day. I'm thinking of seeing if there's some brown airplane dope.

"I haven't had any letters from anyone . . . Say again; I missed that. You're speaking so fast, and it sounds like you've got a cold . . . You're what? . . . Are you certain? . . . Slow down, please. How far along? . . . I can't say I'm ecstatic. It'll take a bit of getting used to. How do you feel? . . . I'll try for maximum delay en route . . . Are the kids aware? . . . Any more surprises? . . . I'm worried about you; I wish I were there.

"In fact, I wish I were anywhere but here. Time's moving backwards. I've seen it all before. But I guess now you can say the same in some respects. I never thought it would turn out this way . . . I understand your position. Believe me I do. Intellectually I understand completely. I suppose it's selfish to want it the way it was. Or maybe I'm just getting old. Enough of that. Write when you get a spare moment. Take care of yourself."

After hanging up he pulled his gym bag from under the bed and rummaged for a clean pair of white socks. He settled for a pair stiff with dried sweat, then slipped into his shoes and tennis shorts. He left his room without locking the door.

Should do some stretches. Why bother? Wonder where the action is tonight? Up near the Fish Hook as usual. Nixon's pulling out twenty-five thou this month. Beginning of the end. Some secret plan. Stand by boys in blue. In your B-Fifty-two. Not just a few. But the G-models too. And that means YOU. Boo Hoo, Boo Hoo. So you better practice your running, Old Boy, 'cause if you go down among the bad guys after dumping a load of five-hundred pounders, they're gonna be some pissed.

The cool breeze on his chest enticed him to increase the pace, but he maintained a prudent gait, not yet breathing hard, not yet feeling the pounding along the front of his shins. His mind seemed separated again and running along beside him, bounding from subject to subject like a logger skipping across a mill pond trying to reach and break up a jam. *Wonder how Wootan's making out with Monique? Dumb move, extending. Spooky woman, strange hang-ups. Could have had her if I'd pressed. She, almost ready. I, shocked by the bomb Lane dropped. More devastation than all the VC rockets that night. Dear John, dear John, dear, dear, dear, John. Really needing a woman if only to see if I still function. Any woman at all. Even Long. Where's she tonight? Doing whose laundry? Whose boots? With no time for hang-ups. What lay behind those slanting brown eyes? Real feelings, or was she like some pig, or cow, or chicken? Brutus had feelings. Do pigs, and cows, and chickens know we tolerate them only because they're in our food chain? Do all the Vietnamese Longs know they're in our wash chain, our boot chain, even sometimes our sexual relief chain? Or, not being round eyes, do they count for anything at all?*

Friendship counts. The only counter in the game. Long was my friend. And Wootan. And Monique. And Glenn. Even Archer. Friends never split up. Unless one meets the Golden BB. Or steals what be-longs to his friend.

Friends. Wootan and me. Monique was his woman. Would he sleep with Merrilane? He's suave; she'd like him. Maybe all she needed was a fighter pilot in the first place. Someone never to have treated her as anything but a wingman who could be replaced.

CHAPTER FORTY-FIVE

ON THE MORNING of October 15, 1969, *The New York Times* reported the nationwide antiwar moratorium march. That evening Strategic Air Command's management control system would record a mission of Tinker 24. Neither mattered a great deal to Alex Cannard who, while shepherding the bomber's huge bulk between parked rows of her sisters, was thinking of hogs: specifically the Blue Ribbon winner he had once seen at a county fair ponderously following a trail of yellow corn.

Ahead the FOLLOW ME truck, impatient at the pace, suddenly accelerated and whipped into the slot reserved for the aircraft. Alex trundled past the curving yellow line until he judged the wheels of the gigantic forward main truck to be intersecting it. Then he eased the nosewheel steering control clockwise to swing the long snout ninety degrees to the right until it picked up the trail again and homed on the spot it had left over eight hours previously. Halfway through the turn, he spotted the blue staff car waiting beside the crew bus.

"Radar, This is AC. We've got a reception committee. Better check the bomb scores and have your low-level charts handy in case some turkey farmer's complained." He hastened through the engine shutdown knowing that, whatever the news, it would be bad. SAC did not waste an operations officer's time just to tell a pilot he and his people had been voted Crew of the Month.

As he pulled off his helmet, he was surprised to see the outstretched hand and smiling face of the commander of the training squadron.

"Congratulations, Colonel. Your wife's presented you with a baby boy, both fine at the Academy hospital. If you folks filled all the squares on your checkride, you can be out of here tomorrow."

"Thanks for coming out, Hank. I must be getting paranoid; I just assumed you were here to kick ass."

"I know what you mean, but this is the new SAC. The computer says every squadron commander has to pay a compliment or extend congratulations at least three times a week."

"I've been confused over the due date. Any idea of the specs?"

"Eight pounds fourteen ounces, twenty-one inches long. Big baby. Got any names picked out?"

He had started pulling himself out of the damp tangle of parachute harness and survival kit but paused, bracing himself on the ejection seat's headrest. "Little guy needs a name. I guess I'll just have to give him mine." Then he followed the squadron commander through the hole to the navigation deck, and down the ladder to stand stiff-legged on the oil-stained concrete. Beside him the power cart labored and coughed something like a newborn infant trying to clear its lungs.

The flight back to Colorado Springs was a repeat of the last phase of his journey from Vietnam, except he arrived at dusk just about the time the Spookies would be taxiing out for the early patrol. He was glad to see Frank had come alone to meet him.

"Congratulations, Papa! Where's my smoke?"

"Thanks, Frank. No cigar this time."

"What kind of father are you? Being away all summer, you didn't have to do anything to get ready. Guess who ended up painting the baby bed?" Frank chuckled as they waited for the baggage to be distributed. "Now I bet you'll go off to Barksdale and miss all the three-o'clock feedings."

"That's the new marriage style, Frank. Obviously you haven't read how glamorous it is to spend half your life yo-yoing back and forth in airliners or standing around terminals when the schedule's bollixed up. Homemaking's passé, along with the idea of living with one man on a long-term basis."

"Sounds like you're specializing in feminine liberation history." They walked out to the car, Frank carrying the B-4 bag, full he suspected of dirty laundry. Alex had the bulging aviators kit slung over his right shoulder.

"It may sound that way. But if I ever return to academe, I'll make my specialty some insignificant moment in the life of an unknown mystic who lived in the mountains of Peru two hundred years ago. I'm staying away from all things contemporary."

"Any particular reason?"

"Because whenever I think of the sociological and political movements of the time, I want to cry. And you know how difficult it is to work with wet manuscripts." He flashed a weak imitation of the mischievous smile that had intrigued Frank some four years previously when he first interviewed him. "Tell me, Frank, have you seen the little guy? Who does he look like?"

"Yes, I've seen him. This afternoon as a matter of fact. Like all babies, he resembles Winston Churchill."

"Let's hope he thinks like him. The world could use a good statesman. I hear he's a big boy."

"Surprisingly big considering he's not quite term. But you're a big man, so that's to be expected." Frank pulled the Corvair into traffic and accelerated. "The engine overhaul really put some zip in the old gal. She's got no rust so she should be good for another hundred thousand regardless of what Ralph Nader says." He patted the steering wheel. "I think we've both had our warranties renewed."

"You're feeling good then?"

"Never better. Iris and I are settling into our "golden years," and I've rarely been happier."

"Don't say it too loud. The gods may be listening."

As the car sped out Academy Boulevard, Alex noticed the neon sign of the Blue Fox Motel with the poor fox still running in place, but tiring as the sign now flashed on and off in no particular rhythm.

"The investigation, Frank," he had shifted in the seat, resting his shoulder against the door and watching his friend's face in the light of on-coming traffic. "Did anything come of it?"

"No, I'm sorry to say. *The Falcon Code* ceased publication. The Supe pulled the OSI agents off the case. Whatever stir the paper caused has been forgotten. New scandals have a way of taking over. Right now everyone's in a twitter about the banishment of a young Mormon instructor. Evidently kicked over the traces and tried to make up for lost time in the drinking and oat-sewing departments. Tomorrow it'll be something else. Even in this showplace, our people are still human."

"You think the publisher of *The Falcon Code* slipped into the force on graduation day?"

Frank slowed at the gate, switching to parking lights so the guard could see his sticker. "I believe he did. Let's hope the challenge overcomes his immaturity." He returned the guard's salute, flicking back to headlights as he smoothly ran the gears. "Yes, he slipped through our fingers, but it was a near thing. I think our man would have made a mistake eventually."

"You're speaking of Pinski?"

"Yes. It's conceivable you'll run into him someday. He's in pilot training, but he went out of here like all the rest, determined to fly nothing but fighters."

"You know what they say, Frank. The needs of the service come first. It may be Mister Pinski's penance is to spend his life in SAC flying BUFFs. And if that happens, I'll be waiting for him."

Iris' car was still in the hospital lot as they pulled in to park. Inside the main entrance, Alex was stormed by his excited children who had been waiting for him after seeing their baby brother.

"What's the verdict on the new arrival, kids? Do we keep him or throw him back?"

"Keep him," Kim shouted bright eyed.

"Throw him back," Jeffrey said straight faced, but then broke into laughter as his father stooped down and gave his head a violent Dutch Rub.

"You're the one I ought to throw back. What happened to all the letters you were supposed to write me? And you, young lady," Alex hugged Kim. "You weren't much better!"

"Oh, Dad, there's been so much to do getting ready for the baby. And Mom didn't stop working until last Wednesday. You're going to have to get someone to do the house; it's a pig pen, and Jeffrey never picks up anything."

"I've got someone to do the house. It's called the Kids Cleaning Service."

"Dad!" Kim stood before him frowning, with her lower lip stuck out. "Sometimes you make me think everything Mom says is true!"

He broke away from the children, rising to kiss Iris on both cheeks. "I guess you got the short end of this as usual?"

"Not at all. But you'd best run if you want to see the baby. The nursery closes its curtains in five minutes. You'll find Merrilane in a double room, but the nurse said you could stay until ten if you're quiet."

"I'll leave the Corvair for you," Frank said as he tossed the keys. "Stop in for a beer when you get back."

Following the yellow arrows to the nursery, he arrived at the long window and stood trying to detect signs of life in the bundle resting under the placard identifying "Baby Cannard." An older woman, wearing the starched cap and broad black band of a civilian nurse, came into the room to draw the curtains. Seeing Alex, she nodded and smiled. As he began to walk uncertainly away in search of Merrilane's room, the woman appeared carrying the sleeping infant.

"His Daddy ought to be able to hold him despite the rules." She extended the child to him.

He accepted the bundle awkwardly. "Yes, his Daddy should see him. Thank you, nurse." He felt nothing. No emotions of joy, awe, or wonder. No curiosity to see if the child had a full set of fingers and toes. He felt as if he were a stranger asked to hold a baby while his mother made a place to change a diaper. The child's eyes were shut and seemed to have some sort of rash about them. From time to time, he imitated a fish, pursing his lips in and out.

"Hello, Buddy," Alex said. "Do you read me?" The baby didn't answer. He adjusted the blanket and passed the child back to the nurse. She smiled again and started to turn away, but he touched her arm and leaned in to where the child lay doing his fish imitation. "Don't worry, Buddy," he whispered. "I'll take care of you."

Following the nurse's directions, he found the room without difficulty. Its door was open six inches, but he hesitated before entering. In the past, when visiting for the first time after the births of Kim and Jeffrey, he had shaved and picked up roses before presenting himself to his wife. Tonight there hadn't been time. *What difference does it make anyway? Time to stop treating everything as if it were a movie script with lights, wardrobe, and background music.* He pushed the door open a bit further and slipped through. The woman in the first bed had long dark hair and appeared to be sleeping. He stepped past the curtain separating the two mothers to see Merrilane lying on her side, face in shadow, bleached hair grown to a reasonable length.

"Are you asleep, Lane?"

"No. I was wondering if you'd come tonight."

"You didn't get the flowers I sent?"

"You sent some? No, not yet."

"Roses go with babies; you told me that."

She smiled. Alex felt the dampness on her cheeks as he leaned to kiss her. "Are you feeling better?"

She rubbed her eyes with the back of her hand, "Yes, I feel fine. He's a nice baby."

"Yes, I've seen him, held him."

"How . . . how did . . . "

"The nurse saw me at the window. Said the father should see the baby." He felt inhibited by the presence of the woman in the next bed. It was as if he were trying to discuss intimate details in a quiet restaurant where the only other patrons had been seated immediately next to them. He could feel Merrilane's eyes on him. *Locked on and tracking,* he thought.

"What do you think? What are your plans?" she asked.

"I think he's a fine baby. Big and bald. The others had lots of dark hair didn't they? As for my plans, I think I'll have a beer with Frank when I leave here."

She seemed to be sobbing, lying motionless in the dark as if a nurse had syphoned, bottled, and stored away her vitality in some laboratory's deep freeze. He sat on the side of the bed, grasped her perspiring left hand and squeezed it. "Don't cry. I never want to see anyone cry again." He patted her hand for a long time wanting to lower his chest to hers and hold her. But he held his position searching where her eyes should have been for a green flare to clear him in. He saw no flare, heard no voice, made no move.

After a long interval, during which the woman beyond the curtain shifted and sighed, he rose from the bed. "I'll let you get some sleep. Maybe the flowers will be here by morning. We don't seem able to communicate even through Tele-Florist."

"You're right, Alex. But I want you to understand this doesn't change anything. I'm still not going back into the kind of life you offer me."

He turned away, but stopped at the edge of the curtain. "I'm truly sorry, Lane, and I hope you'll reconsider. The invitation's still open. The baby needs a father as well as a mother. You may be right that this doesn't change anything, but it sure as hell clarifies a lot in my mind."

CHAPTER FORTY-SIX

"CANNARD!" THE RASPING VOICE startled him as he sat nursing a cup of coffee in the deserted Alert Force dining room. "How much Fifty-two time you got?"

Alex jumped to his feet as he recognized the Wing Commander. "Good evening, sir. You're keeping late hours."

"I get paid to keep late hours. And you get paid to answer my questions, not engage in idle chit-chat."

He had heard Colonel Culpepper wasted no time on pleasantries. "About four hundred hours, sir."

"That's not much for a SAC light colonel." Culpepper looked askance. "How much total time?"

"Almost five thousand. I figure the two thousand hours in B-Forty-sevens could be added to the Fifty-two totals since the airplanes are similar."

"Not in General Morant's book. He says he wants the most experienced Fifty-two troop I got runnin' the wing's standardization division, and I don't make a policy of ignorin' the Old Man's druthers." Culpepper slid into one of the chairs at Alex's table and motioned for him to sit down. "I need me a Stanboard chief that'll kick ass and take names, and I need him yesterday."

"What happened to Colonel Westbrook? Everyone says he's the best in SAC."

"He is, damn it." Culpepper's voice was mid-way between resignation and rebellion. "That's the problem sharin' a base with the higher headquarters. You get somebody up to speed, and them peckerwoods steal him."

"And you're thinking of me as his replacement? I'm flattered."

"Don't start rearrangin' his office furniture. I been goin' over your flying records and effectiveness reports, and I'm not so sure I want to take a chance on you."

"Why do you think anyone else would be less a risk? My lack of Fifty-two time?"

"Cannard," the wing commander cast a quick look over his shoulder, "I'll level with you. The amount of time don't make a rat's ass to me if you're smart enough to know when to ask somebody else a technical question. What I want is a manager who can keep every swingin' dick eatin', drinkin' and sleepin' his job. Stan-eval's my quality control. I don't know squat about Fifty-twos, low level bombin', and all that other square fillin' you do. I'm a tanker man. I could put a tanker task force at the north pole if Morant said do it. I know the war plan and all the shortcuts in runnin' a base. I know how to make visitin' fire-men feel like they're bein' rocked in their mama's arms. In other words, I'm general officer material, and this bomb wing's my ticket except I don't know diddle about bombers. That's why I need a mean som'bitch to make sure no ill-trained, faintly-mo-tivated peckerwood knocks that star out of my deservin' hand."

"And, if I read you correctly, you don't know if I'm mean enough."

"You got it, Cannard. It's that tour out of SAC that's botherin' me. Four years screwin' off readin' ancient history."

"It wasn't all ancient history, Colonel. My interest was in the military aspect, especially recent times. I did my thesis on command leadership."

"Well, the pitcher I get from readin' your records is a 'Nice Guy.' Even your official photo shows a big, shit-eatin' grin. Do you know what percentage of officers smile in their official photo? Point zero zero two. Part of your job in stan-eval is to scare the drawers off everyone else in the wing. Including the squadron commanders. And most especially the trainin' people, so they don't try to run some dullard by you when they know I'm in a bind for aircrews."

"You forget I was in the 'old SAC' before General Morant's campaign to emphasize integrity. I flew Forty-sevens when the only people you trusted were your own crewmembers and the final controller in the radar shack."

"Well that's what I want here. I want the whole wing to hate the guts of the Chief of Standardization. I want them to spend half their waking life figuring ways of catching him in a technical or judgmental error. As for integrity, fine. I can compete with anyone as long as the reporting's honest. But that means we meet the impossible quotas fair and square. No backing in nav legs or fast-counting the distance on refueling rendezvous. If we don't meet the norms, we'll take our lumps. But I'll give you a small clue, Cannard. When I get zinged, I call for my Stan-eval Chief. And I squeeze him till his eyeballs pop out."

Alex closely observed this self-styled backwoodsman whose country-boy conversation slipped away when he abandoned showmanship for problem solving. "Are you telling me terror is the only way to motivate our people?"

"I'm not saying it's the only way. I am saying it's the easiest. I'll take care of the carrots, but my Stanboard Chief has got to handle the stick."

"What specifically are you telling me, Colonel?"

"I'm telling you, my fine hero, I've had my eye on you since you got here. Mostly I like what I see except for your piddling time in the aircraft and your schoolmarm OER's. I'd planned to send you to Arc Light as soon as you got a little more time in the aircraft, but now I'm tinkering with the idea of making you Stanboard chief even though you don't have enough experience to drop bombs on Ho Chi Minh."

"We can drop bombs south of the DMZ till the cows come home, Colonel, and it won't do any good. If you want me for stan-eval, I'll give it my best shot."

"I said most of what I've seen has been impressive. It's what I've heard that bothers me."

"I don't understand."

"It's about your marriage, Cannard. Normally I don't fret much about what an officer does with his life outside duty hours. But I'm thinking seriously of putting you in the most important staff position I've got. The one that'll affect this wing's performance, and my own personal career, more than any other. I hear you're involved in one of those newfangled, two-career, two-location marriages. I want a stable man I can count on, as well as a mean som'bitch. Are you planning on running to Colorado every whip stitch to play with the baby's mama, or shack up with one of the Bossier Strip dollies, or play footsie with the lame-brained wife of some second lieutenant?"

"I could say that's none of your business, Colonel. Or that I can't predict the future. But since it is your business, and since I see the future clearly, I'll assure you I know my priorities. I won't embarrass you."

"Your last OER out of 'Nam says you 'overcame high-level harassment' to get your job done. What's that mean in words I can understand? You got a mean streak in you?"

"It's nothing I'm proud of. But I guess I can be as mean as the next man. Maybe meaner."

"How mean are you, Cannard?"

"I'm mean enough to bust you on your next stanboard if you don't know your procedures or bring less than a professional attitude when you come to fly."

"That's not mean, Cannard. That's downright foolish. But if I can get a waiver on your lack of time, you're the next Chief of Stan-eval." Culpepper got up quickly, almost tipping his chair onto the floor, and left the table without sealing the bargain with a handshake.

The months following his posting to standardization duties merged into one seemingly never-ending blur of briefings, staff meetings, conferences, arguments with the Chief of Training, and late night sessions with the Wing Commander. Punctuating these activities were countless checkrides—blasting off at dusk always with a different crew on a surprise basis, riding hunched in the jumpseat, grading each phase of the flight and documenting it on the printed forms.

Often he was called out of meetings to discuss an airborne emergency with an aircraft commander trying to break loose a hung outrigger gear, or experiencing pressurization difficulties, or attempting to repair a balky refueling system. On occasion their radio conversation evolved into a conference call with the main SAC command post deep under the headquarters in Omaha and with a team of technical representatives located at Boeing Wichita. Always during these hook-ups, he stated what he planned to recommend and then asked if anyone wished to modify his conclusion. He seemed instinctively to know not only the technical operation of the various aircraft systems, but also the current and forecast weather along the route and at any feasible alternate landing base.

In the grim-faced process of establishing his reputation, he picked up his nickname. It started among the aircrews, but shortly spread to the squadron commanders, schedulers, and even his own evaluators who began to refer to him as "Alexander the Grate." The name didn't bother him. Someone had to guard the entry into the fraternity of combat crewmen, to screen and grade the raw material, to make sure the heat stayed on so the product remained pure. He knew he could be legitimately called much worse.

Radio transmissions, bastardized by the adoption of truckers' CB jargon, became the subject of Alexander's first campaign. Those loath to change ingrained habits were treated to private interviews with the Chief of Standardization. Those irritated by his perceived arrogance took solace in knowing soon the wing would be hit by "CEG"—SAC's Central Evaluation Group —which would fly not only with a sampling of crews, but also with the chief himself.

"Alexander's got less stick time in the BUFF," observed the commander of the Twentieth Bomb Squadron at a scheduling meeting, "than most any other pilot in the wing despite all his sandbagging on evaluations. We'll see if he can hack CEG, or if he just talks a good game."

"Better wish him luck," his counterpart in the Forty-ninth Squadron replied. "If he rips it, the entire wing will have to pay the price."

"Well, I don't know what the sonofabitch's trying to prove, but he's sure making the rest of us look bad by comparison."

"He's welcome to whatever it is, but you know what they say: 'use it or lose it.' And as seldom as he gets home, I think Alexander's losing it."

To process the details of his frenetic schedule, Alex habitually dedicated the moments after his prayers and before sleep to a recapitulation of the day's activities—a mental re-evaluation of his performance, taking into consideration the salient issues, their options, the emotions involved, and how he could have better understood or responded to the individuals concerned. Frequently—unable to restrain them—images of his wife intruded: Merrilane smiling at his puns, Merrilane concentrating as she applied her make-up, Merrilane teasing him with kisses. Whenever he realized she was with him, he would drag his consciousness back by focusing on specific facets of information and technique, so the memory was smothered under the overpowering minutiae of checklist responses, grading tolerances, and positive control procedures. And the next time his thoughts disobeyed and tried to conjure up her likeness, he would find it just a bit harder to get it exactly right.

As the months fell away, the job became in one way easier because of his experience and technical knowledge. But the youth of the arriving replacements, and the advancing age and associated malfunctions of the bomber and tanker fleets, dictated he tighten the screws of compliance upon himself and his associates.

Occasionally, however, when the wing was not vulnerable to an exercise, he would slip off to Colorado Springs in hopes of spending some meaningful time with his children, perhaps seducing his wife, or—as was most often the case—keeping up appearances. Little Alex seemed to care more for him than Kim or Jeff, who were remote and involved with their own friends.

Merrilane's career continued to skyrocket, often obligating her to make out-of-town trips that seemed to coincide with his visits. Frequently, therefore, he spent much of his time sitting in Frank Harbinger's library living in the past.

Culpepper won his star, subsequently giving Alex a pair of his lucky eagles as a clear sign of forthcoming promotion. His replacement was a gentleman, Al Diamond, who continued most of Culpepper's policies but opened the lines of communication. He, too, was general-officer quality.

CHAPTER FORTY-SEVEN

"ALEX!" FRANK HARBINGER'S VOICE exploded from the receiver as if he were still in England shouting into the army phone net. "How about joining me in Hartford on the twenty-fifth for the meeting of the Society of Military Historians?"

"Sure, I'll let you go," the Deputy Commander for Operations said. "Provided the ORI has hit and we've maxed it." Alex knew better than to quibble about the details of pre-registration, non-refundable hotel fees, and airline reservations. SAC's world revolved around the annual Operational Readiness Inspection. So he simply nodded, went back to work, and quietly made preparations to attend.

I've got two chances of going, he told himself that night after he snapped out the light. *Slim and none. SAC just hit us with a standardization evaluation, so they know we're good. Chances are they'll catch us toward the end of the cycle when we're bored from practicing bombing runs in the trainer. Better to get it over with. Is Your inspection system like this, God? Is life just one long ORI that You score to see who gets his star?*

The next morning he scheduled his standardization crews to attend a weekend "GI Party" to give the office a thorough housecleaning. Sad stories asking exemption flooded his office. "Consider this the yearly premium on your professional insurance policy," he told the supplicants. "Spend a day with me now, rather than every weekend for the next six months with my successor."

"But, sir," Hank Allison said, "we never get any time at home."

"Your story has touched my heart," he replied. "Tell everyone families are invited. They can clean the offices while you guys check every signature, date, and evaluation item on every record in our files."

When he arrived shortly after eight on "Clean up-Ketchup Day," Alex found the office overrun with people who were removing draperies and blinds from the windows, stripping wax from the floors, and preparing the walls for painting. Hank Allison's arthritic wife, Miriam, smiled sweetly from her wheelchair, wished him a cheery "Top o' the Morning," and resumed tracking the various tasks on her PERT charts. Precisely at noon, a contingent arrived with hot dogs, chips, baked beans, soft drinks, and two cases of Heinz 57. By 4:30 windows sparkled, floors reflected buffer swirls, and semigloss beige had supplanted institutional green.

"Your worries are over, boss," Hank Allison called from the doorway. "Two officers have separately checked each form. If those inspectors find one discrepancy, I'll kiss a pig on the front lawn of Second Air Force Headquarters. From now on Lou Katz or I will countersign each folder before it goes into the files. It'll give us something to do in our spare time."

"Major Allison," he pushed back from his desk, "you may find a little extra something in your pay envelope this month."

"Thanks, boss, but Miriam gets the credit. She orchestrated the whole thing."

"She's a remarkable woman; reminds me of someone I once knew."

As the vulnerability date for the massive flight exercise and compliance inspection drew near, he detected the Wing's peaking. Holding its sharp edge for an extended period would be difficult. Scheduled to assume alert on the Thursday morning coinciding with the first day of vulnerability, he knew his lead standardization crew would be the first launched should the exercise be called. More probable, however, were the chances of spending an uneventful week of 24-hour duty caged in the alert quarters while some other unit put its reputation on the line. Having lived so intimately and for so long with the abstract concept of Mutual Assured Destruction, he seldom considered the possibility of being dealt a hand in a final game of nuclear annihilation.

"You want to get some lunch before we go to target study, boss?" Alex looked up to see his radar navigator.

"I think I'll skip it today, Phil, and go running instead."

As Major Donaldson turned away, Alex called to him. "What say we get the crew together after target study and go over the ORI once more?"

"I'd vote to hold off till tomorrow when we're on alert. We won't be eating home cooking or sleeping in our own beds for another seven days—eight if you count flying a training mission off alert. We just had CEG, so there's no chance of our getting hit."

"Sorry, Phil. I can't buy that argument. If the Viet Cong taught me anything, it was to expect the unexpected. And SAC is easily as sneaky as the VC. If I were commanding SAC and I wanted to take a close look at Diamond's star qualities, I'd hit his wing when it's most vulnerable. That's tomorrow during alert changeover."

"That's easy for you to say," Donaldson's cheeks flushed red as if he had been drinking too long at the O Club bar. "You don't have a wife to pacify or kids who ask straight out why you never have time to play with them. You're letting the fucking job SACumcise you. When are you going to get tired of sucking up to the Old Man?"

Alex jerked to his feet, propelling his chair back against the baseboard. "You're out of line, Major! It's easy to criticize when you're not in charge; but if you disagree with my judgment, give me an operational argument not your personal problems."

"Look, Colonel, I'm going . . . "

"When I talk to you," his voice spiked then dropped back into its normal range, "I don't expect to be interrupted. If your first instinct is to fight me, I suggest you remember who you are, and where you are, and who in the hell I am. And in case you don't recognize me, I'm the best friend you've got."

You smug son-of-a-bitch, Donaldson's eyes flashed as if the words were a tornado warning trailing silently along the bottom of a television screen. "I'm sorry for whining," he said.

"Laura's bitching sometimes gets to me. I'll tell the others we'll be reviewing the ORI."

"If it's any consolation, I'm suggesting the DO have all the crews join us in taking a look at the route this afternoon."

"That won't make you any friends."

"Maybe not, but it'll make you feel better. Besides, the more I think about it, the more I'm sure we're gonna get hit at changeover."

"Care to wager a small sum on your belief?"

"Not on that, but if you get a pool started, I'll put fifty bucks on our crew to get the best bombing scores."

In bed that night, he played and replayed his encounter with Donaldson thinking of alternate ways he could have responded. Sometime before dawn the asthmatic air conditioner belched violently, shaking the entire window frame as if rockets were dropping in from the Dong Nai.

Shortly before eight, sleepy eyed and moving slowly, he joined the crews assembled for change-over briefing. The routine items were disposed of quickly, the meteorologist signaled for the lights to be dimmed, and Alex was startled by the appearance of his boss kneeling beside his chair.

"Your hunch may pay off," he whispered. "The ORI team's airborne out of Omaha filed to Dyess. That flight plan's close enough to allow a quick diversion in here. I'm cutting this wuz-wuz short and getting ready for the real war."

The briefing broke up with men streaming out of the underground facility as if they were answering the klaxon horn. Alex sprinted across the ramp while the remainder of his crew piled into a pickup loaded with dumpy bags of cold-weather clothing, satchels jammed with flight manuals, and jet helmets encased in their protective bags which caused the ritual to resemble nothing so much as an amateur bowling team departing for a tournament.

"How's the bird?" he yelled above the huffing power cart.

"Pretty good shape," the crew chief pulled the huge Mickey Mouse protectors off his ears. "We changed the starter solenoid on number seven engine after the practice alert Monday and had some radar maintenance yesterday. As far as I can tell, she's a goer."

He clambered up the ladder onto the flight deck meeting Captain Jim Wright, who had lived with the bomber for the last seven days. He had the combat mission folders and communications documents ready for Alex's inspection. Hank Allison and Technical Sergeant Herb Lorenz, the gunner, had begun stuffing the aviators kits and briefcases through the entrance hatchway to Phil Donaldson who was sorting them out. Skip Thorp had squeezed in beside Alex to verify all the required war plans were in order. Once satisfied, Alex signed the receipt giving a carbon to the agitated captain.

"Okay, Colonel, she's all yours, and you're welcome to her."

Rising from his crouch, Alex saw the crew chief pop through the hatch frantically rotating his right fist above his head. He slapped Thorpe on the shoulder and pointed to the cockpit. "Alert," he yelled before scrambling into his seat and hitting simultaneously all eight starter switches. As the RPM indicators shook themselves and began to creep up, he spread the earphone pads and jammed the plastic headcover over hair that each day seemed more nearly to match the helmet's flat-white color. The reaction message was already crackling over the command frequency. He ignored the sounds, knowing both navigators and the electronics counter-measures officer were copying and decoding them. He had enough trouble—number seven engine was hung up at twenty percent. The bomber parked next to him was already rolling forward, lurching as its pilot tested his brakes, then sweeping out in a wide arc tumbling yellow chocks in its wake and causing its crew chief to clutch his headset and bend his back against the whirling jet blast.

"AC from Radar. Message checks, Cocoa alert: taxi to the runway and simulate take-off."

"EW agrees. It's the fucking ORI."

"AC, Roger." he tried to control the tone and pace of his words, but knew he was talking from a hole. "Crew chief, number seven's hung up. See any signs of fire?" The Maintenance Control bread truck had seen the delay and pulled beside his right wingtip spilling green-suited men like June Bugs from an overturned can. All the other bombers were moving now, with tankers filling in wherever a break existed in the stream. If this were war, the large wall clocks at SAC Headquarters would be counting down the time until Soviet missile impact as controllers carried out their tasks with a sense of resignation and even contempt.

"Crew chief. Clear those technicians out of the way; we'll taxi on seven engines." He flicked the landing lights signaling his intentions. "Crew from AC, standby for taxi. Co-pilot confirm seven-engine take-off data."

Twenty-six minutes later, dripping perspiration, Alex wheeled Billy 16 back into its parking slot. Despite his delay, all alert birds had simulated takeoff within the established limits. As SAC had removed the wing from its nuclear war commitment, now began a game of musical chairs with maintenance teams downloading weapons, adjusting fuel quantities, and repairing malfunctioning items tolerated for an emergency launch but deemed necessary for peacetime safety.

Alex and Phil Donaldson walked together across the ramp as the visual heat lines contorted the control tower reminding Alex of the Moroccan belly dancer he had watched out of boredom some nine years ago.

"Wright's crew sold us a sick radar," Donaldson said bitterly. "Unless it clears up when we get airborne, we may have to dead reckon around the horn. I wish there was a way to get maintenance to look at it when they fix the engine."

"Engine's safety of flight," he said. "A weak radar's the breaks of the game. Unless you're suggesting we cheat."

"This here's come-to-Jesus time. Lots of promotions on the line. Diamond's—yours."

"Spit it out, Phil. You're the radar expert. What do you recommend?"

"You puttin' me on, Alex?" Donaldson's head was cocked; he had that incredulous East Texas country boy look. The lid of his up-wind eye squinted in the sun.

"No, Phil. None of us wants to be penalized by a screwed-up radar that could be like new if we played our cards right. But it's illegal, and they'd burn us and crucify Diamond if we got caught."

"You're actually telling me to get the radar fixed?"

"No, that's too easy. You said you wished it was fixed. I'm saying I'm delegating the decision to you. The responsibility's on your back. You might as well get used to making command decisions; you won't be spending much more of your career on a crew."

"If I get caught even suggesting it to one of the maintenance men, I won't have a career. Look, Alex, I know you're shittin' me. You wouldn't let me cheat even if you knew I could."

"I don't know what you're talking about, Phil; I just said I wish the radar was fixed. Now it's up to you. I'm dealing myself out of it."

"Shit, Alex. You know I can't do anything like that."

"Yeah, pal, I guess I do. But it sure would be nice . . . "

"Alex, you sly son-of-a-bitch. You might as well kiss your fifty bucks goodby."

"It's not just the radar," Hank Allison had caught up with them. "It's the airplane itself. Everyone knows she's a Hangar Queen. It started when Arlie York stalled her in, almost breaking her back. He screwed up every vacuum tube and wire connection there is in the avionics system. Pilots say she even refuels flying sideways."

"Well, gentlemen, there's not much we can do about it. She's ours to win or lose. You wouldn't want some brand-new crew to have her would you?"

"You bet your sweet ass we would," Donaldson said.

"Grab yourselves some crew rest, and I'll see you in the wing briefing room tomorrow at seventeen hundred. By the way, Phil, I'm doubling my bet. When the story of our weak radar gets out, I'll get some great odds that'll pay for my trip to Hartford."

That night after turning off the bedside lamp, he began his monologue with God. His thoughts were as dispassionate as if he were on a conference call to SAC. *Nine chances out of ten, Lord, they'll have the engine fixed. But it's a repeat malfunction; what does that do to the odds? It's the radar that bothers me. And the weather. I could use a little luck in the refueling area and on the low-level route. Bad weather and weak radar'll make it sporty. You're cleared off frequency if You want, Lord. I know You're busy, but I guess You've got lots of channels and simultaneous translation capability. I hope You still have Your sense of humor.*

What if You're really Female like the astronaut joke says? Knowing my recent luck with women, I'm probably damned already. You may recall I used to be a pretty humorous fellow, but I seem to have lost all but the sardonic kind. Lost a lot that year. Didn't know most of it was slipping away. Like the color in my hair, draining out so quietly I didn't even notice. Like losing glycol in a Spitfire. That's the plane to have flown. By myself. Happy to slip the surly bonds, even with Huns behind every cloud. Worth risking it all to have flown the Spit and touched Your face.

Tossing and turning, he lay on the verge of sleep. Then he was letting down through turbulent clouds, lower and lower, his co-pilot's masked presence bathed in the bright glare of reflected instrument lighting, his own darting eyes seared by constant lightning. Someone was calling the scoring site over and over. The time-to-go needles ticked toward zero as the heading pointer slued ten degrees either side of track. High-pitched warbling tones, like the buzz of a cornered rattler, shredded the voice of the radar navigator. Overpowering the cacophony, the cloyingly feminine voice of Ithaca Bomb Plot cleared him to run against her. Ear-splitting, oscillating waves of electronic jamming crashed inside his head, wrenching his concentration from the life-sustaining instruments and riveting it on the woman's seductive voice. He broke out of the dream several times but never far enough away to escape being drawn back into the spinning vortex illuminated by the insistent flashing of the radar altimeter triggering on the rocks below.

Finally he roused himself sufficiently to grope in the dark until his hand found the lamp's elusive chain. Blinking away the dream, he rummaged for a beer in the small refrigerator beside his bed. "I can't believe I bought Black Label," he mumbled as he levered off the cap and sipped slowly, analyzing the taste really for the first time. *Good*, he mused, *just never thought about it before.* Images crowded into the room as he drank: Hubbard, Blackie, Tiny Temple, SugarFox, Glenn, and— sitting in the shadows off by himself—Wootan.

He blinked again, chug-a-lugged the remaining beer, and snapped off the light. Immediately he felt her presence sitting on the bed beside him, trembling in the darkness as she recovered from the shock of the rocket attack and the memory of his weight upon her. He moved to touch her, then felt embarrassed at having given way to the impulse. He continued to sit holding his head in his hands trying to conjure her image like an early morning insomniac flipping from one snowy channel to another. All he could bring in was the halo of dark curls. He lay down, wondering if his head would clear enough to lead the wing against odds that kept stacking against him. He awoke at seven thirty to the muted drumming of the shower in the next room, the taste of stale beer in his mouth, and nine-and-a-half hours to kill before he had to report for flying.

He was out of sorts at the mission briefing, but that was the chief facet of his personality lately. He recalled less and less of himself as he used to be: the smile, the good words, the dumb little jokes. He knew those characteristics had leaked out one night when he had other things on his mind. And as they drained, they cauterized their channel like a vasectomy that can never be repealed. Easier for a sperm to jump the severed canal than a spontaneous smile to wrest control of those tightly closed lips.

The dream's premonition, fertilized by the TV weatherman's hyping of a menacing cold front, and incubated in the recesses of his mind all day, hatched full-grown at the forecaster's words during the pre-takeoff briefing. Pilots cannot give way to premonitions, he reminded himself. Do it once and, like adultery, you've indelibly marked yourself.

Number seven refused to start: this time not even turning over. No chance to bluff, an inspector stood beside the engine watching the mechanics breaking open the cowling to get at the starter solenoid. The remaining two ships in his cell called ready for taxi.

"Billy Control, Billy One Six; no rotation on number seven."

"Roger, One Six. Wait one." Alex fidgeted in his seat, feeling already the itching hemorrhoid he had been planning to have fixed.

"Billy One Six, Billy Control. DO directs you shut down for maintenance. Plan to launch as last aircraft at zero eight hundred Zulu. We're sending a bus for your crew. Billy Control out."

He passed his instructions to the crew chief, directed external electrical power be restored, and stop-cocked the throttles. As he completed the shutdown checklist, he counted six assorted vehicles drawn around the aircraft. He wished there had been a seventh.

"That's it for now, Sportsfans," he called on interphone. "Let's check weather at Ops and maybe pick up a few zees. We've got a long wait and a longer night."

Four hours later, he rousted his crew from the lounge where they had been draped over the furniture. No one spoke on the ride to the aircraft that was still surrounded by what seemed to be every maintenance truck and staff car on the base. The last cell was thundering down the runway and lifting off in a veil of engine exhaust. Low scud swallowed their navigation lights almost immediately. The DO left his car and walked over to intercept him. "It's gonna be a near thing, my friend."

"Why's that, sir?" he wiped the back of his gloved hand across his chin, feeling the stubble beginning to sprout. "Any bomb scores yet?"

"Diamond told me the first two over the target were turning at release and the bomb plot couldn't score them. That means the aiming points are showing late in the run, and the pilots are honking her over trying to center the PDI." The DO, like Alex an old B-47 pilot, said "PDI" whereas those with only B-52 experience properly called the small needle synchronized with the radar cross hairs simply the "Heading Pointer."

"I guess he's pretty uptight."

"Not so's you can notice. Culpepper would be screaming at me by now, but Diamond just called to have the club ice the champagne. We'll get the bubbly regardless of the scores."

"He's a class act."

"That's not all. He's concerned about the weather and that sick engine of yours. He said for you to abort on the runway if you have any hint of malfunction, even if it doesn't smell right. He'll back your judgment."

"Thanks for the good words. I'll see you in the morning. Save us some champagne."

CHAPTER FORTY-EIGHT

JET ENGINES ROLLED THUNDER, rumbling and skipping and finally thrusting the aircraft off the tire-streaked concrete. Alex shifted his seatback and closed his eyes, grateful to be only a paying passenger. Fatigue, as tangible as g-forces in a tight turn, pressed him into his seat, sagging the crinkled pockets beneath his eyes. He had reason to be happy: the threat of an operational readiness inspection could be forgotten for another year; his crew had prevailed over marginal weather, an intermittent radar picture, and degraded ECM equipment. Their fellows had doused them with champagne.

He recalled the trepidation he had felt descending through massive clouds into the low-level route, the obstinate number seven engine lazily windmilling after flaming out during refueling. Torrential rain, reflecting back their depleted radar energy like nature's own iron curtain, poured from solid ranks of cumulus buildups. Sharp downdrafts buffeted Billy 16, rattling the crew as if they were dice being shaken inside a leather bar cup before the final toss to decide Hal Diamond's survival. Mercifully unknown, a deadly combination of late-blooming offset aiming points, faulty equipment, and impatient crews had lowered the wing's bombing effectiveness to the limit between satisfactory and marginal. The Second Bomb Wing's honor rode with Billy 16.

As the airliner's captain reduced power to cruise, Alex's mind tracked down the climactic bomb run, simultaneously analyzing and incinerating each instant like a sputtering fuse that would expunge the performance from his active memory. Rapid, hollow-sounding thumps of the oscillating radar antenna hitting its stops announced Donaldson's reaching out for the target. Alex had only to hold what he had: altitude, airspeed, and heading. Having played cat and mouse with teasing swipes from the site's missile-tracking simulator and then blasting it with his jammers, Hank Allison's contribution was complete. The bomb run belonged to the heavy-breathing radar navigator who tuned and refined and fumed over his ghostly scope like a medium sitting in circled trance probing the fast-approaching future.

Hal Diamond had stood at the bottom of the crew ladder shaking each man's hand as he deplaned. To Alex he whispered, "I won't forget this." After a half-hour of maintenance debriefing, an hour of ceremonial champagne and the resolution of bets, he had returned in anti-climactical loneliness to his room, showered, and packed his bag for Hartford.

At midmorning of the meeting's first day, while browsing through the displays of booksellers with a randomness born from having learned that Frank Harbinger had been unable to get away, Alex felt a presence behind him.

"Hello, Alex Cannard."

"Hello, Monique Delepierre." They embraced for a long time, not kissing but simply holding each other and letting the tape of memories play.

"I was hoping you might be here," he whispered into her hair. "But my luck since returning to the world hasn't been good." He backed off—looking intently at her soft black waves of hair, heavy eyelashes, finely chiseled nose—then embraced her again, this time kissing her cheek and petting her back gently as he often did the rabbits he raised as a boy. Many in the crowded aisles, embarrassed by the superficial screeching that usually marked conference reunions, watched enviously as the couple continued holding hands after separating.

"I was hoping you'd be here too, but my own luck also turned bad, and I've learned all over again how to exist without it."

The crowd seemed to be moving toward the lecture rooms, but he steered her to a seat beside one of the tall windows. "What do you mean? Has something happened to Wootan?"

"I thought perhaps you didn't know, or you would have contacted me . . . " She looked vacant, too embarrassed to finish her statement. "Adam was shot down escorting an RF-Four on a reconnaissance north of the Demilitarized Zone about two months after you left. They heard a personal locator beacon as a parachute deployed. Couldn't tell if it was Adam's or the lieutenant who was with him. It stopped after a short while. I found it hard to get information as I wasn't his next of kin . . . or any kin."

"Oh, Jesus, Monique, I didn't know. I've thought of you both so many times. I just assumed things had worked out well. I can't believe they got Wootan."

She was still holding the book she had been looking at when she first saw him, nervously turning it over and over as they talked, so its cover began to resemble a reference dictionary in a student's paperback library.

"I finished out my contract, getting the project operating and even publishing our first report. All the time I kept pestering the casualty reporting people, the men in Adam's directorate, and even the generals I briefed. They were all sympathetic, but they gave me little information. I guess they had little to give. The reconnaissance pilot had reported gunfire, and Adam immediately attacked the site. He didn't make any calls after that. They launched a search and rescue operation, but nothing came of it. Only photographs of the crash and a destroyed gun emplacement. Imagine trading one F-Four and two crewmen for a measly Soviet anti-aircraft gun. It doesn't compute."

"Nothing computes anymore, Monique." He took the book and walked to the cashier to pay for it.

Her eyes followed. He looked shorter than she remembered, and grayer—much grayer. In fact she could not remember his having been noticeably gray at all. She had never seen him in civilian clothes before, and his appearance surprised and violated her fashion sense. His dark blue suit was too severe for the occasion, ill-fitting, and narrow lapelled. A dingy white shirt, frayed collar, and carelessly knotted tie identified him as a man not inspected by a loving female. Only his shoes, obviously most usually part of his military dress, showed a gentleman's care. It was not that he was so much out of place among the academicians, but she could not help comparing him unfavorably to the image she had treasured of the tanned, youthful officer in starched fatigues and glistening jungle boots.

"Would you like to take a walk, Monique? I can't say I'm in any mood to listen to assistant professors stumble over scholarly articles."

"A walk would be fine, maybe up by the capitol building."

"Anywhere there's not jackhammers and bulldozers. There's so much construction. Nothing's happening around Barksdale except a few houses and rumors of a new racetrack."

They walked northwest from the hotel, strolling hand-in-hand along the busy streets until they found themselves in Bushnell Park. Mothers and children brushed by them, drawn by the strains of the distant carousel. He removed his coat, slinging it across his left shoulder and holding it with his index finger through the hanger loop. He loosened his tie.

"I don't know when I've felt so free, Monique. Maybe not since the last time I cut classes to take Lane boating. Same kind of afternoon. Same kind of feeling."

"What feeling, Alex?"

"I should have known you wouldn't let me speak in generalities. You think I don't remember the feeling? Simpatico, complete congeniality. No sham, free to be myself." He paused, waiting for a comment that did not come. "Do I take you too much for granted, Monique? Do you know how wiped out I am about Wootan? Or have they regimented you, or beaten you down to the point where you demand all the proper answers in the exactly prescribed format? Are you like all the others, looking over my shoulder waiting for me to deviate twenty feet off my altitude?"

"No, Alex. You don't take me for granted. I share your feelings for Adam. God knows I share them. Among friends it's not so much the individual words. It's the overall package." They found an empty bench on a knoll with sunlight.

"We've been together for over an hour, and you've mentioned your wife's name only once," she said raising her voice to be heard above a passing group of young children and their teachers. "How is your family? Do they like the Shreveport area?"

"They're fine. Kim's almost thirteen now. Jeffrey's just turned eleven. He used to want to be a cadet, but now I don't know. He wears his hair long. Longer than Kim's. Lane has done quite well for herself. I guess you'd say she's the one they designed the new jogging shoes for. You know, the ones with the rounded heals."

"Alex! That's a horrible thing to say even in jest."

"Sorry if my crudeness offends you. We're not living together. Seems she meant everything she said on the infamous tape. We've never taken any legal steps. I guess it's just a matter of time. I go home—home, funny name for the place anymore—I visit every now and then. Otherwise my life's like the last three months in Saigon. I wrap myself in the job and try to fly as much as I can. Damn poor way to live."

"I'm sorry," she squeezed his hand. "I know loneliness. I find lately I go out of my way to mold even more isolation around myself, as if I were constructing an igloo somewhere above the arctic circle. Married friends compliment me on my apartment, my clothes, my knowledge of world events and current literature. They laughingly offer to trade their children and mortgage payments for my independence. And I follow the script by disdaining their proposals and then telling them my vacation plans. They never perceive the heartache of my seeing my fertility ebbing relentlessly away. To them, swamped in their own households, they see my life as one of precious silence and blessed privacy."

"Roger on the loneliness. There's not much to be said for a room in the bachelor officers' quarters. Would you believe, sometimes when I'm sitting in front of the tube watching again some idiot commercial I've seen eighty thousand times, I wish for a rocket attack. Something to break the monotony, to get the juices flowing again, to remind me of what's important."

Spotting a vendor setting up shop in expectation of the lunchtime rush, he rose from the bench and pulled her after him. He bought them each a hot dog and a soft drink, a "soda" as the man called it. They crossed the street, finishing their meals and stuffing the cups, napkins, and tissue into a corner trash can.

"Ever been in Connecticut before, Monique?"

"Yes, when I was in graduate school at NYU. A group of us used to come up for the theater, or boating in the summer, or pass through on the way to Vermont for skiing. I always wanted to stay in a country inn, but we patronized motels. Usually the cheapest."

"I've been to New England only once before, and then hardly got off the base. Brought a B-Forty-seven up to Westover. Went in to Chicopee for dinner one night. Must have been around Christmas. Houses decorated, smoke curling out of chimneys, snow piled all over the place. I've about given up hope of ever being stationed here."

Their aimless walking seemed to be taking them back toward the hotel when they happened upon an automobile lot devoted exclusively to used sports cars. He drew her into the narrow passageways and soon they were browsing just as they had been some two hours previously among the books.

"What can I do for you folks," the booming voice came from a giant—six four at least—who could not possibly fit into any of his wares.

"You can lease me that red Spyder for the next three days," Alex said.

Thirty minutes later, they were heading north with the top laid back, the sun shining, and the radio playing some symphonic arrangement unfamiliar to Alex but completely fitting his new-found mood.

"Where are we going?" she yelled across to the smiling driver.

"Somewhere my friend at the car lot told me about, my dear lady. Think of it as being carried away on the prince's red charger, saved from the reluctant dragon of academic boredom."

"But we'll miss this evening's banquet and the guest speaker."

"Dammit, Monique, that's history. This is real. You're being kidnaped, and I didn't even leave a ransom demand. Just think of the romantic stories you can tell all your grandchildren."

"You've forgotten, my dear Prince, I'm not married, and a thirty-five-year-old school teacher doesn't have many prospects."

"Then tell it to your fellow geriatrics when you retire. Most of them will be acting like children by then."

"Alex, be serious. What have you planned for the afternoon? I've got to attend the banquet."

"I've acted serious ever since I've been back, and what's it got me? Two years of lost time and a reputation for being a certified bad-ass. In Saigon I always wanted to take you to a nice place to eat, somewhere they wouldn't throw a grenade into the room while we were waiting for dessert. So that's what I'm going to do. And if there's a chance, I'm going to talk you into sleeping with me tonight."

She slumped in the black vinyl seat feeling the slipstream burbling over the windshield ruffling the long folds of her linen skirt as she remembered the faces, the lips, of men who had in the past made the same proposal. Tentative, fumbling acquaintances from undergraduate days, gruff and demanding associates in graduate school. Some had been sober, sincere, maybe a little pathetic. Others egotistical, drunken—sometimes abusive. All ended with the same sterile result. Then the rumors began, the words spoken behind the backs of upraised hands, the cessation of invitations, and finally the frightening and unwanted attention of other females.

She had tried to sort it out, spending money for therapy she could ill afford after landing her first post-doctoral teaching position. Afraid to confide her need, she randomly selected a name from the phone book, arranged weekly sessions with the obese, un-kempt psychiatrist, then cursed her luck in absolute certainty he would be of no help. He kept forcing her back into childhood, trying to trip her up by suddenly interrupting her long silences with questions about Father or Mother.

"And what did your father say when you won the lead in the sixth-grade play?"

Who cares what he said or thought? That was a long time ago, and he was busy. Principal of the High School was a responsible job in those days. A job calling for a man of his personality and talents. He expected me to win the lead—and make top grades. That was my responsibility. I was his girl—more even than his girl—his boy too. Living in his presence, eating at his table, worshiping at his feet. I didn't need extra fondling: being his daughter—his most secret friend—was encouragement enough. Mother? She was his too. She served him and made the household run smoothly. He didn't have time to worry about small things when matters of educational policy had to be studied. No, I don't want to talk about either of them. What's wrong with me right now? Yes, I understand psychology. It's an imperfect science dominated by old men revering older men. Aren't there any women therapists? I'm not hostile. I'd just like to spend my time talking to a woman who knows how women see things and experience them. What do you know about loneliness and my longing for something I can't define because I haven't experienced it? And you haven't experienced it either. I don't know. If I knew, I wouldn't be here. I don't know why I come anyway. To be infuriated. You say little, never recommend, never tell me if I'm getting hot or cold, whether I'm close to understanding or moving away from it. Why do you keep bringing up my father? Yes, I see him when I go home. Two years ago; why? Look, I come here for insight. I want a lecture and some homework. Something I can research and pin down. If you recognize my problem, why don't you tell me, so I can start doing something about it? No, damn it. That's your job. You're the doctor. You've been the doc-

tor for over a year, and the patient isn't getting any better. No, I never have dates. Never have offers anymore—from men—or women.

"Why so quiet, Monique? I don't often divulge my game plan. But having slipped up, I thought I'd see some reaction. You did hear what I said didn't you?"

"Yes, Alex, my good friend. I heard what you said, and I was thinking about it."

CHAPTER FORTY-NINE

THEY DROVE IN SILENCE as the panorama of rural scenery bathed in brilliant sunlight seemed to inspire meditation. He felt a grinding, expanding exhilaration building inside him that short-circuited the voice of conscience that had once reverberated in high fidelity stereo inside his head.

He thought what a fool he had been, leaving her that night when she had clung to his arm, not wanting him to go. Just to maintain his string of negative victories, he had walked away, leaving her unsatisfied and afraid as he held stubbornly to the illusion that remaining celibate made him superior to others. During the past two years of close examination, he could find no nobility in his decision, only the fear he had held of attracting the notice of perverse gods to a miserable straight arrow. Overthrowing the conventions—committing blatant adultery with another man's woman—could cause the gods capriciously to block his way home, turn his wife into a harlot, remove his children from him forever.

He had always believed turn about was fair play, his breaking of the vows would entitle Merrilane to a penalty shot—a chance to get even. Now he believed much of his past behavior had been determined by his instinctive understanding a woman with her strong sexual urges could easily run wild if her passion were ever given free rein. He had lived with the premonition of her unfaithfulness since pilot training, from the day he saw her preening herself at the pool, trading quips with the bachelor officers, and lowering her straps so they could rub her back with glistening oil. He had repressed the paranoid fear that someday, someplace, with someone, she would give herself if only to have the experience. Driving now up the winding road with his second chance riding close beside him, he wondered whether he had nurtured his paranoia, living for the inevitable confrontation when he would be able to lord his extramarital virginity over her—breaking her spirit and pulling her repentant form back to lie forever at his feet like the dog one sees etched on brass grave markers of medieval knights.

He whipped the little car off the main route onto a narrow country road but maintained his speed, increasing it if anything, slipping low in the sweeping turns, accelerating explosively on the long upgrades. Cresting a hill with nothing but woods on either side, they dropped into a broad valley of cultivated farmland, dotted with weathered red barns sited near houses of white clapboards. Only a staggered rank of utility poles confirmed they had not regressed a hundred years in time. She realized at once their destination was the gray colored, white trimmed country inn resting on a rise several hundred yards off the road. He downshifted smoothly, swept into the gravel driveway, and approached the building slowly, so she could memorize her first impression.

"Like it?"

"Oh, Alex it's lovely. How did you know about it?"

"Easy. I asked Honest Al."

"Honest Al!" she shrieked with delight. "Is that some name you made up?"

"Of course not. You met him, the owner of the car lot. Honest Al Halworth. I told him I wanted directions to the finest country inn within the Fiat's radius of action. So he whipped out a map of New England, traced the route, and told me to tell Amanda he'd sent us."

"Alex," she laughed, "I don't believe a word you're saying."

As he glided to a stop, a thin woman in a faded pink house dress called from the wide front porch. "Welcome to the Boston Post Inn!" She approached holding out her hand, "I'm Amanda Metcalfe; Al called from Hartford to say you and your wife were on the way, Mr. Cannard."

He took her outstretched hand in both of his. "Thank you for your hospitality. I'm Alex, and this is Monique."

"What an absolutely gorgeous country inn," Monique managed to say scarcely looking at Amanda before returning her gaze to the weathered boards, the slate shingles, and the strutting rooster topping the cupola. "It looks like the set of a movie. Has it been in the family for ages and ages?"

"Goodness, no!" Amanda laughed showing sparkling eyes, perfect teeth, and deep dimples. "Hunter and I bought it five years ago as our retirement dream. We moved up from The City, and we've been working harder here than we ever worked on Madison Avenue. But it's beginning to show promise, and we're building a clientele: mostly friends from New York who don't know when to throw in the sponge."

"You'll be able to cater to a couple of weary travelers then?"

"I think I can squeeze you in. We're between seasons now, so all our rooms are empty. We've three other couples coming for dinner, but that still gives us plenty of space. Are you ready for a drink now, or would you like the specialty of the Inn—afternoon tea?"

"Sounds wonderful," Monique said quickly. "Alex allowed me only a hot dog for lunch, and I believe riding in that bouncy convertible drained my strength."

"I guarantee my afternoon tea will hold you until dinner. You'll be staying the night?" Amanda looked from Monique to Alex, then back to Monique again as she saw hesitation in their expressions.

"Well, you see," he started to waffle, hoping Monique would commit herself.

"What Alex hesitates to say is we did all of this—the leasing of the car from Al, the driving up here from Hartford—without any planning or even any luggage."

"This isn't exactly the Waldorf," Amanda said casually. "It's a long drive back to Hartford, and you can't get the flavor of a New England inn unless you stay overnight. If it's just a lack of luggage that bothers you, I can live with it if you can. Let me show you your rooms, and you can decide while I'm making tea."

Amanda preceded them up the uncarpeted stairway pausing at the landing to give general directions. "We've three single rooms down this corridor. Right here at the top of the landing is your suite: sitting room, bedroom, and bath." Pausing to allow the drama to build, she opened the sitting room door displaying a colonial simplicity that appealed to Alex's sense of order and caused Monique to put her hands to her lips and draw in a deep breath. The bedroom was even more spectacular with dark-stained armoire, chest, and rocking chair—obvious antiques. The focal point was, of course, the canopied bed of burnished wood, intricate quilted spread, and frilly pillows. The bathroom was modern with colonial decor carried out in the wall paper, the exposed beams, and the sheer curtains.

"Feel free to refresh yourselves regardless of your decision," Amanda said. "I'll have tea on the screened porch off the main dining room in about twenty minutes." Pausing at the doorway, she looked back at her guests who were standing by the fireplace holding hands like two innocent school children. "In case you decide to stay, I just might have two new toothbrushes and a razor. If you want more than that, the general store down in Titusville should be open until six. Dinner's at eight."

"How do you feel, Mrs. Cannard?" he asked with an embarrassed grin after Amanda departed.

"Like the butler in a murder mystery, when I should be feeling like Martha Washington on her honeymoon."

"That makes me happy," he said. "At least they both did it."

"Alex! That's an atrocious thing to say. Your seduction techniques need refining."

"It goes back to what I told you before. I feel comfortable around you, and I haven't felt that way with a woman in almost three years. I'm being entirely selfish, I admit, but sometimes in the last several months I've thought I'd explode unless I put my arms around a woman who had some kind of feeling for me."

Pulling his head down to hers, she kissed both his eyelids. He would not let her disengage, but held her so she shared his involuntary tremors.

"Are we absolutely committed to afternoon tea?"

"Yes, we are, love. All because you allowed me only one hot dog for lunch."

They laughed, wordlessly agreeing to act as proper adults for a few hours more. She retreated into the bathroom to repair the ravages done to her hair by the journey. He waited in the sitting room leafing through a travel booklet until she returned, then disappeared to relieve himself. When he rejoined her, she was seated on the sofa in front of the worn cobbler's bench calmly pouring tea into cups entirely surrounded by small finger sandwiches and fancy cookies.

"I trust you take your tea in the English fashion with milk and sugar," she laughed. "It seems Amanda thought we'd prefer our refreshment here in case," and now she imitated their hostess' high-pitched voice, "'we might wish a brief nap before dinner.'"

He managed to maintain a civilized veneer, but his desire for the beautiful woman seated beside him talking gaily of inconsequentialities had robbed him of his sense of taste. He fumbled the cookies badly, sending crusty portions of one cascading down the side of the sofa. Then he managed to grind it into the braided rug as he sought to retrieve it. Finally, as she was beginning to pour him a third cup, he restrained her hand, dumped his napkin on the tray, and drew her beside him.

"We really should have a shower before we nap," he said. They showered together using lots of soap and pausing often to slide their glistening bodies together. She lathered him over and over, stroking him as if she were unaware of the effect she was having, looking up frequently, grinning impishly, and then going back to her task. They stepped out of the enclosure, dripping great quantities of water onto the mat, and began toweling each other. Her hair fell in glistening strands much longer than he had believed it to be.

Realizing her inexperience, he fought to restrain his own passion by thinking of the clear, blue waters of Tahoe on a November dawn, crisp and cool and remote and serene. She was beginning to show traces of nervousness, turning away from him, attempting to hide her generous breasts. He kissed her then scooped her into his arms and carried her to the bed. Easing her feet onto the smooth, wide flooring, he stripped off the quilt, scattering the clustered pillows. When he turned again to her, he found her rigid, eyes wide and sightless. He lifted her to the bed covering her with the sheet.

Sliding in beside her, he raised himself on his left elbow and began skimming his right hand lightly across her nose, her right cheek bone, and into the hairline around her ear. She did not respond. Instead she lay tensed, eyes tightly closed. He felt his passion ebb, being replaced by a deep sense of concern.

"Monique," he whispered, "it's me . . . your friend . . . Alex. Are you all right?"

Beginning to shiver, she moved onto her left side and drew up her knees. He pulled up the quilt and tried to tuck himself in beside her. She moved away, rolling onto her stomach, hands forming a chastity belt beneath her body.

"Monique," he whispered again. "It's Alex, the friend who needs you."

He saw her back heaving before he heard the sobs. *It's Wootan. Crying for Wootan, her lost love who's most probably a pile of bones encased in decaying cloth all jammed together in the bottom of some water-filled crater. And here I lie consigning him to an unmourned grave when he could be enduring the limbo of a Hanoi cell. So I force myself on his woman because it's easier to steal from a mixed-up friend than to salvage what's still rightfully mine.*

He began to stroke her back: long, confident, smooth strokes that took away the goose bumps and finally put her to sleep. His mind wandered, looking to find the brass ring, the key, or the word that would move him back in time to when his life was right. But he had difficulty deciding when that was. So he tried to project a time in the future when things would once again be ordered. But he could not foresee when that would be.

The war will go on and on, and my country will be destroyed. And Merrilane will go higher and higher, reaching for her own brass ring. And Kim, and Jeff, and Little Buddy—that poor little bastard—what will happen to them? Who will they have to confide in? Other kids? And who will those other kids have to talk to? Kim and Jeff and Little Buddy? And what will happen when Merrilane's got the brass ring? Will she discover what I've come to know—that nothing equals having a friend to hold on to when the memories flood? And will she find, as I've found, that kids don't stay kids, don't wait for parents to get smart enough to raise them? Will she find they had grown up wild, like ignored seedlings, and of no more use than weeds—dandelions that blossom, go to seed, and get blown away? And if the great Alexander is already so goddamn smart, why doesn't he do something about it while there's still time?

CHAPTER FIFTY

MANY TIMES AFTER THE NIGHT at the Boston Post Inn, Alex had tried to put the pieces together. They had dressed for dinner. His blue suit looked presentable in the candlelight. She swept her hair into a bun, applied just a bit of coloring to her cheeks and lips, and wore the long sleeved white blouse open at the top and without her jacket. Amanda strategically placed her guests so each party had the privacy it deserved.

Monique was a charming dinner companion, discussing her doctoral dissertation and commenting on the wonderful research facilities at NYU. He delighted in watching the movements in her neck as she talked, relished the way her eyes sparkled in time with her short bursts of laughter, and marveled as she skirted any subject that might cause them seriously to consider their circumstance.

She chose the wine, a dark red New York State Cabernet Sauvignon perfectly complimenting the pot roast they both ordered. He was tantalized by thoughts working at cross purposes. One line of reasoning strengthened his decision to withstand temptation. The other, growing stronger as he consumed his second glass of wine, dictated he take her regardless of her squeamishness, treating her as spoils of war to harden a growing insensitivity within his character that could fuel the final sprint toward his star. If Monique could read his thoughts, she gave no indication. Instead she continued to introduce new subjects, generate from him smiles and outright laughter, and stoke his boiling sexual appetite.

They decided to have after-dinner drinks on the screened porch, finding the pure air and change of scene worth the discomfort of the crisp temperature. Amanda brought a handmade afghan for Monique's shoulders and mugs of steaming Irish coffee. Afterwards, somewhat unsteady from the drinks and the accumulated stress of the past several days, he led her up the stairs.

She stayed a long time in the bathroom. Succumbing to the great press of fatigue, he dropped into fitful sleep. She arrived not as a lover but as a shade, a dream dimly perceived. He barely felt her slide into bed, keeping to the far edge, destroying any hope remaining that she would move close to him and invite the first overtures of foreplay. He lay still, wondering if he were imagining what seemed to be tremors issuing from some hidden epicenter thousands of miles or tens of years away. He reached to stroke her face but his fingers encountered only the tangle of hair she had released from the tight bun. She was on her stomach again, trembling. He patted her shoulder three times, then extracted her icy hand, cradled it in his, and recalled the deep waters of Lake Tahoe.

He awoke to the sound of her shower. They shared a country breakfast, and pulled onto the road in time to make the first sessions of morning lectures. In the evening they drove to New Haven to stroll the Yale campus and jostle among students at Pepe's to verify stories of his fabulous pizza. His soul reveled in her company, whether sharing a booth in a noisy pizzeria, hunched in the small car when an unexpected shower forced them to raise the top, or walking through the deserted hotel corridors late at night, his arm loosely resting on the firm curve of her hips.

She had invited him into her room that night, both of them smelling of pizza and beer, both kissing with such passion he began to feel deep aching he had not experienced since college. Yet, when he pulled her onto the bed, she had turned on him, arching her back as a cat might do when forced into a corner, and slapping away the hand that had drifted ever so casually onto her inner thigh. He resisted the urge to force her, stifling her screams in an overpowering kiss and holding her wrists as he had once done with Merrilane. He realized her actions were reflexive, not motivated by a desire to deprive him. Propping himself against the headboard with pillows, he pulled her into him and held her crouched tightly against his chest while patting her back as he would a child who had awakened during a thunderstorm. He could again detect her sobs and, after a while, feel the wetness of her tears filtering through his shirt. When she was asleep, he laid her gently in a still-clothed bundle on the bed, covered her with a spread, and lay down on his back beside her. He wanted to be there when she awoke.

The third day was a replay of the second except he spent his time not following the obtuse arguments sketched in droning conference monologues but deep in thought trying to make sense of Monique's actions. What had she said after the rocket attack and again that last night in Saigon? Something about no one ever having held her as he had done. So he had spent two nights with her—unproductive in one sense, yet in another, perhaps initiating some movement toward trust. Someone had hurt her badly, leaving scars that were beyond his ability to decipher, much less mitigate. What strain had he put her under? A pressure to keep up appearances among colleagues, all of whom were no doubt gossiping about their disappearance before the banquet and their constant attention to each other? An ordeal to face him each morning knowing she had disappointed, discomforted, and perhaps even insulted him?

That night they prolonged the final separation by joining a theater party at the Hartford Stage Company. Afterwards they lingered over a late supper at Honiss' Oyster Bar and then made the final trek through the red-carpeted, dimly lighted corridors to her room.

"I'd like to talk it out if we could, Monique." She was blocking the doorway, and he felt within a whim of being shut forever out of her life. "Somewhere without smoke, and drinks, and loud music."

"Come in," she said.

They sat in armchairs separated by an octagonal table and a lamp that cast grotesque shadows on the wall over the bed.

"I want you to know, Monique, these past three days, as unorthodox as they may have seemed at times, have meant a great deal to me."

"That's the start of a nice speech, Alex Cannard, but I'd have expected it from you. You're a dear man sadly miscast in a role that's changed since you tried out for the part almost twenty years ago."

"That's quite perceptive. Did you know I was on the verge of changing roles when I went to Hawaii? But we never got on the subject. When my new orders arrived, the window closed, and she never even knew it had been opened. So now I'm trapped playing the role of professional son of a bitch, tightening the screws, and nailing the meek to their crosses. I'm so good in the part my name's up in lights, and I'm forever typecast, always to be the ironass when my nature tells me there's a better way to direct the show. Sometimes I think even my previous role as killer is preferable. But that thought lasts only a moment, and I hear the voice calling me in closer, and I know being a son of a bitch is better."

"I'm fortunate to have you as a friend," she said, "although I don't know why you put up with my quirks."

"We're a lot alike. We both have something in our past that's poisoning our present. We're both so damn independent, we feel we have to work it out by ourselves even though our intelligence tells us it's impossible."

"Alex, I'm ashamed of the way I've treated you. Believe me, I've programmed myself to give you what you want, to love you and purge all the bitterness. But it hasn't worked. The moment you touch me where he touched me, my body just rebels."

"Who's the 'he,' Monique? I can't believe it was Wootan."

She cried hard then, head buried in her hands, spasms racking her body, rasping sounds animating the shadows over the bed. He gave her his handkerchief and waited for her to stop. Finally she did.

"No, it wasn't Adam. I tried to give myself to him with the same success I've had with you. And he was just as understanding. Maybe not quite as understanding, but at least as forbearing. A sweet man. What a paradox. Finding two of the most tender and empathetic of men clothed in the warrior's uniform. The others I've known on a professional basis—doctors, professors, men of God—all were unfeeling, unbending, unenlightened fools mouthing the same old routines. All of them wanting to put me in a pigeonhole, tape a band-aid on my shattered wing, and shunt me off to someone else."

"You're the victim, Monique. You're letting something you're not responsible for keep you from fulfillment. You've got to get a handle on it. You're needed. Whatever's stunted your physical lovemaking has stimulated your spiritual understanding. You've got a lot to give a man who needs you."

"What man, Alex?"

"Oh, Jesus, Monique. I wish you wouldn't ask me that."

"What man, Alex?"

"Wootan if he's alive. Me if he's not."

Again she cried, but for a shorter time as if she were filling in while getting her thoughts together. "You know," she said finally, "I feel like Jake Barnes in the Hemingway novel. Only worse. He was impotent, but at least he had memories. I don't have even that. Just questions, and longings, and a secret life of shame and frustration, and no one to write my story so I can study it and try to dope it out."

"Was it your father? Was he the one who took advantage of you when you were young and would have done anything to gain his favor?"

She looked at him vacantly, beginning to twist the handkerchief he had given her.

"You don't have to say anything. It fits together. Like following the schematic of the hydraulic system, tracing it backward to find the malfunction. I hope you know you're not alone in this. Men, even fathers, can be brutes for so many different reasons, some of them maybe even excuses."

She bowed her head, covering her face with the handkerchief.

"I've seen my own Kim, just beginning to emerge from childhood, testing her feminine wiles, eager to please, anxious for a word of praise, trusting her Daddy as she'll never trust another man. How easy it would have been to have compromised her, to take out my frustrations against her mother. Whatever his motivation, you've probably called him nothing but 'bastard' ever since you were old enough to realize what he was doing. And now, when you see him, there's just a shell of the virile man who used to be your Daddy, and maybe you even feel some pity for him."

"I'll never pity the pious bastard."

"Maybe you blame yourself for succumbing to the sensuous feelings that rolled over you, or indict yourself for being somehow guilty for allowing it to happen, or chastise yourself the way I do every night in the last instant between consciousness and sleep when I almost cry out in horror and shame for not having been better, more perfect, superhuman on a night when fate conspired against me."

He slipped from his chair to the floor, sliding against her closed legs, folding his arms around them, and holding tightly as his mind once again painted a grotesque montage.

She placed the damp handkerchief in his hand. "Have you told Merrilane?"

"No, the time's never been right. I was close once in Hawaii, but I lacked the courage. I tried to say the words. It's almost like a physical restriction, like you can't speak until a timer allows you. I had the words composed in my head, but what came out was lost in translation. We may have had sex then. It seems when I'm depressed or trying to express the inexpressible, I tend to resort to another kind of intercourse as if the thoughts could be transmitted along with the sperm, and the words would never have to be said in case anyone else were listening. But it never works. That's why you've not really missed anything. You and I have had some of the foreplay and part of the afterglow. We just missed the messy part that sometimes doesn't do what you expect."

She said nothing. So he continued, talking not particularly to her but just to keep the silence away. "Silly what the mind will do. Mother Hubbard said to forget it. Easy as that. Yet I know he wouldn't be able to forget it. Killing the black hats is bad enough when they're on the attack and overrunning the good guys. But killing the good guys too isn't acceptable. Like cannibalism, it's taboo."

"Strange you should choose that word," she said. "Taboos. We're both trying to resolve the ultimate taboos."

CHAPTER FIFTY-ONE

SKIP THORP MET ALEX'S return flight with news that SAC Headquarters had alerted the wing to move its G-model bombers to Guam, all leaves were canceled, and maintenance was working around the clock generating aircraft. "It's running just like an ordinary readiness inspection," he said, "with no glitches I'm aware of." He also said Diamond had asked for Alex to see him at ten that evening.

Diamond's outer office was dark when he entered, but he could see the commanding officer hunched over his desk.

"Come in, Cannard. Good to see you looking rested."

"Thank you, sir."

"Sorry to be cutting into your plans for the evening, but I wanted to talk when we had a chance of not being interrupted. Sit down."

He seated himself in the armchair beside the desk wondering what was so important it could not be passed through his boss, the Deputy for Operations.

"I said I wouldn't forget you, but that was last week when I was still in the generals' race."

"Yes, sir." He had learned not to show surprise or interrupt a senior officer who had something on his mind. If he wanted to philosophize, let him talk; if he wanted to give direction, take notes. Diamond, leaning back in his chair and looking out onto the broad ramp where Billy Mitchell had trod, obviously wanted to talk.

"When I took over this wing, General Culpepper gave me a sketch of all the major players. You were the only one he singled out as being indispensable. He said he put you in Stanboard on a hunch, and it paid off. You did everything he wanted without complaint even though he knew much of it went against your grain. I thought at the time you were just his fair-haired boy."

"Yes, sir."

"But I've learned he was right. You're one of the few people I know who honestly tries to do a good job regardless of who gets the credit."

"Thank you, sir."

"I had big plans for you, as well as myself. But now the president's reducing ground forces in-country, and he's taking up the slack with more bombers. I won't be leading them."

"I'm sorry, sir. The troops need someone with your knowledge and perspective to inspire them."

"That's kind of you to say, but I'm sure they'll be well taken care of by those already in place."

"They'll need to be sir, especially when the president loses patience and commits them against Hanoi and Haiphong. When that happens, we'll take horrific casualties using our present Arc Light tactics. I've already seen too many friends sacrificed."

"That's got to be expected in a military environment."

"With all respect, sir, the environment's political not military; and it's lost its moral dimension."

"You're too much the humanist, Cannard. General Culpepper warned me you were."

"What else did he warn you about?"

"That you were the saddest person he'd ever seen."

Alex regarded Diamond, wondering what went on behind those gold-framed glasses and broad forehead. "That covers a lot of territory. Did he say it affected my work?"

"No, but he asked me to keep an eye on you; and if I liked what I saw, to get you out of standardization."

"So?"

"I happen to think you're of more use to the Air Force off a crew. You've paid your dues; you won't be of any special value flying milkruns out of Guam. They've got their own standardization people, as they have their own commanders, so there's nothing there for you."

"Yes, sir."

"On the other hand, the operations plans directorate in Second Air Force Headquarters has an opening. You'd stay right here at Barksdale working for a friend of mine. With a more normal schedule, you could have your family join you."

"What about my crew?"

"I'll rely on your judgment. Pick an aircraft commander you think will be compatible, and we'll do some shuffling. Okay?"

"Yes, sir. Dropping bombs on people from thirty thousand feet's not my idea of combat. Maybe in plans I can figure out something different."

Within two days Diamond had worked a crew change and produced the promised orders to the headquarters. On the evening his crew was to deploy, the DO gave him a ride to where they sprawled on the ramp in front of their aircraft killing the last few minutes before engine start.

They did not get up as he approached. He felt overly dressed in his blouse and wheel hat with the embroidered silver clouds and lightning flashes on the visor. For a moment he wished he once again wore a sweat-stained flying coverall with checklist jammed in the lower leg pocket and refueling frequencies scribbled on the back of his hand. But only for a moment.

"Hi guys," he tried to sound casual. "Still speaking to your old pal?"

"Are the effectiveness reports all signed?" Donaldson asked from beneath an overseas cap that seemed balanced on the tip of his nose.

"Yes, finished the whole bunch this afternoon."

"In that case, why should we want to talk to anyone who gets himself a cushy job at Second and sells his buddies down the river?" The men rose slowly to their feet.

"He didn't sell us down the river, Major," Herb Lorenz said. "He sold us across the pond."

The sergeant's remark broke the tension, and Alex threw his arm across Lorenz's shoulder. He drew away. Alex dropped his arm. "I wanted to wish you well."

"It's nice of you to come out, Colonel," said Wilcox, the major Alex had selected to take over his crew. He tried to check his watch unobtrusively and blushed when Alex noticed.

"I know it's almost time to button up, but . . . as I said . . . I just wanted . . . "

"We know what you're saying, Alex." Donaldson extended his hand. "And we appreciate it. Most headquarters weenies wouldn't have bothered."

"Thanks for all your help, Phil. I enjoyed flying with all of you, and I'll be here to welcome you home in the next month or two."

He shook each hand, not looking at the man, afraid his eyes would betray his fear their separation might be forever.

He watched their takeoff from the balcony in front of base operations. Watched as the three-ship cell waited at the north end of the runway for clearance, then trundled heavily toward the white hold line with Wilcox's ship crossing just as the second hand on his watch hit the twelve numeral. It thundered down the long concrete slab trailing dense smoke as the other two bombers followed at one-minute intervals. Soon they were only glistening specks pulling thin comets' tails as they climbed west chasing the setting sun.

He looked skyward long after the cell disappeared and the faint rumbling ceased. Inside he registered empty.

The cry of a child distracted him. Below on the ramp stood a few of the wives and children who had lingered as if they had nowhere to go. A shapely woman, her thin duster pressed against her body by the freshening breeze, sobbed openly as a little boy and taller girl clutched at her legs. He pulled his hat lower until its visor weighed hard upon his glasses, descended the outside stairs to his Spyder, and drove to his room. *Seven o'clock in the Springs*, he thought. *They should be finished with dinner.*

"Lane? Did I get you at a bad time? . . . I'll make it brief. I've got a new job at Second Air Force. Should have weekends off and no alert to pull. . . . Thanks. How are things going with you? . . . That's good to hear.

"Listen, this is important. Do you suppose you might like to come down for a few days? We could . . . What about if I come home this weekend? . . . Can't someone else handle . . . No, I don't think I'm being demanding.

"Would you put Kim on the line? . . . Doing her homework? And I suppose Jeffrey's not available either. . . . I don't care. They're still my kids. . . . I don't give a damn. It's still my money paying the bills, although I guess you're so far up the fucking hierarchy you think you're self-sufficient. Well, you can take it from an expert, no one is.

"Damn it, Lane. Haven't you had enough of the fast track? Haven't you had enough of a fling? . . . If that's the way you really feel, I guess it's time to get our lawyers together. . . . Mad? You're goddamn right I'm mad. I should've got mad before all this got out of hand.

"You're throwing your life away, letting the kids raise themselves, and twisting the dagger in my heart every time you treat me like this. . . . Ashamed?

"Hell no, I'm not ashamed. I saw five of my best friends— the only friends I've got left as far as I know—takeoff for that fucking war, and now I'm supposed to take a ration of shit from someone I used to think was all I wanted out of life.

"There's no harmony anymore, and I can't get it back no matter what I try. . . . Yeah, name your second, and I'll name mine. Thanks for the glove across the face. Take care of yourself."

He leaned back in his chair, expelling pent up energy and trying to process the conversation. *Is it all my fault? She was my wife and I lost her. If I'd only been stronger, more competent, smarter. Smart enough never to have tried to make something of myself.*

He undressed quickly, throwing the blue blouse with the silver wings and colored bits of ribbon onto the bed and leaving the trousers in a heap on the floor. He pulled on a pair of Levis, a plaid shirt, and his boots. Slamming the door, he stormed down to the parking lot, raised the Spyder's top, and headed out to the Bossier Strip to see if he could find someone to talk to.

CHAPTER FIFTY-TWO

THE STAFF WORK at Second Air Force Headquarters lasted eight months. Beginning in April, 1972, he worked a variety of projects such as phasing FB-111 bombers into their new home at Plattsburg, New York, preventing anti-war activists from barricading runways, and assisting families of men declared missing or prisoners of war. In mid-July he shifted to the logistics directorate, the much maligned supply organization that tried to inject reality into the schemes of planners. There, poring over stacks of inflated requisitions, cajoling suppliers, and mollifying wing commanders, he discovered the true meaning of the word "unsung." Joining a team of always overworked, and often cynical magicians, he learned to anticipate and cover shortages that otherwise could degrade the bomber or tanker fleets. Self interest, the awareness that he was being groomed for future command, acted as an aphrodisiac spurring him to grasp any lead that would provide inside information or extra experience toward the day when he would be calling the shots.

He lived on the job, working eighteen-hour days, ignoring weekends, and becoming the long-distance confidant and savior of staff officers and commanders from Bangor to Saigon. He had no peers, no competition from normal men. His associates grumbled at his dedication but tolerated him when they realized he made no move to exploit or embarrass them. As he made himself more and more indispensable, he became a familiar actor on the lecture platform mesmerizing visitors to the headquarters and charming critics with the candor and depth of his answers. Inside the darkened command post, where piercing questions flashed like thunderbolts from the shrouded, glass-enclosed balcony, he was most often the officer singled out for a response.

Sometimes he was tasked to augment the Inspector-General's team in no-notice compliance inspections at one or another of the command's bases. Putting on his SOB hat, he inspected paperwork, grilled personnel, and searched for discrepancies. He knew they existed because of the reduced level of experienced staff caused by Vietnam's recurring levies. In the process he learned the system and the ways units had devised to meet it—or beat it. Unexpectedly, his reputation seemed to rise among the outlying bases as the old-boy net circulated the tart words "Cannard sees everything but teaches more than he reports."

Merrilane never named her second. He continued wearing his wedding band and sending the lion's share of his salary to their Colorado bank. For a week in June he had toured Mexico City, Taxco, and Acapulco with his children. Kim was quite grown up, seemingly perturbed at having been pulled out of circulation by a man she used to think knew everything and now considered completely out of it. Jeffrey showed no interest in athletics, flying, or becoming a cadet. Affecting long hair and a weak handshake, he declined eye contact during the infrequent times he had anything to say.

Having always believed his children would intuitively do their duty and make him proud, he realized he had once again been wrong; and he filed that naive conviction along with the other he had once held about the purity of his motives and his invincibility. For all he knew, Kim relied on the pill and Jeffrey abused drugs. They seemed neither to acknowledge him, nor appreciate the position he held in society and the virtues he had sworn to uphold.

Periodically he called Monique, sometimes when she had already retired for the night. Twice he asked her if she would meet him in whatever locale she desired. Both times she claimed previous commitments. Once he called on Thursday to ask if he could visit her that weekend. She hesitated, saying she was checking her calendar, then said she would be out of town. On occasion, he would pull up the Spyder's top and head for the Bossier Strip, just an old, white-haired cowboy.

When his name appeared on the list for promotion to full colonel, he accepted the obligatory congratulations from his office mates, and was pleased to get a few calls over the military telephone network from acquaintances scattered around the world. Most, he thought, came from people who stood to gain if he continued to rise and to remember they existed. The call that surprised and truly affected him came person-to-person over the commercial line from Mother Hubbard, still a lieutenant colonel at Logistics Command Headquarters.

That night, after missing dinner and working late coordinating the modification of B-52 electronic countermeasures equipment, he celebrated in his room with a piece of dried cheese he found in the refrigerator and two bottles of Black Label. An intelligence briefing earlier in the day had caused him to think of Wootan. A prisoner in Hanoi had encoded information in a letter telling of isolation, starvation, and torture. Sitting alone in the darkness, holding a cold bottle to his burning forehead, he wondered if Wootan also sat isolated in a dark cubicle seeing his life dribbling away like a casually sipped beverage. The first ring of the telephone startled him.

"Lieutenant Colonel Cannard speaking . . . Is that you Lane? What's wrong? . . . Oh, that. Thanks. Anybody at the Academy make it? . . . Too bad. Kids okay? . . . What'd he do that for? . . . It's his life I guess, but I doubt he's mature enough to make that kind of decision. Think it'd make any impression if I talk to him? . . . I didn't think so either . . . Should pin them on in November. No, I don't know how much the increase is.

"You all right? . . . That's nice. Makes it all worthwhile . . . No, don't jump to conclusions. I'm not trying to be 'snotty.' Crude, insensitive, perhaps, but not snotty . . . For Christ's sake, Lane, let's not get into that. I got a promotion and you got one, too. Congratulations. If it makes you happy, I'm happy for you. Probably aren't many female VeePees, huh? . . . That's surprising; even the most enlightened organizations seem to allow only one female into the inner circle . . . That complicates matters; but I'm sure your sensitive and caring personality will unruffle her feathers . . . Take it easy, Lane. I sympathize that you've run into a personality conflict, but that's all it seems I've encountered for the last two years. It goes with the territory.

"Let's drop this sorry subject. I know you have a lot on your plate; you'll just have to handle it . . . No, I'm glad you called. I was just sitting here with a couple of old friends . . . Not to worry; they're gone now . . . No, but I imagine they'll be sending me to Guam . . . Don't know for sure. Probably to parachute behind enemy lines and burn more bridges . . . Just a little humor . . . No, there's a difference. This time I don't give a ratz. Take care of yourself."

The first of December, he received his eagles in a brief ceremony in the front office with the general's secretary standing in for Merrilane. The next morning he had orders to join the 72nd Strategic Wing on Guam as special assistant to Colonel Chris Lambrite, the commander and a friend from B-47 days. By the ninth, he was ensconced in the Senior Officers' Quarters at Andersen Air Force Base, had flown a disturbing mission with one of their premier crews, and had come to realize he had been dropped into a smoldering powder keg of low aircrew morale and overworked support personnel.

Phil Donaldson was not ecstatic to meet his former aircraft commander in the officers' club bar, but he knew his phoned invitation was another in a continuing series of command performances that were rubbing off successive coatings of his civility.

"Colonel Cannard, sir," he said putting his glass on the bar but refusing to extend his hand. "Is there something wrong with my Seiko? Back at Barksdale you told me you'd see me in a couple of months; and here we stand on Guam, and damned if I don't believe it's almost Christmas."

"Hi, Phil. Good to see you sporting those silver leaves. I called Laura before I left. A man answered."

"Alex, you bastard, I don't have to take that from you even if you are a full bull."

"I'm glad to see you laugh. I was beginning to think every-one around here had forgotten how."

"They damn near have. It's a war of attrition, and we're the ones getting ground down. You know a lot about military his-tory, but I defy you to find a precedent for this."

"What's the problem besides fatigue and dé jà vu?"

"Same ol' same ol'. Never get any feedback on what we're accomplishing. No idea when this fuckin' tour'll be over."

"Have you heard about that fiasco I flew with Ragsdale?"

"Christ, who hasn't? I always knew you had big balls, but from the way his radar nav tells it, with you turning the mis-sion into a standardization check and not moving out of the jumpseat all the way home, you must have a bladder the size of the BUFF's aft main fuel tank."

"Is that what I'm famous for?"

"That and the fact the entire crew hasn't been court-martialed yet. How'd you manage that?"

"Lambrite's an old friend from better days. I told him we had complacency problems and convinced him to let me work with the crews for a few days. Starting tonight I'm conducting Come-to-Jesus meetings along with the regular mission brief-ings."

"What are you going to threaten 'em with? They're already in SAC, they're flying the BUFF, and they've been on Guam since Easter."

"I don't know I'll threaten them with anything. Although if we wanted to, we could put a few in Leavenworth."

"No federal prison's big enough to hold the entire SAC bomber force, Colonel."

"It's an option, and I know some guys who'd use it. But I agree it's not a good option, not even as a scare tactic."

"Then what are you going to do?"

"I don't know yet, but my first briefing's not for another hour."

Leaving Donaldson at the bar with a fresh drink, Alex drove to the "Arc Light Building," the large planning and briefing facility where aircrews manning two cells of D-model B-52s congregated. After completing the usual routine, he dismissed the strap-hangers and the enlisted man who operated the slide projector. The room hummed like a hornet's nest when the hive is penetrated. He dimmed the overhead lights and descended from the podium to stand on a level with the flyers who continued to buzz. The air-conditioning system labored to pump frigid air that was immediately ingested by the stagnant humidity dominating the room.

"I know you've got a long trip ahead of you, so I won't take much of your time. Most of you have heard about me by now. I'm the man with the biggest bladder in Strategic Air Command." The audience chuckled encouragingly. "In other words, it takes a lot to piss me off." Some groans from the back row. "But two nights ago I almost became a statistic because of pure complacency: what I call the 'milkrun syndrome.'" He paused for a five-count. "You've heard the story: hit-and-run MiG skipped two heat-seeking missiles through one of our cells bombing just south of the Demilitarized Zone. You've probably also heard the lead crew was sitting fat, dumb, and happy with safety pins in their ejection seats, parachutes unhooked, and helmets stowed."

One, two, three, four, five. "The point is Captain Ragsdale was sending me a message from all of you. That you're tired—disgruntled." Even the refrigeration system was quiet.

"Gentlemen, we can get into a pissing contest, but I'd win." The room exploded in laughter. "Okay. Now that you've conceded defeat, let's address the problem. It's a fucked-up war against an enemy who's tough, smart, and motivated. He's out to win and to kill us in the process. He'll surprise us by doing the audacious as his MiG fighter did against Ragsdale's cell. If we go north again, he'll contest every inch of airspace over Hanoi and Haiphong. He'll aim his propaganda at our sense of fair play. Or, failing all else, he'll let us drop on him day after day until boredom and complacency destroy the most disciplined military force ever forged."

They were contrite now, looking down at the floor in embarrassment. "Gentlemen, you may not consider South Vietnam a high-threat area for BUFFs. But as far as I'm concerned, anytime you're standing within a half-mile of a Fifty-two, you're in a high-threat area. Those of you flying the D model, make that a three-mile radius." More laughter: nervous, wary.

"One other thing. This is just my gut feel, but you know my gut . . ." They rocked with laughter, shouts, and whistles like a high school pep rally. "I think there's a developing sense we've diddled around with the North Vietnamese long enough . . ." More shouts. Spontaneous clapping. "It wouldn't surprise me to see us going north before long. Those strikes back in April against Vinh and the Bai Thuong airfield just proved we could do it. So you'd better have your procedures honed. And you might start treating your Electronic Warfare Officers with a bit more respect because your EWs will be the guys pulling the SAMs off your tails. Do you have any questions?"

A hubbub arose as each man looked left and right. A single voice arose from the pack. "Are you for real, Colonel?" Everyone laughed.

"Sometimes I wonder, my friend. Sometimes I wonder." Then he added in a voice only a few on the front row heard, "God Bless You."

He conducted all the briefings for the next two days making a version of the original speech each time. He was happy afterwards when individuals and sometimes whole crews would seek him out to discuss procedures that might eliminate some little irritant or inefficiency. Soon he had three volunteer crews investigating a list of fourteen specific suggestions he believed had merit. Hearing rumors that "Alexander the Grate talks the crewmember's language," the Flying Safety Officer asked him to speak at Beer Call. Alex enjoyed the diversion, recalling a long-forgotten store of anecdotes, flying stories, and jokes each of which seemed to point out some truism of flying while, at the same time, serving to bond the crews further to him.

With Lambrite's approval, he put the Wing staff to work reviewing the contingency plan for a massive attack on the Hanoi-Haiphong complex. He interrogated electronic warfare officers and avionics technicians concerning the status of ECM equipment needed to support a maximum effort. The results displeased him, and he directed the Chief of Logistics to call his former boss at Barksdale with an emergency requisition for additional jammers.

Simultaneously, he assembled a small working group of training officers and volunteer crew members, charging them to design an explicit ground school and flying training program to requalify crews for low-level tactics.

On the night of the eleventh, Chris Lambrite invited him to the Club for a late supper. When they had been seated, Lambrite came to the point. "Alex, what the hell are you up to with this latest project on low-level retraining?"

"You know about that, huh?"

"Of course I know about it. I'm the Wing Commander. I learned of it two days after you started planning."

"It's not entirely my initiative. My old boss in Plans called to remind me that many of these crews have been out of the nuclear war plan a long time. Some of the new aircraft commanders have never flown the BUFF on the deck. If our Vietnamese missions start dwindling, we're going to have to find something for the crews to do before they go home. So we might as well start preparing them for a return to the nuclear deterrence business. It's going to be a hell of a job, but I thought after we got the basic plan scoped out, you might like to take it to Air Division to get their blessing."

"I'm surprised you've got all the volunteer help. It's been like pulling teeth to get them to do anything in the past. What's your secret?"

"I don't know I've got one except maybe taking them into my confidence. Someone said that my namesake, Alexander the Great, led by indulgence as well as by example. Liberal or lenient treatment isn't such a bad idea when you're working with intelligent people. I don't know when I've felt this good or been so enthusiastic about anything. I feel so damn strange. If I didn't know better, I'd almost think I was happy. I was thinking . . . " He stopped abruptly and stared at a group filing into the dining room.

"What the hell's wrong with you? You look like you've seen a ghost."

Alex pushed back his chair, arranged his napkin beside his plate, and rose from the table. "I think I have. Would you excuse me?"

CHAPTER FIFTY-THREE

"MISTER PINSKI," Alex spoke to the broad back and cropped blond hair he had scrutinized on the glider flight over the Academy.

"Captain Pinski, or hadn't you noticed, Colonel."

Alex scanned the officer's face, locking onto his eyes with such cold intensity his companions scattered leaving the two standing toe-to-toe and bending into each other like fighting cocks the instant before release. "You'll always be a cadet in my book."

"Suit yourself, Colonel. How's Merrilane? Still practicing to be Miss Liberty?"

"My wife's activities are no concern of yours, Mister."

"You can never be sure can you, Colonel?" Pinski reached his right hand across his chest, unzipped his upper left sleeve pocket, and pulled out an almost-empty pack of Marlboros. Shaking one loose, he pulled it from the package with his lips and extended the pack to Alex. "Smoke?"

"No, I don't indulge. Is that all you're smoking these days, Mister?"

"All us ol' cowpokes smoke only Marlboros. What's this I hear about you running a dog and pony show at the mission briefings, Colonel? My crew just got back from three weeks in the World. We too late to catch your act?"

"You've missed the 'act' as you call it, but I imagine I'll be giving you a special performance from time to time."

"I doubt that, Colonel, unless you're the decorating officer whenever my crew does something exceptional."

"You surprise me, Mister. I thought a man with your competitive tendencies would be flying Phantoms."

"Had my choice, but it takes forever to accumulate time in fighters. BUFFs will build up my resumé for Pan Am."

"The air lines is it? I'd assumed you were career military. Think of all the people you can lean on when you're a colonel."

"You mean like you're trying to lean on me?"

"Precisely."

"Well, Colonel, I've got a mission briefing in fifty-five minutes. You wanna come down and see us off?"

"I don't believe so. Just remember, Mister, fate's pulled us together, and you'd better not make any mistakes because I'm going to be looking over your shoulder when you least expect it."

"I'm flattered by the attention, Colonel, because I'm the best BUFF pilot on the island, and I've got the best crew. Tell Merrilane I send her my very best."

Pinski sauntered off to where his crew had clustered around a table. He was laughing as he sat down. Alex made his way back to Lambrite, realizing as he reached to pull out the chair that his hands were still doubled into fists.

"What was that all about?"

"Just an old friend from Academy days."

"If that was a friend, I'd hate to see you meet up with an enemy. You had your jaw stuck out about three feet."

"What do you know about him? Name's Pinski."

"Don't know anything bad if that's what you're asking. Been an aircraft commander about three months. Up-graded in minimum time. Sharp as a tack, courteous, always gets the job done."

The native waitress was trading quips at Pinski's table, standing close against his shoulder as he massaged her thigh.

"You listening to me, Alex? What the hell's come over you?"

"Sorry, Chris. He just brings back lots of sad memories. Not his fault I suppose. Glad to hear he's good. I may ride with him in the next day or two."

After dinner he walked the short distance to his quarters, a large room with bed, wardrobe, chest, desk, and ceiling fan. The windows were the usual tropical design, louvered and screened. For his amusement, bright-eyed geckos scampered up and down the walls, cute little buggers who watched him as he undressed, erotically flicking their tiny red tongues at him.

He lay in the dark on his back for a long while reviewing the day's activity: meeting with the committee on the retraining program, working with Isaacson's crew and the Food Service chief to revise the in-flight lunch menu. Everything had been going so well since the consternation of his initial mission with Ragsdale. He had recognized the complacency problem and was mitigating it. He had got the men thinking like SAC crews again and sharpening their procedures for the inevitable missions against Hanoi. They would probably come just after the first of the year unless Le Duc Tho got serious at the Paris conference. Then along came Pinski. Everything he had started, especially the good reputation he had begun to acquire among the crews, could be compromised or destroyed by a man with Pinski's charisma.

He tried to reflect on other subjects, but Pinski's image, standing like Lucifer in arrogance and open defiance, refused to fade. In trying to expunge Pinski, he opened the tap releasing Mother Hubbard, Merrilane, Rod Pike, Monique, Wootan, Tiny Temple, SugarFox, and—try as he might to stop the rushing torrent—the voice of Buddy. Giving it up, he threw back the sheet with which he had covered himself and snapped on the lamp. He sat on the side of the bed, running his hands through his hair and rubbing his eyes trying to purge all the unwanted visions. He picked up a magazine, leafed through the pages looking idly at the advertisements for clothing, automobiles, and cigarettes, then sailed it, pages ruffling like the wings of an attacking hawk, at a startled gecko hanging inverted on the ceiling.

"What's wrong with me tonight?" he said aloud. *Gotta knock that off. Starting to talk to myself. Gotta take up running again. Late at night when it's cooled down.* He heard the first of the three-ship cell begin its takeoff roll. No need to look at his watch, he knew the launch schedule. Strong sound, undulating as the wind scattered or concentrated the roar. Number two now hurtling down the runway both pilots scanning their instruments, cross-checking acceleration with elapsed time. *They're committed by now. Number three's on the roll, engines churning at a hundred percent, exhaust gas temperatures right up near their limits, sound registering a deeper tone as the water injection clicks in. Oh—shit!* Silence.

Three's aborting well into the roll, throttles to idle, brake chute streaming out, all needles reversing, speed dropping now that the chute has blossomed. Listening hard, he heard the cycling screech of the anti-skid mechanism as the pilot stood on the brakes. *Power already coming up on the taxi-spare, crew grumbling over their having to fill in, rolling now scarcely three minutes behind number two, bumping along until the drooping wing rises, lifting with it the thin outrigger wheels, and finally the main trucks which skip off and begin their ponderous retraction.* Three miles off the end of the runway, rising and falling in the swell, the ever-present Soviet trawler taps out its report of another cell outbound for Vietnam.

Could have been Pinski. First mission after a three-week layoff. Chance they missed something on the checklist. Burn his ass if he did. Harass the bastard until he wishes he'd never heard the name Cannard. No, the Pinski's of the world never abort. They charge on, ignoring the instruments and the warnings, doing precisely what they please, always coming out on top of the heap.

Turning off the light, he lay naked on his back, eyes open as if waiting for the feature to start. No picture, only words came to mind as he drifted into a familiar monologue. *Hello God.* He felt his lips moving, heard the soft tone of his own voice within his mind. *I swung on a sucker pitch tonight, didn't I? You threw me another curve, or maybe a screwball. Why do I have to face Pinski again? I could use a little burst of wisdom—like water injection— just to get me flying again. I won't bother You about mental peace anymore. I know I have to make my own. Is this my sentence? Al-*

375

ways to live isolated in a one-room cell. Could you give me a vector and a clear frequency? Alex listening out.

He lay visualizing the dark waters, this time in sharp focus, almost as if his forward motion had stopped. As if he were on the verge of a stall. But he must have dropped instead into sleep. He woke up once, hearing some late arriving transients slamming van doors, shouting raucously, and moving into the quarters across the drive. But he drifted off again. When the alarm clattered, he was dreaming of the lithe waitress entwining herself around an exultant Pinski.

He ate breakfast at the club reading *The Stars and Stripes* and listening half-heartedly to the chit-chat on the command net. He was lucky having his own brick. Two-way radios were a status symbol on the island, but inconvenient as everyone was on the same frequency. The Division commander could monitor any conversation, so the chances for privacy within the wing were zero.

Later he went to the avionics shop to check into the ECM situation. Allison had promised to meet him there to make sure the maintenance men were not blowing smoke when they briefed him.

He lost track of time as he worked with Allison and three technicians to devise procedures to reprogram the wing's jammers should the enemy shift frequencies on his missile tracking radars. The brick's squealing tone summoned him. When he answered, Chris Lambrite's terse voice asked for a call back by telephone. Allison was dialing the command-post number even before Lambrite dropped off the net. He handed the phone to Alex as it began to ring.

"Colonel Cannard for Colonel Lambrite . . . Hello Chris, what's up? . . . Still at avionics. You need me? . . . Okay I'll be out front."

Picking up his notebook, brick, and cap, he excused himself and went outside to await the Wing Commander. Within a minute the white-topped Ford sedan whipped around the corner and swung to the curb beside him. An ashen-faced Chris Lambrite reached across the seat to open the contrary passenger door.

"Oh, shit, Alex. I knew something was going to happen before I got out of this place. Damned if I wanted to come back here again." He talked at three times his normal speed, words tripping over each other, like an asthmatic who had been given a shot of adrenalin. "I had a chance of making general on the next list. Good chance. Damned good record. Nobody with more bomber experience: B-Forty-seven, B-Fifty-eight, B-Fifty-two. A year in Thuds bombing the North, dodging the flak and the SAMs. All the schools–Squadron Officer, Command and Staff, War College. Right up the ranks to Wing Commander. Getting the birds off on time regardless. What more could they want?"

They accelerated through the guard post onto the flight line and still Lambrite had not named the problem. But Alex could imagine. *Only two cells airborne. Not the early launch, or we'd be on the radio. Pinski's cell's landing. Oh, God, not a bombing error. Not again!*

"Why does it have to happen now? I thought I was out of the woods when you got here." Lambrite was still talking to himself thinking he was filling in the details.

"Chris, take it easy. Was it a short round?"

"For Christ's sake, Alex, weren't you listening to anything I said? One of our planes must have bombed direct instead of off-set. He put the whole load in the middle of a village just south of Tay Ninh."

The first bomber was clearing the runway as the second flared for landing. The third was smoking inbound on short final. Alex could see the helmeted head of the pilot of number two as the aircraft decelerated on its roll-out, brake chute a billowing black mushroom rather than the usual faded yellow or dirty white.

Lambrite's brick shrilled. He looked sideways at Alex, pulled out the antenna, and switched to the transmit position. "Colonel Lambrite."

"Colonel, this is General Wilhoyt. I'm directing you to isolate Argos 64 and put a security team around it. Off-load the crew and have them taken directly to the base hospital. Lieutenant Colonel Mucklewhite's there to receive them. I don't want that airplane touched until I give the word. No one enters the bombbays except to install the door locks. Have you got that?"

"Yes, General. I'll tell the crew . . . "

"Lambrite, I don't want you or any of your staff talking to them. My JAG is meeting the aircraft to read them their rights."

"General, they don't even know what's happened. I can't allow them to get hit with this and then think the wing's treating them like criminals."

"Colonel, you heard my orders. The Associated Press is already reporting upwards of two hundred casualties. So the Air Division's taking over the investigation, and we're going to hang their guilty asses unless my men find an aircraft malfunction. Now you do what I told you to do. Out."

"That pompous son of a bitch. He sits up there on his fat behind letting us do all the work while he takes the credit. Then we have an incident, and he's ready to sacrifice us all."

"Maybe he's just trying to protect the crew from self-incrimination. He did ask us to isolate the aircraft systems until they're checked out."

"You think I was born yesterday? I'd already had the command post transmit those instructions as soon as I got the call from SAC ADVON. He listens to our network all the time, so he's just acting like he's on top of things. I got my JAG people meeting the aircraft too, but at least I was going to be with them. This is one of our crews, for Christ's sake. They haven't just dropped in from Mars."

"Chris, you haven't told me who the commander of Argos 64 is."

"Sorry. Thought you knew. It's your friend, Pinski."

CHAPTER FIFTY-FOUR

RETURNING TO WING HEADQUARTERS, Alex found a message instructing him to report to the Air Division Commander. When he arrived, a sergeant ushered him into the general's office. Wilhoyt, thin-faced under a shock of coal-black hair, returned his salute with a detachment reminiscent of the humanoid robots he had seen at Disneyland three years earlier.

"I've got a job for you, Cannard. As of now you're attached to this division to investigate the short round we had last night."

"Yes, sir." Alex understood the futility of complaining; Lambrite would probably have given him the investigation anyway.

"You don't seem overjoyed, Colonel."

"No, sir. There are other things I'd prefer to do."

"Such as?"

"The projects I'm working in the wing. ECM modifications on the G-model, an up-date on our contingency plans to hit Hanoi, a requalification program in low-level tactics for when we go back into the nuclear delivery business."

"You're saying you're too busy?"

"No, General. It's just that I've lived too close to short rounds when I flew Spookies. They traumatize the individuals involved if they're not handled right. Or even if they are."

"Well, Colonel, it's up to you to handle this one properly."

"Yes, General. Do you have any other instructions?"

"No, your personnel folder says you're a take-charge guy. That's what I want you to do here. I want a preliminary report on my desk first thing in the morning and something I can get off to SAC before close of business. You don't have to worry about maintenance malfunctions; all systems checked normally. Just to be sure, I told Lambrite to fly a test tomorrow dropping live bombs in the practice area. If the system works properly, I'm releasing the aircraft for routine operations."

"You seem on top of everything, General. Do you really need me?"

"Yes, Cannard, I want a man with a reputation as an SOB to put the fear of God into these crews. I've seen them screwing off in the club and walking around the base uncovered and wearing flight suits unzipped to the navel. They're sloppy and complacent. I'm surprised you haven't picked up on it."

"I had noticed it, General. Chris Lambrite's got a lot . . . "

"Don't try to blow smoke, Colonel. I've had my eye on Lambrite for several months. He's worn out—running scared, worrying about the generals' list."

"There's a couple of things you need to know, General. First, I've tried to get away from the SOB mold, and the crews here don't perceive me as such. I don't want to compromise the rapport I've built up."

"Oh, heaven help me," Wilhoyt rolled his eyes and stood up to take the height advantage away from Alex. "Don't tell me I've got a colonel who wants to be one of the boys."

"No sir. I'll never be one of the boys again, but I like having the option of tailoring my leadership style to fit the situation."

"Well the situation here is a clear case of incompetence which made embarrassing headlines all over the world. Someone's head is going to roll, and it's not going to be mine. So I don't care how you get to the bottom of this thing. I don't care if you tell them you're from *Time* magazine, but I want to know precisely what happened. Understood?"

"Understood, General."

"You said there was something else I needed to know."

"I'm acquainted with Mister Pinski from my tour at the Academy. We're not on the best of terms, so he may think this investigation's a witch hunt if I'm running it."

Wilhoyt started to say something, thought better of it, then stood rubbing his chin with his right hand. Alex saw the massive West Point ring looking like a deformed knuckle as it moved slowly back and forth. "That's your problem, Colonel. Seems to me his being a former cadet will simplify your job."

"How do you figure that, General?"

"Come on, Cannard! It'll guarantee you at least one of them will be telling the truth."

"Do I have your permission to release them to their quarters after I've read their written reports and spoken to them?"

"No way. I want them isolated until I decide what to do with them. Let the crew force know we're serious about this short-round business."

"What about Colonel Lambrite? May I allow him to visit?"

"I'm beginning to wonder about you, Cannard. No! I said 'isolation,' and I meant 'isolation.' No Wing Commander, no reporters—got that—reporters? No calls home. Nothing but medical personnel or chaplains. Now get with it."

Ten minutes later Alex paused at Lambrite's office door. Framed between the national colors and the wing's flag, his friend sat leaning back in his chair, eyes closed, feet on the cluttered desk.

"Come on in Alex. You want a statement from me?"

"You know about my new job?

"Yeah, Dudley called me."

"You mean the general?"

"That's what the crews call him, "Dudley Do-Right." Always looking at the big picture, like flight suit zippers, not wearing caps, and flying over the Agana hospital on final approach."

"I tried to get out of it, Chris."

"I bet you didn't try too hard."

"No, I was too busy trying to cover your ass. He thinks you're worrying too much about the generals' list."

"That's nice to know. You two must have got on famously to have discussed my professional shortcomings."

"I tried to tell him you were stretched thin after he mentioned he thought the crews were complacent. That's when he cut me off. I was trying to get him to soft-pedal this whole thing, but he thinks we're all in jeopardy unless he's got a completed investigation off to SAC within forty-eight hours."

"No need to investigate. It's obvious who's going to take the fall for this one."

"Nothing's obvious. Unless I miss my guess, there's enough blame to be passed around, so no one needs to be sacrificed."

"I tell you, I'm pissed at the way he's quarantined those guys. Isolated as if they'd flown through a radioactive cloud."

"It's a closed issue with Wilhoyt."

"You know the area south of Tay Ninh. It's nothing but VC, NVA, or sympathizers. Pinski's crew ought to get the DFC for taking them out."

"Chris, I've got to get going. But I need you to keep pushing our revision of the Hanoi-Haiphong contingency plan. We can't attack in a bomber stream betting our ECM will handle their missiles."

"I've been thinking it over. We don't have the manpower to put that together. Especially not now. That's SAC's job."

"But it's our crews who'll be hanging it out. At least send a priority message to SAC to get them hustling."

"It won't do any good, those weenies never listen to us. But if it'll make you happy, I'll call Kiefer in Ops Plans and see if I can get him interested."

"That won't hack it, Chris. Phone calls are too easy to ignore. Right now we need to get them thinking of something besides short round. A strong TWX sent under the General's name will get you back in his good graces and the SAC staff off dead center."

"I'll think about it."

"Don't think too long. The red flags are springing up like poppies on Memorial Day."

He started his investigation by reading the handwritten reports each crewmember had completed without reference to the others. In different lengths, literary styles, and grammatical correctness, they told the same story from six viewpoints. For all practical purposes, he could forget the gunner, Electronics Warfare Officer, and perhaps the co-pilot. They had been along for the ride. To a certain extent, so was Pinski. Flying above a solid undercast, he had no idea where the crosshairs were lying or what bombing mode—direct or offset—the radar navigator had selected. Outside of maintaining proper altitude and airspeed, he had only to see that the heading pointer was lined up as the time-to-go indicator stepped down to bomb release. He probably thought the mission just another milkrun until he stepped into the hostile ring of strange faces as he emerged from the aircraft.

Using the scrambler telephone which allowed discussion of classified information, Alex called the SAC Advanced Echelon, the bomber office in Saigon. He felt like Dorothy trying to talk to the Tin Man, a mechanical-sounding alien whose reconstituted voice seemed as though it had been transmitted through a string tied to a can a thousand miles away. His patience paid off, however, when he learned the beacon transmitter serving as the off-set aiming point for the bomb run had been mistakenly placed within the village itself rather than in an unpopulated area as regulations stipulated. Charge that responsibility to the ADVON liaison people. If the beacon had been properly positioned, an improper switch position in the bomber would have resulted only in a demolished beacon with no loss of life.

Going next to the hospital ward where the men of Argos 64 were confined, Alex found five of them in a small lounge. Pinski spotted him first and called his companions to attention.

"As you were, gentlemen. I'm Alex Cannard. The Division Commander has asked me to investigate why your bombs fell outside the box. Captain Pinski, which crew member are we missing?"

"The Radar Navigator."

"I beg your pardon?"

"The Radar Navigator, sir."

"Would you please have someone ask him to join us?"

"He's asleep."

"I beg your pardon?"

"He's asleep, sir."

"Would you please have someone wake him and ask him to join us?"

Pinski glared at him but turned to a blond lieutenant who was evidently the navigator. "Do as the man says, Smitty."

Alex snapped off the television, then turned toward the sullen-faced men. "Would you please gather around, so I can get a few facts cleared up." They took their places while Alex remained standing.

The blond officer returned, stopping to hold the swinging door for his teammate, an exceedingly thin, ebony-hued captain. When they had settled themselves, Alex asked Pinski to introduce his crew.

"Colonel Cannard, may I present Captain Budd, Radar Nav." The officer pulled himself from his seat but avoided looking at Alex. He continued standing and was joined by each of his associates as Pinski called roll. "Lieutenant Smith, Navigator; Lieutenant Tokas, EWO; Lieutenant Russell, Co-pilot; Staff Sergeant Hienrich, Gunner."

"Please sit down, gentlemen. I regret having awakened you, Captain Budd. I know it's difficult sleeping in strange surroundings." The officer did not acknowledge his apology. "Let me remind you that you've already been briefed on your rights under the Uniform Code of Military Justice and anything you say may be used against you. Any questions?" No one spoke.

"I don't know how long you'll be here, probably until I've submitted my report tomorrow afternoon. General Wilhoyt asked that you be kept here, so we could get a complete story from each of you before it was possibly diluted by conversations with your friends in the wing."

"You sure we got any friends left, Colonel?" Pinski asked.

"You've as many friends in the wing as ever. Probably more. Any of us who fly in combat share the risk of being involved in an investigation such as this."

He paused to see if Pinski would challenge him again. When he did not, he continued. "The preliminary ground checks found the bomb-nav and release systems operating properly. We're flying a test hop early tomorrow to see if anything shows up in the air. SAC ADVON admits the aiming beacon was mistakenly placed inside the village rather than in an unpopulated area. Additionally the briefed attack heading had you tracking directly toward the off-set aiming beacon. If the heading had been properly divergent, you may have detected that the aircraft was lined up with the off-set itself rather than the target."

The navigator was looking at Budd, who sat staring at one green tile as he polished it with the sole of his right boot. Of the other crew members, only Pinski was looking directly at Alex.

"That, gentlemen," he raised his voice, "leaves the matter of the position of the bombing mode switch which wasn't addressed in the statements of either member of the bomb-nav team. Because of a scope-camera malfunction, we have no pictures of the bomb run to assist our investigation. Captain Budd, are you certain you positioned the switch properly to off-set?"

"Yes sir." Budd looked him in the eye momentarily but broke contact and returned to polishing the tile.

"Lieutenant Smith, do you remember visually checking the position of the switch prior to bombs away?"

The lieutenant hesitated perhaps thirty seconds before answering. "I think I did. It's just mechanical to check it as we run the checklist, but I can't swear I checked it."

Reasonably satisfied with the discussion and confident he had gained all the information the men were prepared to give, Alex had retrieved his hat, sunglasses, and brick when Budd spoke in a low, almost inaudible voice.

"Do you know how many I killed, Colonel?"

"If your question is how many casualties resulted from the bombing, first reports estimate some two hundred, including wounded. Anything else for me? I'm having your uniforms sent over, so you can get out of those flying suits. If you need anything you're not getting, have the ward orderly call me through the Command Post. That's all I have. Thank you gentlemen."

The crew rose. "Captain Budd," he said as he passed the man, "will you step outside with me?" They passed through a second set of swinging doors leading into an empty reception room.

He stopped beside a humming Coke machine. "I want you to know," he placed his hand on the officer's shoulder causing him to look up in surprise, "I've walked where you're walking. You're going to be thrown on your own internal resources, and it'll be rough. The outcome of this investigation, however, will have little to do with the resolution inside your mind. It's something a man must deal with on his own. If you ever need to talk with someone you can trust, I'm available for the remainder of my lifetime."

He had alerted the General's executive officer that he would need a stenographer for the early evening. She was waiting when he walked into the office they had arranged for his use. She remained seated, legs crossed, chewing gum which seemed to synchronize her pumping jaw with her swinging calf.

Introducing himself, he thanked the woman for agreeing to work overtime, then took a seat facing the window overlooking the parking apron rather than inward toward the rapidly swinging leg. Still her perfume momentarily scrambled the sentences he had composed.

"Ms Thurston," he began, "this is a secret message from the general to CINCSAC, subject: B-Fifty-two Short Round Investigation. I want to make it a final report rather than an interim one. Once I've dictated the basic message, we'll put a cover sheet on it with a short paragraph for General Wilhoyt explaining the case and my rationale. Got it?"

When she did not respond, he turned to see her large brown eyes regarding him as she brushed her pencil across her thickly painted lips. She nodded, lowering the instrument to her pad like the mechanical facsimile devices which mindlessly scribbled observations transmitted from the base weather station.

"Okay, stop me if I go too fast."

"That's all right; I can take it as fast as you give it to me."

Realizing ripe women like this had never before distracted, never even existed for him when he was living with Merrilane, he took a moment to compose himself, then fell easily into the netherworld of military jargon:

Paragraph one: At Thirteen slash one two three five, Zebra, December, one nine seven two, Argos Six-four, second in a cell of three B-Fifty-twos of the Seventy-second Strategic Wing, using ground beacon offset bombing techniques, placed its entire load three point two nautical miles northwest of the desired target impacting in the South Vietnamese village of Cal Truong. Subsequent ground and airborne tests of the aircraft produced no system malfunctions. Neither weather nor enemy action were a factor on the bomb run although solid undercast complicated pilots' ability to perceive an error in heading.

Paragraph two: Crew records, standardization checks, and beacon bombing training all complete. Crew rest adequate. Mission briefing normal. Crew participating in first mission since return from twenty-one day ordinary leave in CONUS.

Paragraph three: Primary cause. Radar Navigator most probably failed to place bombing mode switch in offset position resulting in bombs being released in direct mode subsequently impacting on the offset aiming beacon itself rather than the target. Contributing causes: Number one. (Put that in parenthesis if you please, Ms Thurston). Navigator did not ascertain bombing mode switch in offset position. (Paren number two) SACADVON did not assure beacon properly placed away from inhabited locations according to current regulations. (Paren number three) Seventy-second Wing planned an attack heading improperly divergent by less than thirty degrees from a heading directly aligned with the aiming beacon's designated location.

Paragraph four: Recommendations. Actions for Headquarters SAC (Parenthesis number one) Direct Commander Seventy-second Wing to issue written reprimands and remove bomb-nav team from combat-ready status for retraining and subsequent assignment as individual replacements on separate crews. (Paren two) Issue written reprimand to Commander, SAC ADVON for improper placement of off-set aiming marker beacon. (Paren three) Instigate immediate IG inspection of all related ADVON bombing procedures concerning off-set beacon and Sky Spot radar delivery. (Paren number four) Issue written reprimand to Commander, Seventy-second Wing for failure properly to monitor operation of Bomb Nav Branch. (Paren number five) Direct Commander, Third Air Division to inspect all procedures of Seventy-second Wing Bomb Nav Branch.

"Got all that, Ms. Thurston?"

"Sure. What do you want on the cover sheet?"

"Working late I see." Wilhoyt stood in the doorway. "What do you have so far, Cannard?"

"I'm putting a final report together, General, betting we don't find any discrepancies in tomorrow's test flight. I need to coordinate it with your JAG and Bomb-Nav folks, but I think it'll fly."

"Read it back to me will you, Betty?"

The woman began to read in a husky voice putting more emphasis on the words than they probably needed and punctuating each recommendation with an energetic swing of her leg.

"Okay, type that up, but stop at the recommendations section and bring the message to me. Cannard, let's talk."

Wilhoyt settled himself behind his desk and began looking disinterestedly through a stack of personal mail. "I thought I gave you the impression I wanted the guilty bastards hung."

"It might be a bit sticky to hang the Saigon ADVON, General."

"Who said anything about hanging the ADVON? They didn't salvo on the village."

"True, sir. But if the ADVON had verified the beacon's placement, all we'd have had was the loss of a homing beacon and a load of bombs that could possibly have done just as much good as those dropped inside the box."

"I don't care for impertinence in my officers, Cannard. I want people who can carry out orders."

"I like to think my job's to use my head, General."

"When you work for me, you follow orders. Do you understand that?"

"With all respect, General," Alex could feel the constriction in his groin, "I don't understand your reasoning. You picked me for this job when you had any number of other officers who were certainly qualified and who were already under your supervision. I assumed you wanted my particular skills."

"What's the reason for only a reprimand for Lambrite? Friend of yours?"

"I've known Chris for a long time and consider him an outstanding officer with a proven record. I'm trying to get us past this thing without wrecking any more lives and careers—and maybe even the command."

"What do you mean by 'the command'?"

"Crew morale's been rock bottom. You've seen some of the indicators. To crucify a crew or a popular wing commander might be all we need to start an outright revolt."

"Cannard, you're talking through your ass. SAC crews'll do what we tell them to do for as long as we tell them to do it. That's what they get paid for."

"General, there's not enough money to pay those men to keep doing forever what they've already done for too long. They read the papers and the news magazines. It's a young force. More in tune with the anti-war movement in many ways than they are with us. We've got to lead them. We can't give the impression we eat our young. You sacrifice Budd and Lambrite, and you've lost the crew force."

"You're not intimidated because he's black are you?"

"I hadn't noticed, General."

Wilhoyt leaped from his seat, shaking a finger in Alex's face reminding him of drawings of Ebenezer Scrooge chastising Bob Cratchet. "Look you poor excuse for . . . "

Seeing Betty Thurston entering the outer office with the typed message, Wilhoyt recovered his composure. "I don't buy any of this crap you're slinging, Cannard. I'll write my own recommendations, and that misfit crew will wish they'd paid more attention to the bomb run checklist."

Ms. Thurston stopped in the doorway, tapping impatiently with the foot of her high-heeled pump a message of missed dinner and two hours' overtime. As Wilhoyt motioned her to enter, the outer office door crashed open, hitting the wall with enough force to dislodge a framed B-52 picture which shattered on the floor. A red-faced major brushed past the woman, waving a sheaf of message forms not yet separated from their carbons. "You'll want to see this, General. Flash precedence from CINCSAC."

Wilhoyt read the message, stopping twice to check details. "Would you mind waiting outside, Betty," he said, then turned back to Alex as she closed the door. "Your short round just got pushed off the front page. Nixon's going against Hanoi with a sustained max effort. Get your ass back to the wing. I'll hold your message until we see what's going to happen."

CHAPTER FIFTY-FIVE

ALEX FOUND LAMBRITE bent over the map table in the Ops Plans shop surrounded by somber-faced staff officers. "I'm assigned back to the wing, Chris. What can I do?"

"Pray for me."

"If we're sending these guys to Hanoi in a bomber stream, I'd better pray for them. Did you get a message off to SAC yet?"

"Of course not. Who'd have thought Nixon would bomb just before Christmas, for Christ's sake?"

"When do you expect the frag order from SAC?"

"They're probably putting it together right now. Anyway you look at it, I've got less than three days to figure how to put a hundred BUFFs over Hanoi without running 'em into each other."

"What about the tactics?"

"Screw the tactics. This morning I kissed goodby to a tanker full of flight crews going home for the holidays. Where am I going to get enough bodies for a sustained max effort?"

"You've recalled them of course."

"The moment I got the word, but I'm still scraping the barrel for the first day's launch."

"What should I do first?"

"Run over to maintenance and see how many sorties they can generate for the first day. I figure Thailand will produce about thirty. While you're there, see where we stand on the ECM modification for the G-models. I already got the word there's no maneuvering for the last four minutes of the bomb run. Everything'll be riding on electronic countermeasures."

"Don't they know an elephant walk across Hanoi could turn into a turkey shoot?"

"Don't ask me. My job's to launch the sorties and lead the gaggle."

"Chris, you know as well as I do if we fly our bombers over the same track, at the same altitude and airspeed, and with the same interval between them, the Vietnamese will barrage fire missiles without turning on their tracking radars. ECM can't defend against stations that aren't broadcasting."

"You may be right, but it'll take the dinks a while to figure it out. They'll think even we can't be that dumb."

"How long will it take?"

"Hard to tell. But I'd rather be leading the first wave than the third. What say we quit worrying till we actually see what the frag order says? I'll need you back by twenty-two hundred for a meeting of the senior battle staff to pull this thing together."

The maintenance hangars crackled with activity as men swarmed over the bombers like children preparing their wagons for a Fourth of July parade. Alex made his way toward the avionics shop where technicians would be programming black boxes for an invisible duel with enemy radars and missile-guidance transmissions. He slipped into the air-conditioned assembly room and stood for almost two minutes before anyone noticed him.

"Oh, hi Colonel," the young sergeant looked up as he closed the case of the transmitter he had been troubleshooting. "I didn't hear you come in."

"Don't let me disturb you, Sergeant Meiners. I just need some idea of whether we can configure a hundred plus for day after tomorrow."

"It'll be tight, sir. The major's on the horn to U-Tapao seeing if we can borrow some jammers, but I wouldn't bet on it. They'll need to outfit their own guys plus keeping some in reserve. You know how that goes."

"How's the modification on the G-model? They're the ones I'm sweating."

"About fifty percent complete, I'd say. The figures are on the board."

"Good evening, Colonel Cannard." The sad-eyed major's short sleeved shirt was rumpled; a white plastic insert, jammed with odd-size pens and grease pencils, protruded from an unbuttoned breast pocket. "What can I do for you?"

"Brief me on our ECM status if you please, Major Rossi, and tell me what you think we'll run into."

"No problem on the D-models. All modified and fully equipped although I don't have any spares and UT says they can't loan me any. We're in deep-serious on the Gs. Fifty-eight percent modified. By cannibalizing, we should be able to configure the first day's strike pretty well. But it'll take a lot of manpower playing musical chairs."

"How good's the modification?"

"Gives us a chance to program the jammers in flight and not have to depend on fixed-frequency transmitters. The Russians will be switching frequencies on us like crazy and probably using some we haven't seen before."

"You think the Soviets are operating the air defense system?"

"Wouldn't you supervise if you were in their shoes? Opportunity to test their equipment, deflate SAC's balloon, and destroy the Fifty-two's credibility as a nuclear penetrator. You don't believe they'd leave that to the locals do you?"

"You think they know we're coming?"

"What difference does it make? The trawler will transmit the exact number in each wave, and Hanoi will have eight hours to get ready. Probably expecting us to do something really daring like coming down Thud Ridge just like all the TAC drivers have done before us."

"You don't sound too happy about our tactics."

"Who, me? I'm just a passed-over major. What do I know? All I'd like is for my equipment to have a reasonable chance. Give me a little help: vary the attack altitudes and headings, cross the inbound tracks, program simultaneous drop times, provide good electronic support from EB-Sixty-sixes and Wild Weasels."

"Anything else?"

"Yeah, Colonel." The major was searching about his cluttered desk.

"They're on your head."

"Oh, yeah; thanks." He pulled his glasses down so he could examine Alex's face. "Don't use three-ship cells in trail like we do in the South and expect to mask them with a little bit of chaff. And for the love of God, don't let them make a hairy turn off the target. It'll give the enemy's radar their profile while causing our own jamming signals to go sailing off into the boonies. Better to fly right across the city than to turn."

"You've been a big help, Major. Just one thing more. What about evasive action on the bomb run?"

"I've got to have faith in my equipment, Colonel. Evasive action's okay maybe against one SAM site, but you're going against thirty or so—that's at least two hundred individual launchers! If some pilot waltzes outside the chaff and mutual jamming support of the formation, I guarantee the SAM's will nail him. We've got to remember the job's to put the bombs on the target."

Alex slipped into his seat five minutes before Lambrite's planning meeting was to start. Precisely on time the Wing Commander strode into the room looking as if he had just showered after a quick game of handball.

"You're wondering, no doubt, why I've called you together." He waited for the obligatory chuckles to subside. "By now you know in general what we're going to do. Here's the message from the Joint Chiefs laying on a max effort starting at twelve hundred hours Greenwich mean time day after tomorrow."

Lambrite began to read: "Object is maximum destruction of selected military targets in the vicinity of Hanoi/Haiphong. Be prepared to extend operations past three days if directed . . .

Exercise precaution to minimize risk of civilian casualties . . .
Avoid damage to third country shipping . . . ."

Lambrite paused, looking around the room as if soliciting
questions. Feeling strangely detached, like a member of a theater audience incapable of interrupting the inexorable events
unfolding before his eyes, Alex sat mute trying to remember
anyone ever before telling him what the overall object was.

"This isn't just our show," Lambrite continued after placing the message on the conference table before him. "Tactical
aircraft will hit airfields, rocket sites, and flak emplacements.
But we're getting top billing. Colonel Enthoven, will discuss
the targets, route, and number of aircraft we anticipate launching."

Enthoven moved from his seat near the door to stand beside the rear-projection screen. "First slide," he said animating
the sleepy-eyed airman who swapped the colorful SAC shield
transparency for one showing the route from departure to coast-
in just below the DMZ. "Pre-strike refueling off the Philippines
as usual with KC-One thirty-fives out of Kadena. We'll launch
eighty-seven bombers, to be joined by forty-two out of U Tapao.
Together they'll comprise the largest formation of attacking
bombers launched since World War Two. First takeoff at fourteen forty local with one-minute intervals between aircraft and
five minutes between cells to allow spacing for refueling. Next
slide."

Oh shit! Alex thought as the second slide materialized showing the route west across South Vietnam, north at the
Cambodian border, and finally southeast into the target. Others in the room voiced his expletive. Enthoven did not wait for
silence before continuing. "We're going north almost to the Chinese border before turning down Thud Ridge. We'll be in cells
of three aircraft separated by five hundred feet in altitude and
one mile in trail between attacking cells. Four flights of F-Fours
will fly close cover and spread a chaff cloud between twenty-
five and thirty-five thousand feet from the IP into the target.
We'll have a MiG cap of three flights of four F-Fours each."
Pausing, Enthoven called for questions.

"We all know the enemy SAM capability around Hanoi," Alex spoke as he pulled himself out of his seat. "I'm concerned about attacking in trail across the SAMs clustered along Thud Ridge. I'm also concerned with that one hundred and thirty-five-degree, post-target turn."

"This is the plan we got from SAC, Colonel. Any other questions?"

"None that I care to discuss with you, Colonel Enthoven."

"Alex," Lambrite jumped to his feet, motioning for the lights to be brought up, "I've already discussed the route with General Wilhoyt. It's out of our hands."

"I find that difficult to accept, Chris. What kind of loss rate do you contemplate?"

"We're forecasting three percent."

"At thirty-six thousand feet we're in the SA-Two's optimum performance envelope. With that horrendous post-attack turn and the marginal capability of our ECM in the G-model, we're looking at six percent at least."

"You're forgetting about the chaff cloud, Colonel Cannard," Enthoven interjected.

"With the forecast wind and the number of aircraft we're trying to protect with only sixteen F-Fours, your chaff cloud will be thin cirrus at best."

"Alex, come off it. Even with a six percent loss ratio, we're way ahead of anything comparable. We lost nineteen percent on the Regensburg-Schweinfurt raid and thirty percent when we hit the Ploesti oil fields."

"That nineteen forty-three analogy won't wash, Chris. Both those missions were mass screw-ups. If we take a few extra days to line up our ducks, we can pull this off without losing anyone."

"Colonel Cannard," Lambrite glared, "we have our orders. The crews are used to these procedures, and we're going to have enough trouble just generating and launching a force this size without getting into a pissing contest with SAC." Lambrite turned away from Alex.

"Stormy, can you give us a quick weather briefing?"

The meteorologist repeated a litany that most in the room could quote from memory. Typical weather patterns, possible thunderstorms in the refueling area, northeast monsoon involving the entire northern portion of Vietnam. Alex wasn't listening.

The Chief of Maintenance followed. A short-tempered giant with tufts of gray hair spilling over the neck of his white undershirt, Amundsen looked as if he could shove a B-52 into the sky if absolutely necessary. "Getting the aircraft to the runway in the proper sequence, is a major problem," he barked without benefit of visual eyewash. "We'll use normal procedures for sparing the cells. If a primary bird craps out early in pre-flight, we'll move to the ground spare. If there's not time, or if the pilot aborts his takeoff, we'll launch a backup crew in the taxi-spare. Being short on G-model ECM equipment, I can configure only the primary aircraft. If we use any of our spares, I can't guarantee they'll have a full set of jammers."

"Thank you, Harvey," Lambrite was back on his feet again. "If you've got work to do, you're free to go."

The maintenance chief grunted, picked up his brick and grungy cap with its grease marks and frayed silver braid, and left the room before someone could ask a question that would further complicate his life.

"That brings us to the matter of aircrews," Lambrite continued. "We were caught short because I'd released as many as I dared to go home for Christmas. Fortunately the sick, lame, and lazy are coming out of the woodwork to fly this mission. They figure it's going to bring the POWs home."

"Colonel," Enthoven asked tentatively, "what's the status of Captain Pinski's crew?"

"General Wilhoyt's releasing them to fly in the third wave of our first day's attack. If there's nothing else, let's get back to work."

The staff left the briefing room quickly, but Alex waited to see Lambrite. "I'm glad to hear the general took my recommendation, Chris."

"He wouldn't have if this Hanoi thing hadn't come along. He was planning to burn the whole crew. But he managed to attach a bit of his warped sense of humor as a stipulation."

"I'm waiting."

"He wants you and Pinski to lead the third wave."

CHAPTER FIFTY-SIX

LITTLE HAD HAPPENED EASILY since the meeting of the battle staff. Alex met briefly with Pinski's crew for target study and a discussion of emergency procedures—bailout, escape and evasion, and Code of Conduct should they be captured. Otherwise he roamed the base all day doing odd jobs for Lambrite: working the crew manning problem, selecting the cell leaders, and overseeing the review of each crew member's training and currency records. Regular meals and proper sleep became the first casualties.

Early the next afternoon—Day One of the attack plan and just six shopping days until Christmas—he joined Pinski's crew for their mission briefing as the first of the scheduled eighty-seven B-52s lurched out of its parking slot and trundled down the taxi lanes leading to the take-off point. Its movement marked the beginning of the launch sequence that was to last almost two hours before the final aircraft lifted into a sky polluted by the residue of six hundred ninety-six J-57 jet engines operating at maximum take-off thrust. Some fifteen thousand ground crew and base personnel lined the runway to watch, photograph, and cheer the departures.

Complications began shortly after the crew chief applied power to Pinski's aircraft. Budd reported blanking on his scope, and radar maintenance technicians soon arrived to troubleshoot. The ramp sweltered under the tropical sun as a valiant air-conditioning cart puffed cooling air through long yellow conduits that curled up the ladder into the crew compartment. Alex stayed out of the way, sprawled with drooping eyelids in the shadow of the wing. Lulled by a light breeze and the muted surging of the auxiliary generator, he closed his eyes remembering the crashing of the tropical ocean when he lay beside his wife on a perfect Hawaiian beach just before the storm that ripped his life apart. Reaching into his left leg pocket, he pulled out a crumpled crew roster and began writing on the backside.

18 December 1972

Dearest Merrilane,

By the time you receive this, you should know my fate. Within the hour I depart on a mission long overdue. Because of that delay, the enemy is well prepared. Death will be riding with us tonight, and I have a strong premonition of disaster. So this note could have the validity of a death-bed confession.

My thoughts are of you, and I ask you to forgive me for the suffering I've caused. I believed my duty called, and I too have suffered from that belief. A great trauma drained my humanity, stilled my hand, and paralyzed my tongue. It ruined our time together in Hawaii and has prevented my reclaiming your love.

During our time apart, I've become a distrustful, almost desperate, man. I've lost my only love, and I don't know how to find her again even if I'm granted the time. I've failed the only test of manhood—nurturing you and my children.

Think not harshly of me,

Alex

Maintenance waffled and hoped and finally surrendered to a bag-drag twenty minutes before scheduled engine start. He joined the line forming a bucket brigade to pass the personal gear, flight bags, lunches, water bottles, secret communications kit, and all the equipment necessary for the crew to operate seven miles above the earth for the next sixteen hours. After loading the bus, they rumbled out to the hardstand where the replacement aircraft squatted, already preflighted by another crew. Pinski and Budd hastily scanned the aircraft's records then climbed aboard. Alex checked only the loading of electronic countermeasures. The aircraft carried full chaff dispensers but was not yet modified to support the new AN/ALT-22 jammers.

As he handed the forms back to the crew chief, a disheveled Major Rossi appeared. "I guess you saw the bad news, Colonel."

"Luck of the draw. Any suggestions I can pass to Lieutenant Tokas?"

Nothing I can think of. He's a sharp kid, but you can't play in the symphony when your horn's busted."

"Could I impose on your good nature to mail a letter for me?"

"Sure thing."

"All I had was some scrap paper. Could you provide an envelope and address it for me?

"Got it," Rossi said as he buttoned the sheet into the left breast pocket of his fatigues. "I'll get it out tomorrow."

"It's important. You won't forget?"

"Forget what?" the major said with the bare hint of a smile.

Engine start, taxi, and takeoff were uneventful. Except for the feeling of flying into the pages of history, this could have been any of the hundreds of missions he had flown in the instructor pilot's jumpseat. He had talked little with Pinski other than to clarify their respective duties. The captain commanded the aircraft and was responsible for its crew, whereas he would make decisions concerning the wave as a whole. "I want you to understand," he had said, "that split seconds will make the difference in an emergency. If we're badly hit, only the ones in ejection seats have a chance. Get 'em out quick and don't wait for me."

Pinski ran a tight ship. No extraneous conversation: just checklists, hourly station checks, and business. No first names, no speculation, no backtalk. What transpired, Alex wondered, within the gray matter protected by his white plastic helmet? What fantasies, remembrances, ambitions swirled? What recurrent visions coalesced? Was there a long-haired woman sprawled on a crumpled bed?

No chatter accompanied the maneuvering for refueling rendezvous. Hook-up and transfer proceeded under radio silence with boomers flashing their director lights and nodding their booms up and down to invite contact. The tankers simply swept into view, mimed their mournful lines, then exited stage right.

As they accelerated away, climbing and turning toward bright lights, hot coffee, and clean sheets, he wondered if his innermost soul yearned to join them rather than participate in another night's killing. He knew the answer. If the tankers were meant to be the chorus, he was fated to be the tragic hero plunging doggedly forward encumbered by the flaw he could no more jettison than he could mollify. Pulling his thoughts away from the twinkling lights, he wished there were more for him to do. At least Pinski could set up a mechanical scan of the instrument panel, perhaps tracing the almost imperceptible drop of an oil pressure gage, but he was left to his own devices: thinking, remembering, thinking again.

Approaching coast-in the crew began to stir, each man in turn going off interphone to crawl to the relief tube on the lower deck. He slipped into his survival vest, patting each pocket to be able to locate its contents in the dark and feeling the walnut handle of his .38-Special nested under his left armpit. He struggled into his parachute, cinched the leg straps, and rearranged himself in his uncomfortable seat.

Leading the third wave was good therapy for the crew: enough activity to keep them from thinking extraneous thoughts, enough responsibility to let them know they were back in the fold. Banking northward the bombers plowed long, billowing, condensation trails through the moonless night like a full-rigged armada sailing majestically toward their turn southeast and the final run down Thud Ridge.

"AC, Radar requests to go off interphone."

What's that all about, Alex wondered. *Probably a nervous kidney.* Pinski had the cockpit illumination turned so low, it was like working under distant starlight. As he strained to see the small clock on the instrument panel above the pilot's artificial horizon, he was startled to feel a bony hand on his right shoulder. Turning his head, he perceived the massive white dome of a jet helmet close to his face, but he could determine no features within. For a moment he was Lawrence Olivier on the battlements cringing from a dead king's apparition. He slid his own helmet aside, better to hear the hoarse voice whispering to him. Deciphering the gentle breaths falling on his cheek was like feeling the distinctive shape of each word, like learning to hear in braille.

"I just want you to know . . . I appreciate what you said to me, Colonel." The hand patted his shoulder three times, then the spectre vanished.

"Radar back on interphone."

"AC," Alex called, "put the formation on the primary tactical frequency, so I can talk to the fighters."

"Roger, IP." Pinski answered on interphone, then thumbed his mike button in the opposite direction to transmit on the command radio. "Black lead to all cells, come up on primary."

He knew from the cacophony exactly when Pinski switched radio channels. A hodge-podge of calls, warnings, and expletives cascaded over each other on the attack frequency. "Walker Lead, this is Black Lead, over."

"Welcome to the party, Black Lead. Walker flight dispensing your chaff now. You'll be bombing through solid undercast with the dinks barrage firing sometimes fifteen missiles at a time."

"Black Lead, this is Idaho Lead providing MiG cap. Don't sweat fighters; you'll have wall-to-wall SAMs."

"Walker and Idaho, Black Lead listening out."

"AC from Navigator; in one minute start your turn to a heading of one three seven degrees."

"This is Black Lead," Pinski called on the command radio, "turning inbound now."

Rocket trails filled the windscreen and side windows. Like most things dangerous—snakes, thunderstorms, avalanches— the firings were supremely beautiful. First the carpet of clouds simmered red, then bubbled sparkling orange as it spat out dark splinters leaping upward at twice the speed of sound.

"AC, multiple SAMs eleven o'clock, Two Rings. Headed right for us."

"Roger, EW. In sight."

Tokas ejected an aura of chaff to lure the racing missiles toward a false target and worked his transmitters in hopes of breaking the weapons' guidance signals.

The fiery shapes passed close by their right wingtip drowning its blinking green navigation light in the intensity of their blazing engines. Watching their passage, Alex braced for detonations that never occurred. Scanning forward again, he the counted missile tracks: *two, four, seven, eight, nine, eleven,* losing count when Russell shattered his concentration.

"Two more coming in at three o'clock. They got our names written all over them!"

"Copilot, glue your eyeballs on the instrument panel, control the throttles, and keep my airspeed on the money."

Alex reduced the volume level of radio chatter assaulting his eardrums, intent on culling information concerning only his third wave. As yet no parachute beepers screeched their maddening, overriding squeal on the emergency channel. Closing on the target, he rotated his interphone wafer switch to monitor the navigators' private channel. "There it is," Budd's voice had lost its rich baritone to the acoustics of his tight-fitting mask and the forced pressure of pure oxygen, but the confidence of an exceptional teacher bolstered and instructed his teammate. "See the offset just beginning to bloom under the cross hairs? Okay . . . let's check the dropping offset. See the pointer system? Just like target study." Satisfied, he switched back to the main interphone.

"One eighty TG." Pinski called. Three minutes of straight and level flight before an electrical impulse would ripple through the bays sending their load of high explosive bombs whistling onto the Yen Vien rail yard. Russell nursed the throttles, seeking to peg the airspeed needle. Occasionally he flinched as the cockpit illuminated, but he did not look outside.

"Gunner, this is IP. How's the cell behind look?"

"Holding on centerline," Heinrich adjusted the gain on his fire-control radar, "fifteen hundred yards back, sir."

Good, just hold it in the road.

"Sixty TG . . . Now!" Russell hacked his stopwatch for an emergency release backup. Heading pointer centered, airspeed on the money, altitude pegged. "Thirty TG." The gigantic aircraft shuttered as the bomb doors sprang open. Russell nudged the two inboard throttles to cancel the drag. "Bombs away," Budd called. "Right breakaway to a heading of two eight zero." Pinski's gloved hand rotated the autopilot knob maximum right, tilting the artificial horizon bar into a fifty-five degree angle of bank. "Multiple launch six o'clock, three rings, closing fast." Alex pulled his leg straps tighter. "Black Lead," someone screamed. "Three SAMs homing on you."

"They've got us! Chaff's running; jammers useless in this fucking turn."

An incandescent shark's body flashed past the co-pilot's window, its exhaust freezing the cockpit into the climactic scene chosen for a movie's publicity poster: Pinski hunching over the control wheel, Russell recoiling from his fate, and Alex—an impotent observer—steeling himself to process every detail of deafening sound, blinding colors, and heart-stopping fear in this instant before extinction. The second missile streaked past the high wing on Pinski's side. *The call said three.*

Retina-searing light bleached the cockpit; shrapnel shattered the copilot's side window; Russell collapsed backward, helmet shattered, leg jamming full right rudder. Pinski wrestled the controls. Alex slipped out of his parachute, grasped the dead copilot's lapbelt, and wrenched it free. The aircraft rolled violently left as Russell's leg slid off the pedal. Draping himself over the body, he unsnapped the parachute harness knowing his survival depended upon gaining the ejection seat. The bomber now pitched upward to the point of stall; death throes cascaded throughout the structure as airflow across the wings burbled. He found and disconnected Russell's main oxygen hose, the thin rubber tube connected to the bail-out bottle, and the interphone cord.

Managing to hold the steep left bank, Pinski jammed the control column full forward, arching the aircraft momentarily in a weightless parabolic curve. Alex yanked Russell's lifeless form as he would a side of beef, floating it over his right shoulder. Filling his lungs with oxygen, he pulled the hose of his own mask loose, climbed into the empty right seat, and connected into the copilot's oxygen regulator. Pinski had the aircraft in a dive, wings level and airspeed building. *Twenty-five thousand, altimeter still unwinding.* Groping blindly for the interphone cord, he found it slippery with gore.

"IP on. You read me AC?"

"Roger IP. Strap in while I take inventory." Pinski was breaking the dive, working methodically to avoid a high-speed stall. "AC to crew. Check in."

"Radar okay. Nav's not breathing. Holes all along the right side of the compartment."

"EW okay. Hienrich took shrapnel in the left leg, bleeding like a stuck pig."

"AC, we got a bad leak in the forward main tank. Fluctuating fuel flow on five and six."

"Black Lead, this is Walker Lead. I'm off your right wing. Your inboard pod's on fire. Better think of getting out before she blows."

Red fire warning lights flashed for engines five and six. "AC, number six flamed out, fuel flow dropping on five. Whole underside of the wing's reflecting red."

"Throttles to cut-off on five and six. Pull firewall shutoff valves. Fire extinguishers on five and six."

"Black Lead, fire's spreading to the wing and torching a hundred feet behind. I'm pulling away. The son of a bitch's gonna blow."

"Wing fire. Throttles seven and eight to cut off. Pull fire valves on seven and eight."

Alex ran through the drill just as he had a hundred times in the simulator. "You got it, AC. Forward main tank shows empty. Center of gravity's shifted aft. You're out of nose-down trim. Feel that shake?"

"Black Lead, do you read Walker lead? Your whole wing's involved. You can't save it man. Get the crew out!"

CHAPTER FIFTY-SEVEN

MERRILANE GOT HOME after Kim and Jeffrey had already eaten the last of yesterday's chicken. The cardboard bucket, greasy wax paper, and piles of half-stripped bones lay on the counter along with plates and soft drink cans. She ignored the mess, changed into jeans and sweat shirt, and was on her way to retrieve her briefcase from the front hall when she saw the blue sedan pull into the driveway. She stood in the door, thinking the Christmas wreath should have been up already. Frank and Chaplain Foster approached.

"Is he dead, Frank?"

"I'm sorry, Merrilane." She saw his lower lip quiver. "He's listed as missing, down in the southern outskirts of Hanoi."

"Won't you come in," she stepped back from the door. "Thank you for coming, Chaplain. I haven't seen you in a long time."

"I'm sorry it has to be under these circumstances." He nervously played with the metal leaf on the cap he clutched in his hand. "Are the children home?"

"They're here somewhere, I suppose. I just got in a few minutes ago." She knew she was not carrying it off well—no screams, no tears—just her nipples taut against the warm fleece of the pullover. Where was Iris? Frank must have called her even before notifying Foster. She had not seen her since their blowup over the crowd Kim was running with.

"Mother," Kim yelled from the den. "You'd better come here. They've shot down three B-Fifty-twos over Hanoi."

She led the officers down the hallway, stepping over the scattered Sunday paper, and into the den. Kim slumped on the sofa, bare feet propped on the coffee table, a cigarette smoldering in the ash tray beside her. Jeffrey slept in Alex's chair.

"Oh hi, Uncle Frank," Kim said making no attempt to move. Then, seeing the cross above the left breast of the second uniformed man, she covered her eyes and screamed. Jeffrey bolted upright, blinking, trying to focus against the brilliance of the television screen. Crying hysterically Kim fled into Frank's arms, the first time she had done so in over two years.

"What's going on," Jeffrey kept repeating. Merrilane began to sob, holding on to Kim and to Frank. Foster moved around them, turning off the television as he did so, and put his hand on Jeffrey's shoulder.

"It's your father. He's missing in action."

Jeffrey looked at the chaplain as if his long hair had muted the words.

"I said," Foster raised his voice above the wailing that continued undiminished from the girl, "your father's listed as missing on the Hanoi raid."

"I heard you the first time, Chaplain. What do you want me to do? Cry?"

Foster drew back, then moved to place his hand on the boy's shoulder. Jeffrey pulled away.

"Breaks of the game, Chaplain. Breaks of the game."

From across the hall, came the rasping cries of a young child. Jeffrey kicked a pacifier out of his way and slipped past Foster. The crying ceased. He returned holding a squirming, fat-faced three-year-old whose wide grin was crinkling little patches of dried jelly that ringed his mouth. "Might as well join the party, Buddy. Your old man got his ass shot down."

"That's enough out of you, young man. Let's have some respect for your father."

"He respects him, Mother." Kim hung tightly to Frank, wiping her tear-streaked face with her free hand and dislodging dark smudges of mascara. "Just as much as you do."

Merrilane stepped in front of her daughter and slapped her across the face with her open hand. "I won't take that from you! Precious little you know about respect."

Foster stepped into his familiar role as mediator, moving between mother and daughter and holding up his hands in the manner of the good shepherd. "Now, now. Let's try to focus ourselves . . . "

Merrilane turned on him red-faced. "Get out! Get out of my house." Wheeling on Frank she screamed, "That goes for you, too. If I need any more information, I'll get it from CBS!"

Later that night she sat in the darkened living room trying to recreate the events of the past five hours. She had abandoned the children, retreating into her bedroom, slamming the door, and crying herself to sleep. She woke at 11:30, too late to catch the news. The house was quiet. Even Buddy was still for a change. She roused herself, going into the bathroom to splash cold water on her swollen face. Then she stumbled into the kitchen, got the almost empty jug of Chablis and a processed-cheese jar that was the only glass on the shelf, and walked up the corridor to collapse in the armchair by the cold fireplace. Pouring herself a drink, she miscalculated in the dark and spilled wine over the edge of the chair and onto the woven pile. She had sniffed its bouquet before drinking but could smell only the odor of the partially burned log she had neglected to remove after the last fire a year ago.

Wonder if the wreckage smells like that? Probably not. Most likely reeks of jet fuel. She shivered, wishing she had selected the heavy blue Academy robe Jack had given her. She thought of getting it, but took another long drink instead. *What difference does it make whether he's working on the flight line eighteen hours a day, or sitting in the Hanoi Hilton, or even lying dead somewhere in the jungle? Nothing's changed. He was never here when I needed him.*

"Are you in there, Mother?" Kim's voice startled her.

"Yes, honey, come sit with me."

Merrilane could hear her daughter's rustling nightgown as she took her place across from her. "You can have some wine if you can find a glass."

"I'll clean the kitchen tomorrow. I don't want anything to drink."

"Cigarette? There's half a pack on the table next to your chair."

"No, I just want to talk."

"What's there to talk about? Your father's got himself shot down. If he's alive, he'll have to get himself out. We can't do anything."

Kim didn't answer.

What a bitch I've become. She raised the jar for the third time, drained it, then filled it again. This time she spilled more on the carpet. *Two-faced Queen of Hearts staring wide-eyed in the dark while daughter begs Mother to come home.*

"I called the number in the letter," Kim said. "I called the number in the letter Uncle Frank left. The Air Force casualty office in San Antonio. The letter said they would have information. So I called them and pretended I was you."

"I shouldn't have made you do that, honey."

"That's all right, Mother. I know you're upset."

"What did they tell you . . . Mrs. Cannard?"

"They said Daddy ejected just before the airplane blew up. He talked to the other pilots on his emergency radio while he was still in his parachute. But he never talked to them after he got on the ground."

"Then he's still alive."

"We don't know, Mother. We just . . . we just know he got out of the airplane."

"Your father's a very special person, Kim. He knows his procedures, and he's very brave."

"If he's special, Mother, why haven't we been living with him?"

"It's a long story, sweetheart, and not a pretty one."

"I've got a right to know, Mother. After all, it ruined my life."

"Oh, Kimmy, don't say that. You've been able to stay here with your friends . . . not having to change schools."

"I never wanted to stay here, Mother. We were an Air Force family. I wanted to move to Louisiana with Dad. So did Jeff. And I'm sure it didn't make any difference to Buddy."

"When did you decide that? You never said anything at the time."

"No one asked us, Mother. We were all excited about the move. Jeff was bragging to everyone he was going where he could catch some really big fish instead of just trout. Then Dad came home, and you two seemed to quit talking in front of us. And pretty soon, Dad left by himself."

"It's a complicated story, Kim. People sometimes grow away from each other. Lifestyles change."

"Did Dad find another woman while he was in Vietnam?"

"You've been reading too many Judy Blume books."

"Why not? You've got to get your information somewhere."

"Look here, young lady," Merrilane's voice was hard, as hard as she remembered its being when she last spoke to Alex in this same room. "That's the second time you've put me down tonight, and I'm not going to stand for it."

"I'm sorry, Mother. But I'm not a child anymore, and I don't want to be treated like one."

"I'm sorry, too, Kim. We shouldn't argue like this. Especially tonight."

"We never talk any more, Mother. You're always on the job, or off on a trip, or doing office work at night. I remember when Dad had just left for Vietnam, you'd fix us a snack before we went to bed. And we'd talk about school or what we'd done that day, and we'd add something to the letter you were writing. Then you got the job, and we never saw you again."

She didn't know how to make her daughter realize she was still seeing life through the eyes of a child. The job had been good. It had been her salvation. She couldn't have got through that year without it. Then, when things went sour with Alex, it was the biggest thing in her life.

"I guess I'm being childish," Kim said. "I'm not thinking about how hard the separation must have been for you."

"Kim, I'm surprised. You're growing up. Growing out from under me just like I grew out from under your father."

"Why do you keep calling him 'your father'? Don't you ever think of him as your husband anymore, or even just 'Alex'? Or is the only Alex in your life little Buddy, who you ignore even more than Dad?"

"Oh goddamn Kim! Won't you give it up? Why do you keep twisting the knife in me?"

"You never answered my question, Mother. Did Dad take up with another woman?"

"It's none of your business. That's all over and done with anyway. It's a period of my life I just want to forget."

"It is my business, Mother. We used to be a family. Then all of a sudden Dad left us. Why'd he leave his children? Why'd you always have us involved in something whenever he came to visit? What did he do that was so bad?"

"Oh I don't remember all the gory details, Kim. It's late, and I have a battle to fight at work tomorrow."

"Just tell me one thing. I have to know if he found another woman."

"Why's it so important? You're just fifteen years old. You've got a long time before you need to be engaging in heavy-duty woman talk."

"It's important to me to know if a woman can trust a man."

"Oh, my God, Kimmy. You're not sexually active!"

Kim fell to the side of her mother's chair, buried her head in her lap and sobbed. When she stopped, Merrilane could feel her looking upward in the darkness.

"It wasn't another woman as far as I know. He was different in Hawaii. Acted as if a black curtain had lowered itself between us. He used me shamefully in a sexual way and insinuated I was unfaithful to him. He couldn't accept that I had developed a career that completely fascinated and fulfilled me." She stopped but knew the eyes in the dark were still questioning. "When he came home, one thing led to another, and I saw we'd never be compatible again. He went out of our lives . . . until now. That's my story, and I'm not proud of it. But I never catted around when I was fifteen, or even twenty."

"I don't need that from you, Mother. I just need some information and maybe a little understanding. It's just one boy. He loves me. He treats me nice."

"Is he a cadet?"

"What if he is? You've had yours. Jeff told me about seeing Jack Pinski come to visit you late one night in a thunderstorm."

"You little slut! Don't talk that way to me!" Merrilane kicked her daughter away from her feet, then collapsed backward into the chair, rocking and moaning inconsolably.

Kim withdrew to the fireplace, listening to the rising and falling of her mother's grief and smiling tentatively. But as the cries grew louder, becoming interspersed with great rasping gasps for breath and sounds of fists beating on flesh, Kim's smile froze and her eyes widened. She found her mother in the darkness and captured her hands.

After a while, she quieted. "What more do you know?"

Kim was silent. Merrilane asked again. "What more do you know?"

"Nothing, Mother. Except the man in San Antonio said Daddy was flying with Captain Pinski, and they didn't know if he got out of the plane."

CHAPTER FIFTY-EIGHT

ALEX TRIED TO SURFACE, failed, drifted again into darkness where he choked, retched, fought upward thrashing his arms and dragging paralyzed legs.

"Take it easy, Colonel," a voice murmured.

He swam for the voice. Breaking out with stinging eyes, he found himself lying not in surf but naked on a damp slab with feet restrained. Dried blood filled each nostril. Thick mucus clogged his throat. He hacked to dislodge it.

"Take it easy, Colonel."

"Who are you?" he croaked. "I can't see." He tried to rise to a sitting position but fell backward.

"Bad news," the voice responded. "I'm Captain Pinski, and we're in the Hanoi Hilton."

"I'm hurting bad . . . " He stopped his sentence trying to remember what it was he wanted to say.

"Lie still. I'm in leg irons, too. It's hard for me to reach your cover when you throw it aside." Pinski snagged the blanket, and tossed it onto Alex's chest. But fever flushed the colonel's body, and he pushed it off again.

"I'm thirsty."

"Go back to sleep. We've been here all day, and they haven't given us anything. I think we pissed 'em off somehow."

"Pinski, Pinski. I've heard that name before." He willed his head to stop spinning, then grasped it with both hands. The gyrating behind his eyes began to slow; his vision cleared slightly, but the patterns were jagged, like lightning flashes in comic strips. He discerned a dim bulb covered with yellow dust and dead insects dangling from the ceiling, emitting light the consistency of ultraviolet. The smell of vomit, urine, and excrement mixed with darkness to convince him he was awake.

"We came down close together, Colonel. If soldiers hadn't got to us, the peasants would have done us in."

The ringing in his ears began to subside. He remembered the explosion. "How's Wallingford? Did they get the bleeding stopped?"

"I don't know any Wallingford. Who's crew's he on?"

"Holman's crew. Up on the Dong Nai."

"I don't think you're all together yet, Colonel. Just try . . . "

Pinski stopped speaking as he heard shuffling in the corridor. Jingling keys . . . lock's sharp snap . . . solid door scraping rough concrete . . . two khaki-clad jailers, one with a bright red tab on his shoulder. "You come," Red Tab said as he worked on Pinski's leg stocks.

"Water," Pinski said in a loud voice as they lifted him to his feet. "We need water." The closest guard prodded him out the door.

Alex struggled to remain conscious. He remembered pulling out the antenna of his radio and talking to Walker Lead as he swung beneath his parachute canopy. *What else? What else?* He recalled deploying his survival kit and life raft and feeling them swinging twenty feet below. That's all.

Cocking his ear, he strained to hear the sound he perceived to be building but still hovering just outside his range of frequencies. His slab shook: *Saigon . . . Arc Light . . . B-52s.* He knew the rumble of five-hundred-pound bombs.

From the near darkness, he heard the door bolt slam, felt the inrush of dampness. A bundle crashed to the floor. The bolt slapped home again. "Those bastards sure know how to hold a grudge, Roomie. I got a feelin' this is gonna to be Doolie Summer all over again." Pinski pulled himself alongside Alex and arranged the blanket.

Launched from close beside the prison wall, a surface-to-air missile lit the courtyard and reflected intense light into the cell. Alex saw deep rope marks on Pinski's upper arms.

"What's the drill?"

"The dinks are kicking ass and taking names. And any other information you care to volunteer."

"What did you tell them?"

"To stick it in their ear." Pinski crawled onto his slab and stretched full length, left arm dangling. "That wasn't what they wanted to hear, so they gave me the ropes." He stopped talking for awhile. The thunderous missile launches and sharp cracks of anti-aircraft guns continued.

"What are they asking? Answer me! What are they asking? What did you tell them? Wake up, dammit. I'm on deck, and we've got to get our stories straight."

"Ease up, Colonel. I just got out of one interrogation." A fit of dry coughing racked Pinski's chest. "If the BUFFs hadn't come back, I'd still be trussed up. That's all we got in our favor. They're scared shitless."

"You're not such a big operator now, are you Mister?"

"Your time's coming, Colonel. Let's forget history and try to get out of this alive."

"You'd *like* to forget that part of your life, Mister. Not while I'm alive you don't."

The sounds of battle moved away. Only an occasional flak gun barked like a dissatisfied and previously intimidated watchdog. Lost in his thoughts, Alex did not hear them come for him until the door crashed back against the wall. One stood in the doorway while the other removed the leg irons then stripped off the soggy blanket releasing the pungent odor of concentrated urine. He tried to stall, hoping to rub some circulation into his legs, but the turnkey prodded him off the slab and motioned him toward the door. His fever had passed, leaving in its place an acute sensitivity to cold that overrode the leg cramps and even the stabbing pain etching his right kidney.

The guard shoved him across the corridor and into a crude washhouse with a communal trough, single faucet, wooden pail, and open cesspool. Alex filled the bucket, drank deeply, then doused himself with spasms of liquid ice crystals that jerked animal noises from his throat and reamed the befuddled channels inside his brain. His keeper threw him a thin pair of black pajamas and goaded him into putting them on.

Shivering violently, he shuffled out of the cellblock and into a lighted courtyard some 150 feet long and maybe 60 wide. He saw no evidence of other prisoners. Three-quarters of the way up the yard, one escort slapped his shoulder indicating a passage leading off to the left. It opened into a smaller courtyard and another passageway beyond. He could feel the presence of others as he was directed right, and then right again. Rounding the corner, he saw a gigantic poster of Lenin and realized he was coming to the end of his march.

"Alex Cannard and Jack Pinski, BUFF pilots," he yelled with all his strength. The near guard tripped him, then stooped to pound his head into the rough wall where he had fallen. He rolled hard into the man's legs, upsetting him and commandeering the thick staff he had carried.

"I'll teach you some stick work," he snarled as he jammed the weapon against the guard's windpipe. The referee stepped beside the struggling pair and drove his rifle butt hard into Alex's rib cage. They dragged him into a small room just to the right of the portrait and left him lying beside a low stool.

The old waiting game. His mind retrieved impressions gained from similar circumstances experienced some fourteen years earlier. Then—stripped, shivering, and apprehensive—he had been thrown into an interrogation room at the air force's survival training school in the mountains outside Reno. That room had been painted flat black with yellow zig-zag patterns on the walls. There two enlisted airmen, obviously enjoying the captor's roles, humiliated and badgered him for some twenty minutes. He could recall few details except for thinking he had to endure for only three days, four at most. Back then it was all a game.

This was no game, although similarities existed. He imagined he would be a captive for three weeks or a month. Only as long as it took for the B-52s to bring the Vietnamese back to the conference table. He could do three weeks standing on his head.

Think of it as just another Reflex tour in North Africa, he told himself.

The room's furnishings were few: just the stool, a chair, a small table covered with a blue cloth, and a lamp providing the only light. No chains, no rack, no iron maiden. He was a senior officer; his rank should mean something. Just an initial interview; nothing to worry about. Then he saw the sheets of blank paper and the pencil lying on the blue cloth.

He closed his eyes and immersed his mind into a vision of Lake Tahoe with the light beginning to spill over the eastern ridge. Then Merrilane emerged from the dark waters and filled his vision more completely than she had since his dreams at Bien Hoa. She was preening for him, flirting, swinging her trim body in time with some unheard music, like the dancer he had watched in Morocco. She came toward him, shifting her body and bending backward as she swirled past. For an instant her face was inverted before him, lips glistening under her flicking tongue.

"Stand up, Criminal," a voice close beside him shouted. He pulled himself to his feet. "Bow down, Criminal." Something thin and stinging ripped across his shoulders. The face before him looked like an animal's—a rabbit perhaps or a jug-eared weasel—spiteful, arrogant, dominating.

"Sit down, Criminal." Strong hands on each shoulder pushed him onto the stool. "I represent the Camp Authority," the rabbit said in rapid-fire English. "You represent fascist criminals giving death to women and children. From where you come?"

I am an American fighting man—the words popped into his consciousness. *If I am captured, I will continue to resist by all means available.* "My name," he heard himself speaking automatically without stopping to consider strategy, with no thoughts of whether he would feign loss of memory, or illness, or stupidity, "is Alexander X. Cannard. My rank is . . . "

"We know you, Colonel Can-nard. We know your birth date, and your birthplace, and your aircraft number: three-one-six. We know your wife—Merry Lane—we know your two children.

You are despicable Air Pirate. A scholar, you are more guilty than other lackeys who come in ignorance. You have knowledge of history. But you lick the boots of the criminal Nix-san and, before that, the criminal John-san. You have many crimes—much to answer for."

He shivered on his stool, realizing the man had access to Soviet-collected intelligence. *He's holding the high cards. All the cards, for that matter.*

"I hold all the cards as you would say," Rabbit continued. "But I am reasonable. You may send message to your Merry Lane. You write; we send."

"Stick it in your ear."

Rabbit smiled and nodded. The guards knocked him off the stool, looped a length of hemp rope around his legs at the ankles, forced his torso forward, looped two coils around his neck, pulled his arms straight out behind his back, and tied his wrists together with the tag end of the rope. *It's like yoga,* he thought, *like an inverted plough.* But then came the foot on his right shoulder, the tightening of the rope, the raising of his arms—and his screams. Intense, immediate, overriding agony crashed into his brain. He heard his tormentors grunting as they forced his arms up another notch; he tasted bile, felt the sound screeching from his gaping mouth.

At the zenith of his pain, a typhoon of churning thunder skipping across the rooftops flooded the chamber with a shock wave shattering the tight nucleus of prisoner and persecutors. The explosion and concussion followed immediately. "Blast the bastards," he screamed.

"Be Silent! Be Silent!" Rabbit commanded. Alex's retort was lost in the roar of the second attacking jet. The lamp on the table tottered, fell, and extinguished. They were all in the dark, squirming together on the dank floor. Someone was whimpering. "It's not me now," he yelled.

Red Tab came running with a flashlight. Excited voices conferred. Rabbit issued orders in a high-pitched, but controlled voice. The guards removed the ropes, hustled Alex back to his cell, and threw him inside without waiting to apply the leg irons.

"How'd you make out, Roomie?" Pinski asked, as if inquiring about intermural football.

"Lions two, Christians zero," Alex managed to reply. "Glad the Blue Angels showed up. The bastard was treating me like I busted him on his checkride."

"You get any water?"

"Got some when the turnkey let me clean up. Got some PJs like yours. Good to be in the uniform of the day."

"You're a lot like my dad, Colonel. Good sense of humor, but you rarely let anyone see it."

"Does that make Merrilane like your mother?"

"Low blow, Colonel."

"What's a man think when he's humping another's wife?"

"If you don't know, then you're not like my old man after all."

"No. I don't know, Pinski. I guess I was never that hard up."

"Jesus, Colonel; weren't you ever young?"

"I was young all right, but that was on another planet. Where you had to scramble for tuition, spending money, even food."

"Sounds like Dullsville, Colonel. Worse than this place."

He felt in the darkness for his blanket, then pulled himself up to stand braced against the sleeping platform. "Tell me about Merrilane," he said after a while. "When did it happen?"

"What's with you, Colonel? We ought to be planning how to get out of this hole. You're living in the past. Whatever happened is over and forgotten."

"Not by me."

"Well, I've forgotten the time I spent in the Zoo just like I'm gonna forget whatever time I spend here."

"You think it's fair to take what you want without a thought of the consequences?"

"Fair! You're shittin' me, Colonel. Life's not fair! You think this is fair! Why are we in this cage?"

"You ever think maybe we deserve it? Maybe this is in the master plan? The way we pay our debts?"

"You're weird, Colonel. What have I done to cause some dink to truss me up worse than a pig? I'm too busy living my life to look back on things that might have happened. If you're still worrying about whether your wife kept her pants on four years ago, you've got your priorities confused."

CHAPTER FIFTY-NINE

"WAR'S OVER, CHIEF!" Wootan looked up at a grinning SugarFox who stood holding a tin cup of steaming liquid.

"The slopes just delivered a five-gallon can of hot java." He extended the cup to Wootan. "Just a little dividend from last night's air power demonstration."

Wootan raised the weak brew to his lips, savoring the aroma for which he had often searched his memory. Then he drank slowly to stretch out the enjoyment.

"Thanks Sugar," he said. "Did you get your share?"

"Fuckno. I wanna remember these bastards the way they've been the last four years. They probably mixed rat turds with the beans anyway. Any info about the guys they picked up after the raids?"

Wootan drained the cup. "We've identified two so far. One's our old friend Alex Cannard. Rodriguez heard him yell his name and one other on the way to quiz. Later they heard screams."

"Heavy duty." SugarFox was doing deep knee bends as he talked. "But why go back to the torture routine? Even they gotta realize this thing's coming to an end."

"A confession from Alex would cause every newspaper in the world to yell for Nixon to back off."

"Will Al play ball? He seemed a little soft to me."

"He's complex. He'd let some sort of personal tragedy get to him. He's tough when he has to be, but he worries about the human condition."

"That fuckin' Rabbit'll beat any concern for the human condition out of him."

The tapping of a "shave and a haircut" sequence interrupted them. Sugar answered with an immediate "two bits." The call-up signal was as familiar to Wootan as the NBC radio chimes had been during his youth. The follow-on message came through the wall as clearly as a tape of market averages would appear to a broker. The stream of taps and pauses relayed instructions from the senior ranking American and closed with the shave-and-a-haircut pattern. SugarFox tapped the obligatory two bits, then added a quick GBU—God Bless You.

"Whatta ya think?" he asked.

"Best we can do. Formal complaint to the camp authorities, signal to the reconnaissance bird they're torturing again, coupled with a hunger strike beginning with a mass demonstration tomorrow morning. That should take the pressure off Alex."

"You think everyone will go along with it? The new guys may not know the rules."

"We hold some cards we haven't held before. Better health, communal living, and all of us concentrated in one location because of the Son Tay raid. They don't want to release a bunch of emaciated skeletons when this thing's over.

"Then there's our ace in the hole," SugarFox added. "The BUFFs bombing every night."

Alex cried when they threw Pinski back into the cell. With his face a pulp of puffed skin and coagulated blood, he looked like a forgotten strawberry mashed at the bottom of the crate. This time the ropes had cut deeply, flaying the skin like precise strokes from a lash. They had beaten the captain horribly, so the colonel would be moved to give into their demands. "Serves you right!" Alex screamed. "You dirty son of a bitch! How does it feel now? Bet you've rather be smoking a joint or humping my wife. You dirty bastard! I hope they finish you off!" Then he collapsed sobbing over the senseless form.

He heard the peephole open and leaped to confront the startled guard. "Call your officer," he yelled pounding the door. "Bring him so I can get my hands on his fucking neck."

The cover slammed shut as he continued to beat the door and scream insults. Minutes later he heard approaching footsteps, then the key hit the lock on the first stab, the bolt sprang back, and the door opened. Like a mechanical booby trap, he fell on the tall officer who entered, knocking off his visored garrison hat, smashing a fist into his delicate features, and clawing for his throat. Red Tab kicked Alex in the groin and followed with thrusts to the ribs and kidneys. The officer slumped against the wall, bleeding from the nose, his bald head exposed. The other two guards joined Red Tab in plummeting Alex who had rolled into a ball trying to protect his head.

Their leader called them off, speaking rapidly but with numerous pauses for breath. "You make . . . mistake, Can . . . nard," he said. "Now . . . you pay."

"Stick it . . . " The guards pinned his arms, lifted him to his feet, and stuffed a filthy cloth into his mouth. They dragged him out of the cell, turned left, and headed through the passageway. Instead of crossing the courtyard and entering the opening leading to the quiz room, they turned left again, dragging him toward a small building sitting by itself about three-quarters of the way down the courtyard. One of the guards swung the wooden door open, then helped to lift him up two steps into the low-ceilinged room. They threw him down on the filthy floor, retrieved the gag, and began to attach leg irons.

"Water," he said, his throat constricted with thirst now that the taste of tainted meat had subsided. Red Tab looked down at him, slowly unbuttoned his fly, pulled out a boy's penis, and sprayed him from head to foot.

He awoke shivering to the sound of sirens spilling over the walls from the city and echoing through the cell blocks. The odor and sticky feel of dried urine made him retch. His lower lip was split and his left eye swollen shut. But at least Pinski was not on display.

With one narrow ventilation slit near the ceiling, a bricked-up window on the back wall, and no amenities such as sleeping platform, honey bucket, or blanket, his cell resembled at most a tomb. A bulb hanging from the ceiling emitted what passed for light in North Vietnam. He smelled sour food odors, the kind that had nauseated him every summer at scout camp, but these were soon overpowered by the pungent fumes of cordite wafted through the courtyard as the heavy anti-aircraft guns belched. They fired steadily, joined by smaller calibers as the flak-suppression fighters swept in.

From reconnaissance photographs he knew guns and missile launchers nestled close by schools, hospitals, and the Hilton, where they were assumed to be safe from retaliation. The imminent return of the bombers elated him, but he anguished over their reliance on a single attack corridor rather than saturation tactics. Could these plodding airmen possibly be descendants of minutemen who sniped at redcoats from behind every tree and stone wall in Massachusetts? *No*, he thought, *this is a different race: computerized, mechanized, immobilized in the face of an intractable enemy*. He knew the real descendants were the men in surrounding cells who would prevail over fate by trusting in each other's integrity and devising lines of communication regardless of the cost.

All night he lay in his tomb shaking to the concussion of bombs, rocket launches, and the chills and fevers that racked his body. He had snatches of conversation with God, lucid and amicable dialogues. In between he cringed under ear-splitting explosions, caustic smells, and sure expectation the ground would open and swallow him. In the morning, he could not remember anything that transpired, but he believed something significant, some enlightenment, must have taken place.

Shortly after dawn two strange guards pulled him out for quiz. Rabbit screamed for him to bow down as he entered the familiar room. "You will be punished, Criminal. You can be with us many years . . . after others have gone."

On his stool he swayed to the hypnotic words of his antagonist. Overpowered by thirst, he did not follow the sing-song gibberish.

"Now you cooperate."

"Water," he croaked.

Someone looped a fan belt around his neck and pulled him off the stool. He awoke sometime later lying drenched on the floor. He tried to lick black water, but a hand jerked his head back as his two keepers piled on. The rough cloth of their uniforms grated across his face, gagging him with sour odors of perspiration, mildewed clothing, unwashed genitalia. Searing stabs from his ribs spiked all other sensations as the men jackknifed him. He tried to vent the pain with screams. Both assailants had their knees on his back as they pushed his forehead between his shin bones and jerked his arms higher. He felt the coming unconsciousness advancing slowly, as if he were being squashed by a giant thumb. His brain shut down as pain blew its circuits.

Agony brought him back, reminded him he was nothing, then plunged him again into blackness. He revived, realized they were not working him, but knew blood throbbed stagnant in his arms. With no breath left to scream, he prayed, *Get me out of this.*

Someone fumbled with the ropes. He felt the acute agony of blood seeping into clogged arteries. "Now you write!" Rabbit shouted.

"In your ear," he muttered. "In your ear, you bastard."

They forced him onto the stool and tightened the ropes. In desperation he threw himself backward. He did not feel the fall, did not hear the officer come in, did not comprehend the whispered conversation. But he became conscious of a muffled roar that modulated like the crowd at Falcon Stadium. He passed out again as rough hands lifted him.

Aroused by the prison gong, he found himself lying on the floor of his tomb shivering without a proper shroud, hurting all over, reeking of another man's urine and his own vomit. What had he written? What had he signed? With hands shackled behind his back, he lay terrified his crystallized arms would shatter if he dared to move. Spread apart and constrained by thick manacles attached to a rusty iron rod, his bare legs calcified in ever-darkening shades of blue.

He realized he was no longer the warrior, the guardian of his country's honor. He had become Kauhi, spurned by the lovely Goddess Hiiaka, who went gaily on singing her song of independence. He was now the impotent crouching lion, slowly turning to stone.

I'm ready, he thought. "Come get me again you bastards. I don't give a ratz." Instantly he regretted his bravado as he heard the key in the lock.

The door opened, and a grinning, fair-skinned man entered holding a pot of steaming tea and a small tin cup. The accompanying keeper removed the handcuffs, then both withdrew. As the fluid soothed his dried throat and washed away the compacted bile of the past three days, he could almost tolerate the excruciating pain of congealed blood beginning to flow once again. When he sat the pot down, a slip of wet paper slid into sight. He looked quickly at the peephole, then unfolded the note. Small, childishly printed words barely appeared. But he held the paper to the light filtering from the window slit and made them out: WHAT DID YOU DO WITH MY BEAVER PICTURES? This time he wept for joy.

Later in the morning, the turnkey came back, removed the leg irons, and motioned for him to follow without bothering to gag him or cover his eyes. He hobbled up the path, through the familiar passageway, across Heartbreak Courtyard, and into another passage opening upon a smaller enclosure with a horse trough at the end. The area seemed deserted, but his sixth sense alerted him to unseen eyes. His escort motioned for him to enter an open bathhouse, pointed to a sliver of brown soap, then modestly went outside. He washed quickly in the cold water without bothering to take off his pajamas. Then, seeing he was being given time, he removed the garments and used them to scour himself. He had wrung them out and was dressing when the guard opened the door and again motioned for him to follow.

They retraced their steps, Alex lagging behind trying to establish some visual contact with his fellow prisoners. But the guard signaled him to move along. Back in the cell, his escort replaced the leg irons and left. The grinning man who had served him earlier returned with thin pumpkin soup and a four-inch chunk of stale baguette. He felt as if he were slipping out of the high threat area, no longer an item of interest on the enemy's radar.

Nightly B-52 bombing continued after the three missions the original message had proposed. But the follow-on attacks were decidedly smaller and northeast of Hanoi proper. He theorized they were going after the Gia Lam railroad yard and the Yen Vien military complex. Tactical aircraft continued to sweep in, keeping no certain schedule.

He was given a blanket, a honey bucket, and two meals— pumpkin soup and bread—each day. No more notes accompanied his food, and he was kept in leg irons and handcuffs when not eating.

With no responsibilities, no suspenses, no meetings, he had time to think. He tried to account for the change in his treatment. He had assaulted an officer in front of his men. As far as he could remember, he had not given into their demands. No doubt a raucous demonstration by his fellow inmates had saved him. Despite apprehension concerning his future welfare, he found his mind reverting most often to Pinski, worrying, he realized, like a father about an errant son.

CHAPTER SIXTY

CHRISTMAS WAS JUST TWO DAYS away, but its spirit had not brightened the Cannard household. Everyone except Buddy had slept in, and at mid-morning Merrilane refused to abandon her sanctuary even as the smell of baking muffins drifted into her bedroom. Her normal frenetic schedule shattered by the events of the last five days, she was grateful the schools were on holiday and even her office had closed until after New Year's. Determined to catch up on her sleep, she had ignored the phone's insistent ringing having bargained with her daughter to play mother for just a few days more.

But Kim had judged the call important, so Merrilane took it on her bedroom extension. The caller identified herself as Professor Monique Delepierre, a friend of Alex's from Saigon days. She had read the newspaper account of the first night's bombing and wanted to express her concern and know what further information Merrilane might have.

Suspicious of the caller's motives, she confirmed only that Alex was listed as missing and nothing else had been forthcoming. Attempting to ascertain the nature of the relationship, she was assured it had been professional, as they both were military historians. Alex, the professor said, had been kind enough to provide her with advice and background information that had proved invaluable in her dealings with the military bureaucracy.

Monique then authenticated her validity and captured Merrilane's interest by mentioning that she, too, had faced the situation of a beloved friend who had gone missing on a flight deep inside North Vietnam. Falling victim to Monique's soothing voice and obvious understanding of the casualty notification process, Merrilane soon chatted unhesitatingly. After six or seven minutes of preliminary, Monique made her request.

"Perhaps it's presumptuous of me to ask, but since my classes are over and I live alone, would you think it inappropriate if I flew to Colorado Springs a few days after Christmas and talked with you?" Not giving Merrilane an interval to protest, Monique continued with a justification. "I'm familiar with the Broadmoor, so I could stay there, visit you for an hour or so, and see Frank and Iris Harbinger, who are friends from graduate school."

Having struck a cord with a person who had passed through the same emotional ordeal in which she now found herself, Merrilane was loath to do anything but extend an invitation.

"Thank you for your kindness," Monique answered. "It will mean a great deal to me, and I believe you'll also benefit from what I have to tell you."

After proposing the evening of Wednesday, the twenty-seventh of December, and promising to confirm the time after consulting with Frank and Iris, Monique wished Merrilane well and terminated the call.

Afterwards she sat for some time recreating the conversation and wondering just who this decisive and caring woman could be and how close her relationship with Alex had really been. Was she the elusive "other woman" Kim had interrogated her about? Unable to resolve her curiosity, she realized she had two priority tasks: to prepare an agenda for their discussion and to clean the house.

After Monique's call the Christmas spirit, or a reasonable facsimile, did indeed descend on the Cannards. For the first time in quite awhile the family had both time and a goal—to prepare for a visitor more mysterious than Santa Claus. Deep inside her mind, Merrilane harbored the idea that her recent caller was more than she presented herself to be. Her intuition signaled she was about to meet her competition for Alex's affection, or perhaps her successor. More than she would have anticipated, that thought disquieted her.

Regardless, she determined to show the kind of hospitality for which she once was known. She enlisted Kim and Jeffrey to join her in a three-pronged assault on accumulated clutter, neglect, and dirt. Their carrot was the promise of one hundred dollars each to be spent as they wished during the after-Christmas sales.

Inspired, she invited for Christmas dinner Frank and Iris, whose son was tied up elsewhere. Pleased at their acceptance, she extended the same invitation to Rod Pike, the carefree bachelor who just happened to have nothing else on his calendar. Rod even offered to drop by early on Christmas eve with a fresh-cut tree. After all, he had said, the beautifully landscaped United States Air Force Academy wouldn't miss "just one little blue spruce."

Late on Christmas evening, after the dishes had been washed, the dining and living rooms straightened, and the leftovers refrigerated, Merrilane sat alone by the fire rethinking holidays past to see where this day's activities would rate. From her point of view, it had been fine. She hadn't lost any of her cooking or decorating skills even though this was the first entertainment she had supervised since shortly before her husband left for Vietnam. The children had done well: Kim as assistant chef, Jeff as maitre d', and Buddy as jester. Her guests seemed appreciative of the invitation; she had received many compliments. Alex would have loved it.

Iris had mentioned she and Frank would not hear of Monique's staying at a hotel when they had an empty guest room, and they had prevailed upon her to cancel her Broadmoor reservation and expect Frank to meet her flight. From the weather forecast, one could not presume the roads would be in any condition to drive shortly after her arrival. While helping with the day's clean-up chores, Iris had also sketched Monique's background, emphasizing her status among academicians, her star-crossed involvement with Adam Wootan, and her subsequent seclusion following his loss.

"You'll like her instinctively," Iris had summarized. "She's a beautiful, bright, wonderful creature surrounded, I'm sorry to say, by an aura of sadness."

CHAPTER SIXTY-ONE

ALEX KNEW IT WAS CHRISTMAS EVE from the snatches of carols he heard echoing from various parts of the camp. He lay on the dank floor of his cell shivering and thinking of Christmases past: memories of Santa Claus bursting through the front door, passing out toys, then having a nip in the kitchen before going off to visit all the other good little girls and boys who happened also to be Santa's nieces and nephews. He visualized the variety of food his father had customarily laid in—oranges, nuts, hard candy, chocolates—embodiments of his own childhood dreams in a poor family. He joined the festive table watching his mother serve the massive dinner on Christmas Day. He sampled everything: turkey, dressing, sweet potatoes, green beans, gravy, hot biscuits, cranberry sauce, mince and pumpkin pies.

He thought of the holiday meals he had shared with his family while confined to the alert facility. He, uneasily watching the clock and wondering if SAC would spoil it all with a practice alert. She, trying to keep the children from wasting food, then captivating the wing commander who paused at their table in his once-a-year role as proprietor of a family restaurant.

He saw once again the lighted candles reflected in Merrilane's eyes as they joined the procession singing "Silent Night" at the Academy chapel. He recalled Christmas in Saigon, sharing the meal with Monique and Wootan, then leaving them to relieve Airman Woziniac so he could share the feast before everything was consumed. Solitary meals at Barksdale conjured no soothing memories, only concentrated, all-encompassing loneliness.

To his surprise Christmas fare at the Hanoi Hilton was special: a small piece of stringy meat of uncertain origin on a mound of brown rice. The turnkey removed his handcuffs, allowing him to fold his hands as he gave thanks.

No bombers returned in the evening. The handcuffs did. As if to make up for previous leniency, his keeper refused to remove the restraints when he delivered the next day's food. Forced to root like a pig, he spilled the jar of precious water, then cursed his spiteful jailer.

That night he propped himself in a corner listening intently. Off and on all afternoon the air raid sirens had shrilled the city to hush. He heard flak and distant bomb impacts most likely caused by fighters using electronic guidance to drop through an overcast.

Close to midnight the wailing began again, punctuated by missile salvos and continuous flak. Shock waves engulfed his tiny cell. He heard cheering in the background and Vietnamese guards shouting to control it. Choking fumes invaded his cell as the guns outside the walls blasted the dark sky. Then the first bombs struck, their sound whipping in from the northwest. Simultaneous explosions from the east and the south rocked the prison, dislodging chunks of straw-filled plaster from the ceiling. "Pour it on!" he yelled. "You're cleared in hot!"

The earthshaking rumbling ceased, but missile launches continued. He counted the seconds. After two minutes impacts rumbled again. In his mind's eye, he visualized streams of B-52s plowing a night sky illuminated by white-hot rocket trails.

The second series of impacts stopped abruptly. He counted again, hesitated expectantly at two minutes, then continued. Sixty seconds later another string erupted. His ears found the attack frequency, heard the wave leaders relaying their success codes as they scampered over the fence, outdistancing the rabid guard dogs. He knew the force had taken losses, but he believed they were few. Undoubtedly screeching personal locators—warbling fingernails dragged across a celestial blackboard—signaled the parachute descents of ill-fated crewmembers.

Two minutes more and bombs exploded again. Then a three-minute interval; four; he stopped counting. The missile

launchers shut down, but flak batteries continued firing inter-
mittently, making their crews feel useful but succeeding only
in littering the city with more fallen shrapnel. The tactics had
changed; he estimated over a hundred bombers had struck their
targets in less than fifteen minutes. *That'll give the bastards something to wire their diplomats in Paris.*

CHAPTER SIXTY-TWO

FRANK HAD JUST RETURNED from Peterson Field when the promised snow flakes began to fall. By the time Monique visited, had dinner, and prepared for her eight o'clock meeting with Merrilane, a full-fledged Colorado blizzard enveloped the region. Merrilane called to say her guest should bring a suitcase and plan on sleeping over, as they had lots to talk about, and there was no need to venture even across the yards in the expected white-out conditions.

Looking like the Ghost of Christmas Past in his ice-encrusted parka and hood, Frank delivered Monique, who resembled the Snow Princess in her red ski jacket. Buddy was already hibernating, assuredly with plans to wake up hungry as a bear by daybreak, but Kim and Jeff were at the door to be introduced to their guest and help her with her coat. Kim chatted easily with the professor, Merrilane noticed, whereas Jeff seemed to stare at her while trying surreptitiously to pat his bushy hair into place.

Over coffee in the living room by the fire, with a gale-force wind howling outside, the two women settled to discuss the oppressively hot and sticky Saigon environment and other topics best described in the same terms.

"You have a lovely home, Mrs. Cannard," Monique led off.

"Please call me Merrilane. No one calls me that any more. Iris told me something of your academic career. How did you get to Vietnam, and what position did you hold?"

"Frank recommended me, and I was picked to head a program to gather contemporary history of the war. As for my position, I was the woman who loved your husband."

The logs crackled sending showers of sparks into the copper screen. Merrilane picked up her coffee cup, sipped the contents, and replaced it in its saucer, all without taking her eyes off the woman who had spoken with such surety.

"I thought perhaps it was something like that," she said. "Did he love you?"

"Not at that time."

"You met afterwards?"

"Yes, in Hartford during a conference of military history scholars, but that's getting ahead of the story."

"I suppose after the way I've treated him, I have no right to ask you to continue."

"You're still his wife, you've played a part in the drama, but you've not been privy to the more unseemly portions of the script."

"And you are?"

"Only by chance, but that's appropriate because fate has played such a large part in this. Crowded conditions at Seventh Air Force Headquarters caused my staff to share space with Alex and his colleagues. Adam Wootan, who became my friend, was their boss. The only separation between our two offices was a row of metal lockers. During times of quiet, early morning or late night, one could hear whatever was happening next door. One evening when I was working late, Alex came in from a trip, found the tape you sent, and played it. Once I realized what it was, I didn't know what to do. After it was over, I heard your husband weeping. I knew then I had to phone him."

"So you could comfort him I imagine. So you could get what you went over there for." Merrilane's voice was harsh but controlled because of the children's presence nearby.

"Yes on both counts," Monique said without emotion. "Although I doubted I could achieve either."

"I don't understand?"

"I don't suppose you do. You have three advertisements of your sexual proficiency in this house and another who, like my friend Adam, may or may not be somewhere out there. I'm only half a woman, like a transvestite one would meet at a trendy bar. You see, I was molested—soft word "molested"—rolls easily off the tongue and is meaningless unless one has experienced its horrors. Especially if one is young, inexperienced . . . and a daughter."

Merrilane sat bolt upright, staring with incredulous eyes at the Madonna sitting across from her, a Madonna whose eyes brimmed with tears. "You don't have to tell me this," she said. "Why are you telling me this?"

"I'm telling you because, if your husband is alive, you can still be saved. I'm already lost. I can't react physically to a man. Not to Adam, not to Alex. Once during a rocket attack, I tried to run. Alex pulled me down, covered me, and talked to calm me. Clutching me closely, he called me 'Merrilane.' Then by age-old reflex, his pelvis began to thrust. I viciously repelled him, and he apologized in such an embarrassed manner I know it was spontaneous.

"Later, in Hartford, after you had rejected him and he had been living celibate under such terrible job pressures, he had the opportunity to possess me, and I prayed he could love me like no other had. But then I rose up like a wildcat scratching, and spitting, and biting. He controlled himself and, as I saw his agonizing need for nurturing, I felt as if I had betrayed my entire gender. I doubt you can understand that. Others with credentials far beyond yours could neither believe it or treat it.

"On our last night in Hartford, we confessed our inmost demons to each other. My sin and his shame. He holds himself responsible for the deaths of an American soldier and a Vietnamese patrol. The facts are inconclusive: local commanders dropped the matter without an investigation. Yet he can't forget it. It haunts his dreams. It's drained his humanity, and the one person who can purge his guilt appears to be wrapped exclusively in her own adventure."

Merrilane moved to protest, but Monique continued.

"He told me once I had everything you wanted—position, power, notoriety. Well, my dear, you have everything I'd sell my soul for—a home, children, a good man who may have played his cards imperfectly but who still loves you."

Merrilane sat mute trying to piece together a coherent story that would keep herself in the position of protagonist instead of wicked witch. What right, she asked herself, did this guest in her house presume to shatter her illusions and discredit the decisions that had strengthened her position over the last four years?

"Is that all there is?" she asked.

"There's more. About how he tried to call from Saigon to explain why he had acted as he had, only to find the circuits down or jammed with priority messages. And then he was off to Pleiku and no opportunity to call. Back again in Saigon, he found two of his friends had been killed, which required his gathering their personal effects. He felt drawn to me, the only woman he knew with whom he could talk. Because of that attraction, which he realized was wrong in two ways—adultery against you and disloyalty toward Adam—he stayed away from me, except to say goodby on a night I was so fragile I would have committed any unseemly act if only he'd asked."

"More?"

"His wanting to discuss with you in Hawaii his leaving the air force and settling here, so you could continue your job. But the horrible storm on the beach severed all communication and locked him into his career once orders for Louisiana came through. Louisiana! How I wish you knew of his experience in a job totally foreign to his disposition. That and the effect of recurring refusals from both you and me when he reached out for some human contact."

"More?"

"The circumstances of your baby's birth and your final refusal of a reconciliation. It's a long and doleful situation, one making the minor difficulties of Romeo and Juliet pale in comparison."

"More?"

"Isn't that enough?"

"No, unfortunately that's only half. Mine is easily as sordid, so as sometimes to seem plotted by a vengeful devil. There's my relationships with one-dimensional characters whose names you probably have heard, but whose complexity you can never know. Names like Rod Pike, who once bore the brunt of Alex's jealously. His bravado masks a role known to few, and one I've promised to protect. And Jack Pinski, whose father's death in Vietnam changed him into a renegade cadet who violated my trust, stalked, raped me, and then finally abandoned me just like Alex had done, and my father before him.

"After the baby was born, I suffered a severe and long lasting depression just at the time I was having to prove myself in a new job—again in an all-male environment where big ideas were hatched, then moved immediately to me for fleshing out and implementation."

"I'm sorry," Monique whispered. "I've known in my heart your path has not been easy. Early on, when I was in control of my emotions, I was even your advocate."

"I guess I was naive to have thought my two eldest children would have supported me. Would have taken over part of the load around the house. I did when I was their age. I told them what I needed, but they let me down, preferring their own kind to their mother . . . or their father. Although I must say they seem to have modified their behavior since the impact of the most recent disaster began to register."

"I noticed," Monique said, "in the *Times'* follow-up article, a Captain Pinski was among the crewmembers missing on the first attack. Am I to suppose he's the same young man you mentioned just now and Alex had described in such harsh terms previously?"

"None other. That's one of the reasons I mentioned a 'vengeful devil' as perhaps the source of my trouble. Except always before, Alex and I believed only in a merciful, caring God rather than devils of any ilk.

"My life's been an absolute disaster since Hawaii, when his jealousy caused us to fight and argue until it seemed we were speaking in tongues. I had arrived in the islands completely fatigued from my job in academy sports. My body needed to be pampered and rested and my sexuality carefully regenerated after lying fallow for seven months. Emotionally I needed my man, not his shadow."

Monique leaned closer to fathom the whispered confession.

"I'd never had anyone but Alex, and when things went hay-wire between us, I lost control—became a loose woman. On the flight home, I encouraged a man who had joined me for dinner. Spared with him in conversation, giving every indication of going all the way. And I would if cystitis hadn't flared, causing me to burst his balloon like I'd deflated Alex's ego. My conduct was reprehensible, of course, demeaning, and morally corrosive, but—like cocaine—it made me want more.

"You know, of course, that a woman gets lots of hits. For some reason, perhaps because I was traveling so much, I started getting more than my share. I had my pick, and I learned to pick discreetly with the clear understanding I didn't have time for long-term relationships. So I can now say I've sampled the spectrum, and would you believe it, the memory of Alex still tops them all."

"What about the position you have now?" Monique asked.

"In most ways it's been everything Rod said it could be. We're striving to bring the headquarters of the United States Olympic Committee from New York to Colorado Springs and to establish a Sports Center to house and train athletes. The faint-hearted say it's pie in the sky. They know it's at least five years in the future before we could possibly secure the head-quarters, another year before the first resident training for the U.S. women's volleyball team could be accommodated, and ten years—something like nineteen eighty-three—before the first phase of the Sports Center could materialize.

"It's a hard-sell. Besides the prima-donnas involved in over-seeing Olympic competition, and the state and local politicians we have to pacify, I've had to contend lately with another fe-male on my same level who thinks management is running rough-shod over our own people and marketing is intimidat-ing those whose political and financial support we depend upon. So now instead of just getting the job done and keeping everyone in the loop, I have to endure harassment, undercutting, and innuendo from someone I thought would be an ally as well as a friend. It's plain I don't understand my husband, my children, or arrogant female VPs."

The two women talked late into the night, pausing on occasion to add logs to the fire, or make hot chocolate, but coming back to probe the nuances of the subjects broached in their opening remarks. In the process they bonded as two sisters alone in a deep forest beset by predators, knowing they had only their own resources to depend upon.

Long past midnight when the yawns became more pronounced, Monique realized one subject had been glossed over. During a lull in the conversation, as they both stared at the dying embers, she asked, "Has your infatuation with cocaine continued?"

"Why shouldn't it? They say its not addictive . . . like tobacco. It's easily available, makes me feel good, and allows me to go twenty-four hours a day, several days at a stretch, if I need to."

"I think you're playing with fire. I saw what heroin did in Vietnam, and I've seen the effects of cocaine on some of my associates. It's definitely habit forming and life threatening; I don't care what the culture says."

"I can handle it. I'm used to playing with fire, but I'm beginning to think it may not be worth it. Can you imagine what our Olympic folks would say if they knew my briefings were drug induced? Or Alex? He detests my smoking and suspects I've been dabbling in pot. If he survives, you may yet inherit him. Or do you think my benighted straight arrow would take me back if he knew what I've admitted to you?"

"Yes," said Monique.

CHAPTER SIXTY-THREE

ON THE NIGHT OF THE 27TH, the bombing began as a bell located somewhere across the wall tolled eleven. Again the attacks were along different axes with drop times two or three minutes apart. The bombing was over in ten minutes. On the 28th it began fifteen minutes later and lasted for eight minutes with the sounds of impacts coming from four different directions. After the last drop on Hanoi, he heard the rumbling of far-off deliveries beginning just after the bell struck eleven-thirty and lasting for another eight minutes. Flak was more sporadic, missile launches few, as if the cupboard were bare.

On the 29th, the sirens sounded at eleven. The bombing began sometime after the bell struck the quarter hour and continued only six minutes. The target seemed to be northwest, in the vicinity of the Phuc Yen storage area. About ten minutes later, distant thunder indicated the Lang Dang rail yards were getting hit again. Quiet returned after eight minutes. The 30th passed without attack as did the next day when he, lying manacled, cold, and thirsty, realized that never in his life had he really enjoyed a New Year's Eve.

He spent New Year's Day reviewing his adult life, focusing particularly on the last decade. At graduate school he remembered blowing past the others, none of whom had orders to produce an advanced degree in twelve months. No extensions the Air Force had said. Just read, write, test, and—in your spare time—push the base support C-47 through the night sky. Good duty for Merrilane: another chance to set up housekeeping, do the shopping, cook the meals, and acclimatize two young children to a strange location. This time, however, she got a bonus—the honor of proofreading his papers. *Vacation? With a thesis to write and an instrument check coming up? We'll play in*

*Colorado. Horseback riding every evening. Trout fishing on the week-
ends. Skiing at Vail, or Aspen, or Steamboat Springs.*

Degree in hand, he had anticipated three years flying, teaching, enjoying the family. But other things impinged.
Extra-curricular things. *We've got to remember we're still in competition. With that in mind, I volunteered to coach lacrosse. As a
club, not an intercollegiate team, they depend on the cadre for help.
Why don't you and the kids ride without me? I met the sergeant who
runs the base pistol team. They need an officer to politic for funding.
Won't take much time—just a few weekends a month when I'm not
flying. Say, there's a great opportunity to pick up five acres in the
Black Forest. Terrific location. Perfect for retirement. We might want
to build right away. I know you just got this house fixed up, but you
do it so effortlessly.*

Then came the war. Seven months with the Spookies wasting unseen people, followed by five days in Hawaii killing a
love assumed to be immortal. Five months with Wootan end-
running the egotists, outsmarting the lethargic, getting the job
done. Beginning to rise out of depression before being hit by
the tape. To the flow of words unstoppable, unbelievable, irre-
futable. Afterwards feeling free to think at night more often of
Monique than Merrilane.

Going home to find there wasn't any home: no wife, no place
except back into the hopper to see what jobs SAC would spit
out. And doing them because it was easier to do the impossible
within the system than to risk working where there weren't
any regulations or higher headquarters sitting like Oz with an
answer or a waiver of requirements. And knowing everyone in
the game would excuse him for not being human after a long
day of playing with machines and schedules and performance
criteria. So it became reasonable for the fast burner not to have
a woman or even a friend after a while.

But how come there were others—the Hal Diamonds—doing it just as well, even better, and maintaining their smiles,
and their families, and their perspective? They had what he
didn't have and maybe didn't even want. They really loved
doing everything that went with it: living with the packed

schedules, the imminent readiness inspections, the non-stop social obligations. Paced by their lovely, competent wives who also delighted in being a hospital volunteer, or a United Fund leader, or hostess to visiting brass. And their kids pushing to follow in Dad's footsteps because the life is in their genes. But it never was in Kim's or Jeffrey's. Maybe not even in his. Maybe the bug he had was only to fly—to break out on top and drink in the beauty, not to go immediately into the refueling checklist. And it had taken only two decades for him to see in his character what Monique perceived almost immediately.

The pride that once fueled his ambition had flamed out. But it had taken all this time, four years now, to dissipate the airspeed. And the last several years had been spent living isolated in a succession of ever-smaller cells until he lay in filth, hands and feet chained, but with unfettered eyes beginning to see beyond the clammy walls.

Immersed in thought, he missed the guard's approach until he heard the key being inserted into the lock. The keeper slammed the door open and made a rolling gesture with his hands. Leaning over the leg irons, he removed the heavy top bar, and motioned for him to turn on his side so he could reach the cuffs. Again the man made the rolling sign, ending by pointing to his blanket. Looking like the guide in *Lost Horizons*, he beckoned his prisoner to follow.

The afternoon sunlight, even though filtered by an overcast, inflamed his eyes causing them to water profusely. Following the guard like an injured and mindless crab, he hobbled up the courtyard and turned left into the passage toward the quiz room. His heart sank as he realized the torture was about to begin all over again, just when he had decided maybe he did give a ratz after all. But they angled off into a smaller enclosure encompassing ten individual shower stalls. His escort motioned him into one, handing him a thick bar of brown soap and a rusty safety razor as he entered.

He scrubbed furiously, scarcely feeling the intense cold of the water. The soap gave no lather, but its gritty composition seemed to shove off the accumulated filth as a bulldozer blade would do. He gulped great quantities of water before attacking the two-weeks' growth of whiskers. The keeper beat on the side of his stall, so he finished quickly, shivering in the brisk wind. He wrapped himself in the filthy blanket and followed around a row of cells and through a passage for some thirty feet until he entered a cellblock. The turnkey opened the first door on the left revealing a gaunt but smiling Adam Wootan.

"Happy nineteen seventy-three, Alex."

The two embraced, tears rolling down their cheeks. "Happy New Year, sir. I've thought of you so often."

"It's been rough at times," Wootan said. "Funny what a woman can get you into."

"She was worth taking a chance for."

"I don't know. I knew her for only a short time. Never really knew her. Even have difficulty now visualizing what she looked like."

"That's not hard to explain. Her kind of beauty causes a man to draw his eyes away for fear of embarrassing himself."

"You talk like you're in love with her," Wootan said.

"No, I thought for awhile that I could be, but I have a wife."

"Have you seen Monique?"

"Only once. Two years ago at a conference. I didn't know until then you'd been shot down."

"How did she look? Does she . . . "

The tapping was abrupt, intrusive, but Wootan was on the wall in an instant with his tin cup rapping two short beats. "It's SugarFox—wants to know where his beaver pictures are."

Alex laughed, "Tell him . . . "

The tapping resumed again in rapid starts and stops.

"He says they're moving prisoners out of Heartbreak and New Guy Village. Looks like all the SAC new arrivals, some thirty or so, are being loaded in covered trucks."

"Ask him if he knows anything about Pinski, the captain I came in with."

Wootan tapped quickly. The reply was short. Even Alex could understand a "no." Wootan broke off the exchange and turned again to Alex who had arranged himself to sit on the sleeping platform clutching his blanket about him.

"Why do you think they're moving the SAC people, Adam?"

"Two reasons probably. This place is bursting at the seams, so I'd guess they're reopening another camp. Perhaps the Zoo about two or three miles south of here. The second reason is we haven't had a chance to completely integrate the SAC people into our POW structure. The Vietnamese probably think they can handle them better, keep them more docile, if they don't let us get to them."

"If they're taking Pinski to a place called the Zoo, he'll take it apart within a week. He's had practice."

"He'd better be careful. You never know what these bastards are going to do. They've threatened to keep some of us when the exchange finally takes place."

"Why did they leave me here at the Hilton?"

"Since you're a senior officer, they probably think you'd be able to organize the new camp. That means you held up well under interrogation because they've put you in with us hardcore reactionaries. But enough of business, tell me about the world."

They stayed up all night with Alex covering current events, and his cell mate explaining the policies and methods the Americans used to maintain communication, discipline, and resistance. Wootan explained the history of prisoner treatment from intimidation, starvation, and torture existing until roughly the time of Ho Chi Mhin's death in 1969, then a gradual easing of restrictions, increase in rations, and communal living which gave hope of eventual repatriation.

That morning they were allowed outside to empty their buckets and to wash. In the evening they ate communally in the "overflow room" between "Stardust," where they were quartered, and "Desert Inn," the adjoining cellblock. Wootan introduced Alex to the camp leaders, mostly naval and air force officers who had been in captivity in some cases since 1965. He was asked to give the group a sketch of society's trends.

"You're going to have to maintain your flexibility and sense of humor when you go home," he began. "You'll probably find you have a closer touch with reality than most of the people you'll meet. Society's in transition. For those of you who have children, you'll find their hair much longer. I mean on the boys."

His audience laughed apprehensively. "The war has polarized the country, but the draft's expected end has cooled campuses. Self-interest is at an all-time high: no more John Kennedy-style idealism. Feminism—Woman's Liberation—is big." The audience buzzed. "That means lots of women are attempting to find fulfillment outside the home." Again the audience stirred. "That can be pretty positive in lots of cases. Many of your wives, for example, are active in the POW/MIA arena. If it hadn't been for their stirring the pot, the government most probably would still be sitting on dead center, and torture and solitary confinement may have continued."

"What's the support for President Nixon?" someone asked.

"I'm sorry," Alex said. "I don't do political commentary. Since I didn't return from the first Fifty-two raid, I don't know the reaction to that decision."

"You seemed to be ill at ease in front of the bunch," Wootan said later as they sat on their sleeping platforms. "Did you get things straightened out at home?"

"No, sorry to say. The communication wasn't there. Not talk, not sex, not even a tap code."

"Maybe this interlude will help. It's probably the only place where men can discuss sex and gender relationships rationally. Must have something to do with the diet."

"May be true in Lane's case," Alex said. "She certainly got a belly full of me."

"As one who's lost a mate, I can't understand anything less than death breaking the bond between a loving couple."

"Circumstances trapped us. In Hawaii I was still grieving a short round and living with its repercussions—mood swings, depression, and disenchantment with what the future seemed to hold for us. Back in Saigon, after talking to you and Monique that night, I left the club and tried to call her to get things straightened out. Fate stepped in again—phone lines busy, a rush trip to Pleiku, and a 'Dear John' waiting when I returned. Once home, all I had was orders back to the crew force, whereas she had what she thought was the chance of a lifetime. Turned out she also had been seeing someone while I was finishing my tour in Saigon."

"'Seeing someone?' Isn't that putting it a bit Victorian? You mean she was unfaithful to you?

"Yes."

"You're sure?"

"Yes."

"She told you?"

"For Christ's sake, Adam. Some things you don't have to be told. How would you like to come home from the wars and find your wife on a weekend jaunt with a male cohort?"

"If I could see my Trisha again, I wouldn't dictate the circumstances."

"Oh shit, Adam. You hit between the eyes."

"Maybe that's what you need to bring things into focus. You're telling me you never once kicked over the traces?"

"Never did. Before or after. We had something special. We used to . . . "

"'Used to' is dead, Alex! Killed in action in World War Two. You can't live in the past. I know; I've tried."

"It's not that simple, Adam. There was a scandal. Lots of people—maybe everyone at the Academy—knew about it."

"So you washed your hands and left her to face it alone."

"There was a baby."

"So?"

"I gave it my name."

"You're sure it isn't yours?"
"I'm certain."
"How can you be?"
"It looks exactly like him."
"Who?"
"Pinski."

CHAPTER SIXTY-FOUR

ALEX CONTINUED LIVING with Wootan, discussing the subjects a man of his temperament would probe during four years of captivity: philosophy, religion, ethics, politics, history. Each morning when Alex awoke, cold and stiff from the dampness, Wootan would be sitting with his back against the wall, arms wrapped around his legs, chin resting on his bony knees. Then he would pop the morning question to see what Alex's first reaction would be. After reflecting on the answer, he would follow with whatever position he had distilled over time. Alex found him widely read, precise in his thinking, and receptive to new data and ideas.

To Alex their conversations were unlike any teaching he had done. This time he had an unbiased partner whose emphasis was on understanding the nuances of a subject no matter how long it took to appraise them. He came to resent the interruptions to eat, trips to the bath house, and the intrusive calls to the wall when news would not wait for the evening gathering. He found he had been given a gift, a sabbatical to allow him to organize his mind and determine the way he wished his life to progress. As their conversations ranged far afield, he came to understand that Wootan was really the teacher, the person who seemed most attuned to nature's common frequency.

In mid-January, some two weeks after the B-52 raids had stopped, each prisoner received an English translation of the peace accords agreed upon by Dr. Kissinger and Le Duc To. All they had to do was endure just a bit longer and then they could go home.

The morning after receiving the protocols, Wootan was sitting in his normal position. "What do you think will happen to our side?"

"I think they'll outpace South Korea," Alex said. "Their economy will blossom, their political apparatus will follow the democratic ideal, and President Thieu will be revered for generations."

"You really believe that?"

"No. I think once we're gone the NVA will roll up the country, push the VC leaders out of the way, and run the South like a fiefdom. After a short breather, they'll occupy Laos and Cambodia, and this whole land will be an economic basket-case making North Korea look good."

"No more idealism remaining?"

"None where this debacle is concerned."

"But we've got Kissinger and Nixon . . . "

"And before them MacNamara and Johnson, Martin and Lewis, Laurel and Hardy."

"You're not high on Nixon? He mined Haiphong Harbor, sent the B-Fifty-twos to Hanoi. The man's got guts."

"Spare me, Adam. The man came into office supposedly with a secret plan to wind down the war and bring the POWs home. That was four years ago, about the time you got shot down. We've taken more casualties on his watch than we'd suffered the whole time before he was elected. He's just another politician—the product of the public's ignorance of the lessons of history, our paranoia over godless communism, and our infatuation with silver-tongued rascals who practice short-term expediency. For the last fourteen years, we've frittered away our power and prestige in Vietnam and, until the most recent bombing campaign, have appeared to be the paper tiger Mao said we were. Now we're cutting and running, what LBJ promised we'd never do. Politically Nixon needs to get out of Vietnam in the worst way, and that's how we're leaving." He paused, realizing the depth of venom he had released. "You see it any differently?"

"No."

"What can we do about it? I can't even get my wife back, so what right do I have to criticize anyone with ego enough to take on the world's problems?" Alex expelled a long sigh. "I feel sorry for the lonely bastard. We've got a lot in common. We've both let Vietnam stymie us for the last four years."

Wootan thought for a while. "What are you going to do about your situation when you get home?"

"You tell me. I'm locked in by constraints just like I was in Saigon."

"You're saying you're waiting for a miracle to get your marriage back on track, so maybe then you can get control of your life? You didn't wait for miracles when you worked for me. You went out and got the job done."

"But that was different."

"In what way? You told me you've been hamstrung by constraints. I'm saying you just have to take a fresh look, a new tack. Somehow I don't care for you in the role of Hamlet."

Alex signaled for quiet. They heard the keepers dragging something heavy past the door. Loud voices reverberated in the hallway. Alex recognized SugarFox's high-pitched grousing.

"What's going on, Adam?"

"Beats me. It's late in the game to be shifting rooms."

The key hitting their lock signaled they were part of the equation. "Hang tough," Wootan whispered as the door banged open.

"You come," Red Tab gave the roll-up signal and pointed to Alex.

Grabbing his blanket and cup, Alex shuffled into the corridor. Red Tab shoved him sideways around the corner and into cell number six. Lying naked on the platform in the right-hand corner, his feet encased in leg irons and his body covered with dried blood, lay Jack Pinski.

"Good God, what have they done to you?"

"They don't have any sense of humor at the Zoo, Colonel." Alex saw the tears in Pinski's eyes. "They worked me over, and now they've brought me here, so you can finish me off."

Someone had come into the room and was standing behind them. Alex recognized the man who had brought food when he was in solitary. He extended a pail of water. Alex mumbled his thanks, poured some into his cup and, cradling Pinski's head in his arm, raised it to his lips. Then he removed his shirt, dipped a portion in the pail, and started cleaning the blood from his cellmate's face. Later he soaked the shirt, wrung it out, and applied it to the swelling around the captain's eyes. He covered him with his own blanket then sat shivering as he watched the sleeping youth.

When he awoke, Alex fed him cold pumpkin soup and thought of little Buddy. He had held him once in the hospital. Had there been other times? Not that he could remember.

Alex was not allowed to eat with the group that night. He demanded another blanket and increased rations, but nothing appeared. All night Pinski thrashed and called out, but Alex could not understand what he said. He was better the next day although the puffiness in his cheeks and the split lower lip prevented his talking for more than a few sentences. By the third day, he was sitting up to pass bloody urine in the bucket Alex held for him.

"Why did they do this to you?"

"I seem to have a way of pissing off perfect strangers," Pinski said. "They caught me communicating."

"The tap code?"

"Nothing as crude as that. I used your example. Started yelling at the guys in the other cells." Pinski lay back. "They pulled me out and beat the living hell out of me."

"Why did you draw attention to yourself?"

"Because we were being too submissive. We weren't doing anything to harass the bastards. I guess most of the guys were still in shock from getting shot down. We'd got copies of the Paris accords, and that seemed to make everyone pull inside himself and prepare to wait it out."

"Did your shouting do any good?"

"It warmed me up," Pinski smiled, breaking open the gash on his lip. "The dinks made the mistake of beating me in the open where the others could hear. The whole bunch started yelling and pounding on their cell doors. Some light colonel took on the camp commander and got him to call off the dogs. Then they shipped me over here."

"Sounds like you did good," Alex said as he raised the cup. "Take a drink and try to get some sleep."

That night Alex was allowed out to eat, and Red Tab took the irons off Pinski. Then Alex slipped into the same kind of routine he and Wootan had shared. Now he was the undisputed teacher and mentor. He found Pinski well informed and exceedingly bright. The relationship was strained initially, both feeling each other out, listening for double meanings or veiled insults. They talked mostly about flying: Pinski's experiences in pilot training, the performance of the supersonic T-38, and the capabilities of simulators to prepare pilots for flying a strange aircraft.

In subsequent conversations Alex shared his impressions of directing a standardization division and his technical knowledge of the B-52 and KC-135 tanker. Exhausting the range of technical subjects, they drifted toward the more personal. They discussed the last moments of Black Lead. Pinski seemed comforted when Alex told him they had used up all possibilities. At least Tokas and Heinrich had ejected and were prisoners. Perhaps Budd would turn up.

One night Alex talked Pinski through a complete B-52 pilot's standardization check. They climbed out of Guam, hit a tanker, then did a jet penetration and three instrument approaches. Alex set up the situations and asked the questions. Pinski responded with the procedure, the required technique, and the standards to which he would be held. Alex gave him a "Highly Qualified" rating and allowed him to go to sleep. Then the instructor pilot who had been soaring among the fleecy clouds lay awake on his miserable pallet, staring into the dim light bulb, thinking of the deep waters of Lake Tahoe, and listening to the bell toll away the night.

In the common gathering on the eleventh of February, the senior American officer announced that Air Force transports would pick them up at Gia Lam airport the next morning for the flight home.

Back in their cell, Pinski and Alex seemed lost in their own thoughts. The wind whistled as it swept under the door and out the rear window. The captain was lying on his left side facing the wall. Alex thought he was already asleep.

"This'll probably be the last time we'll be together where we can talk like men, huh roomie?"

"What do you mean? We'll be on the plane together, and our paths will probably cross sometime in the future."

"No, it'll never be the same. You'll be a general soon. And there'll be distractions, like food and drink."

"I grant you there'll be distractions."

"You've been good to me, Alex. I know you jumped that officer to take the pressure off me. You nursed me when they brought me back here. Even gave me your blanket . . . and the shirt off your back."

"You'd have done the same for me."

"Yes, I would have. But I've still got a lot to answer for."

"Not to me."

"I'm not fit to be an officer, Alex. I did things at the Academy that violated everything it stands for."

"That's past. It's where you're going we're interested in, not where you've been."

"You don't understand. I violated the Honor Code. Hell, I smashed it to smithereens."

"You've lived to a higher code here. That's what we were trying to teach."

Pinski was quiet for a long while. The bell struck midnight. "Alex, I think a lot about that village. Over two hundred people wasted."

"Who do you think I am, Father Confessor? I think of them too. I think of the poor, manipulated NVA soldiers and the fifteen-year-old Viet Cong who's fighting because some marine put a Zippo to his home. I think of the human souls I've dispatched from this earth, and the terror is I don't know how many there were.

"You want to think about short rounds for the rest of your life? Then try thinking about a trusting grunt calling you in to protect him. Think of your bullets slamming into his flesh. Think about it till you lose your mind and what little time you've got left!"

"I'm sorry, Alex . . . I didn't know."

"Nobody knows except Mother Hubbard and Wootan . . . and . . ."

"Merrilane?"

"No."

Pinski pulled himself into a sitting position and turned away from the wall. Tears streamed down his face. "I'm sorry, Alex. I'm sorry; Christ I'm sorry."

Alex wiped his eyes on the edge of his blanket. Its smell was sickening, but it was something to hold on to, and he tightened his grip until he could feel his nails embedding the thin cloth into his palms. "The past, Jackie, is a tale told by an idiot." He spoke slowly, picking his words as if he were tapping them into his own brain. "It signifies nothing until we learn to regard it dispassionately. Until we can put aside our selfishness and our emotions, it remains an unfathomable riddle capable of poisoning the present and swindling us out of our future. For some reason, you and I have been spared while better men have been taken. We've been given another chance . . . in my case a third chance."

"Listen, Alex. This is important. About me and Merrilane. It's not like you think. . . "

"It's all right. Don't you understand what I'm telling you? It's in the past. I don't live there any more. And neither do you. And I've got to make sure Merrilane doesn't either. Our job—yours and mine—is to rub the slate clean and look ahead. That's what we've been trained to do. Look ahead and take care of our people. You understand? I'm transmitting. I've finally de-ciphered what the Captain really means."

"I hear you, Alex. But the Captain was only partially right. It's not just the war. It's a fucked-up time . . . a fucked-up world."

"It may be, but we're still players. We still have time. And I'll be *God damned* if I waste any more of it!"

EPILOGUE

UNDERSTANDING HIS MOOD Iris Harbinger had retired early, leaving her husband alone in the dark library surrounded by his books and immersed in memories. Sometime later Frank switched on the lamp, unfolded his morning newspaper, and began to read once again the article that had confirmed his deepest fear and destroyed whatever joy this Christmas day of 1976 had promised:

Omaha—Strategic Air Command Headquarters released the name of the officer swept from a B-52 bomber which suffered an explosive decompression over the polar ice cap two nights ago. Brigadier General Alexander X. Cannard, commander of the Seventh Air Division located at Carswell Air Force Base, Texas, was investigating an equipment malfunction when the locking mechanism of a fuselage hatch failed or was otherwise triggered in the aircraft's cramped navigation compartment. The bomber subsequently landed without further incident at Loring Air Force Base, Maine. General Cannard is presumed dead.

A highly decorated veteran of the Vietnam War recently selected for promotion to Major General, Cannard was known for his personal rapport with the men and women of his command and the frequency of his flights to observe aircrew proficiency and gain working-level views concerning operational and welfare matters. He was slated for imminent assignment as Director of Legislative Liaison in Washington, a prestigious position involving intimate daily involvement with influential members of Congress concerning matters of utmost importance to the Air Force.

His wife resides in New York and is founder and chief executive officer of Merrilane Enterprises, Inc., a leading design group producing exclusive athletic clothing. A daughter, Kim, and two sons, Jeffrey and Alex, survive the general. Memorial arrangements are incomplete.